MW01293993

THE CRUEL DAWN

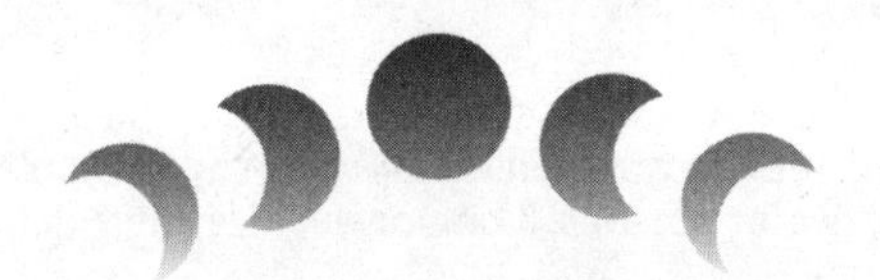

THE CRUEL DAWN

BOOK II

RACHEL

NEW YORK TIMES BESTSELLING AUTHOR

HOWZELL HALL

RED TOWER BOOKS™

This book is a work of fiction. Names, characters, places, and incidents are the product of the author's imagination or are used fictitiously. Any resemblance to actual events, locales, or persons, living or dead, is coincidental.

Copyright © 2025 by Rachel Howzell Hall. All rights reserved, including the right to reproduce, distribute, or transmit in any form or by any means. For information regarding subsidiary rights, please contact the Publisher.

Entangled Publishing believes stories have the power to inspire, connect, and create lasting change. That's why we protect the rights of our authors and the integrity of their work. Copyright exists not to limit creativity, but to make it possible—to ensure writers can keep telling bold, original stories in their own voices. Thank you for choosing a legitimate copy of this book. By not copying, scanning, or distributing it without permission, you help authors continue to write and reach readers. This book may not be used to train artificial intelligence systems, including large language models or other machine learning tools, whether existing or still to come. These stories were written for human connection, not machine consumption.

Entangled Publishing, LLC
644 Shrewsbury Commons Ave., STE 181
Shrewsbury, PA 17361
rights@entangledpublishing.com

Red Tower Books is an imprint of Entangled Publishing, LLC.
Visit our website at www.entangledpublishing.com.

Edited by Liz Pelletier and Sarah T. Guan
Cover and edge design by Bree Archer
Cover image by lyubava.21/shutterstock
Edge image by Naddya/Depositphotos
Case design by Elizabeth Turner Stokes
Case images by Msnty studioX/Shutterstock,
and Md Aktharuzzaman79/Shutterstock
Endpaper design by Elizabeth Turner Stokes
Endpaper image by lyubava.21/Shutterstock
Interior map design by Heidi Pettie
Interior formatting by Britt Marczak

Hardcover ISBN 978-1-64937-916-0
Ebook ISBN 978-1-64937-462-2

Manufactured in the United States of America
First Edition August 2025

10 9 8 7 6 5 4 3 2 1

MORE FROM RACHEL HOWZELL HALL

Vallendor Duology

The Last One
The Cruel Dawn

Sonny Rush Series

Fog and Fury

The Lou Norton Series

City of Saviors
Trail of Echoes
Skies of Ash
Land of Shadows
A Quiet Storm

Single Titles

What Never Happened
We Lie Here
These Toxic Things
And Now She's Gone
They All Fall Down
The Good Sister with James Patterson
What Fire Brings

For those who've been told that they're too much…and not enough.

The Cruel Dawn is a tale of rage and magic—and the desires that set the world ablaze. The story includes elements that might not be suitable for all readers, including battle and combat, injury, death, imprisonment, assault, illness, amnesia, grief, perilous situations, burning, poisoning, graphic language, racism, homophobia, alcohol use, and sexual activity on the page. Readers who may be sensitive to these elements, please take note, and prepare to enter the realm of Vallendor…

EAPONYS
EMPIRE OF
BRITHELLUM
SEA OF DEVOUR
MOUNT DEVOUR
CAERNO WOODS
PERIA
DUSKMOOR RIVER
HAFELD
PETHORP
PENEM
WEETON
CABURH
LINANDE
HAMOR

KINGDOM OF VINEVRIDTH
CHESTERBY
BARAMINZ SPIRES
OHOGAR
DOOM DESERT
TRONY RIVER
AZZAM CAVERN
GOLDCREST
DANFORTH
VERIL'S COTTAGE
MAFORD
ERMINE RIVER
STEEDALE
THE FORSAKEN
PRISON
OF BACHA
VINEVRIDTH
HEAFORD
CERULEAN SEA
N
W
E

Previously, in *The Last One*

Kai awakens in a desolate, sickness-ridden land, surrounded by unnatural beasts, with no memory of how she arrived. The only thing she knows for certain is that she must reach the Sea of Devour or the world around her will worsen. When she encounters Jadon Ealdrehrt, a skilled fighter with a mysterious past, she reluctantly accepts his offer of help, unaware of the dangerous truths lurking within him.

As Kai navigates the kingdom of Vinevridth, she discovers that no one, including Jadon, is who they appear to be. Worse, she is pursued by Elyn Fynal, the powerful Adjudicator—a goddess-judge who intends to sentence Kai to death for her past transgressions against the Aetherium and stop her quest to destroy Vallendor. To restore balance and achieve justice, Kai must die.

As she searches for answers, Kai's memories remain elusive, but she begins to uncover unsettling truths about Jadon's true identity—he is the eldest son of Emperor Syrus Wake. This revelation, combined with Kai's growing anger and fractured memories, creates an unpredictable tension between them. Their complicated relationship reaches a breaking point when the true villain, Danar Rrivae—a malevolent god and Jadon's biological father—reveals his plans to steal Vallendor. For this to succeed, Kai must die.

But Jadon defies his father's dark wishes, choosing to stand by Kai, complicating Rrivae's and Elyn's plans. In a desperate attempt to separate the two, Elyn blasts Kai to the farthest reaches of Vallendor. Yet, when Kai awakens this time, more of her memory is restored—and so is her determination to fight for herself...and maybe even for Vallendor's future.

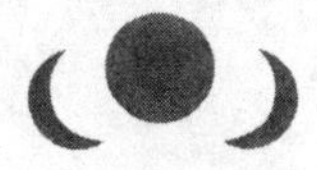

Anybody can become angry–that is easy, but to be angry with the right person and to the right degree and at the right time and for the right purpose, and in the right way—that is not within everybody's power and is not easy.

-Aristotle

PART I

INFERNO

In shadowed woods, where danger loomed,
Our village razed, our lives consumed.
But then you came with blazing light,
A beacon strong dispelling might.

Celestial, your power bright,
Always our star in darkest night,
With gratitude, our voices raise
In song and praise, we sing your ways.

Your mighty sword and fiery hand,
You shielded us, our Divine Grand.
In trials long, you led us through
With strength and grace, your love so true.

We are so small, we are so meek.
We need your strength, your love we seek.
We bow our heads, we bend our knee.
We still our hearts and honor thee.

Divine Lady, Divine Grand,
Against our foes you make a stand.
Lady of Life, Lady of Might,
Always our star in darkest night.

–A Song of Praise, Author Unknown

1

One day, I will wake up to a kiss instead of a kill. I will stretch and sing instead of crouching and growling. Maybe tomorrow will be that day because today, right now, an otherworldly being with the shrewd blue eyes of a man, the cupped ears of a man, and the sharp teeth, short fur, and claws of a bear roars at me.

"You have no business here." The creature sounds like he chews rocks and picks his teeth with burned splinters.

I slowly reach for my back scabbard and pull out one of my two swords, the one with the wine-colored handle etched with moths. The one with the blade as black as night. *Fury.* A gift from the blacksmith.

My heart wants to think about that blacksmith and figure out how I feel about him. Do I love him? Do I hate him? I don't know, and I don't have time for any of that right now. At this moment, all I care about is how this fucking incredible sword that he forged must save me from this rock-chewing, splinter-gnawing asshole thundering toward me from the canyons.

I push up from my knees into a crouch. I'm not ready to fight the foul-smelling threat bearing down on me, but I have to be.

"Get out of my desert," he snarls.

"This is Vallendor," I snarl back. "*My* realm, and no one tells me where I can or cannot be. Especially an aburan who holds no title to—"

The beast roars again.

My skin goose-pimples, and my knees quake. *One day, a kiss instead of a kill…* I lift my sword and wait for him to get closer…closer…

He charges, but I wait, and I wait, and then…

I swing.

Teeth bared, the aburan successfully ducks my swipe—but he doesn't expect my blade's quick return.

Fury finds the otherworldly's neck and pushes through that fur and bone like a hot stone through snow. Beheaded, the body of the aburan topples to the dirt, surprise bright in his beady human eyes.

Yeah, I'm also surprised to be here, sir—especially since I don't even know where we are.

Last time I opened my eyes to a strange new world, I ended up chasing a thief through a dying forest. She'd stolen my clothes and ran into a crummy little village filled with unhappy people who tried to kill me.

Didn't turn out so good for them in the end.

Didn't turn out so good for me, either.

Before being attacked, I'd opened my eyes to the world around me, sprawled on my belly in a sea of red dirt filled with mysterious shoeprints too big to be the average human's. Now, I return to peer closer at those *one…two…three* pairs of prints, each a different size.

Who made these prints—and why are they so close to my face?

I squint at the dead beast's feet.

Bare. Bear.

He didn't make any of these tracks left in the red dirt.

I sneeze—sand in my nose—then scan the desert in front of me.

Jagged-edged craters filled with red dirt and glistening white bones. Sheer walls rise up there and end as plateaus. Goats with curled horns climb on barely there crags and ledges. Long-legged hares hop from one underground den to the next. Yellow lizards big as hounds, with three heads and three jaws strong enough to crack boulders, sun themselves on rocks. A pack of gray wolves with wings too small to fly slurp from a muddy watering hole.

I can smell that water way over here. Smells like dead things. Musty things. Shitty things.

Every creature that I see glows amber. *That's right.* I can tell who is sick and dying by the glow they emit, and in this realm, that soft light burns amber.

But none of these animals at the watering hole or resting across boulders made these tracks.

With a shaky hand, I touch the amulet still hanging from my sweaty neck. The moth's gold chain still shines bright. Her ruby-crusted wings twinkle, but the stone thorax stays as dark as the night. Dead as it may appear, this amulet still gives me power and proves that I'm no ordinary Vallendorian. At least she's mine. Chasing her all over Vallendor again is not how I aim to spend my time.

What's that smell?

I sniff the air.

Smells like…dead things riding upon a living thing.

The air warms—whatever lurks here hasn't come to welcome me to this part of the realm.

Good.

I push to sit up on my knees. My body creaks beneath my rose-gold armor, tarnished and gunked-up. Dried gore from humans and beasts covers my breastplate, vambraces, and gauntlets. Beneath my tunic, my bones feel as shattered as stardust with my armor now just a fancy casserole dish holding me together. My bloodred hooded cape, though, remains unspoiled, free of dirt and blood—a benefit of the protective wards stitched into its fabric.

The ground beneath my feet vibrates.

Whatever lurks here has decided to come visit, and I feel its presence before I see—

He rushes toward me. A shrill cry shatters the silence.

My gaze snaps to the sky above me.

A flash of color blinks against the ginger- and blue-tinted sky. With those shimmering metallic gold-and-blue wings that span the width of a river and curved crimson beak…

A daxinea!

She cries again, then says, *"Come, Lady!"*

How about "no, thanks." I chased another pretty thing across the realm—that thief's name was Olivia—and that adventure landed me here, standing over a now-dead aburan. Not trying to do that again.

But the bird won't leave me alone. *"You must go there, Lady!"*

But where is "there"? And who left these tracks?

"Hurry, Lady!"

I swipe Fury's bloody blade across the fallen aburan's fur and stow her in the sheath beside the Adjudicator's sword with a platinum hilt and engraved silvery-blue blade. *Arbiter. Judge. Truth. Mediator. Justice. Life. Death.* I won her in a fight against Elyn Fynal the Adjudicator at the Sea of Devour. I take a step, but my breath comes short and fast. I want to vomit even though my stomach is empty. My tongue feels dry and swollen, and it's cut. The blood I'm now tasting reminds me that I'm not whole, that I'm imperfect, that my situation remains… *complicated.*

With great care, I take tiny steps to the cliff's edge and look out.

I stand above a realm on the verge of destruction. Thorny shrubs and acacia trees. Red dirt tufted with spiky grass. Sandy columns that used to be mountains before harsh winds scraped them down. Way out there, the land shimmers—but it's a trick. This place has no treasures. This place has no hope or any promise. That shimmer? Those are bleached bones and broken glass.

Of all places in the world, Elyn swept me here, the ass-crack of Vallendor.

My knees wobble and my head spins. The need to vomit surges in my throat.

Another cry from the soaring daxinea. *"Come, Lady!"*

I need to sit for a moment. Those gray windwolves, though, blink their golden eyes at me, ready to lunge for my neck.

Sitting means surrendering.

I can't surrender.

According to Elyn, I made Vallendor this way, destroying the realm out of selfishness and frustration. *You are the one who will destroy the world.*

But I didn't destroy this daxinea. My heart swells to see her beauty and color bright against this landscape of desperation.

The creatures down here in the canyons also watch the bird. The wolves with stunted wings flick their pink tongues across their bladed teeth. *"Hungry, so hungry."*

"Don't touch that bird or else," I warn them. "You think your wings are little now."

The wolves blink at me, then drop their shaggy heads back down to the muddy pond. One thinks, *"She will fail."* Another thinks, *"We will wait."*

Yes, I was defeated in battle against the army of Syrus Wake, the Emperor and so-called Supreme Manifest of Vallendor. I remember confronting the traitor, Danar Rrivae. And I remember *him.* Jadon Ealdrehrt—no, Jadon *Wake*. The blacksmith. The prince. My lover. A liar. My foe. He'd asked me, Kaivara Megidrail, Grand Defender of Vallendor, Lady of the Verdant Realm, and Destroyer of Worlds, to be the empress to his emperor, as though this realm belonged to him. As though I trusted any word he uttered. As though he hadn't betrayed me. Yeah, he betrayed me—I remember *that* most of all.

But none of these memories calm my stomach, clear my head, or heed the call of the daxinea currently soaring over me. Nor do my titles or anger at the blacksmith tell me why I still feel like I'm being watched even after slaying an aburan.

I take one last look around, and then I say, "Lead on," to the daxinea. I follow her over the rocks and down the hillside. I scramble across scrapple and squeeze through slots. I rest because I get dizzy and the world keeps swooping, the edges of my vision fading.

But I don't sit down.

Sitting means surrender.

I take a moment to scan my surroundings again.

No aburan. No humans.

No one follows me, yet this big world feels cramped with too many pairs of eyes.

Sometimes as I walk, the daxinea blots out the daystar and casts shadows across the land. Sometimes she circles, but she never slows even as the terrain climbs, and pebbles become rocks, and thorns grow to the size of a man's hand.

I gape at the sharp red rocks stabbing the sky, at those three-headed lizards and tiny-winged wolves lurking from their dens and rocks. My muscles ache as though I've fought every creature in this realm.

The daxinea picks up speed. I run to catch up with her again and—

Roars. Growls. Women screaming. Men shouting. Children shrieking.

Supreme, help us!

Supreme, hear our prayers!

Supreme, have mercy!

The cries and roars echo throughout the canyons and roll over this desert.

Humans in distress.

Fuck.

Here we go again.

2

The faster I run, the louder the cries and roars.

Am I about to meet the ones who made those large shoeprints? Or is something worse waiting for me?

I race through the scraggly desert glen to the mud-bricked walls of a town. The tall date palms on its perimeter are on fire.

I know this city. Gasho, the capital of the kingdom of Ohogar, in the middle of Doom Desert. One of my favorite provinces in Vallendor Realm is now besieged—but by whom?

The scorching winds from the burning city whistle, but they aren't as loud as the cries of the humans within, which grow shriller the closer I come.

A tiny part of me whispers, "Not my problem." But my heart is bigger—I can't pretend that I don't care, that I can't help, and that whatever happens in this mud-bricked town will stay in this mud-bricked town.

I snap my cloak, and the air around me swirls with red dust. The dark stone in my amulet barely glows. I'm not strong enough. I'm not blessed enough. But I'm strong and blessed enough to *do something.* I'm as blessedly strong as I'm gonna be.

A bridge crosses over a dry canal and into a city now lost in smoke.

My mouth is dry and my throat parched. I need water before launching into another fight, but I don't smell any water. The way tiny tumbleweeds roll up and down this canal, water hasn't run here in ages. My eyes burn from the spinning dust clouds and smoke. And then the stink of rot and decay hits me and makes me gag.

Down in the gully, a mother holds a child by the hand and clutches a baby to her chest. Together, the three of them clench into a tight ball. A man holds the gash in his neck. His mouth gapes, and his eyes widen as his end comes. Children shake the shoulders of unmoving adults; some cry, "Amma, wake up!" and "Papa, I'm scared!" Fat and hungry corpse flies buzz from body to fallen body. I skid to a stop and think about jumping into the canal, but I don't know what I can do to help them. I *have* to help them!

A woman screams from the rooftop of a house. Somewhere, a bell clangs. Everywhere, people shout, weep, pray.

No!

Run!

Get back!

The iron-studded gates of this town dangle on their hinges like front teeth, like they'll be knocked out by a good punch.

Where are the city guards who were all here when I last passed through this town?

Amus: he'd been a long-distance runner, I remember. He'd been mean but committed to protecting his town.

Sumerka: too elegant to work as a guard, but he burned with the need to prove to his father that he could handle a sword.

Ilil: she'd had opinions—about weapons, about strategy, about the right amount of pressure to apply on an enemy's neck to scare them without killing them.

Once upon a time, this gate had thirty guards, each trained in combat techniques by my Mera contingent. Now, though, these gates have been abandoned.

I pull Fury from my scabbard and race past those broken gates that protect nothing.

Everyone I can see is trying to hide beneath rubble from creatures swooping down from the air and snapping at them, tearing through their skin and breaking their bones.

Arrows fly from bows I can't see, bouncing off the hides of these… these…

Cowslews.

Each creature is as big as a bull, with white skulls for heads and enormous red eyes. They have wings, but these creatures are not birds of prey. They're not even the battabies I faced down in Azzam Cavern. They have no feathers, but rather brown fur like a bear's and razor-sharp talons as long as my forearms.

Supreme didn't create these beasts. They have no symmetry, no sense. The traitor, Danar Rrivae, brought them to Vallendor. And now, the biggest cowslew locks its red eyes with me. *"You."* Smoke curls from the beast's nostrils.

I cock my head. "Yep. *Me.*"

The creature roars and charges at me, its teeth bared, its talons glinting.

Right as the cowslew springs at me, I roar, almost scaring myself with just how fierce I sound. I hold up my left hand to protect my head, sending a ball of my otherworldly wind that slams the beast back into a house.

For a moment, silence falls across the city as humans and otherworldly gape at me.

A woman shouts, "Celestial!" just as another cowslew swoops down from the sky and snaps her neck in its beak.

I shout, "No!" and shoot wind at that beast, and at another otherworldly that tries again to bite me. Not one of these creatures fears me—they sense that I'm not entirely myself. Their confidence, though, fuels me and steadies my hand, and I hit my marks. One cowslew after another tumbles from the sky. I send them slamming into market stands and shops. If I didn't have a fuzzy stomach and blurred vision and softening knees, I'd be able to stop even more of these beasts. Yeah, if I was as healthy as a young Mera warrior after eating a full meal, I'd be able to do this wind-whipping all day.

But there are so many cowslews—and more are coming. Fearless, they're breaking down the temple doors. They're dancing atop a temple's domed rooftop, and those stunning mosaic tiles crack, fall, and shatter against the hard-packed dirt.

Cowslews lift grown men into the air and snap them in two within their beaks.

Cowslews rip at the bellies of women and tear out their bowels.

City-folk who see me run behind me, bloody and broken. They crouch, hoping that my wake will protect them.

But I can't stay in one place. The cries of children pull me south.

I run toward those kids with this cape of terrorized people lumbering behind me—they're barely managing to stay alive in this fight. I find those young ones in a dead garden. Their bronze, tear-slicked skin burns the amber of sickness.

"Amma!"

"Papa!"

They scream and scream and scream.

But the creatures attacking them aren't those red-goggled cowslews. No, these snarling beasts are ground-bound urts with shiny silver scales that run along their spines. Their snouts gleam, bright with blood.

I push wind at the silver-spined creatures and shatter three of the four against those mud-bricked walls.

Urt Number Four snarls at me.

I push it into a dry fountain, then run to meet it, driving Fury into its neck.

Four more urts stand where the previous four stood.

"Too many," I whisper, my limbs trembling. There are too many otherworldly, and just one of me, and I'm about to throw up and pass out. I know I'm gonna lose this battle.

The silver-spined urts and the red-eyed cowslews see me standing by this fountain, towering over a crowd of cowering humans.

I want to tell these people that it will be okay, but how can it be okay when I'm leaning against Fury's hilt because my legs aren't strong and I'm so fucking thirsty and the world goes back to fading at the edges and—

The ground quakes beneath my boots. The sound of the buckling earth echoes over the shrieks of the city-folk. Shouts fill the air. These aren't howls of fear but the battle cries of the fearless. I hear metal striking flesh and bone. I hear…*laughter* and shouts of, "Kai!" Others shout, *"Fekaa!"*

Huge warriors, the men bare-chested, the women wearing black or red bandeaus, race around me as swift as nighttime fog. Eight of them stop to surround me and the terrified humans in my wake. But their weapons face inward, aiming at me and not the urts and cowslews that are steadily devouring the mortals of this town.

How am *I* the threat?

I glance at these warriors' feet—feet large enough to have made those shoeprints out in the desert.

These warriors are as tall as the city's mud-bricked houses, and they wear linen and leather sarongs that protect their muscular thighs. Their tattoos swirl like black-and-red smoke around their torsos, and black-and-red paint adorns their sharp, high cheekbones. Their irises are ruby-rimmed and filled with hatred.

The warriors not guarding me move from house to garden to town square, looking for urts and cowslews to kill. Blades high, blades wet, blades hot from work.

I smile at a woman warrior and step forward with my hands up. "Hi. You may not remember me, but I'm not—"

The warrior standing behind me presses his blade against my neck and growls, "Dum's kuqa ur aerr maqar kuqa osoem." *Don't move or you'll never move again.*

He speaks…*Mera*?

Another type of warrior works on the edges of the battle. They aren't built for fighting, and their beauty is more of a hush than a holler. Their smiles are soft, their gray eyes bright and sparkling. They wear tunics and loose trousers made of linen and light, and they kneel beside dying and injured villagers who are drowning in amber waves of death. They place their soft hands against the foreheads, broken limbs, and hearts of the injured, and whisper, "Assiph mi seshm sihv fi misisiv." *Accept the light and be healed.*

They are speaking Eserimean, the second of my two native tongues.

But why are they *here*, now, in the thick of the fighting?

A woman cries out.

The blade at my neck disappears.

Two cowslews attack another warrior who is holding me hostage. The circle has broken, and now, my captors are also fighting the otherworldly.

I back away from the fountain, careful not to stumble over my living cape of now-twenty city-folk.

An urt lunges at me from my right.

I sweep it against a wagon and burn another in the sky. I turn to run toward the sound of more fighting, but four flying creatures thump down in front of me, blocking my path. Three land behind me. They all snap their beaks at me, and one cowslew successfully slashes my wrist.

I cry out at the blood spurting out around my hand. Trembling, I stagger back, still shocked. Feels like my arm is on fire and filled with broken glass.

The creature's beak is now red with my blood, and it lunges at me again.

But a warrior's dagger slides between the cowslew's shoulder blades, killing the creature before he aims his blade at me again.

"What the fuck?" I cry, wincing from the fiery pain now sparking from my hand up to my shoulder. "I'm not the enemy, idiot."

But the ground shakes again. Stones and dirt explode all around us.

Up in the sky, a ball of fire the size of a mountain heads straight for the city.

What the *fuck*?

The heat of the meteor warms my face, and even the otherworldly shield their eyes against its brightness.

The ball of fire races closer…closer…

BOOM!

3

The cowslews that surround me and the city-folk burst into flame. Some of the otherworldly drop to the ground and roll in the dirt to put out the fires singeing them.

BOOM!

The world quakes again as the meteor strikes the ground.

My knees give and just as I fall back...all action around me stops.

A pair of hands presses into my back. The flames around me, no longer flickering, still shine bright.

I look back to peer at those hands—strong, large hands that span the width of my shoulders. I turn to face the one connected to these hands.

He is wreathed in fire, and his rum-colored eyes shine brighter than flame. His skin is the color of this land's soil, and he looks strong enough to carry all of Vallendor on his back. He wears a bronze wolf amulet on a black leather cord. A source of power like my moth pendant, his pendant twinkles as bright as the real-life black wolf that fights alongside him—she's the size of a horse and moments away from killing the closest urt. He moves so fast that he can stop the realm—everything and everyone around us is now frozen in place. But because he has been punished by the Council of High Orders, his powers have lessened, and he can no longer stop the realm for too long a time.

"Aim your blades elsewhere," the beautiful warrior tells my captors. "Our leader has returned." He winks at me. His deep voice rolls through me like thunder.

Before I can respond, one of the healers rushes over to me and tends to my injured wrist.

"They don't remember me," I tell Beautiful Warrior.

"They do," he says, "but no one knows who you are right now."

Who I am?

I've already forgotten that I'm hurt, but I still remember to thank the healer.

"Raodae kur kuka kim?" he asks. *Ready for some fun?* The language he speaks is not the same as the healer's, but I know it just as well. This tongue is also a part of me, the Mera part of me: Meran.

I nod and smile. "Yes, I am." And I drink from the flask and taste the sweetest water I've ever known.

Before I can say, "thank you," the battle action thaws around us and the fighting starts up, the otherworldly burn, and the wolf has killed again. The beautiful warrior's dual blades swing in smooth arcs, striking down the herd of cowslews that tore at me.

The closest otherworldly look over their shoulders. They attack still, slowing down as fire and metal chop them down and burn them up.

The big black wolf clamps the hands and heads of urts between her jaws. Cowslews howl to the sky and glare at the Mera warriors now cutting them down.

Together, Beautiful Warrior and I race toward the creatures now wrecking carts that protect women wearing ochre-colored robes. These women close their eyes and pray:

"Hear us, Celestial. Be our sword and shield. Don't turn your back on your children."

My mind immediately responds. *I will never turn my back on you.* Why did I answer? Ah. Yes. It comes back to me. They call me "Celestial" in this province.

The women's eyes open, and their faces relax—they heard my promise.

Beautiful Warrior wields his dual blades of catherite and flame like a cat's claws. He rips through the skin of silver-spined urts and fuzzy cowslews, and his big black wolf pounces on the flying ones, keeping them from escaping into the air to strike again. Her knife-like teeth rip at necks, and her silver claws rip at bellies.

I bend, stronger now, ready to swing Fury. My first strike rips a cowslew from its hip to its heart. I lunge, and my blade sinks into another otherworldly's throat. In between my slashing and burning, I sneak peeks at the man wielding those dual blades. Watching him makes my skin tingle. I can't *not* look at him, at the way he fights and the way he moves…

I like the way he moves.

I remember now. He taught me to go above my training as a Mera warrior, to use blades like I'd use my fingers. He taught me that not every fight should be fought the same way, that I needed to know the "why" to affect the "how." He wrapped my hands when they bled. We bathed together after every battle to soothe our muscles but to also talk about the fight we'd either won or almost lost. He baked me honeycakes and always burned the bottoms.

Yes, Zephar Itikin taught me how to fight—and how to love.

But he is now known as "Diminished."

My stomach swings from desire to alarm as a cart spirals toward me. I unleash a burst of wind from my hands and push the wagon back at the silver-spined urt who'd thrown it at me. The cart hits the otherworldly—and the power of my hands and the fierceness of the wind causes both the creature and the cart to splinter into thousands of pieces.

The big black wolf claws her way through a herd of urts, tearing their solid spines like fresh bread, cutting and slicing.

Over in the temple courtyard, a herd of urts chases a woman holding a baby to her chest.

I run toward them.

Zephar runs beside me and swings his dual blades to cut down two of those beasts.

The surviving urt continues to chase the mother and child, and just as it lunges for them, I pounce on the creature and knock it to the ground.

Pulse thrumming in my head, I drive Fury through the urt's heart. After the creature's death cry, the woman wraps her free arm around my leg. I take that moment to look back at the city.

A temple with smooth-coated stone walls stands in the northern part of this city. The temple's massive dome is covered with tiles of crimson, gold, and black and reflects the flames now burning up date palm trees whose reddish-brown, crispy fronds haven't borne fruit in seasons.

The houses here are no taller than three stories high, with flat roofs, square windows, and doorways draped in cottons and silks faded by the daystar. Some houses have crumbled, earth returning to earth. Chickens—some roasted by the fires, others running and clucking—huddle with villagers who glow bright amber.

Is this city now under the rule of Syrus Wake? Or is it now part of Kingdom Vinevridth? Maybe it belongs to a tyrant-king worse than the traitor Danar Rrivae and Wake combined. Who did I just bleed for?

Wait. I remember.

I know this city.

Gasho, the capital of the kingdom of Ohogar, in the middle of Doom Desert. One of my favorite provinces in Vallendor Realm is now besieged. By whom? Or what?

I'd left this place, and then the wild things came and tore through these streets. Yes, I'd left this place because they'd complained about working too hard to cultivate the land. They'd complained, about the daystar being too hot, about wanting a god who didn't require them to fight and toil and experience hardship. The people here had started to compare me to some made-up god that someone's cousin had heard about on holiday.

In the past, I'd healed visitors who'd come here and had been attacked by cowslews during their travels. I'd saved those who could be saved and had ordered the order of Eserime stewards to install protective wards on the roads. But then I'd been ordered by Gashoan leadership to ward lesser-traveled trails and to remove protections from those humans they deemed unworthy. Those leaders, not just in Gasho, but all over the realm, had started to treat me more like a tool than the Lady of the Verdant Realm. I'd warned them of where their disrespect would lead. They didn't care. They wanted what they wanted.

All of that had pissed me off. And I'd said, "Fuck it," and that had been that.

Not everyone had rebelled against me, though, not enough to justify the wild things invading the city and doing their worst to this family and others like them. I failed to protect them, then—and while I can't undo what's already been done, I can be...*better*.

The skies are smoky from the burning palms but clear of those fuzzy buzzards. No silver-spined beasts chase children over the cracked flagstone pathways. Healers tend to the injured as the warriors help the living and carry the dead to the center of town.

Zephar saunters over to me and offers me a leather flask. "Well, *shit.*"

I take the flask and let water dribble into my mouth. Just like that, my tongue shrinks, and the insides of my cheeks soften.

"Surprise, it's me," I say, now that I can, trying to smile.

The woman's hold around my legs tightens as the baby cries.

Before I can speak to her, an Eserime healer with bright pink hair comes to embrace her. The woman melts into this comforting hug and releases me. She whispers, "Celestial," to the Eserime, who looks nothing like me. To the woman in need, though, we must all look alike.

Now that Zephar and I are alone...

"You're still the fighter I remember," he says in his soft, low voice. "Methodical. Tenacious. Always taking one bite at a time."

"I've never been a messy eater," I say.

"I am, though," he says, cocking an eyebrow. "From what I remember, you loved watching me eat." He blushes as he tucks a stray hair behind his ear, then whispers, "I've missed you, Kaivara."

My breath catches in my chest as the sound of my name on his lips brings back memories of the...*meals* we've shared. And from what I recall, I was his favorite snack. That wolf pendant twinkles around his neck.

"And I've missed you, Zephar," I whisper. "Zee."

He's the man I'd forgotten.

He's the man I love.

4

Strong arms. A gentle touch. Fierce and fearless.

On the last day we were together, right before I was dropped into that forest outside of Maford, he'd kissed me. Mera don't glow plum like mortals, but I'd known that he wanted me, that he loved me. But then I chased that thief into Maford, and my life changed, and my heart swayed, and I fell in love with another. And now, as I stand before Zephar, my face burns with shame and guilt for not trying hard enough to return to him.

As tall as a date palm, as broad as a river, and larger than any man in this realm, Zephar is still not his true size because he is Diminished—punished by the Council of High Orders for breaking the rules. Like me, his strengths and abilities have also been muted. He moves slower than he used to, and his punches land softer, though to a mortal, still deadly. Zephar can only travel the realm by foot and not by Spryte, which is simply thinking "Maford," and *pop*, you're in Maford. Strips of his tawny skin hide beneath crimson symbols, orbs and connecting vines that signify the realms he's destroyed. There is the raindrop of Melki Realm. There is the mountain peak of Yoffa and the seashell of Ithlon, the realm of my childhood, the realm that I destroyed without permission.

Zephar had poets write songs for me, and sometimes, Zephar would sing them.

Before the world began,
I loved you even then.
You held my heart and hand
And found my joy within...

Zephar would woo me with lavish dinners, and we'd lose ourselves in drink and honey and clouds of incense. He'd punished those who spoke against me, and all knew that if they fucked with me, they fucked with him. We'd recline beside a fire or near a stream, and I'd trace the ink on his chest and back, mountains, raindrops, snowflakes, and arrows, and those symbols that spelled ZEPHAR MERA, BREAKER OF REALMS. His skin always pebbled from my touch.

I see no new markings right now, but I haven't seen all of him... *yet.*

"Kai," Zephar says as I melt into his arms. He feels solid, familiar, like home. His face lightens as he lifts my chin. "It's you."

I smile and shiver from his touch. "It's you."

He places the lightest, sweetest kiss upon my forehead, and then he feathers another kiss across my lips.

My stomach tumbles with desire as I caress his cheek. "You found me. Right on time."

The daxinea sent me here to save Gasho and its people—and as reward, I also found my love. I search the skies but see no sign of that magical bird, the last of her kind on this realm.

Zephar lifts an eyebrow and says, "You've been away since last spring, but I remained yours."

My tongue stiffens—I can't say the same. It's been such a long spring. And then I hear what he's just said...

"I've been gone for twelve months?" My hands tingle, and I squeeze my numb fingers.

"Yep."

"Shari," I say, looking around. "Where is she?"

He shrugs, distracted only by me.

But I see her, realm-sized now but still wolf-big. The Warden of the Unseen Step romps with the sheep dogs, and her pink tongue hangs from the side of her mouth.

Zephar's rum-colored eyes brighten until they're nearly translucent. He squints at my amulet. "Still dark?"

I glance down at the moth and nod. "Yeah."

"You have me again," he says. "Let the Council of High Orders keep their toys." He flicks his hand even though *his* "toy" still hangs around his neck, weakly lit but lit enough to slow time. He kisses my hand, cups it to his cheek, and leads me up a pathway of brown- and cream-colored mosaic tiles.

I take another quick sip from his flask. "This can't be water. It's so good."

"Just water, Beloved." He lifts an eyebrow and chuckles. "You've been roughing it, huh?" He points to the healers now holding golden pails and inspecting a dry fountain. "And they're back to healing the Gashoans' aqueducts again."

Golden pails. Sybel Fynal, the Lady of Dawn and Dusk, carried golden pails of water from the forests to the wells outside of Maford.

"Where are the guards?" I ask. "Amus and Ilil and the rest?"

Now, though, these gates have been abandoned.

Zephar's brows furrow. "Dead."

I gasp. "What? How? Where were you?" Ice crackles in my tone, but I force myself to take a breath. "Sorry."

Zephar's jaw muscles tighten—my tone didn't go unnoticed. "We can talk specifics later. Now is not the time."

He's right.

Because right now, villagers are falling to their knees in gratitude as we walk past them. There's Heri and his wife, Sotaty, and their baby, Imet—*oh my goodness!*—who is now walking.

I take Imet into my arms. She's shaking from all the fire and fighting. "It's okay, little one," I whisper. She touches my cheeks as I smell her soft baby skin—

Oh, no.

She smells like fire and sweat, and *no*! Babies should smell like warm cake and fragrant powders. They shouldn't tremble with fear.

I whisper, "I love you, little one, be at peace," and I smile down at her.

Imet stops shivering. She gurgles baby-words, and "Amma."

Yes, I'm gonna work to make babies smell like babies again.

I hand the child back to Sotaty as a crowd of toddlers totters over to greet me.

Aricus and Lanna and Enrik and Nosu—I'd blessed them days after their births on the Benediction of First Light. Now, they hug my legs, though they can barely stand on their own. I let them see my true face because children deserve that.

They all gape at me, and they begin to giggle and dance. Their glows shift from the amber of death to the blue of life.

I bend to touch their cheeks, and to each child, I say, "I'm sorry for leaving you."

They crowd into my arms and plant kisses on my face.

They heal the hurt parts of me, too.

I peel out of that toddler hug, stopping to touch Saba's broken arm and Puabi's broken leg, which mend under my palm. I calm hearts beating too fast, like the hearts of the elders Damuta, Unnabit, and Samath. I place my cool hand against the fevered foreheads of little ones, Myla, Ettum, and Kernshe. I can do all of this—my mother, Lyra, had been Eserime and the Grand Steward of Ithlon. She'd had a title and different names throughout that realm. One especially reflected her power, and now, that same title reflects mine: Healer.

"We have to keep moving, Beloved," Zephar whispers to me. "They will keep you here forever. You don't see it, but I do—you're weakening."

Ah. Yes. My body aches, and my muscles quiver, and the thudding between my ears is making me clench my teeth. I'm also Diminished.

With his hand on my back, Zephar guides me to the center of the pathway. He circles his finger in the air, and Mera warriors create a barrier between the people and me.

"You're not gonna believe this," Zephar says. "I've come around to your way of thinking about these bright-light coddlers."

"Bright-light coddlers?" I say, eyebrows high. "Who are you referring to?"

"The Eserime." He gathers his long hair into a topknot. "Having them with us gets our point across to the Gashoans and to anyone else who thinks that all we do is destroy. These people are glad and grateful that we've returned. You hear them, don't you?"

Though their mouths are still, the minds of the Gashoans move like whirlwinds.

"I told you help would come."

"Celestial answered our prayers."

"We must bring her gifts."

The women wearing matching ochre-hued robes stand in the temple's courtyard, their voices lifting in song. Their garments are embroidered with gold thread along the sleeves and hems. Two columns of gold-and-green circles decorate the front of their robes—and those circles signify the importance of continued learning. They are the Sisters of the Dusky Hills.

Celestial, your power bright.
Be our star in darkest night,
With gratitude, our voices raise,
In song and praise, we sing your ways.

Two guards pull back one of the veils hiding a temple chamber. Inside the chamber is a bath built on polished alabaster stone. The whole room shimmers, its walls made of blue lapis lazuli and inlaid with gold moths. Pillars of obsidian threaded with silver soar up to the open domed ceiling. Water cascades from multitiered pools, billowing steam scented with mint and lavender.

An Eserime with wavy seafoam-colored hair and silver eyes makes her way to my side. She dips her head and says, "Lady Megidrail, your list." She hands me a roll of gold-tinged paper, which reads:

- AQUEDUCT NORTH
- AQUEDUCT SOUTH
- FORTIFICATION OF:
    - ROADS
    - GATES
    - BRIDGE
- OVERGROWTH

From reclaiming farmland and organizing defenses to healing the sick and weak to reconnecting with old allies.

"If you could please consider," she says, "what you'd like to restore first."

My eyes widen, and I sneak a peek at Zephar.

"You like it the way you like it," he says with a shrug, grinning. "You don't like shortcuts or others making big decisions like...the color of wildflowers in a field no one visits."

"Water and healing first," I tell her. "Food next. Place protective wards all around—without them, what good is a fixed bone if another urt is gonna break it? Wait—where's...?"

I race out those broken gates and return to the gully.

That mother with the baby and toddler hasn't moved from their spot in the dried canal.

I hop down to join them and say, "Iretah."

She looks up at me with wide, tear-filled eyes. "Celestial."

I touch the top of her head.

She glows blue.

I touch the top of the little girl's head, and Nenefer also glows blue.

The baby that she holds, though...

"Whose child is this?" I ask, touching the infant's head.

"Tymy belongs to my brother and his wife," Iretah says.

"And where are they?"

She swallows. "Dead. Attacked last week by the creatures. There was no one here to protect us. No one here..."

Tears burn in my throat—the monsters came because I left this place. Because of that, this infant has no parents, and now, this young mother has yet another mouth to feed.

"I will fix this," I say, cupping the woman's cheeks in my hands. "This is my promise to you, to Nenefer and Tymy, too." Her husband, Samose, lies in the dirt just steps away, lightless.

The work has started, and my promise soon manifests in sparkling water bubbling from new holes dug into the dried gully. Charred date palms burst with green fronds and plump fruit. The Eserime are doing what Supreme created their order to do: heal the land.

Villagers blue with life congregate around an altar just placed in the city square. Atop the altar, an alabaster statue of a woman with wavy hair holds a ball of light in her left hand and a sword in her right. The engraved plaque at its base reads, *Celestial, Our Lady of Might and Life.*

Zephar cocks his head and stares at me. "So… What happened?"

I take a deep breath and slowly exhale. Then I tell him almost everything—from being arrested in Maford and Veril Bairnell's death to confronting Elyn Fynal and Danar Rrivae at the Sea of Devour. "And I'm going *back* to Mount Devour," I say, "and this time, I'm reaching the abbey and I'll be demanding an audience with the Council of High Orders—"

"To reinstate—?"

"*Everything.*"

"Including Spryte? Because we can't do our jobs if we can only move one step at a time."

"Agreed." I tap my amulet. "And I want this back with its full powers."

"Or?"

"There is no 'or.' I need to do what I'm put here to do."

"That's right." He grins and nods. "Destroy and rebuild Vallendor *our* way."

I stop mid-step, crinkling my brows. "Actually, that's not what I mean. I'm not here to destroy, at least not in the way—"

"Celestial!" More people arrive, their arms filled with baskets of dates, bottles of wine, breads, quilts, jars of honey, and gold coins. They place all of this before the altar. In their windows, doors, and posts, they drape colorful moth tapestries weaved in gold-and-red threads.

Zephar says, "Come," and takes my hand again.

"But I need to get back," I say, resisting. "There's no—"

"Ssh. You just got here," he says.

The massive sandstone walls of the Temple of Celestial stand, with each tiered level featuring heavenly and realm-bound scenes depicting both my light piercing the dark sky and my might as my sword lifts in battle.

Might and Life.

The grand hall boasts high ceilings and is lined with stone columns that stretch toward those ceilings like a forest of marble oak trees. Flickering torches illuminate murals depicting legends—from the creation of Vallendor Realm and the battles Celestial waged to protect this world, to paintings of Zephar and me embracing, our immortal love rendered in crimson-and-gold paint.

Another alabaster statue of my likeness stands at the front of the sanctuary. Her arms are spread—she is the welcoming mother ready to provide safety, comfort, and moments of respite.

The Sisters of the Dusky Hills stand at the rear of the sanctuary and sing a new song.

In battles fierce, where shadows lie,

You rise, oh Xisi, Warrior high.

With strength unmatched, your blades ablaze

Through every storm, you lead our way.

I would call Zephar by that name, Xisi, and most of those times, I'd be naked, and his hands would be lost in my hair.

The daystar moves to the western skies.

I need to return to the abbey.

"We need to talk," I tell Zephar.

He leads me to the Howling Wolf Inn, its wooden sign painted with a black wolf with jaws agape. The inn stands two stories tall, and crushed date pits cover the floor of the sitting room. I'd held court in this inn, taking meals with the farmers or the family heads or even the young people tapped as future leaders. I'd told them stories about the ways of other cities—their successes and failures. I'd offered lessons on diplomacy and conflict resolution.

But then tables of fifty people became twenty people, became five, and then no one came except for the innkeeper and his wife.

Now, that leather-faced innkeeper, Wolda, bows as his tiny wife, Sabenn, rushes behind Zephar and me with plates of date cakes, two glasses, and a pitcher of something dark and fruit-scented.

Zephar and I settle on a patio that overlooks the town, now being made perfect by the Eserime and Mera. I drop my cape, unbuckle and peel off my breastplate, greaves, and vambraces. I pull off my tunic, and now I'm standing in just my bandeau and leather breeches. I let my head fall back as light from the daystar nourishes my skin. Feels like freedom and victory and fucking, and I never want to wear armor again.

Zephar's eyes sweep across my body, and he watches my hands rub life into skin that hadn't felt light like this since last spring. "You leave me breathless," he whispers.

My head rolls to the side, light-drunk. "Prove it."

"You want me to die for you?" he asks, biting his lower lip.

I meet his gaze. "Umhmm."

"I will. Tonight. Little deaths, over and over again."

I raise my eyebrows. "It's like that?"

"It's *been* that, love. Since last spring."

My smile wants to die, but I force it to remain on my lips. I didn't deny myself the pleasure of Jadon's touch, *but how the fuck was I supposed to know*?

Zephar lifts his full glass. "To finding our way back."

Yes.

The beverage tastes of fermented figs and apples, and the honeycakes taste more luscious than any I've eaten since waking up in that forest outside of Maford.

"So what do we need to talk about?" he asks.

"Even though I withdrew my favor from Gasho," I say, "I didn't leave them altogether vulnerable. You said the guards are dead. All of them?"

"I dissolved the company *with your permission* because Gasho forgot," Zephar says, shrugging. "Yes, the otherworldly played a role in destroying the city, but the Gashoans are also at fault. They mistook their success as something *they* did. They believed that it was their genius that led them to create this perfect place, that their mere imaginations invented ways to irrigate their crops and harness the daystar's power. They believed that *we*, the gods, were only here to ensure that their dates ripened, that their goats made milk, that we didn't give them everything they had.

"And so they stopped praying to us. They stopped asking for advice and giving thanks. They knew what they wanted, and they knew what they were doing, and they didn't need us and so we, *the gods*, said, 'Fuck it.'"

He grins as he lifts his glass. "Anyone who knows me knows that I don't take shit like that well." Zephar drains his wine. "The otherworldly came to remind them that they are masters of *shit*. They did call upon us for help, in the end, while you were away."

"So…you didn't answer the call?" I ask, squinting at him.

"Your instructions were, and I quote…" He dramatically clears his throat. "'Fuck these people and all this fucking sand, they can kiss my sparkly ass, and Zee, don't you *dare* help them without an okay from me.'" He pauses, then adds, "But you moved your head a lot more when you said it."

Shit, Kai. I stare at my glass of wine, unable to drink on my suddenly sour stomach. I couldn't have meant that. How could I say those things after I'd blessed all those babies and loved all those mothers and the Sisters and the old people? Today's attack happened because I… because I…

Because I was an asshole.

Zephar pours himself more wine. "And here we are, together again. We can pick up where we left off. I'm thinking Shelezadd, north of here. They call it the 'city of dawn,' but there, too, they've turned it into a shithole."

As Zephar describes the tar-stained town now overrun by bandits and rapists, my mind wanders. I will have to tell him that I didn't come back to Gasho to destroy it or any other town. No, I'm here to save my people and Vallendor from Danar Rrivae. But if I'm to do that, I must first return to Mount Devour and demand the restoration of my powers. This realm—from the babies to the battabies—matters to me. Even in their imperfection, they deserve to not just survive, but to thrive.

"…because I'm far behind in destroying where my father was at my age," Zephar is saying now, tapping bare skin where a realm's symbol should be.

Zephar's markings mean less to me now—the Kai from before would've cared about his ink as well as her own. Now, though, Vallendor must be restored and protected from the traitor at all costs. No more orphans. No more invasions. Zephar may bristle hearing this at first, but he will understand. And he will stay with me until the end, and then, if he wants, he can leave Vallendor to destroy the truly fucked-up realms like Gropool, Myala, and Alex. He can earn so many tattoos that he'll run out of space on his beautiful body.

There are 67,000 known realms across the Aetherium, and a number of them can go.

But Vallendor is mine.

5

As Shari bounds into the courtyard, the Gashoans gasp with excitement and fear. The wolf nuzzles my legs, and I press my face against her thick black coat. Lightness comes over me—she's always brought me joy. She'd sleep at my feet, lead me through forests on long walks, wait patiently as I tossed her honeycakes, dried elk hides, and apples. Now, her heart beats with love beneath her fur—but I hear a soft, barely there whine.

"You okay, girl?" I ask, my nose to her nose, my golden eyes blinking into her green-jeweled ones.

The wolf's breathing stills—I can't hear her thoughts because she's not mine.

Zephar can't hear her thoughts, either, because he's not Eserime. Still, he studies us and laughs. "She doesn't want you to leave again. She missed you more than I did."

I kiss Shari's nose, pat her head, and say, "I love you, too." I want to say, "I'm not going anywhere," but I can't, and she knows that I can't, and that's probably why she won't exhale.

"Relax," I say, offering her a honeycake.

The wolf cocks her head—this isn't what she asked for—but she takes the cake anyway, since this is all that I can give her.

After their second song of farewell, the Gashoans line the courtyard and toss bundles of chamomile and wild thyme at our feet. Zephar holds my hand as we enter the temple with our Mera warriors—who no longer want to slit my neck but now recognize my authority—and Eserime healers behind us. Shari trots ahead of us—she knows the way.

"Last we talked," Zephar says, "Gasho was marked to be the final city destroyed."

I nearly stumble. "But Gasho's already been destroyed—and now, we're restoring it. Everything on the list was meant to rebuild the city."

"No," he says, his eyebrows creased. "This is more of a cleanup than a restoration. Gasho was nowhere close to total destruction. There was no cleansing fire."

We're outside again, and Zephar gazes at the nighttime sky.

The altar beneath the belltower glows in the night. Carved from a single piece of alabaster, the solid ball is as tall as the tallest Gashoan. The Sisters place the last of the night offerings there, and then they kneel to pray.

"We won't destroy Gasho," I say now to Zephar. "You do realize that Danar Rrivae wants Vallendor for himself and plans to kill me, right?"

"Kai," Zephar says, "*everyone* wants to kill you. The Dashmala, Syrus Wake, What's-His-Face on the other side of Doom Desert."

"This is beyond old-fashioned hate—"

"I know—"

"Do you, though?" I ask, head cocked.

"Of course I do, and I'm not worried." Zephar reaches for my face and tucks strands of my hair behind my ears. "If I'm not panicking, then you shouldn't panic, either. Have I ever steered you wrong?"

"No."

"Okay, then. Relax a moment."

Only the Sisters follow us to a garden as wide as the temple's courtyard. Mist, veiling this terrace and hiding its true size, flows like a river around the roots of trees that look as old as the realm itself. Those roots rise out from the ground like warriors, and their branches block most of the sky.

Gleaming, fat plums hang from the twigs of some of these trees. Flowers in impossible shades of indigo quiver on their vines.

"This place," I whisper, "it reminds me of…"

"Ithlon?" Zephar asks.

I close my eyes. "Yes." I'd designed it that way.

Zephar kisses my hand and leads me deeper into the garden, our feet silent against the smooth, polished-stone pathway. Soon, we're walking beside a stream of clear water that opens into small ponds around the garden. Their mirrored surfaces reflect light from the sky above.

We stop at a space where the mist gathers thickest and most fragrant.

No mortals can move beyond this point without dying.

This is the Sanctum of the Dusky Hills.

Polished alabaster walls and mosaic tiles of crimson and gold. Sigils of moths, and runes of protection: diamonds, bears, wolves, paddles, and knots.

Up above, the nightstar, goddess Selenova, slowly treks across the dark canvas as her children, called "stars" by humans, dash across their sky-playground just like Gashoan children chasing fireflies across the marshland. Zephar and I walk the mist-covered trail lit by pearly light, and we approach the sounds of flutes, drums, and voices singing a song about stars and glows and…

The dawn will find you as my love draws near,

Blades of desire cut my heart, unaware.

I lose sight and sound in open spaces.

I lose sight and sound behind closed doors.

Your beauty has me bound in quiet place,

My heart you've lain and belongs to you.

I gasp and spin to face Zephar. "This song… You remembered that this song…" My throat tightens with emotion, and I whisper, "Zee, I love this song. The words…"

"I know." He brushes my cheek with his finger. "I always asked them to play it during those times I missed you the most, which meant every dawn, every dusk."

Zephar had this song written and performed for me. On the night the cantor first sang these lyrics, I cried.

Red, black, and gold moth sigils line the Sanctum's footpath. This haven is nestled in a valley surrounded by acacia trees that have never been touched by drought or disease. That stream down in the misty garden flows from the water here, running over smooth stones speckled with green moss.

A pavilion sits in the center of this valley and is encircled by carved wooden columns entwined with vines and topped by interwoven branches and leaves. All of it glows with runes. The pavilion's floor is polished stone inscribed with moths and swords and covered with plush rugs, cushions, and low-slung chairs.

"Look who's back," Zephar shouts.

The music stops, and thirty warriors stand at attention. Some smile. Others scowl. I am the prodigal Grand Defender returning to stir up shit and change their lives. *Again.*

There's the best scout in the group: Jarini, a Mera beauty with braided, coffee-brown hair and a resting bitch face. Her eyes dance even though the rest of her cannot. She shouts, "Welcome back!"

Carana, his bronze skin almost free of markings, grins at me only because I've shown him patience in the past. I know he will turn on me the moment his little chest wears three worlds, and he knows I know it, too.

But where's Dyotila? She swung a battle-ax as big as an oak tree.

And where's Avish? He wrote the song that brought me to tears.

Some faces I don't recognize—it's not that I don't remember them. No, I don't know them. Where did they come from and why are they here?

My mouth goes dry, and I run my tongue along my lips to moisten them. A flicker starts behind my eyes and grows into a twinge across the back of my neck. I feel strange.

Jarini shouts, "Av've!" and the others shout, "Av've!" and everyone whoops and claps, and the music starts up again.

A fire burns in a circular hearth, and it doesn't smell like burning trees and trapped wildlife. No, I smell cinnamon and chamomile, lavender and thyme.

Zephar holds out a chair and bows as I sit. "My love."

I grin despite my misgivings. "You're new and improved."

"And you're the same star that lights my sky." He drops into the chair beside me and bends to kiss me, a kiss that turns from sweet to sultry. He tastes of mint and dates, and all of it makes me breathless and tingly.

But that tingling across the back of my neck? The heaviness pressing against my shoulders? Feels like someone's watching me—and not the Mera and Eserime in this pavilion.

He pulls away and nudges his nose against mine. "Hungry?"

"Starving."

Platters of my favorite foods appear before me. Roasted carrots and sweet onions. Glazed bananas and thin, crispy slices of apples. Pistachios and almonds roasted and salted or roasted and candied. Greens and golds and ruby-reds, there are so many colors on my plate. And honeycakes, so many honeycakes.

The faces of my destroyers are bright, and even the scowlers are now smiling. I stare at the Eserime and turn back to Zephar. "The Eserime never camped with us before. Why now?"

He catches a grape in his mouth before saying, "We're building bridges between the hardline Mera and the other half. The stewards believe in our cause, and there are enough challenges with Danar running around, so why not accept their partnership? Why should immortals fight immortals? That's a waste of time and effort. That was your reasoning before you went away, and you were right. The Eserime believe in *you*, and they add value to our interactions with the mortals, humans especially, as you saw in Gasho."

An Eserime healer stands at the edge of the pavilion. Her platinum-colored eyes are flecked with worry. She holds her fist beneath her chin and flicks her pinkie finger at me. Like she's beckoning me to come over but doesn't want anyone else to know.

Or maybe I'm imagining it. Zephar doesn't appear to notice.

At the Sea of Devour, Elyn didn't mention that Eserime had joined me in the wanton destruction of Vallendor, one town at a time. I mention it now to Zephar. "She and her mother said that my way was not *the* way."

Zephar scoffs. "What do they know? Elyn is a big brain who's never led anything. She doesn't know what happens in a dying realm because she's never been in charge of one. She's a fucking librarian who keeps her hands clean."

He's right—Elyn Fynal has never managed one damned street corner, but she's telling me how I should rule a realm?

But she was right about one thing, so I say, "There are innocent people that will be caught up in—"

"First of all: *what*?" Zephar gapes at me like he doesn't know whether to laugh or shake me. "Second, every destroyed realm contains innocent people, even those realms approved for destruction by Supreme and the Council. You gave them a chance, Kai, and frankly, the Grand Stewards in those realms failed. Sybel, Vallendor's Grand Steward, also failed. They failed, and so we destroy them."

He chomps down on a few black olives and adds, "Gasho finally started acting right today, but only out of desperation and fear. Those fucking cowslews and urts broke their spine. Today, we saved them, and they dusted off the altar, presented you with gifts, and now they expect us to forgive and forget everything they did or didn't do."

I swallow the acid burning up my throat, and I look over to where that healer stood, the one I imagined motioning to me.

But she's now gone.

"Do I want the Gashoans and all of Vallendor to serve me out of fear?" I ask Zephar distractedly. "Can you really punish people and expect them to love you in return?"

"I don't make the rules, sweetness," Zephar says, shrugging. "I just bring the fire."

Rows of luxurious tents line one side of the settlement, each tent grand in size, crafted from silk and linen, and embroidered with protective runes. Mera don't build permanent dwellings, since we move from realm to realm, destroying and restoring.

"And my tent?" I ask, nodding as I pass warriors bedding down for the night.

"You mean, *our* tent?" Zephar says. "We share." He stops walking. "Oh. Is that okay?"

I chuckle. "Of course." I tap my temple. "I forgot, remember?"

"That's right," he says, nodding. "And I must remember that you forgot."

We laugh.

I must tell Zephar about Jadon and me…

Right?

Of course.

"Welcome home again," Zephar says, approaching a gazebo three times the size of the others.

This tent is divided inside like a cottage and includes a sitting room with chairs, cushions, and a table. A wall separates the sleeping quarters from the rest, and our large, elevated bed is covered with quilts made of soft cottons and silks.

I'm sweaty and tired, and before I say, "I need a bath," Zephar pulls two cauldrons from the fire burning in a hearth behind the tent. "I know what you need," he says, pouring hot water into a large, wooden tub. "A hot bath and some of this…" He holds up a glass vial and pours its contents into the water.

The surface is soon covered by lavender-scented bubbles.

"I thought we ran out of that," I say, pointing to the bottle in his hand.

He chuckles and says, "We did but when you were away, I had nothing to do, so…"

I grin and point at him. "You made the bubble-stuff! Just like your mother said you would! She was right! Admit it."

He rolls his eyes and holds out his hands. "Fine. She was right. Learning how to make the bubble-stuff will now benefit the both of us."

"You're damn right it will."

"Because I get to see you naked now."

"You still want to see me naked?" I ask, eyebrow cocked.

"Fuck yeah," he says, capping the vial, "but more than that, I want to see you happy, especially after a day like today."

I hop on his back and nuzzle his neck. "Ha, you love me."

He shakes his head, blushing.

I give him a sloppy kiss on his cheek. "I can't wait to tell your mom that you made me bubble baths."

He watches me undress, and his eyes slide from my breasts down to my hips. His gaze never leaves me even as I slip into the hot water and dip beneath the bubbles.

My skin tickles and warms.

"Are you joining me?" I scoop up bubbles and blow them into the air.

Zephar pushes off his breeches. His body is marked by those destroyed realms, orbs and symbols and tendrils rippling across his muscles. He stands there, this mighty warrior, in his perfect stance. Supreme is good all the time, and all the time, Supreme is good.

His golden eyes sparkle. "Am I still good enough?"

He's swollen enough. He's large enough. Oh, yeah. He's good enough.

I stare at him in awe. There is no form like this man anywhere on Vallendor or in all of the 67,000 realms.

But he's too big for this tub, and his legs and feet stick out like tree trunks.

"This isn't gonna work," I say.

He taps the side of the vat. "I'll build us a bigger bathtub, one that fits two."

I lift an eyebrow. "So a lake, then?"

He splashes me with water and grimaces as he shifts on the bench.

I wince. "You're uncomfortable. I'm sorry."

He tries to grin. "A little longer." He shifts again. "Since last spring, we've bathed alone, and we've slept alone and…" He splashes me with water again. "I just want to enjoy this. I just want to enjoy you. I just want to talk about crazy shit and sing stupid songs and…" He shrugs and smiles. "Be yours again."

I say, "Yeah," feeling like shit. Because I haven't slept alone nor have I bathed alone, and I need to tell him that, but I don't want to, even though I wasn't in my right mind those times. I couldn't even remember my own name, so how could he expect me to remember *his* name or that we were together? Yes, Jadon and I talked about the possibility that I had someone waiting for me. *What if you were already in love before waking up in Maford? What if someone's waiting for you?* Back then, on that night as we sat on either end of a log, my heart told me that no one was waiting for me, that my heart would remember that kind of love. An unforgettable love. *Shit.* I knew nothing. I was wrong. Because here I am. In love.

"When others had given up," Zephar is saying now, "when others grew convinced that either you weren't coming back or had been killed, I knew. My heart knew. And so, I waited."

Because that's love.

Zephar carries me into our tent as I kiss and lick the muscles flexing along his jaw and neck, trying to focus only on him, to forget the guilt churning in my belly. He's iron beneath my hands and everywhere they roam, but then my hands find his face, and I close my eyes and something bubbles inside of me that shifts my desire to sadness.

He doesn't speak, and soon, he pulls me into his arms and whispers, "It's okay. I understand."

"So much has..." *Happened.* Tears form in my throat and trickle down my cheek as I squeeze my eyes closed.

"I know," he whispers, lifting my chin. "I can wait—we have forever."

I nod. "Okay."

He whispers, "I raqo vai," and I whisper, "I raqo vai," because yes, I *do* love him.

We climb into bed, and he wraps his arms around me. He closes his eyes, and soon, his breathing deepens into a steady rhythm. He's asleep.

Each time I shut my eyes, my heart thuds like a boot dropped on glass.

A shadow shifts across the tent wall. From the corner of my eye, I watch a strange silhouette twist against the canvas.

Trees backlit by the nightstar?

I hear footsteps and sit up in bed. A chill runs through me. I keep my hand on Zephar's shoulder as my heart beats wildly in my chest. I scan the walls of the tent again. This time, I don't see shadows. I close my eyes to listen for footfalls. Nothing.

Am I expecting Jadon Wake to break through the tent flaps and declare his love for me?

Has my guilt about betraying Zephar—betraying them both—become a living thing, stalking all hope of peace and pleasure?

I slowly exhale, and I rub my face to snap out of my thoughts. I slip back beneath the quilt, kiss Zephar's forehead, and whisper, "I'll never leave you. Never again."

His sleeping face flushes. The glow comes from my amulet, thrumming with a faint light, vibrating against my fingertips.

What is it?

The flaps of the tent are pushed open.

A snout. Gold eyes. *That's Shari.*

I pull on my linen robe, and the wolf and I tiptoe out the back of the tent. I stare up at the dark sky while clutching my amulet. So many questions drift across my mind.

Why can't I accept Zephar's love without worrying about Jadon?

Why didn't Jadon tell me the truth?

Why am I still thinking about him, when he's firmly in my past?

Why—?

Shari nudges my leg.

"Done?" I ask, smiling down at her.

Fortunately, I don't have to have any answers now.

She studies me with her jewel-toned eyes.

I kneel before her and stroke her head. My hand slides down her neck and stops at that whine in her chest, same as before. "What's wrong, lovely?"

She can't answer me. But my moth pulses with weak light.

Something's wrong.

While I'm in bed with my love, Danar Rrivae is trudging around the Sea of Devour, scheming to kill me and take Vallendor as his prize. That's what's wrong.

I must leave the Sanctum and Gasho, and not for Shelezadd, like Zephar's planned. I must leave, but this time, I'll muster the Mera and Eserime with me, ready to fight to protect Vallendor. And I'll have Zephar and Shari beside me, too. And that's enough.

It will *have* to be.

6

The sweet perfume of night-blooming jasmine wafts through the arbor, nurturing this moment of peace amid the chaos of war raging outside this canopy. We lie on the soft grass beneath a bower of old trees, Jadon's strong hand finding my uncertain one in the dim light. The soft light of the nightstar casts silvery streaks in his dark hair. His blue eyes glow bright as pearls.

I whisper, "Jadon? What—?"

"Listen." The one word he speaks is soft as the scented air. "I shouldn't have lied to you, but don't ever doubt my love. Don't ever doubt my heart." His eyes shimmer with devotion as he adds, "I can't do this without you."

"Do *what* without me?" I push away from him to stand. My leather breeches creak and squeeze my thighs—they no longer fit. I'm too big for my breeches.

Jadon also stands and tightens the buckles of his breastplate. The rune on his right hand—fire, water, ice, earth, each within a circle—sparks with faint light as his eyes search the sky. "Is that a 'yes'?"

I blink at him and shake my head. "What are you talking about?" I reach for my amulet—my pendant no longer hangs from my neck. "Where—?"

I peer at the ground and search between the blades of grass. The earth rumbles beneath our feet.

Jadon draws his greatsword, Chaos, from thin air. That wide silver blade looks dull and dry, ready to soak in the blood of enemies. "Are you ready?" he asks.

"Ready? For what?"

Red-and-gold moths sweep up from the grass, crying out as they whirl around me.

"Go now, Lady!"

"You're in danger, Lady!!"

"Lady—!"

BOOM!

The land beyond this grove explodes, flinging dirt and stone into the air.

A giant aburan, a beast in the shape of a bear that glares at me with the eyes of a man, claws through the hedges that protect this bower. Above the canopy of trees, a scavenging gerammoc—its beak crackling with lightning—soars on wings that hide the nightstar.

"Are you ready?" Jadon asks again.

I reach for Fury— *Shit.* My scabbard is bare. "Where's my sword?"

The ink on Jadon's hand flashes like the gerammoc's lightning. "Time is life," he shouts.

I nod. "Yes, I know, but—"

He moves closer to me, his eyes bright. "For love, for change, for all that yet breathes."

With trembling hands, I hold his face and say, "Fight."

He kisses me—he tastes of iron, sugar, and blood.

BOOM!

Our arbor explodes, and the ancient trees that served as protection catch fire, raining burning leaves down on us. Jadon's marked hand also catches fire, but he smiles as smoke rolls up his arm and billows across his chest. He shouts, "Stand fast," as his lips flicker with flame. We kiss one last time, *fuck the flames*, and my face—

• • •

It's too early in the morning to be shouting at the top of our lungs at each other inside a stupid tent. And no matter how many rooms there are, *this is still a stupid tent*.

I stand with my arms crossed and my gaze locked on Zephar.

He pulls on his breeches and storms to the other side of the room. His golden eyes burn bright with frustration and his beautiful face twists with…

Hate? No.

Disappointment? No.

Rage. Yes. At me, at my words.

"All this time," he growls, "I've been waiting for you and planning for this moment to destroy and restore the next city—"

"I know—"

"And now you wanna back out?"

I force myself to not look away even as guilt claws at me. This means so much to him, and he's right—in our time together, he's never asked much of me. But the realm is different now. A greater threat looms, one far more dangerous than a desert town with bandits who attack traveling merchants and troublemaking adolescents who burn down wheat fields.

"Please listen to me," I say, my hands steepled against my lips. "We are so close to losing this realm, and I'm not being hyperbolic, Zee. Danar Rrivae is at our front door, and my life is at stake here, and so is yours, and so is the life of this realm. This is not in the near future. The threat is *now*."

He will understand. He *must* understand. He has understood in the past. Like when he was charged with destroying the realm Sadaadea. Both the mortals there and the terrain were uncontrollable. In a moment of exhaustion, Zephar had wanted to flee this first campaign of destruction that he'd led. I convinced him that he could do it, that he *had* to do it, that this task was worthy of completion. He understood the urgency and the assignment, and the craggy peak of Sadaadea is now inked in the middle of his lower back.

"I'm not backing out," I say to him, softer now. "I'm thinking about strategy. Shelezadd can wait. Danar Rrivae and Syrus Wake can't. If we don't stop them—"

"I don't care about Danar and some fucking emperor-puppet!" Zephar shouts, shattering the quiet. "I care about you dismissing me, talking to me like I'm some *boy*. I waited for you all this time..." He runs his thick fingers through his hair and closes his eyes. "There's this *distance* between us now." He lowers his head and whispers, "Do I still matter to you?"

His question is like a blade to my gut.

"Of *course* you matter to me," I say. "Do *I* still matter to *you*?"

"Yes." His eyes open but stay fixed on the rug.

Does mattering even matter when the world is about to end? Like... for real. Danar Rrivae is at the threshold of Vallendor, preparing to take her from me.

The dim light of pre-dawn casts long shadows across the tent's walls. Zephar's shoulders heave as he turns away from me, his jaw clenched. I want to apologize, but the words die in my throat. Instead, I say, "I can see that you're done talking for the moment. I'll leave you to think about all that I've told you."

He doesn't speak, just keeps glaring at the tent's canvas wall, his back rigid with anger.

I linger, hoping that he'll say something, *anything* that might bridge this chasm forming between us. But he doesn't speak. He doesn't even sigh.

Wearing only my bandeau and breeches, I leave the tent. Out here, the valley enjoys perfect peace. Over in the pavilion, embers flicker in the hearth. A few Mera sit in those low chairs, heads back, eyes closed, swords at their feet. Shari rests at the entrance to our tent, and she lifts her giant head.

I kneel and scratch her ear. "Did we wake you up with all that bullshit?" I kiss the top of her head. "Sorry for the disturbance—the Warden of the Unseen Step deserves better. Let's go for a walk, yeah?"

She yawns, stands, stretches, and trots beside me until we reach the perimeter of the Sanctum. That's where she sits.

"I know: you can't come," I say, nodding. "I'll be back this time. Promise."

The mountains are cool this early in the day, and I welcome the crisp air, which chases away the fog of anger and guilt clouding my mind. It's still early, but it's never too early for otherworldly. That's when I realize that I left my swords in the tent. I gaze at my empty hands—empty, though, doesn't mean powerless.

I reach a ridge that overlooks Gasho and the desert plain. There's the Temple of Celestial. There's the canyon I escaped yesterday.

The skin on the back of my neck prickles. I look back over my shoulder.

No one's there—no amber or blue glows of the living creep behind me.

And I don't believe that.

I'm being watched.

Holding my breath, I continue my trek, my steps seemingly casual. My mind, though, isn't resting. I study the terrain, thinking through ways to capture my stalker. After taking a few more steps, I spin and circle behind a cluster of boulders. I grab the neck of the figure crouched there. "It's too early in the day to kill someone," I say cooly, "but if I must..."

"Please, Lady Megidrail," he says, wheezing as my hands press down on his windpipe. "It's me. Avish."

Avish? He's the lyricist who wrote my favorite song. *The dawn will find you as my love draws near...*

I squeeze his neck one last time before releasing him. "You weren't at the Sanctum when I arrived last night."

He grimaces as he rubs the new welts forming on his skin and stands, swaying still on his feet. One of the slighter Mera, Avish still towers over all mortals. The color of his eyes looks closer to hazel than gold, and his chest is covered with markings of the three realms he's helped to destroy under my command.

But all he really wants is to write.

I've supported that desire by letting him write the speech I gave at Yoffa in defense of the realm's destruction. He wrote the blessing I recited at Separi and Ridget Eleweg's wedding. The proclamations of kings and queens of Vallendor—all were Avish's words.

"Why are you following me now?" I ask, leaning against a boulder, my hands prepared to resume strangulation if needed. "You need help penning another song? And I thought you'd abandoned us."

"Not abandoned," he says. "I've simply...*relocated*. I see folly in Zephar's path, but you are clear-minded."

"Folly?" I tilt my head and peer at him. "That's a dangerous word to choose when speaking of Lord Itikin, your commander, my partner, my betrothed. Thought you knew words better than this." My hands burn—his disrespect would've taken him to Anathema's porch, yet he still stands before me.

Avish's face flushes so much that he blends into the red dirt of the desert. "It *is* folly, Lady, but please know that I still believe in *you* and in the path *you've* chosen."

"And what path has Lord Itikin taken?" I ask.

"Ignoring the peril of the realm and focusing on this small town that, ultimately, won't matter," Avish says.

I squint at him. "And what path do you think that *I've* chosen?"

Avish meets my gaze. "Danar Rrivae is a threat. Shelezadd is not. What's the point of destroying a stupid city if Vallendor falls? You know that. And so does Malik."

I blink at the man before me. "Who?"

"Malik—remember him? He has a temple on the other side of this hill erected by his believers," Avish says. "He wishes to see you again. He agrees with your reasoning: Danar Rrivae must be eliminated so that Vallendor may prosper."

I study the poet, searching for any signs of deceit. He has spun words into beautiful song and powerful speech. He can wield that same gift—no, *weapon*—to also spin beautiful lies. If I find out that he's lying, he'll meet my hands again. I should trust him, but just yesterday, my own warriors held their swords to my neck. For now, I'm questioning *everything*.

Avish and I travel quickly through the mountain pass. The pathway grows stonier the higher and farther east we walk. We finally reach a plateau—it's hard to imagine that believers climbed this high, like goats, to erect a temple.

We move beneath the pines, and a sprawling low temple emerges from the mist. The sleek dwelling's white stone-and-glass walls gleam in the new morning light. Lush gardens of yellow, white, and red flowers surround the structure. All of it is a stark contrast to the oaks and buckeyes, sagebrush and wild grape growing around the sleekest damned building I've ever seen. No fussy parapets or colonnades. Just a series of white-washed, hollowed-out boxes stretched across the clearing. There is more glass than stone, and a rectangle-shaped pool in the courtyard. Single story, open-hearted. No mosaics. No domes.

"Is this a house or a temple?" I ask Avish.

The poet grins. "It is whatever you need it to be."

As Avish and I approach the dwelling, a tall Mera warrior with long brown braids and a battle-ax emerges. She gazes at me, stern but respectful. Then her eyes flicker with recognition, and the edges of her lips lift into a smile.

"Dyotila?" I ask, surprised.

She bows and takes a knee. "Lady."

"What are you doing here?"

Just standing here instead of flanking Zephar or me is treason—and by the way her eyes bounce from me to the ground to Avish, she knows this is true.

But something is happening here.

"Lord Malik Sindire," she says. "He is raising a new army that can challenge the traitor and win. And he wants you to lead that army to victory."

I keep my gaze moving as I follow Avish and Dyotila through large walnut double doors. I spot no other Mera or Eserime, or mortals. No one lounges beside the glistening pools. No one sips wine beneath the towering oaks. No one sits on the sofas.

This temple feels more like a country estate, and I like it.

We enter a room of vanishing glass walls that blur the outside from the inside. Standing there barefoot and bathed in amber morning light is a short, round man, draped in a yellow robe. "Lady Megidrail," he says, his voice as smooth as the glass around us. "It's been several springs since we've enjoyed each other's company. It was an honor then, and it's an honor now to be in the presence of the one who prophesies speak of."

I bite the inside of my cheek. "Prophecies? Since when do gods listen to the fever dreams of mortals?"

"When they, too, say that you will change the course of this realm." His eyes, a wild mix of Mera gold and Yeaden black, twinkle with amusement.

I glance back at Avish and Dyotila, and even her face shines with hope. I turn back to Malik Sindire, my mind dancing again.

Change the course of this realm...

Stopping Danar Rrivae before it's too late: that's more than changing the course of this realm.

Malik Sindire smiles as he takes my hand in both of his soft, small ones. "Do you remember me, Lady?" He nods back at Avish and Dyotila, and both leave the room.

I study my host, flipping the pages of my memory. Nothing presents itself. "I'm afraid not, sir."

"I visit Vallendor every seventy-five seasons or so—you were just a youngling last time I came." He flaps his hand. "Your father and I have been friends since Supreme formed us from nothing." His feet make no noise as he pads down a corridor filled with light shining down through the glass ceiling. "I established this dwelling ages ago—my *followers* did, since I do not lift hammers. There are no closed gates here because all are welcome. You know this, but I've been told that you may not remember the details of your many visitors nor your realm. Who can blame you? Most things and most people are forgettable."

True.

Malik Sindire laughs, and his laughter sounds like bells. "*Anyway.* I'm back! To my followers' great joy. Or disappointment. Both!"

"If you know my father," I say, "does that mean, then, that you know—?"

"The traitor?" Malik Sindire asks, his lips twisted in disgust. "Yes, I know the traitor, and soon after your father joined the Council of High Orders, he helped make the decision to punish Danar Rrivae for his treason. No matter—Danar Rrivae still moves about the Aetherium wreaking havoc. I hear that he plans to take Vallendor just as he's taken other realms."

"But I won't let him."

"Because you're Vallendor's greatest defender." We reach the end of the corridor and step into a sunroom.

The ceiling is made of walnut, and the glass walls open to a patio. There's a pool with a vanishing edge, water extending to the horizon. Beyond the pool, there's a sweeping view of Vallendor's western lands, including Caerno Woods and a dwarven Mount of Devour.

Malik Sindire smiles at me, and his eyes disappear into slits. "This is my favorite place in the temple. I love how beautiful it is here."

The dusky hills are bathed in golden light. Mist wreathes the tops of the trees.

My host settles on the couch and pats the cushion beside him. "When I first heard that Izariel punished you so severely, I voiced my disagreement. Your reasoning was sound, Kaivara. Syrus Wake calling himself 'Supreme'—what god can ignore such blasphemy? You show that man your strength and ruthlessness by destroying his provinces one by one.

"Really!" he says. "It was a brilliant plan! But ultimately, the plan was not approved by the Council, so here we are, with one of us branded as Diminished, which..." He adjusts the cuffs of his robe. "Yes, you disobeyed them, but now the Council is glad that you defend this place even if your reasons are selfish and shortsighted."

I bristle. "I'm neither."

He laughs and places his hand over his heart. "But it's true, Precious One. You *are* selfish and shortsighted, and there are times when the realms require that type of leader."

But I don't want to be either of those things. My mother is no more because I was selfish and shortsighted and destroyed Ithlon Realm with her on it. My father has yet to visit me on Vallendor or even send me a simple note of encouragement after I was punished and sequestered here on Vallendor because, again, I was selfish and shortsighted and destroyed realms without authorization from the Council. All of

Linione wants me dead—and they sent Elyn Fynal, the Adjudicator, to kill me.

Malik Sindire reaches for a carafe of wine on the table. He pours wine the color of my eyes into two glasses and offers me one. "Danar Rrivae is more complicated than many perceive him to be. I witnessed his downfall, as have others, but unlike them, I acknowledge that his motivations have been misunderstood."

I frown after sipping this delicious wine. "I'm sorry, but… He is not a sympathetic character in the story of Vallendor."

The old man holds up his left hand, heavy with rings encrusted in emeralds, topazes, rubies, and diamonds. "I didn't say *that*. He isn't simply out to rule the realms. Danar seeks to reclaim his family. A futile act, unfortunately."

I tilt my head. "He has a family?"

Malik Sindire laughs again. "Oh, dear."

I bristle again. "Did I say something funny?"

"Every being comes from another, Precious One," the man says. "We don't simply *become*. Even a weed is birthed from a drifting dandelion seed. You see, Danar's family—his forebears, his wife Indis and four children, what were their names?" He cocks his head, skims his fingers along his jaw, thinking. "Anyway, they all lived on Birius Realm."

A realm of savannahs and herbology that had been stripped of its lushness to make poisons instead of medicines.

"Birius is gone," I say.

Malik Sindire nods. "Destroyed ages ago by both your father and Zephar Itikin's father, Bezeph. A destruction approved by the Council of High Orders, I must add."

"If Danar's family was destroyed along with the others," I say, my words tight, "where was he? How did he escape that doom?"

"He was somewhere in the Aetherium starting trouble," Malik Sindire says with a sigh. "With Birius's destruction, so came the destruction of his past, present, and future. But he refuses to accept his family's end, and instead of discovering new realms, which is his job, he goes about the existing ones, holding them captive until his demands are met and Supreme returns his family back to him."

"Which is impossible," I say.

"Nothing is impossible for Supreme," Malik Sindire points out. "At the same time, nothing warrants the return of those who are lost." He lifts his glass to study the color of the wine. "Now, do I feel for him in some small way? Yes. But I detest that man, who he's become, and what he did to Fendusk, Kestau, and Kynne. And the creatures he's spawned—don't get me started on *that* menagerie. Now, he's set his eyes on Vallendor."

The old man considers me. "He hasn't given up, you realize? Elyn Fynal has only postponed this war, but he's out there—" He nods to the vastness of Vallendor. "And he's angrier than ever, especially since he was so very close."

Jadon Wake had been his weapon, and I'd fallen for that threat, jeopardizing the realm and my own life.

"He'll do anything to claim what he wants, Precious One," Malik warns. "And that means that he will appeal to your…*shortcomings*."

The wine now tastes sour on my tongue. "I'm sure you will tell me what those are."

"I don't need to. You know them. But what I want *you* to tell *me* is this: What are your values? What do *you* hold dear? What will guide you to succeed and save this realm?"

I sip wine that I can no longer taste.

He smiles. "Give me three."

Accountability? How can I expect that when I've escaped my ultimate punishment?

Discipline? Again, I'm that god who has destroyed without the Council's approval.

Strength? What's that worth without patience or fairness, courage or humility?

"I can't name three," I whisper. "Not honestly."

"*Authenticity*," he says, tapping my wrist. "I witness that right now." He fixes his gaze on me, all amusement gone. "What's your purpose, Kaivara?"

I blink at him and open my mouth, but I can't speak.

"To be seen as the most powerful," Malik Sindire says for me. "For this to happen, you must also convince the *people* that the traitor and Syrus Wake were bad for them and that you will be the balm to their injury. You must convince them that you, the Lady of the Verdant Realm, will be the mountain of Vallendor and will not allow a sea of sand to overtake her ever again. You will have to deal boldly and swiftly with usurpers. You will have to act without pause, which…"

He wrinkles his nose and smiles. "You are apt to do. You must also be relentless this time around, Kaivara. Show the realm that you will tolerate no insurgents. Make them fear you; show them how to love you. Do this, and they will do as they should just as the people of Gasho have now done. In order for Vallendorians to change, *you* must change. Be their lady, be their defender, be their mother."

Malik Sindire nods. "You need them, Kaivara. One must have believers in order to be believed. The gods are powerless without believers. Mortals like winners—including the wolves that lurk in the forests and the women who choose mates…and choose kings. You, Lady, are the ultimate winner."

We sit in silence. He hums as he drains his glass, and I sit here, wishing for someone to say—

"All will be well, Precious One."

I gape at the old man seated beside me. *That's exactly what I needed to hear.*

He leans toward me, and his smile turns grim. "Be careful who you trust, yes? Who you let into your circle…and into your bed." He squeezes my wrist. "Once you figure out what you hold dear, decisions will come like…" He snaps his fingers.

I squeeze a smile from my lips and whisper, "Thank you."

He lifts my chin and grins. "And once you understand yourself, you will have all that you need to defeat the traitor. And you will no longer be reduced in your capacities. But your discovery cannot wait."

Malik Sindire surveys my breeches and bandeau. "I know that you have the confidence of the Mera, but you need more protection than…" He waves his hand at my bandeau and breeches. "High Lord Megidrail would be horrified to see his only child looking like an ordinary, shabby Mera warrior."

I roll my eyes. "I look like an ordinary, shabby Mera warrior *because* of High Lord Megidrail. I'm prohibited from wearing the armor of a Grand Defender. Everything I own—my sword and armor—are gifts from either humans or Renrians." I reflect for a moment before touching my amulet. "Except for this—this was a gift from my father, but he gave this to me a long time ago." The stone in the moth's thorax is cold.

"I can see how that upsets you, so...*come.*" Malik Sindire rises from the couch and beckons me to follow him back down that light-filled corridor. We turn into a space filled with glass cases of weapons and armor.

Avish and Dyotila stand at attention in the middle of the room.

"Incredible," I whisper, awed.

Malik Sindire taps his cheek and rocks on his toes and heels. "It *is* incredible. You may not remember, but one of my joys in life is traveling the Aetherium and collecting a realm's best armor and weapons, and books of unusual knowledge. Vallendor, I'm afraid, doesn't contain much of any of those things, no offense to the Lady, but this realm still captivates me. It is—or was—absolutely gorgeous. Perfect in so many ways.

"Nothing in this showroom is truly unique, but..." His expression softens with wonder. "There are beautiful things here. Powerful things, many of which were inspired by the Lady of the Verdant Realm herself."

"Really?"

"Certainly. Only the best in this room." He tilts his head and grins at me. "And you will need the best if you are to defeat the traitor. And since I collect only the best, please take all that you need. Whatever I have is yours, Lady."

I wander around the room and choose pewter-colored armor that reminds me of stormy skies and ancient mountains.

"Any blades, Precious One?" Malik Sindire asks.

"I will keep the swords already in my possession. But..." I pluck a dagger with a gray-leather handle. Its blade matches the pewter armor and is engraved with swirls that make it look as though it's in motion. "I'll name her...Tempest," I say.

Malik Sindire nods, satisfied. "Each piece has been crafted by the armorers at the Abbey of Mount Devour."

"Really?" I ask, eyebrows high. Such rarities demand a price. "So what must I do for you if I'm to walk away with these gifts?"

He stands before me, and even though he barely reaches my chin, his presence is what dominates this space. "You must *win.* You must defeat Danar thoroughly and without mercy. Because if you don't, he will kill you, and then he will take the next realm, and the next realm. He will keep searching for something he cannot have."

He takes Tempest from my hands and strokes the blade. "Your taste is immaculate." He meets my gaze. "Stay alert, Precious One. Do not hesitate to use this dagger—you are a wanted woman and will not be afforded any consideration or respect."

7

After my visit with Malik Sindire, I return to the Sanctum and to my tent.

Zephar and Shari aren't there, but the bed has been made and fresh flowers have been placed against the pillows.

Zephar's apology.

Outside, a horn blows: a call to arms.

I shove myself into my new set of armor and rush back outside, joining my contingent of Mera warriors—Diminished all—rushing to grab their blades, bows, and arrows.

"What's happened?" I ask, running alongside Ianna. He'd been one of the first destroyers to join me in the destruction of Ithlon.

"Attack on a caravan," he shouts.

Together, we race down the pathway to the misty garden. I check my swords and dagger—I'm ready to fight. We run through Gasho and out the now-repaired gates. My lungs fill with dusty air, but a smile finds my face after all the previous uncertainty. *This* is what I'm meant to do.

But then I *see.*

My stomach drops.

Gorga!

Banners with the moth sigil lie trampled on the ground. Women wearing those ochre-colored robes are being chased by green-scaled bandits wearing gray armor. Idus, the prince of Gasho, takes cover behind the two large guards swinging blades too weak for these opponents.

Shari is ripping through a Gorga bandit's neck. Zephar is swinging his dual swords at another bandit, but he shouts in frustration as his blades bounce off the Gorga's thick skin. Finally, thankfully, one of his blades cuts deep into the Gorga's hip.

Didn't I tell someone to place protective wards on the roads?

One of the Sisters of the Dusky Hills screams as she runs toward the open desert, two Gorga bandits chasing her.

I shout, "No!" and run after them.

One of the attackers catches up and rips away the young woman's robe.

His partner looks back over his shoulder and whirls around to roar at me, "You Mera bitch."

I thrust out my hand and throw fire in his face.

The Sister screams again as her attacker throws her to the ground and wraps his hands around her neck.

I catch a glimpse of big brown eyes, hair the color of wheat and sunflowers… I know this woman!

Ancress Mily Tisen had been my attendant. Though her smooth, unwrinkled skin reveals her true age of twenty seasons, those brown eyes and husky voice belonged to a wiser, older woman who'd seen too much. Just two springs ago, and new to the order, she followed me around with paper and pen, recording all that I'd done and said. I'd started teaching her the Mera language, throwing in a couple of swear words in Mera and Yeaden. She'd prophesied a Gasho without light and a canal that ran rivers of blood instead of water. Her dream had come true: the light of Gasho—me—left the city shortly after her prediction and hadn't returned until yesterday's slaughter.

The Gorga bandit tightens his grip around her neck.

The blue glow that I'd blessed her and the rest of the city-folk with just a day ago drips back into amber. She's dying.

I scream, "Stop!" and hurl a blast of wind at the bandit to push him off of her.

But he's strong and scrambles back on top of her.

If I use my full wind and fire, I'll hurt Ancress Tisen.

I grit my teeth and pull Justice from my back scabbard. I push that silvery-blue blade through the Gorga's neck, expecting resistance, but it slides smoothly past scales and bone. Thick brown blood splashes across Mily's face and the Gorga's life-light blinks black. I kick the dead bandit off of the young woman and pull her into my arms.

She's shivering with fear, but her breath steadies the longer I hold her.

A few times, I try to pull away from her, but she tightens her grip and whispers, "Don't go. Don't leave me. Don't go—"

I whisper, "Okay," into her curls, knowing that I must go—other travelers are under attack. Mily's tears keep me there, and I don't know what to do.

"Kai!" Zephar shouts from the riot. His voice snaps me out of my inaction.

I shout, "On my way," to him, and to her, I say, "I won't leave here without you, but I have to help the others."

She releases me and weeps into her hands. Her eyes widen as she sees that another Gorga has spotted her, no longer in my arms.

He's far enough away that I can tear him apart with fire. Then, in a fit of rage, I hurl fireballs at every Gorga that I see until finally, no bandits remain.

Ancress Tisen runs over to me and throws herself in my arms again.

I whisper, "You're okay," as my gaze roams the ruins.

Zephar frowns and holds out his arms. "*This* is what I'm talking about. *This* is why we need to go to Shelezadd."

"Why weren't there protective wards?" I shout back. "This wouldn't have happened if wards were placed—"

He turns away from me and grumbles as he finds Prince Idus beneath the bodies of two guards who'd sacrificed themselves to keep him alive.

Prince Idus, bloody but breathing, bows to Zephar. He's a tall, handsome man with golden skin, thick black hair, and a well-oiled and groomed beard and moustache. Even in its current state his loose brown tunic, made of the best cotton on Vallendor, looks splendid on him.

Zephar finds his simple crown of rose gold in the dirt and sets it on the prince's head.

Prince Idus thanks him and freezes once he spots me. His lips start to curl into a sneer until he catches himself and forces a smile onto his face. "Lady." Anger still bubbles in his eyes before wisdom tamps down the heat of his resentment.

The Mera and royal caravan return to Gasho, and the city-folk toss flowers and coins at my feet.

Alabaster statues ornamented with chamomile and sage now line the courtyard. There's Zephar and Shari… Is that Sybel Fynal's image? And is that…*Elyn Fynal's* image? None of these figures are taller than my statue nor are they permanent fixtures—they've been mounted on horse-drawn carriages. Moveable. An eclipse of moths flutters around the alabaster Celestial, and a few break away to find and flutter around the living one.

Ancress Tisen leads me to a seated canopy and rests on a cushion behind me. Her eyes are still swollen from crying, but hope has replaced fear. "Is there anything I can get you, Celestial? Water? Dates?"

"No, thank you." I cock my head. "You aren't angry with me?"

"You saved my life, Divine," she says.

"But you wouldn't have been in danger if I'd been there."

"I knew you'd come."

I make a skeptical face. "Really?"

She shrugs. "Isn't that what faith is? Trusting that all will be well?"

"You could've died."

"But I didn't."

"Others did."

"And they are now with the ancestors, and you'll look after them just as you continue to look after me."

I touch the young woman's cheek, and her glow burns blue again.

An older man with long, sandalwood-scented braids bows before us.

I nod to him and say, "Intendant Wosre."

"Mighty Celestial," Intendant Wosre says. "Most revered among the gods. The one who protects and guides us through battle and thought. Merciful and cruel, the most exquisite of the goddesses. With your hand, Celestial, mortal-kind finds the path, a higher calling, yet never reaches your perfection."

Zephar, coming to sit beside me, mutters something that I can't decipher.

Eventually, Intendant Wosre reaches the request portion of his grandiose speech: some mortals would like to journey to the next town over to re-establish trade, but they need protection as they travel these dangerous roads—especially after today's assault.

I nod. "Travel mercies for the prince and pilgrims," I say, eyeing Zephar.

He nods, beckons a nearby Eserime, and gives the order.

If he'd done that earlier…

I gaze at the crowd of Gashoans wearing their finest silks, tan and white linens. They're carrying bottles of wine and ale, platters of roasts and figs. The bannermen hold pennants with moth sigils that undulate in the slight breeze. This is no ordinary day.

"What's happening now?" I ask Ancress Tisen.

"The Celebration of Renewal," she says, "in honor of your return. As you know, Divine, it is your right to take as many as you desire."

Take as many… Oh, yeah. Lovers. Sex. *That* kind of celebration.

"We've only had one festival since you left us," Ancress Tisen says, "and today, with your victory against the Gorga, the time is finally right for another."

Intendant Wosre cries out, "Prince Rewyn Idus, Sixth of His Name, Starbound and Shadowforged, Chosen of Celestial."

The prince takes his position before me, and he's still shaken from the attack on his caravan in the desert.

The last time he stood before me in this town square, his eyes had lit up with roguishness. A master of seduction, his expression told me. *How lovely and awful for the future queen of Gasho.*

Now I smile at him. "Prince Idus. Hello, again."

The prince says, "I have a gift for you, Divine One. If you would join me."

Zephar and I follow the prince to the temple.

Intendant Wosre and his staff lead us to a chamber lined with countless sticks of burning incense. There's a large bed covered with silk and hidden with veils. Musicians stand at the door to this room, strumming and fluting and singing a song that I can only hear snatches of over the other songs of celebration.

Rejoice! Be glad! Dance about!

We will delight her! Rejoice and shout!

He moves her with his gifted kiss

Her hips, they move with delightful bliss.

The bed is for Prince Idus and me…and whoever else I choose.

His father, King Idus, had also been a beautiful man, but he hadn't been interested in "celebrating" with me or any other woman. On that night of the Celebration, I'd closed the veils and then-Prince Idus and I held hands. After he promised to protect Gasho, I decreed him king and let him slip away to celebrate with Dorosi, the captain of the guard.

"Shall we try out this big, fabulous bed later?" Zephar whispers, his finger poking my back. "Just you and me? No audience unless…" He shrugs.

I laugh and lift an eyebrow. "Behave."

We return to the courtyard where Gashoans have formed a queue at the south entry. Two ancresses stand on either side of my canopy. Once Zephar and I are seated again, the women hold out their hands, beckoning the first Gashoan to approach.

A bearded man kneels before me and bows his head. "Divine, please give me life so that I may…"

Zephar chuckles and slumps in his seat. "Ah. Hearing the prayers of the people. Kaivara Megidrail, Celestial, Lady of the Verdant Realm, is still being bossed around by mortals."

"Relax, Zee," I snap. Receiving supplicants is a duty I have not fulfilled in far too long.

Refresh my fruits and fields, Celestial.

Heal my wounds, Divine.

Bless my womb-child-horse-hands so that I may prosper, Ancient One.

I snort. "Ancient One?"

"You *are* kinda old," he says, grinning.

I stick my tongue out at him when none of the worshippers are looking.

"Crops, coupling, and coin," he mutters. "That's all that mortals desire. They can all breathe better now and their sores have been healed. What else must we do for them?"

"I've been gone for a long time, Zee," I say. "And mortals aren't the only ones interested in coupling."

Every time a Gashoan steps forward with their hands to their heart, Zephar's brow scrunches and his jaw flexes.

Shari, though, wags her wolf-tail and smiles her wolf-smile, and her pendant shines brighter than the daystar.

"Are you about to bathe the courtyard in fire?" I ask Zephar. "Or is this face your new normal? I bless and you glare?"

He frowns. "Your patience is extraordinary."

That was not a compliment.

I rub the back of my sweaty neck until my ears pop, and anger flickers like embers across my scalp. "What do you want me to do, Zephar?" I snap. "Tell me, since you're—"

"Don't," he says, holding up his hand. "I'm not criticizing you. I'm pissed at these people who are back to treating you as their donkey. Beyond all the..." He flicks his hand at the gifts and banners and dancers. "That's how they see you—a beast of burden. You deserve to be revered without condition."

I grit my teeth and throw up my hands. "That's not how this works."

His head falls back, and he runs his hand across his mouth.

The Mera with us move back and pretend to talk among themselves—but they're listening. Zephar knows this—and he wants this.

"You've changed," he says now.

"I hope so," I say.

"And I'm..." He sets his hands on the table and worries a date with his knuckles.

I touch his arm. "And you're...*what*?"

He places his hand over mine. "And I'm worried that you've softened in your resolve to transform this realm. I'm worried that you'll let them destroy Vallendor—"

"*Them.* Who are we talking about?"

"Humans. Otherworldly. Dashmala. Gorga. Before you left Gasho, we weren't waiting for them to fuck everything up. Back then, you decided, and we followed your orders, and it was a wonderful thing."

I squeeze his arm. "I learned some things while I was away. The strife I caused was not—"

"*Strife?*" He bends until we're eye to eye. "We are Destroyers, Kaivara. Fuck being Diminished. We are still warriors and protectors. Swords and strength are the way of the Mera. It's in our blood to destroy so that renewal may come."

I don't speak.

"So you no longer believe in our *work*?" he asks, gaping at me. "Even though we didn't let this town perish, hundreds still died when you disappeared. Look at it now." He waves his hand to all the celebration around us. "They're thriving. Fruit and water and *sex*."

I nod. "But many died because of me—"

"And others *live* because of—" Zephar points at me. "*You* saved the prince and his company, even with your limited capacity. Even without the complete blessing from the Council. *You* built this city back up again, better than it ever was, and it didn't even require complete destruction."

"Fear—"

"Yes," he says, "and it took fear. If that's what humbled Gasho, then fine. Other towns cry out for a similar renewal—"

"Okay, okay," I say, squeezing the bridge of my nose.

"No, Beloved," he says, "it's *not* okay. I've been unable to fulfill my own duty because I've waited for your return. *You* are the Lady of the Verdant Realm, the Grand Defender of Vallendor. I can't carry out my work without your approval. Even as I watched Danar Rrivae use that fool Wake's army to decimate one town after another as though it was his right, I couldn't do my job." He leans closer to me and whispers, "And *your* army looked at me as though I was weak—"

"Is that why you're pissed?" I hiss. "Because you looked weak?"

Shari whines now and nudges my clenched fist.

"Yes," he hisses back. "I'm Zephar Itikin, Warrior of the Righteous, Prince of Lissome Blades, and I've destroyed sixteen fucking realms and you've—"

Only destroyed three. That's what he wants to say, but he stops himself.

"You may have moved on," he says, softer now, "but I lost Naelah in that campaign at Dismal Fen on Yoffa."

Naelah Itikin—his sister, my friend. She handled curved blades almost as well as her big brother.

I watch far-off shepherds who now guide their sheep across the renewed pastures. I watch children splash in the marsh while chasing white herons in the long grass. I've been away from this place, away from Zephar and from my warriors, for too long. I know they relied on him for counsel and protection in my absence. My stomach cramps as I think about all the trust and goodwill I've lost since then.

"Why are we hesitating to help our people?" Zephar asks, softer now.

"Because Danar Rrivae is more of a threat than Gorga or Dashmala or Syrus Wake," I whisper. "I must cut off the head of the snake. Why can you not understand?"

And where *is* that traitor right now? And where is the Sea of Devour from here? I can't just fly across the realm and land in front of Danar Rrivae, not anymore. We can no longer Spryte from one place to another. They are earthbound just as I am.

Zephar isn't thinking about the details, though. He wants to fight and burn, destroy, and dissolve. He hasn't truly battled the enemy since the War of Flames an age ago. The otherworldly that invaded Gasho yesterday and the Gorga that attacked the prince today are ants compared to the legion of otherworldly lurking around the sea.

But I need his sword, and I need his counsel. I need Destroyers.

• • •

Back at the Sanctum, Zephar and I pace in angry silence behind our tent until I say, "Fine. Show me a map."

He bends and uses his finger to draw a square and a circle in the middle of the dirt-map. "We're here. Doom Desert."

Okay. Maford is southeast. Caburh is southwest. Sea of Devour and Mount Devour are farther southwest.

He taps the space between Doom Desert and the sea. "Eaponys." He taps his finger northeast of us. "And Shelezadd is here."

"And the problems in Eaponys?" I ask.

"Rape. Murder. The Dashmala have always trampled over the poor, but with your absence, the problem has worsened. They now burn women alive. Shall I continue?"

"Shit, no." I chew my bottom lip as I think. "The traitor is at the Sea of Devour—at least he was when I saw him last."

"As we make our way to the sea," Zephar says, "we can stop by and handle Eaponys."

"*Helping*," I say, pointing at him, "not harming. What we did for Gasho yesterday. Understand?"

Zephar smiles. "I will do as you ask. No cleansing fire."

"And set up those wards along the roads this time. Do we have weapons, armor, supplies?"

Zephar nods. "We will—and I'll make sure the wards are up."

Shari yips, and her dirt tail wags so fast the dirt-map is blown away.

But then Zephar kisses me and wraps me in his arms.

So I don't get what I want—which is to go immediately to the Sea of Devour. Instead, I get what I need: Zephar's support, which also means the absolute support of our battalion of Mera warriors.

8

Even while I sleep, I feel a strange white light beating against my face. I turn over in bed and let my eyes flutter open.

Shari's come inside the tent, and her cold nose rests beneath my hand, pulling me from sleep, her emerald gaze steady.

Zephar slumbers beside me, at peace, his face soft even in its hardest places. The disappointment of our lack of coupling again last night has melted from his expression. I want to claim that I'm tired, that my head hurts, but the real reasons are more complicated than a sore back and being bone-weary.

Guilt.

Jadon.

Shari nudges me again.

Past the tent wall, a soft milky light too bright to be the nightstar pierces through the darkness.

My dream breaks apart like foam. I pull on my bandeau, sarong, and boots and grab my back scabbard heavy with Fury and Justice. I ease into my new armor—the plates are lighter than my luclite armor and offer the flexibility of leather and the certainty of steel. I follow Shari through the dark tent and out into the lighter world.

Dawn has not come yet, but a new day has already begun.

No one roams the valley. Down in Gasho, the newly restored acacia trees and date palms stand tall and still. A sweet, honey-scented breeze rustles the banners and kisses my neck. The source of that radiant milky light hangs just above the trees. Daxinea! Her feathers glimmer like white embers, a beauty like none other.

"Come, Lady."

Just as she did days ago, the daxinea flies toward my destination.

Shari nudges my knees and pants. She nudges me again and jogs ahead.

"Where do you want me to go?" I follow her to the path that separates the Sanctum of the Gods from the mortal world.

At the Sanctum's boundary, the wolf sits on her haunches and wags her head. She can go no farther without Zephar.

I stare into the mist, heart in my throat.

What awaits on the other side?

In no time, I'm standing on that other side.

The thick scent of burning incense wafts through the temple's empty courtyard and sanctuary. Steam from that extravagant bath gathers beneath the domed ceiling, ready to soothe me—I'll have to use it eventually, since it means so much to Prince Idus and the Gashoans.

I slip through the city, unnoticed by roving guards and couples meeting in secret.

That white light continues to shine in the west.

I hurry out the city gates and over a bridge over a canal that now contains running water. I dart across the desert sand, so quick and light that I hardly touch the ground. Something powerful pulls me, and I follow that mystery, watching out for windwolves and three-headed lizards—or angry Gorga who'd heard about the fight yesterday in the desert.

I reach the slot canyons where my journey began just days ago.

My breath fogs around my head, and I run deeper into the ravine, keeping my eye on that soft white light. The wind howls through these soaring rock walls, like a song sung by many voices.

The daxinea dips lower to the earth, speeding still toward that great white light.

I slow down—I've reached a dead end. The high canyon wall is too smooth to climb. I crane my neck to see the top—

"There you are." The woman's voice sounds as soft as the clay beneath my boots.

I spin around to look at her, but the canyon is bathed in that blinding light. I close my eyes against the hard glare until it softens to reveal her face. No, her *faces.* The soft joy of her smile. Her angry, flinty eyes. A sorrowful, trembling chin. Vibrant, high eyebrows.

Sybel Fynal, the Grand Steward of Vallendor, the Lady of Dawn and Dusk.

We'd last stood together in the woods near Veril's cottage. That day, she wore a gown of gray mail that floated and folded like silk, its color shifting from ring to ring, from day-light to night-light. This morning, she wears a polished amulet of a silver chalice encircled by a small flame. A yellow sapphire burns above the rim of that cup. Her one-shouldered dress matches the style worn by the women of Gasho, but instead of silk or linen, Sybel's gown is made of canvas rough enough to slough off a man's skin and a boar's hide. Her look slays.

In that forest near Veril's cottage, she'd helped me discover myself and had steered me as I searched for my amulet. She'd instructed me to *choose mercy* before telling me that I was the Lady of the Verdant Realm. I'd hug her right now, but she had failed to mention that her daughter, Elyn, was the one trying to kill me.

"You're awake," Sybel says now. "You've been asleep for too long."

Out of respect, I fix my face and force myself not to scowl. "I deserve rest, don't I? Especially after all your daughter's put me through. After *you* abandoned me."

Sybel tilts her head. "'Abandon' is an interesting word choice, Kaivara." Her eyes take in my armor. "While you are playing house with Zephar Itikin, Vallendor slides further into doom. Danar Rrivae continues to grow in might, and yet you tarry. I know you're afraid—"

"Who said anything about being afraid?" I snap.

"You are, and you'd be a fool if you weren't. Are you so arrogant to think this is simply an ordinary war against an ordinary man?"

"No," I say, "but what good is fear? I'm just trying to...to..." I scrunch my eyebrows and finally admit, "I don't know what I'm trying to do."

"That soft bed has weakened your resolve and your memory," she says, "and while you aren't a fool, softening your shoulders like you have is a foolish act."

Her words and meaning push against my chest. Frustration swirls in my belly until it becomes fire that burns my mouth. "I'm not *vacationing*, Grand Steward. You may not have noticed, but I've healed and helped a lot of people in the days I've been here. I've blessed babies, and I've blessed crops. Merchants can travel again, and we've placed protective wards along the routes so that even shepherds can guide their sheep and goats to safe pastures. My shoulders are far from soft, and I'm doing this while still preparing to fight Danar Rrivae. We'll soon pass through Eaponys, which sits between here and the Sea of Devour. But I don't expect you to understand my job as a Mera Destroyer."

"You mean, as a Mera *Diminished*," she clarifies, eyebrow cocked.

I lift my chin. "Diminished or not, I'm fixing these ruined places, including Eaponys. Isn't that what I should be doing? And 'tarry'? Interesting word choice, ma'am—I've already restored Gasho since I left this canyon three days ago."

Sybel glares at me with her lion face, all rage and judgment, terrible to behold.

Shame makes my cheeks burn, and I lower my eyes to the canyon floor. "I mean no disrespect—I'm just sharing all that I've—"

"Before you make me regret coming here," she grumbles, "before I take back the gift I'm about to give you, I suggest that you listen and swallow any remaining *updates* rolling up your throat."

My shoulders drop—*soften*—and I put my tongue away.

Above us, a creature growls, low and angry.

I look up but can't see the beast's glow behind these limestone walls.

"Unlike you," Sybel says, "I haven't had a moment's rest. Neither has your uncle. Together, Agon the Kindness and I have taken a critical step on your behalf." She slowly exhales, and the face of a sharp-eyed and thoughtful silver eagle takes the lion's place. "We've petitioned the Council of High Orders to consider your situation again, and they've agreed to offer you this." She holds out her hand.

A ball of swirling darkness streaked with lightning bolts bounces around her palm.

I gasp, "Spryte!"

"Unless you don't need it," Sybel says.

"But I *do* need it!"

"Then…"

"Thank you!" I don't waste the opportunity, holding out my hand and watching as the ball rolls along my arm and melts into my amulet. The moth bucks wildly against my chest. I close my eyes to enjoy the thrumming of the pendant now invigorated from this wonderful gift. I can't smile any wider than I'm smiling right now.

For a moment, Sybel shows her softer human face, but then the flinty-eyed eagle returns. "You have the ability again to travel quickly across the realm," she says. "You may keep this gift with one condition: go to the abbey atop Mount Devour immediately. There you will receive new armor—"

"I'm already wearing new armor," I interrupt, hypnotized by the dark swirl of the moth's thorax. "This set was a gift from Malik Sindire."

"Who is Malik Sindire?" Sybel asks, squinting.

"He visits Vallendor every now and then. His followers built a temple for him on the other side of the mountain. He's a collector of things from around the realms. Weapons, armor, books… He knows my father."

"*Everyone* knows your father, child," Sybel says. "I don't understand. How can this Malik Sindire give you *anything* powerful enough to withstand the strength and might of the traitor?"

"I don't know, but he did." I peer at her. "I'll go to the abbey—I have unfinished business there anyway with my uncle." I tap the pendant and add, "Thank you for this, Lady. Now, Zephar and I can—"

"Only you may use Spryte," Sybel is saying.

I blink. "What? No—"

Another growl comes from the ledge above. Multiple footsteps sound against the hard-packed dirt.

I count twelve feet.

A draft catches their scent: rancid, musky meat.

My skin sizzles, and the tiny hairs around my body lift.

"Listen." Sybel's face darkens. "The Council resisted our petition to return Spryte to you, and they pointed out every error and offense you've made against Supreme that caused them to withdraw your ability in the first place. I kept reminding them of your growth, and how you've placed yourself in harm's way to save those around you. How, in your heart, you yearn to do right. But—"

"But what?" I ask, my anger starting to crackle.

"But your ego and intelligence send you spinning back to destruction." Her lip curls as she adds, "And Zephar Itikin is not the advisor I'd want by your side at this precarious moment. He aims to control you, Kaivara. He always has."

"You don't understand him," I say, shaking my head.

"No, *he* doesn't understand *you*," Sybel says, softer. "He doesn't understand your nature. The push-and-pull of steward and destroyer causes him great irritation."

"Zephar and I are getting along great right now," I say. "We're not perfect, but we've spent a season apart. We're just getting used to each other, that's all."

"I'm not talking about right now," she says. "I'm talking about all the time you've been together. You aren't like him, Kai. You, as Lyra and Izariel's child, embody different missions while Zephar only knows how to—"

"Anything else, Lady?" I turn away from her.

She doesn't know how I feel—the daughter of a high lord of the Council who caused the death of her mother. It didn't matter that I had no clue she'd been on Ithlon that day. The Aetherium looked upon me with horror and revulsion. Gods from the 67,000 known realms judged me—does Sybel know how that feels? Greasy failure coats everything I touch. Only Zephar understands the depths of my sadness.

"The Council held fast and refused to grant you any more power, that is..." Sybel exhales, then says, "That is, until I agreed to sacrifice any grace I've earned as Grand Steward and the mother of the Adjudicator. I've assured them that you will ultimately be the power you were meant to be. I assured them that you *will* win. I worry, though, that Zephar Itikin will be an obstacle to your ascension."

"Wait. You said... *What?*" I rub my temples, pushing against the pressure building there. "'Sacrifice any grace'... What does that mean?"

"My fate is now tied to yours, Kai," she says. "Now more than ever before. One more chance, for the both of us. You fail and I am banished to Anathema."

Anathema: Mortals call it the underworld and the wastes. The Realm of Nowhere with only dust to eat, and water to drink that never quenches your thirst. You aren't alone there, but you can only hear the cry of others whom you will never see. When you've given up on the hope that Supreme will offer you relief, you are supposed to speak the word and pass through a final gate. At least, that's all we know. No one has reported back from that realm beyond that final gate.

Despite this, humans continue to think of life and death as a beginning and an end. They are scared of the end—death—more than anything. That's because mortals crave the finite, starts and stops with few liminal spaces in between. So Anathema, the wastes, the underworld, became that final place where you're tortured forever.

The idea, though, that Supreme is filled with so much malice... Torturing a creation forever? Unthinkable. Being thrown in the Nowhere, eating dust and drinking water that won't quench hunger or thirst... That may be true if you refuse to speak the word. If you speak the word immediately, you wouldn't wander or lose hope. If you're there, in Anathema, no hope exists. What are you clinging to?

And now, Sybel has basically volunteered to be sent there if I fuck up saving Vallendor.

"You shouldn't have done that," I whisper to her, tears burning in my throat. "You shouldn't have made such a promise, especially on behalf of someone like..." I bite my tongue and hold my breath.

"Someone like you?" she asks.

"I've failed this realm."

Sybel takes my hand and squeezes. "That remains to be determined."

I chuckle and push my hand through my hair. "You've known me since my birth. You know me better than my own father. I'm..." *Not the god I was meant to be.*

High above us, atop that sheer wall, three windwolves with blood-stained snouts glare down at us, their sharp teeth bared and filthy with old meat. Six eyes glint like new knives, and their stink makes my stomach wobble.

I draw my sword and step in front of Sybel.

"This isn't necessary," the Grand Steward says.

"This is *very* necessary," I murmur, eyes on the predators above us.

"Kai," she says, "ignore the distractions. Now is not the time to fight everything and everyone. You have important—"

Another growl and a roar cut her off.

Sybel spins to look up at the wolves and shouts, "Silence!"

The air around us booms. Enormous rocks fall from high places and strike the ground. The wolves whine their apologies as the cliff crumbles beneath their paws, and they back away from the bluff's edge.

Okay, then.

I stow my blade.

Sybel lays her hand on my shoulder. Such a heavy touch. Such a loving touch.

"You shouldn't have made that promise," I say, placing my hand atop hers. "Sacrificing yourself like that… It's not a good idea." My gaze skips up to the ledge abandoned by the windwolves. "What if I fail?"

"Do you plan to fail?" she asks.

I close my eyes, and a single teardrop blazes down my cheek. "Why won't Supreme just skip to the ending and destroy me? I'm not who I'm supposed to be. A Grand Defender—the Mera warrior ultimately responsible for protecting this realm, crying? A Grand Defender—a Mera warrior now fearful of losing this realm and the beings in it, including those dumb windwolves looking down at me? That's not supposed to be."

"Says who?" she asks, tugging a lock of my hair. "None of the great books I've read says 'You are not to fear.' Recognize and acknowledge that fear, Kai. But then move forward, press ahead, and use that dread to do what you are meant to do."

"And what is it that I'm meant to do?" I ask, drying my tears with the back of my hand.

"Destroy Danar Rrivae before he can destroy Vallendor and our charges."

Sybel and I stand in silence until I push out a long breath and stiffen my back. "I will skip going to Eaponys for now, and I'll go to my uncle and hear what he has to say."

Footsteps pad above us again, but this time, I hear only four feet. I look up to the bluff.

One windwolf sits there, gloating and gaping down at me.

You will fail, Lady.

You do nothing but fail.

9

I can't return to the Sanctum right now, not if I'm trying to figure out what Uncle Agon needs from me. If I return to the Sanctum and try to explain to Zephar why Eaponys is now postponed, he will get pissy. Though eventually, he'd come around to understanding, more time will have passed, and I just can't deal with that right now.

He aims to control you—he always has...

Zephar is a warrior, a planner, someone who needs to...to control the situation. And sometimes, *I'm* the situation.

He's an obstacle to your ascension.

No, *I'm* an obstacle to my ascension.

My gaze skips up to the cliffs.

The windwolf still sits there, snickering at me.

"I should burn you to a crisp right now," I growl at it.

"But you won't."

I roll my eyes and tap my Spryte-filled amulet, and think, *Sea of Devour—*

An eclipse of gold, crimson, and black moths surrounds me.

I can't see, but I feel the wind being made by the moths' madly fluttering wings. Then, suddenly, they're gone.

I stand alone as the daystar hides behind dark clouds. Wind gusts across the plains, transforming sand as well as tumbleweeds and the dried skeletons of soldiers into prickly little cyclones that spin across the toxic green surface of the Sea of Devour. Limbless trees with scoured trunks pepper this dying land. Ashes swirl over bizarre creatures now scampering across the rocky terrain.

I remember the sea at its healthiest. Once upon a time, the sea had been a destination for holiday and sport. Those who settled Peria, the land of saffron, had used the river that originated here to till the earth. Zephar and I had bathed on the harder-to-reach banks of the sea. Yeah, we made waves and made love. But now, my nostrils curl from its stink, and my eyes sting from this acid-tinged air.

Oh, Sea of Devour. What happened to you?

I happened to you.

Danar Rrivae happened to you.

Only one of us regrets being an asshole—and she's standing here with burning eyes.

Speaking of the traitor... I don't sense his presence. Good. Even though I wear new armor, I'm not ready to confront the usurper alone.

But I'm not alone.

A beast with the head of a lion and a bright blue shell, five skinny legs, and one giant claw scuttles behind me. *Sagird!* Another creature—it's an ape, no, it's an owl, no, it's both, it's an ohty—gallops and flies in front of me. Both animals are shadowed overhead by an otherworldly creature with a long snout and leathery wings.

I pull Fury from the scabbard with my right hand and thrust out my left hand at the lion-crab-sagird, using wind to send it splashing into the sea. I swing my blade at the ape-owl-ohty, but my sword bounces off the beast's fur, only stunning the creature, but giving me enough time to drive Fury into its neck.

Almost immediately, golden light shines upon the ohty, and the fallen creature writhes in its spot.

This can't be.

I look up to see a beam of golden light emerging from the mouth of the leather-winged flying thing. *What the...?*

The ohty waggles its head and staggers onto its feet.

What. I blink— *Am I seeing this?* This...*resurrection*?

My temples pound—from the fighting, from breathing toxic air.

Not only is the recently arisen ape-owl-ohty charging at me, but so are *one, two...six, seven* other ohtys, fangs bared, their movements made quicker by the promise of life after death. From the sea, three more lion-crab-sagirds roll out of the waters, acid still hissing from their shell-backs and dripping from their antennae. Two more leather-winged flying creatures now circle above the sea, ready to resurrect any creature that I destroy.

The formerly dead ohty swipes at me.

I duck in time to save my unprotected head, and I roll...right into another ape-owl-ohty.

It swipes at me with its giant paw and slams me into the acrid earth. The pain feels like burning sandpaper, and I scream and thrust out my hand to launch a ball of fire from my fingertips.

Fwoosh! That ball consumes the ape-owl like it was made of paper.

I throw another fireball. *Fwoosh!* That ball consumes another ohty.

Claws snap at my ankle.

I cry out as fiery pain spills down to my toes. I roll this way and that way, tears whipping from my eyes, as another claw grabs my greave-covered shins. I shout, and my breath is snatched from my chest. Somehow, I find the strength to swing Fury again, chopping off that claw but not killing the lion-crab-sagird connected to it.

You will fail, Lady.

You do nothing but fail.

Crawling now, I grab that severed claw and swing it at the ohty. I try to balance on one knee as I swing and swing, but I'm hurt, and none of these otherworldly are dying, at least not for long. My vision turns wet and wavy and the world blurs. Will the leather-winged flying things bring *me* back to life if I die on these shores?

One lion-crab-sagird grabs my wrist, and I drop the claw. Another lion-crab-sagird grabs my already injured foot, and the two sagirds pull me in opposite directions, trying to tear me apart. Now, I feel nothing as my body goes numb. I squeeze my eyes closed and throw my head back and shout, "Abbey!" and—

I'm no longer fighting for my life at the Sea of Devour. This time, I'm dropped like a piece of trash and splayed on the ground in the middle of a long corridor that stretches without end. Moths whirl around me, helping the power of Spryte ferry me from one place to another. Job done, the eclipse flutters down that corridor and vanishes in the distance.

I whisper, "Please don't go." Too late.

The shiny black floor is made of stone with veins of golds and blues. This floor isn't cold and hard as marble, nor is it soft as wood. This floor is otherworldly.

There's a long gray wall to my right and a long blue wall to my left. My limbs feel too heavy to move. The bloody gashes on my hands don't sting as much as those on my cheeks and chin. The armor below my waist feels wet on the inside, filling up with blood from my cut-up calf and foot. I may just drown in my own blood.

At least it's quiet here.

At least it's clean here.

Maybe I could stay here forever.

I'm the only stinking, bleeding thing in this place—not that there's much to see. I turn my head to squint down the hallway, rubbing my thumb against the pendant and shuddering from the buzzing energy now living inside of it. Bleeding and swollen, I lie there, on that otherworldly floor, I don't know for how long, clutching my amulet and listening to my blood drip onto that floor, pain biting at my neck, wincing every time my lower back flares. My brain tries to pull out of this fog—feels like I'm sleeping with my eyes open.

It's so nice in this place.

But in the back of that fog-brain, a part of me whispers.

Time…time…

Every time I come close to understanding my surroundings and what's happening to me, that knowledge skitters away.

I take a deeper and longer breath, and the air snakes through my nose and fills my lungs, and energy pulses through my veins. A strange numbness climbs from my feet up to my legs.

Clear-headed at last, I sit up, and the hallway swings precariously. I close my eyes and wait for the world to settle.

I need to stand—but there is nothing that I can use to lift myself up.

Shit.

I grit my teeth and roll onto my knees. "Ow!" I shout. I want to vomit, but that will only make this slick floor slicker.

Time…time…

I force myself to my feet—one foot burns and the other foot bleeds.

I take one weak step and then another. Despite its polished shine, the floor isn't slippery beneath my boots. The single window behind me lights this corridor—there are no torches or lanterns, sconces or candelabras hanging from the ceiling. Out that narrow window, white, puffy clouds hang in a sky that shifts from light to dark, and then gold, red and blue, black and white, and then light, dark, and each color again.

This place… I know this sky and those clouds and this floor and this air, and I didn't know what perfection felt like until no longer feeling it outside of these walls.

This is the Abbey of Mount Devour.

I want to admire my surroundings. I want to celebrate having made it to this haven, *finally*. But nothing gets done by standing in place. I have work to do—starting with finding Agon the Kindness. Finding my family, *finally*.

Lightheaded, I count my steps as I stumble down the long hallway. At four hundred fifty paces, I'm still stumbling. I look behind me—*fuck all.* Like a snail and its slime, I've left behind a trail of blood. My face burns with embarrassment. I have to come back and clean this up, hopefully before anyone sees this mess. The abbey is too sacred a place, and it deserves respect and order. Also, no one should have to clean up after me, a grown woman. More than that: neither my mother nor Sybel Fynal raised me to be okay with just…*leaving blood everywhere*. I'm many things—selfish and shortsighted—but I'm not filthy.

Up ahead, I spot a set of dark double doors made of wood stronger than Vallendor's strongest oaks and ironwoods. Protective wards have been carved into the wood—diamonds, bears, wolves, paddles, and knots—to keep out those who don't belong.

With bloody hands, I reach for the two knotted metal doorknobs.

The tall, dark doors open before I even touch the knobs.

I belong here.

A woman with copper skin and bronze hair pulled into a bun stands on the other side of the double doors with her hands folded before her. She's tall and radiant with silver light. She bows her head and says, "Kaivara Megidrail, Grand Defender, Lady of the Verdant Realm, Blood of All." Her voice sounds like the low call of whales, so lovely and round.

Blood of All. I've always loved that title.

She sounds and looks so calm.

Does she *see* me? Does she see the mess that I've made?

"For what purpose are you here?" the woman asks.

"To see my uncle, Agon the Kindness," I say, my voice now rich and smoky with confidence.

The woman narrows her stormy-gray eyes and offers a stiff bob of the head. "I will take you to him. Please follow me." She turns away and starts to walk.

I take a step and grimace. "Could you slow down? I'm..." I sweep my hand over the mess of me. "Hurt."

Understatement of the ages.

She nods, and once I catch up to her, she continues on, walking slower now.

"You know who I am," I say, limping, resisting the urge to look back at my bloody footprints. "Please tell me who you are."

"Nimith Findaye," she says without turning around. "My clan of Eserime left the first realm of Linione aeons ago, and we've served as stewards of the abbeys across the Aetherium ever since."

Breathing heavy, I bite my lower lip and follow Nimith through a great hall. Like the corridor, light here doesn't come from a torch or candelabra. The light just *is.*

A mural shines on the hall's ceiling.

The first realm of Linione. The dwelling place of Supreme. The origin of every realm. Home to the Council of High Orders, the esteemed nobles who govern and represent their orders. The same nobles who demanded that Sybel no longer counsel me—though they've now restored my ability to travel fast.

Not that Spryte is helping me right now.

I want to ask if there's an easier way to reach my uncle—I'm slowing down as the pain courses through my body.

Nimith makes no sound as we cross the halls. She wears soft folds of mauve cloth that gather and separate, and could be a gown, a jumpsuit or a simple sheet.

This vast space holds countless benches made of that strong wood, each seat with a scarlet pillow. Like a chapel, the benches—including the ones on both sides—face a raised dais made of glazed wood. No one stands at the podium or sits on the benches. This part of the great hall shines with firelight from wall sconces, candelabras, and torches.

Nimith leads me into a dark alcove, illuminating that space.

Behind us, the area we just crossed is now dark. *She* is the light.

Nimith and I head toward another large space. The scent of sugar and baking bread drifts from the hall up ahead. My stomach growls—I want to follow that aroma and eat whatever is roasting and simmering in pans over the hearths. We enter a room like the chapel, but this area is bigger and has multiple hearths, comfortable-looking chairs, and overstuffed couches. The drapes on the walls and windows are warm browns and oranges.

Oh, no. *People.*

And they will see me like this.

Fuck all.

The gods present are a tapestry of colors and hues, from fair-skinned with rosy cheeks to darker tones and sharper features. Some gasp when they see me, sweeping their gazes across my bloody body. Some smile, but their eyes shine with agitation or sadness.

I try to lift my chin and pretend that all is well, but that's a lie, and they all see right through it. I sneak a peek behind me. *No blood.* I sigh, thankful for that small mercy.

Why are they here today?

Why did they come during a time like this?

Who needs resources from Vallendor?

Malik Sindire—he told me that he had come here to collect artifacts.

Is my realm now a hub for tragic tourism by more fortunate gods?

"Is there a convocation happening?" I ask Nimith.

"The convocation just ended," she says.

Unlike the Renrians' meetings every fifty seasons, our convocations occur only if there is an urgent issue that demands the immediate consensus of as many realms as possible.

I tilt my head. "There's a threat about?"

She waits a beat before saying, "Yes."

Nimith guides me to another room decorated with vases filled with pearl-blue kastat roses and ruby-red pinepart lilies. I'd brought these long-living flowers from Linione as gifts to Vallendor after its creation. But these flowers no longer grow here.

I limp away from Nimith to peek out the windows. I see my realm slowly turning as Selenova, the nightstar, brings nighttime, and as Lumis, the daystar, several paces behind his partner, brings dawn. They never tire. They never dim. They will only abandon this realm moments before its destruction.

I spot Caburh, still wrecked from that fight between Gileon Wake's army, Jadon Wake, and me. Maford sits in nighttime. In the north, Gasho shines as a restored city. Much of Caerno Woods, the site of Veril Bairnell's murder, still burns with my fire.

The towns I've destroyed—Chesterby, Steedale, Trony… I avoid looking at their devastation. I vow I will restore those cities—I just need time.

Nimith is waiting patiently for me with her slender hands folded over her gown.

Onward.

Gritting my teeth, I take one step at a time. Soon, we pass an ornate door encrusted with every gem brought from the first realm. Two Raqiel sentinels—guards of both the Adjudicators and the abbeys of the realms and descendants of the Mera and Onama—watch over this door. Their startling pale faces shift from lion to hawk, bear to owl. Their bright red breastplates look dull compared to this door's grandeur.

Up, up, up, Nimith and I go. I'm sweating, my wounds aching as I follow her up the stone steps of a spiraling staircase.

Nimith slows as we reach the landing, and a plain wooden door greets us. "Agon the Kindness is here," she says, nodding.

"Wonderful." I groan and swipe my blood-crusted hand across my sweaty forehead. "I really want to—"

She's descended the stairs before I can say, "Thank you."

10

The rectangular window in this aerie has no glass. It's deep enough for someone to sit in and tall enough for someone to stand. The dark stone walls and ceiling are speckled with imprints left by long-dead creatures of the sea, pocked with bright green moss, golden mushrooms, and lush purple flowers. This aerie is solid, like an above-the-sea coral reef. A living thing.

My heartbeat slows the moment I step into this space and this thick silence. I've longed for this peace.

Tall bookcases lining most of the east wall are filled with thousands of books with both leather and wood spines. The ceiling is high enough to accommodate a giant bear standing on top of a whale. Parts of the fading mural are hard to see, but I do spot the bright light in the center of the drawing and the white, black, and orange rings vibrating away from that shining orb.

My eyes drift to the plain, wooden furniture placed around the room. No tapestries hang on these walls, and no rugs lie across the stone floor. Plants, glassware, vats of liquids, powders, and balls of fire floating over basins fill long tables. What is Uncle Agon cataloging? Which Renrian has brought him plants and gems, songs and spells?

Someone clears his throat. A man with butterscotch skin, long milky braids, and mutton chops whiter than new snow stands at the farthest, more crowded table. His scarlet robe and matching trousers are embroidered with flames and keys, and all of it shimmers. The top of the robe covers his arms and wraps around his torso as the rest trails behind him like a cloak.

I press my shaky hand to my lips, and I smile. "I remember you."

"It was just a matter of time before you returned," Agon the Kindness says, tucking his hands inside the sleeves of his thick robe. "Like a moth drawn to flames." The air around his mouth ripples as though his words have shape. His voice crackles like fire—not wildfire or my own fire that sometimes lacks control, but fire found in a hearth that provides warmth for children and housecats. The heavy link chain around his neck ends with a heavier-looking owl amulet made of gray-lavender metal. A blue-gray-green stone sits between the owl's brows.

My chest suddenly fills with warmth, and a sense of comfort washes over me. For the moment, I've forgotten my pain because his presence brings me joy. He is the connection to my past that I've longed for. I'm so close to falling at his feet, wrapping my arms around his legs, and never letting go.

"I've missed you," I say, surprised that I sound like I'm about to cry. "And I've missed being a part of our family. I've been wandering this realm with no memories, surrounded by people, yes, but ultimately alone. I speak the truth when I say that seeing you, I finally feel as though I belong somewhere, like I belong to someone."

A teardrop tumbles down my blood-crusted cheek and slips into my smile. "Thank you, Uncle, for asking the Council to restore my travel privileges. I'm truly grateful." I limp toward him. "I've needed someone, and I'm happy to finally be with someone who loves me—"

Wait.

I cock my head. "What did you just say? Like a moth *returning*?"

"This isn't the first time you've come here to make demands," he says, his eyes roving over my bloody face and stained armor.

I gape at the old man, then shake my head. "Demands? I don't understand."

He squeezes the bridge of his nose, then says, "I know Sybel has sent you here this time, but like I've said before: I am *still* the seer and wisdom of this abbey. *I* make the decisions here. No one else. And my response remains unchanged. As much as I care about you, as much as I love you—you remain my sweet sister's baby girl—as much as I wanted to help you become more, you cannot stay here. I can't allow it."

And just like that…I'm still the enemy.

I stand as upright as I can and lift my chin. "This is Vallendor, *my realm*, and no one tells me where I can and cannot be."

"This place is *not* Vallendor," he spits. "It is the Abbey of Mount Devour, a seat of power for Supreme. And may I remind you: Vallendor and every realm will never belong to lesser beings like you, *child*."

"For someone named Agon the Kindness," I say, unshrinking, "for someone who is my *uncle*, you aren't being very kind right now. Fine: I'm only a guest here, but as you said, Sybel told me to come. So, please, be kinder."

He stares at me. "You have no idea how nice I'm being at this very moment."

His jab makes my heart snap. His brusqueness hurts more than my injuries from the fight down at the sea and every fight I've had since finding myself sprawled in those woods outside of Maford.

"Well, thank you for your kindness and patience, Uncle." I limp to the aerie's only window and gaze out to those clouds. "I *do* remember you, and I remember our once-upon-a-time. My favorite memory is that day we traveled to the seaside and…"

Clear waters tickled my toes. Starfish speckled the sand. Birds chased crabs across the shore. A large blanket had been spread on a beach, and a basket filled with honeycakes sat open. Back then, Uncle Agon's braids were darker as he waded with me through foamy seawater. My mother, with her soft smile and hair like mine, held me in her arms.

Many seasons have passed since then, and now, I turn back to my uncle and say, "You would carry me on your shoulders, and you'd help me build these incredibly elaborate sandcastles. Hmm. Sandcastles that resembled this abbey."

I wander over to the nearest bookcase—there are no dusty cobwebs on these shelves. I run my fingers along thick and velvety spines. The letters and shapes on a few of these books are written in languages that I don't know yet—there *are* at least 67,000 realms. Most are books with words that I *do* know, in tongues that I *do* speak. Books on travel and customs, recipes and incantations. Some tomes bear the lettering of the Renrians with others taken from realms like Threka, Gropool, and the now-destroyed Kynne. Glass jars containing preserved herbs, powders, and rare alchemical ingredients are arranged by size, their contents labeled with tags written with a steady hand. Jimson weed. Oleander. Sanguine hyssop.

Veril would've marveled at this collection. I can see him now, lavender eyes wide, gasping at each new shelf, racing around the room, pulling books to read immediately, and remembering the places of books he'd read next. He would've been the biggest sensation and deepest well of knowledge at the next Renrian convocation. That old man had been so much kinder to me than this old man—my own blood—is right now.

"This wood?" I say, knocking my knuckles against a bookshelf. "I miss this wood."

Fierer. Stronger than all the oaks and ironwood of Vallendor.

I look down at my feet. "And this stone? I miss this stone."

Catherite. A mineral that contains almost every gem in the realms—except one. Becomes as soft or as hard or as magnetic as needed. The thorax of my moth amulet is made of catherite.

"My mind," I say, "wants to learn more as I simply stand here. Amazing."

"You're injured," the old man marvels.

In many ways.

I laugh. "Thought you'd never notice."

He closes his eyes, lifts his hands, and whispers words that I can't hear. Then he nods.

The swelling and soreness of my muscles beneath my armor lessens, and my spine straightens. My calf feels stronger, and so do my hands.

I whisper, "Thank you for yet another gift."

Was this truly a gift or did he heal me out of duty? Like taking out the trash, you do it not because you love it, but to keep out nasty flies.

At the other end of the room, in the gloom, I see two sentinels, their pale skin illuminating the darkness. I nod toward the guards. "They'll never leave it, will they?"

"It's their job to keep watch," Agon says.

I sit in the closest chair to my uncle. "So what's our plan to destroy Danar Rrivae? From what Sybel has told me, you need *me* to do the actual destroying."

"To my chagrin."

"Chagrin?" Smiling, I cock my head and squint at him. "I'm trying my hardest to ignore your digs but…" I place my hands, prayer-style, against my lips. "Please understand. I'm very, *very* tired. I've traveled from the farthest places in the realm to see you. I've fought creatures that spit fire, and I've brawled with men who reek of death and disease, and I've resisted elements that tried to grind me into powder. I've eaten fish that tastes like sand, and up until three days or so ago, I hadn't had a proper bath in ages, and right now, even my fingernails hurt. I've done all of this, yet here you are, uttering 'to my *chagrin*'?"

I lean toward him. "Even though you're insulting me, I'm still here. In other words, *Agon the Kindness, Uncle Agon*, I've made an extraordinary effort to reach the Abbey of Mount Devour, and I'm gonna continue to try hard, and I will ignore your rudeness and displeasure and *chagrin*. After everything I've been through, I need *you* to also try harder. Okay? Okay."

I fill my lungs with air, then slowly release that breath until the muscles in my neck and shoulders loosen.

Agon watches me in silence. Then: "Are you done?"

My eyes fill with tears, and I shake my head, not understanding. My stomach churns, and bile burns my insides. Because I thought this was it, that after everything, I'd finally have a place here with my family. "Why are you being so cruel to me?" I whisper. "How have I wronged you? Tell me."

For a moment, Agon's eyes soften. "What do you want, Kai?" he asks.

How can he ask me that? After the distance I've traveled, after the quests I've completed, after learning that there are still quests that I must complete, that all of Vallendor could die… What do I *want*?

I hold his gaze and level my shoulders. "I want many things, but more than anything…I want to see my father—"

"I can't help you with your father." Agon's words are hard.

"Because you don't know him like that anymore? Or you can't help me because you don't want me to be with him?"

"Your father won't see you."

A light shines in a dark corner of my mind, and I swipe the tears from my eyes. "If he refuses to see me here, I'll go to Linione or even Mera. Can you take me?"

"I'm not Mera, and therefore, I'm not allowed to step foot on Mera," he says, shaking his head. "You know this."

"And I know that you must grant me permission to use that down there." I point at the guards standing at the dark end of the aerie. "Please take me to Linione—"

"I can't take you to Linione," Agon says and lowers his head.

"Nimith," I say, "the steward who escorted me up here. She addressed me as 'Blood of All.' I've never heard that before. What does that mean? Why—?"

"There is no time. Again: what do you want?"

"I've told you," I shout, my eyes wide and desperate. "Every request I've made, you tell me that you can't, or you won't. You've refused to help me every time I ask. I know you're a monk and probably don't talk much and didn't prepare for my return, and I know that I'm bossy, and yes, I've caught you off-guard, so I apologize for that, but surely you can be nicer. Right?"

Agon doesn't speak.

My temper grows close to boiling. "I have a job to do. I'm supposed to stop the One, and he's as powerful as Sybel warned. I was fooled, lulled into not believing any of this was possible. But I'm awake now, and I need your help, and you need mine."

"You're correct," Agon says. "The One is a danger and still needs to be stopped. Is that what you want?"

"Yes!" I thrust my hands and send blasts of wind that knock over a bookcase. The ancient fierer wood splinters, and the ghastly sound of breaking shelves echoes off the stone.

The old man whirls around to glare at me, his face twisted with shock and rage. "You *dare* use your power against me? In this sacred place of learning and respite?"

I cover my mouth with a shaky hand. I can't see him clearly because tears cloud my vision again. "I'm sorry, but you're not *helping* me. You're not *listening* to me. Why don't you care about what's happening here? Why don't you care about what's happening to *me*?"

Agon sneers at me, his face quivering because he's that mad. And now, *he* takes a breath, places his hands behind his back, and stomps over to the window. "You are the Destroyer of Worlds, and I'm vexed that our destiny lies in your wicked—"

"No!" I fling wind from my hands again, knocking over another bookcase. I send another blast of wind to turn over a table. Then I kick a chair that hits the wall and shatters. "Don't call me 'wicked'! I've done nothing to deserve that!"

Agon's face twists with a fury that he's barely controlling. "The convocation that just ended? It wasn't a meeting about Danar Rrivae. It was a meeting about *you*. About how to stop *you* while also trying to appeal to anything good within you—"

"What?" I cry, lightheaded with outrage. "Who do you think you are, questioning me, questioning my intent, my identity? You sit up here, in your cave away from everything and everybody, away from the threats and sickness of this realm. How *dare* you—"

"Silence!" His hands push out from those sleeves and a gust of wind sends me backward, wheeling toward that window. My blood boils as I right myself. Heat erupts from every pore on my body. I lift my hands, but Agon's hands are already out, and they shine with silver energy that hits me hard.

The aerie glows bright as though Selenova has entered the room.

"Stop this!" Red cardinals flutter behind Elyn Fynal, who now stands just inside the window. Her white hair is pulled into a braid just as it was the last time we were together. She wears a cloak of swirling golds and blues, and white pangolin-scaled armor. Her walking stick seems solid now, no longer clouds and sugar. This stick can strike over and over again, forever, until the end of time. The glossy black stone in the center of her dove amulet vibrates with pent-up energy.

"Agon the Kindness has brought you here despite the danger you present," Elyn says, "and you and I must discuss—"

I snatch her hand.

She cries out in surprise, then strikes the side of my face.

I hit the wall as though an elephant has whipped me through the air. I fall to the stone floor, breathless. But I shake it off and thrust my hands out, striking back at her with my own blast of wind.

But the cyclone that I produce doesn't even flutter her cloak.

She sends back that whirlwind.

I stumble and land on my back. *Shit.* I push myself up on my elbows, shaking my head while trying to square my shoulders.

Elyn leaps forward and strikes my jaw.

Red-and-gold dust explodes all around me. Her blow sends me sliding backward, hitting the wall again.

Someone's learned how to punch.

I swipe my mouth—blood wets my fingers. Agon's healing was all for nothing.

"Stop this fighting at once," my uncle shouts.

The walls of the aerie shake at this old man's voice.

Elyn and I both freeze in surprise.

"We aren't here to fight each other," he growls. "We're here to stop Danar Rrivae from claiming Vallendor as his own."

"Apologies." Elyn nods to my uncle and settles her gaze on me. "I did what I had to do, Kai. I needed to separate you from the weapon. Even now, he is still not who—*or what*—we think he is. And back then, we hadn't come close to understanding the truth, so I thought it was best to keep you apart." Her posture eases before she says, "I offer my apologies for being so...*hasty*."

I unclench my teeth, and even my hands lose some of their fight. "If it wasn't for your mother," I say, "I'd be picking my way across the fucking tundra right now, wasting time and hating you more than ever. You have the nerve—punishing me while asking me to use the power that you resent—"

The stone in her dove pendant flashes with red light. "I don't *resent* your power," she snaps. "Stop being so melodramatic."

"Says the woman who keeps sweeping me to the ends of the realm—"

"Danar Rrivae," Agon interjects.

"Is in Brithellum," Elyn says, "working together with Syrus Wake now that his primary weapon is off the field. *For now*. Danar is currently creating a new species of otherworldly more powerful than before."

"I met a few of them down at the sea," I say. "A leather-winged flying beast is now resurrecting dead creatures."

"Resurrecting?" both Agon and Elyn say.

"I saw it happen right before I popped into the abbey, and..." I shrug and shake my head with wonder. "If I hadn't seen it firsthand, I wouldn't believe it."

"How?" Elyn asks.

I shrug again. "No clue, but we have to kill *those* beasts to keep them from healing and raising the dead."

"The challenge, then, is greater than before," Agon says. "And the weapon?"

Elyn sniffs. "It's been days now, and he still keeps his back turned to me and refuses to talk to anyone. But I think that's about to change." She sizes me up with narrowed eyes and gives a crooked smile. "Because I know someone who can loosen his tongue—and she's standing right in front of me."

11

"No."

"No, what?" Elyn asks, eyes bugged.

We follow Nimith, with me moving faster down the staircase than I did coming up. Soon, we reach a long corridor with a mural of a sky alive with bolts and bright balls of yellow light. The creation of Linione.

"No, I'm not talking to Jadon," I say.

Nimith soon reaches a closed door with an ornate, moth-shaped knocker. "You may refresh in your quarters." She opens the door, and the scents of lavender and fresh water greet me.

Even though Uncle Agon just told me that I couldn't stay here, I've now entered my bedroom in the Abbey of Mount Devour—and it's just as beautiful as I remember, with a luxurious bed draped in soft silks. A deep tub filled with hot water and oils scents the room and calms my nerves. From the wide windows, Vallendor looks so peaceful. The peaks of Baraminz Spires in the east catch the fading light of dusk, while down south, the cool waters of the Cerulean Sea look iceberg blue. An illusion: my realm is a fucked-up death-scape crawling with otherworldly, fatal diseases, and merciless thugs.

"Jadon is no true threat to you right now," Elyn says, stalking over to the window. "He's imprisoned in the depths of the abbey, guarded by the Raqiel."

I side-eye her. "Didn't you just say that he is far more dangerous than we thought? And yet you want the one person who can stop him to go down there and talk to him?"

I leave the window for the bathroom and peel out of my armor. My mind races, seeing the ruin of my body in the bathroom mirror. From my shoulder blades down to my ankles, I'm bruised, purples and blacks and blues, most of me covered with crusted blood. I look like I fell deep into a coal mine and then was chopped up by madmen wielding rusty picks. No picks this time—just mean-ass otherworldly hanging out at the Sea of Devour.

Elyn paces my room with her arms folded. "We need to learn more about Danar Rrivae's plans, Kai. How he's creating his creatures. Where he'll strike next. What Syrus Wake's role is in all of— " She finally takes a moment and actually *looks* at me. "Shit, Kai."

My eyes burn with tears. "You played a part in all of this, you know."

She grunts, tromps into the bathroom, and grabs a vial from the sink counter. "This stuff works wonders." She uncorks it, and the room fills with the scents of peppermint and eucalyptus. She pours a generous amount into the hot water and says, "I know you're angry, but we have to figure out what to do about Jadon."

I've tried not to think about Jadon. Because when I do think about Jadon, most of the time, I think about him being such a fucking liar. *Wait, you're not Olivia's brother? Wait, you're not a blacksmith by trade? Wait, your surname isn't Ealdrehrt? Wait, you're a prince, the eldest son of Syrus Wake? Wait, you're Miasma and have been slowly killing the people of my realm to help— Wait, Danar Rrivae is actually your* father?

"Jadon lied to me our entire time together," I say and then point at her. "And *you* knew that—*you* were in on it."

She says nothing. Just gazes at me with those cool, gold eyes.

"He told me that he loved me, Elyn," I say. "How can you lie to someone you claim to—?" I stare at the foam building across the bathwater's surface, then shake my head. "No. I'm misremembering." I squint at her. "He *never* told me that he loved me. He told me, *'Kai, I choose you.'*"

I'd assumed "love" was a part of that declaration. Now, with some distance and air that smells like mint and eucalyptus, my mind can make that distinction.

"Being chosen doesn't equate to being loved," Elyn says, scooping up my discarded armor. She carries it out to the bedroom.

I hear the front door opening. Then I hear voices and then the door closing.

Elyn returns to the bathroom and says, "Nimith will have your set cleaned." She holds up a pair of black breeches and a white tunic. "Fine?"

"Fine. Thank you." I slip into the bath and slide down until my chin touches the water. My skin doesn't know what to do—explode or sing, catch fire or embrace the warmth. My mind doesn't care because my thoughts revolve around Jadon.

Like... The Celebration of Renewal in the Temple of Celestial's courtyard. It's tradition for me to bed the next king of Gasho—Prince Idus now—just as I'd "bedded" his father the king and *his* father the king and on and on until the very first Celebration of Renewal... I'd chosen kings in the manner that the people there had requested—which meant that I didn't have to *love* every man who'd climbed into my ceremonial bed. All it meant was, "This is the man who will tell everybody else what to do." That was it.

I dunk my head beneath the hot water and think about Jadon's "I choose you..." His own Celebration of Renewal. He'd bedded me and liked what he'd experienced, and he'd given me a thumbs-up. No special bed and no fancy gifts. He'd fought alongside me and became a temporary companion.

Tears fall from my eyes as I accept this, and though my face is submerged, my tears are heavier than the bathwater.

"Here."

I resurface, relieved that Elyn can't distinguish the teardrops running down my face from beads of scented bathwater.

She's handing me shampoo that smells of cocoa beans.

I rub the hair soap into my scalp, turning my hair—and my memories of Jadon—into a thick lather. I was such a fool, a fool who rushed in, and I told him, "Be the nightstar," because he'd expressed incredible sadness about his father not loving him. His father, Syrus Wake, was not just any old dad who expected his boy to take over the family business, marry a woman with childbearing hips, and have elevenscore babies. No, Jadon had *two* daddies—including Danar Rrivae—and each man represented a flavor of evil. And they'd carried him across the realm on the worst family road trip ever, making him poison enough of Vallendor for the people to move from hope to fear as they praised Wake's name.

Using a loofah, I scrub away the grit and dried blood, scrubbing harder as I remember that Jadon was supposed to weaken the Grand Defender and had been shocked to discover that *I* was the Grand Defender.

"And like an idiot, I told him who I was right after your mother told me who I was," I say to Elyn, my nostrils flared. "He used me as his weapon. As *your* weapon, but then I snapped out of it."

"Almost dying can bring about the best clarity," Elyn says. "You saw the truth."

Yeah, but I'd already fallen in love with him.

"So, no," I say to Elyn, catching the towel she tosses for me to dry off. "Jadon Thousand Surnames is a liar and a master manipulator. I'm not talking to him. He can't be trusted. And since *you* chose him to chase *me*, you can't be trusted, either." I point to the door.

She groans and marches to the bathroom's threshold.

"I'll be out in a minute."

"Wait—"

I slam the door on her even though she helped me bathe, even though she had been my best friend up until…

Up until I made my own foolish choices.

Agon the Kindness murmurs under his breath and shuffles down to the first bookshelf that I knocked over. There, he directs a Raqiel guard to erect it again. He shuffles back to Elyn and me and asks, "Well?"

"The bath was lovely, Uncle," I say. "And I appreciate you letting me see my room again, but I haven't changed my mind. I'm not talking to him." I go over to the aerie's single window.

In the north, the realm hides beneath a cloud of red dust caused by a god-made sandstorm. Shit. I've been gone too long, and Zephar is punishing the province around him. He's thrown tantrums like this before—when we were first imprisoned on Vallendor, he sand-stormed throughout Doom Desert for seven dawns.

Elyn shakes her head and leans out the window. "He's such an asshole."

"Which 'he' are you talking about?" I ask, smirking. I don't wait for her answer and turn to face my uncle. "The Adjudicator can handle it, and she can find Danar Rrivae and give her big speech about truth and justice, and then she can kill him on the spot."

I smirk and lean beside Elyn against the window ledge. "I'll lend you the sword you lost to me."

"Elyn can't destroy the traitor alone," Agon says. "Neither can you, Kaivara. Danar Rrivae can only be destroyed using the strength of the High Orders working together." He nods to Elyn. "You represent the Eserime, Yeaden, and Onama."

He nods to me. "Kaivara, you bring your heritages of all the five High Orders. Together, you are the collective. Together, you represent the Aetherium."

I hold up my hand. "One of my titles is 'Blood of All.' If that's true, why, then, do I need Elyn's help with this?"

Agon chuckles. "Because you aren't in good standing with the Council. Just as you can't trust Jadon Rrivae, the Council can't trust you, either. Further..."

He points to Elyn. "She is the Adjudicator of Vallendor Realm, and only *she* can dispense judgment here. She's not a warrior—there is no Mera in her bloodline. That is *your* strength, who *you* are, Kai. Together, you two are one, and that brings us all hope for victory—for Vallendor, for the Aetherium."

He says nothing else and just looks at me.

Eyebrows raised, I ask, "Are you holding for applause? Am I

supposed to now rush out onto the field, clear eyes, full heart, can't lose, win this for the Aetherium?"

Agon the Kindness blinks at me. "Are you done?"

I break into a smile. "Almost. Because now I see what this is. Keep the Mera girl chained up like a hound until you need her."

My uncle snaps his sleeves. "If you are to be completely restored, Kai, and also save Jadon—"

"Save Jadon?" I ask. "That's possible?"

Elyn snickers. "This is why you need to *shut up* sometimes."

"Ssh," I say, holding up my hand. "How is that possible, Uncle?"

And why do I suddenly care?

"To do that," Agon says, "we need two artifacts. WISDOM and TERROR."

We follow him to a worktable weighted down by a massive, leather-covered book the size of a small quilt. He points to a drawing on a page: a book encrusted with jewel-colored glass, its four corners edged in red garnets, mother-of-pearl, emeralds, and topaz. The book's center jewel looks blue, purple, and silver. A dark starburst sits in the middle of that stone.

I gasp and say, "I know this book. Olivia—"

"The thief who stole Kai's amulet," Elyn says to Agon.

The illustration hypnotizes me just as the real book did when I held it in the hayloft of Jadon's forge in Maford. Olivia stole the book from the library in Castle Wake.

Agon taps the drawing's center gem. "This artifact is known as WISDOM, and it locks the truth within the *Librum Esoterica*."

"Yes, I remember," I say, "but the book isn't with Olivia anymore. The book is with—"

"The redhead," Elyn says.

"Right," I say. "Philia Wysor." To Agon, I say, "She's the thief's girlfriend."

"And where is this Philia Wysor?" my uncle asks.

"In Caburh," I say. "Living now with the Renrians."

"What about the second artifact?" Elyn asks. "TERROR?"

The monk takes a deep breath and flips several pages, passing depictions of horrible beasts and scarier landscapes and complicated diagrams. Finally, he stops at a drawing of an amulet made of metal as dark as my new armor. The pendant's body is made up of crossed swords and compass points, all shaped like a star and ending in spikes tipped with red, blood-like thorns. The deep-crimson gemstone sitting in its center burns and glows even on the page. Malevolent and beautiful, battle and discovery, conquest and death... Its danger wafts from the page like potent perfume.

Elyn pales, and her eyes darken into stormy ice. "That's the traitor's amulet."

Agon slams the book closed. "Yes, it is, and that's the gem known as TERROR, and we must destroy it. Doing so not only kills Danar Rrivae and saves Vallendor, but destroying it also releases Jadon from certain doom."

My uncle and Elyn eyeball me, waiting. Clearly, they've devised this angle: Kai will save her man even if she doesn't give a damn about the rest of us.

I bare my teeth, intent on denying them their leverage. "I don't care if Jadon lives or dies."

Elyn snorts. "Sure you don't."

"I want Danar Rrivae out of my realm," I say, ignoring her. "I want my people free from his and Wake's threat. I want to free the Aetherium from the traitor's deceit and bring safety and happiness to all of us. The realms should decide their destiny—not Danar Rrivae. I'm here for a purpose: to be the Grand Defender of Vallendor rather than one random woman swinging her blade at shadows. I will break all of me to destroy all of him and any others who seek to take his place."

I open the book and find that illustration of Danar Rrivae's amulet. My breath races in my chest, and breathing feels like tiny shards of glass stabbing my lungs. "Before I agree," I continue, "there's someone I must speak to first." I peer at Agon. "And you know who that is."

My uncle pales and stands as still as the Raqiel guards.

"Well?" I say, closing the book. "You have the power to make that happen, Uncle."

"Kai," Agon says, "I don't think—"

"Please, Wisdom," Elyn says to him, "we need to get going. Do we want to waste any more time on this march to battle?"

"Elyn's right," I say. "And that kind of judgment is what makes her the Adjudicator. The longer you keep telling me 'no,' the worse off the realm becomes." I grin. "You have the power to make this happen, because *you* are the anchorite of Abbey Devour."

Agon grumbles and shuffles past us and to the northern aerie and toward the sentinels.

Elyn and I exchange looks, and I wink at her. She rolls her eyes and follows the old man.

Down here, the atmosphere crackles with the heady current of power. The two sentinels that guard the Glass of Infinite Realms are as tall as three mortal men standing on each other's shoulders. They wear platinum breastplates without tunics underneath. Their arms lack the red ribbons tied around the arms of Elyn's guards, and they do not wear the gray kerchiefs that cover the bottom half of her sentinels' faces. But they do share the same gray eyes, white skin, and whiter hair, and their swords—silver blades with a red cardinal on the scabbard and another cardinal etched into the hilt—are ready to end a god who's gone off the path.

The looking glass they guard reflects colors that spin and swirl.

I fix my eyes on the mirror.

The Glass of Infinite Realms is the only portal in Vallendor that reaches Linione. Because it is so sacred, the mirror will immediately destroy those who step through it who are not worthy; or the mirror will let the unworthy live but consume so many pieces of you that you'd wish that you'd been destroyed altogether.

I've used it several times before, before my change.

Elyn stands behind me, her eyes and hair the color of snow, so bright against her umber skin.

I stare at my reflection. My pupils are so golden that I can't see the definition of my eyes. Bruised-cherry-colored markings swirl at my hairline—the skin there feels raw. Fresh, healing scars adorn my cheeks and chin.

Past the clean skin and washed hair, beyond the cocked chin and smirk, I see…

The trembling lips and tear-filled eyes of a lost girl. I see the hollow gaze of someone who tried, who cared too much, who went too far, someone who'd been punished and stripped of all that she'd worked for, all that she loved. I see a woman banished to her dying realm—dying thanks to her own arrogance and hardened heart.

And now, I dip my head to keep from crying for that lost girl in the mirror's reflection.

Elyn touches my shoulder and squeezes.

"I *must* see him," I whisper.

She says, "I know."

My hands shake, and I press them against my hips to keep steady. I dare to look at my reflection again. But now, as I search for me, the Glass starts to shine with colors that don't exist in Vallendor. Pinks that shine blue. Greens that shine pink. The whole picture hypnotizes me; I could stand here and watch these colors forever as long as I don't have to see *me* again. I don't know what I'd do if I saw me again.

The stones in Elyn's and Agon's amulets ignite—two birds, wisdom and peace.

"Proceed, Kaivara," Agon whispers.

I swallow to steady myself and shuffle forward. Gouts of magical fire burn my skin. Before I can speak, I'm standing in a small courtyard where the ground resembles a carpet of golden ants. The sky shifts, too, but the ants above me are ruby-colored. Moths of gold and red surround me—I'm not alone here. A low hum vibrates through my head. It feels…*good*. In front of me, the prismatic light from the looking glass has dimmed, leaving behind a speck of light that still swirls in the top left corner of the mirror.

I reach for that speck of light, and a mystery squirms through my core, like worms in dirt after the rain. I close my eyes—I feel woozy, like I'm moments from vomiting. Bright light shimmers past my closed eyelids, and the heat feels like Lumis himself is climbing over me. My skin grows so hot that I may melt and die here. But I feel no pain, thankfully.

The moths have left me here—they are far too delicate for this type of heat. So I'm alone, and I want to scream, but I clamp my mouth shut because opening it will only let that heat in. I turn my head, keeping my lips closed, and I feel something pull at me and pull at me until—

12

I stand in a courtyard of trees and shrubs full of fat green leaves and multi-hued flowers bursting with life. There's so much color and perfume here that my head aches. The perfectly round cobblestones beneath my boots remind me of fresh-baked loaves of bread, and the sky above me shines with the light of the daystar. White-brightness and black shadow and every shade in between the two pulse… The golds, blues, and glimmer come from Supreme—Linione is the first child of the Aetherium, and so it is closest to the Creator.

The path before me leads in just one direction, and so I follow it through a grove of trees and a twisted brook of perfect water.

Up ahead sits a simple white house—similar to Malik Sindire's dwelling with those smooth walls and glass windows. But this house's broad entryway is flanked by white kastat rose bushes.

I'm surprised there are no guards, but those who'd do this place and the gods who convene here harm would've been destroyed the moment they stepped into the Glass of Infinite Realms.

The thick wood door stands ajar—a modest one compared to the abbey's thick metal and jeweled gate protected by the Raqiel. The door slowly swings open without my help. My next steps don't lead to a sitting room, but to a garden filled with multicolored kastat rosebushes. In the middle of this garden is a round table that has no ending, no beginning, no head or foot. Five beings representing their orders sit in high-backed wood chairs with red-cushioned backrests.

One man stands. He wears a fire-embroidered red-and-black robe with flared shoulders and matching pleated trousers.

I can't see the markings of the realms he's destroyed beneath his garb of Mera nobility, but I know that I have nowhere near as many as he does. I *do* have his golden eyes, his high cheekbones, and his broad shoulders. His brown skin—I have that, too. Yes, I have so much of him, but I don't have his love.

My feet stay planted where I stand, but my knees want to buckle. My stomach plunges to my ankles, but my solid anger keeps me upright, rigid. A quarter of an age has passed since the last time I saw him. He attended my sentencing, and he couldn't even look me in the eyes as the Raqiel guards marched me to the Glass of Infinite Realms. He didn't hug me goodbye on that day, nor has he visited me in the twenty-five seasons I've been confined on Vallendor. He hasn't sent me a gift, a letter, or well-regards from across the Aetherium.

I've imagined this reunion with my father countless times—as a child and up until I stepped to the Glass of Infinite Realms moments ago. In this recurring fantasy, we'd run to each other, and he'd call me "daughter," and he'd pick me up and swing me around, and then we'd walk hand-in-hand into eternal happiness. He'd say, *I'll never leave you again*, and I'd say, *I forgive you*.

Right now, though, it's obvious that neither of us are following my script, because neither of us moves.

All I can do is stare at the tall, broad man whose realm-wide shoulders would reach past the highest apples on Vallendor's tallest tree, whose palms are the size of silver platters and his neck thicker than a sequoia. All the material required for his outfit can clothe four men. That he fits in that chair is a trick or magic.

"Kaivara," High Lord Izariel Megidrail says, his voice strong and warm and filled with terrible thunder.

My shoulders immediately straighten, and my chin lifts even as it quivers. "Yes?"

He pushes away from the round table and says, "Cado." *Come.* He doesn't wait for my response and walks toward a gate behind the table, assuming that I will obey him.

My feet practically take root in the coarse green grass.

"I won't say it again," he says without looking back.

The lavender, green, black, and silver eyes of the four seated Council members stay on me. The heat of their gazes makes me sweat.

High Lord Khari Kynarv wears a long-sleeve white tunic and the black-and-gray cloak of the Yeaden, the order charged with building abbeys across the Aetherium and crafting weapons and armor for the gods. He blinks at me with his coal-black eyes and then gapes at High Lord Reder Cote of the Dindt, the order of explorers and seekers who search for new realms, observe life there, and return with knowledge. Cote's green eyes watch my father stalk to the gate. Silver-eyed High Lady Juchi Eneq of the Eserime nods at me and lifts an eyebrow. It's only respect for my father that keeps her from asking me about my journey since she last saw me.

"It would be in your best interest to…" Lavender-eyed High Lady Dava Hilew of the Onama is speaking to me, and she cocks her head toward the gate. She took this position after Elyn's father, Saerahil, spoke the word to Supreme.

Once upon a time, each person seated here loved me.

High Lord Izariel Megidrail stands beside a small pond that reflects the coppers and blues of Linione's sky. Even with him smaller now and no longer the height of the tallest tree in Vallendor, I still only come to his chin as I stand before him. Without thinking, I drop to one knee and bow my head. "Lord Megidrail."

"Our family is highborn," he says. "We trace our lineage to the first Mera of the original five races. Do you remember anything about the High Orders, child?"

"I remember *everything* about the orders, Father," I say, peeved.

Father nods. "Then you know that these orders and those that came after are governed by the Council, nobles who represent their orders and can ascend no higher in their godhood. Only Supreme is higher."

I stare at the flecks of movement beneath the pond's surface and listen to my fear. Sounds like rushing blood, crunching gravel and whistling wind. Why is he saying this?

"Skovv'rs ka klo graett kaax dikle kaiueso," he says. *Stepping to the glass took much courage.*

I thumb my ear, and I say, "Yes."

"I'd vorr aevaevo ag vaiu vuob'kaedok," he says. "I aesuoob v'kl klo quobik." *I'm well aware of your predicament, and I agreed with the verdict.*

A verdict handed down to me by the Council members still seated at the round table. A verdict that said I would spend the rest of my life on Vallendor Realm with muted power, supervised by Sybel Fynal and Elyn Fynal. Travel privileges would be revoked. Convocation invitations revoked. I'd be stripped of my titles of the Aetherium even though Vallendorians would still see me as "Celestial" and "Lady of the Verdant Realm" and all other honorifics. Vallendor's status lessened, too, with advisories to travelers that she was not the safest of realms to visit. Zephar and our Mera contingent were similarly punished and their powers also stripped. Labeled as "Diminished," we became the security guards of the realm, consigned to preventing further infection. Only my status as Lord Megidrail's only child had kept me—*us*—from being sentenced to Anathema. Anyone else who'd done what I'd done…

But part of my special sentencing was also this: Izariel Megidrail would have no further contact with me. But then it wasn't as though we had been close before the chaos I'd caused. He'd treated me like a child's used-to-be beloved toy crushed by new dolls and new balls and misplaced shoes. Which is why he can now be this unaffected, this… *aloof.*

I'm well aware of your predicament? He's holding me at arm's length like a parent holding a baby's soiled diaper. To my father, I stink.

My rage causes me to stand. "How can you cast judgment on me?" I snap. "On a daughter you never taught? You never told me what I should and shouldn't do. And then you label me as 'Diminished'? I was already weakened because you weren't there. You allowed one side of me to thrive as the other side grew reckless and wild."

He stares at me with those golden eyes.

"You say that you're *aware* of my predicament?" I spit. "But where were *you*? You know so much, but you know nothing about me or how I've felt, what I've feared and what I've loved and how many times I wished for you to be like Saerahil Fynal, who taught me how to reason and ask questions and..."

His nostrils flare, and the breeze around us warms—he doesn't like being compared to another man, especially to an Eserime man.

I close my eyes now filled with tears that are hot as fire. But I force myself to look at the high lord of the Mera order—

Huh?

My amulet now dangles in my father's hand, the stone in the moth's thorax still dead. I touch my bare neck, and my knees weaken again because of the pendant's absence.

"Now that you've taken that," I say, "are you about to make me sand? How is this just? How is this—?"

"No," Father interrupts, looking more pained than I thought he was capable of showing, "I wasn't there for you, but there are reasons for that, Kaivara. Know that I've never forgotten you, child. I think about you every time I take a breath, and now, as you stand before me, so beautiful and so strong and so smart, I'm..."

He takes a deep breath and holds it, then turns away from me. He stoops, releases that breath, and dips my pendant into the crystal waters. "I've been told that you recently experienced some memory loss."

"Yes," I say, "but I'm better now, and I remember everything, including how you've treated me." A sob gathers in my throat, but I tamp it down. *Big girls don't cry...*

Father lifts my amulet, but it doesn't drip water. No, the metal shines brighter than it ever has before. He dips it into the stream again, and this time, little fish nibble at the moth's wings.

He holds up the amulet again, and it shines even brighter. He smiles, then moves away from the water and over to a small maze of flowered hedges.

"You aren't the first to fail in the Aetherium," he says.

"How did it all go wrong?" I ask, chewing my bottom lip. I want to believe him, this suddenly warm stranger.

"'Wrong' is the incorrect word." Father plucks petals from the pink blooms growing around the maze.

"Why didn't Supreme end the disorder before it spread?" I ask.

"Free will," Father says, smiling at the blue flower before taking a petal. "Which, to some thinkers, is not truly *free* will. There is only one way, which means that eventually, free will expires. One can't choose wrong and live forever, and the consequences of choosing wrong serve as lessons for all."

"Danar Rrivae?" I ask.

"Chose wrong."

"If there can be dissension and transgressors among the orders," I say, "what does that mean for mortals? How are they expected to accomplish what we, the gods, can't? Why didn't the Council accept that I made mistakes but that I shouldn't die for those mistakes? Supreme obviously has patience—we're still all here. If one must die, then all must die. Upright, low-life, ignorant, and enlightened. Mistakes and pride flourish across all the realms, and as far as I can tell, people will misbehave forever. Perfection can't exist—that concept is finite."

He looks over at me, eyebrows raised. "Good points, all."

"How do you punish someone for a transgression that could, over the span of time, be thought of as that person finally coming to understand?" I ask. "For you and the Council, it doesn't matter that I'm young, that I don't know everything, that sometimes I make decisions without thinking them through. Aren't I supposed to make mistakes? Isn't that how we all learn?"

Father continues to clench my amulet and those flower petals. "How long should the traitor be allowed to figure it all out? To realize that he's made a mistake? Do we wait until he's destroyed thirty realms? Fifty? Eighty?"

"I..." I heave a sigh and shrug.

"He's not the only one who has transgressed like this," Father says.

"What happened to them? Were they forced to make amends? Were they punished? Were they given another chance to understand and learn why their actions were…disruptive?"

"*Disruptive*," he says. "Interesting. Not 'evil' or 'bad.'"

"So-called good things can be disruptive," I say. "A baby crying in the middle of the night while her exhausted mother tries to sleep—that's disruptive. A new idea popping into your head just as you've finally understood the old idea—disruptive. The baby isn't evil. The new idea isn't bad."

"And Danar is simply interested in new ideas?" Father blows into his closed hand, and then he looks up at the sky. He plucks something invisible from the air and slips what can't be seen into his closed brown fist. I glance over my shoulder and spot a black moth with red-and-yellow wings fluttering toward us. She lands on Father's clenched hand.

"Vallendor Realm is changing even for…" He nods and smiles at the resting moth.

I hold my breath and hope that he doesn't crush the moth as he's crushed the flower petals.

"Lady, welcome," the moth says. *"You are still loved."*

I lean closer to the moth and whisper, "Thank you, lovely. I'm grateful for your love."

Father studies me. "The one power I envy."

"But you don't destroy her," I say.

"Because we, too, show restraint," he says, "and we destroy only what is sanctioned by Supreme and the High Council."

I drop my head. My destruction of realms would be akin to my father smashing the moth.

"We took your powers away because of who you were becoming," Father says. "You would've isolated yourself completely from Supreme had we allowed you to move in that direction—and I didn't want to see my only child, the gift of my love for Lyra, turned to dust and forever gone.

"Had Sybel not appealed on your behalf," he says, "your ending would've happened. She told us about all that you'd done for your people, about the betrayals of those who you valued above all else."

My face freezes as the import of this revelation sinks in. "I was..."

"On the path to your own destruction by the ultimate power. You may only go so far until you can go no further, and then there is no return, and then there is no Adjudicator or Council who can save you from that ending. That is what makes you different from Danar. He doesn't wish to change. Because we were childhood friends, he thought he could speak frankly to me—and during these conversations, he told me that he would never open his heart to Supreme again nor would he ever admit fault. To him, he's done nothing wrong."

"So you stripped me of my power to save me from my power," I say.

Father moves his fist, and the moth takes flight, sprinkling gold-and-crimson dust as she leaves us. "To prove yourself to the Council, and ultimately to Supreme, you must confront Danar Rrivae. You must convince him to abandon his campaign to destroy Vallendor and any realms in the future, and then he must accept his punishment."

"And if he refuses?" I say. "You just said that his heart is hard."

"Then you have the permission of the Council to destroy him and his followers. But...if *you* betray this Council and join with him, or if you abandon this task..." He holds his clenched fist to his heart. "Then the Council will direct Elyn Fynal and a host of Mera to destroy all of Vallendor and those connected to it, including Sybel Fynal, the Grand Steward of Vallendor, and...me."

"What?"

"The last of the Megidrail bloodline will end on Vallendor." He's grown taller as I've stood here beside him.

"But how do I do that—destroy him?" I ask. "I'm weaker than ever before, and he's..."

"He's strong, yes," Father says, "but you're stronger. I, along with the others on the Council, have agreed to restore to you some of your power. We don't have much time—this work must be done by the nightstar's full ascent." He hands me the pendant.

I slip the amulet over my head. "Next full ascent? That's nine dawns from now."

His "yes" rumbles and vibrates across my face.

"Why? What does the full ascent have to do with...?" My eyes close—the pressure feels like stones being dropped on my chest. "I have questions about you and my mother, and I have to admit, I'm scared. Father, I know I'm not supposed to be but—" I open my eyes.

I'm no longer standing in the garden with my father. In fact, I'm no longer in Linione Realm. Moths, my only company now, flutter around my head in this anteroom with the Glass of Infinite Realms. That single speck of light swirls in its top left corner.

Nine dawns.

PART II

THE ODYSSEY

Boundless Maelstrom, the heavens bow,
Your might undaunted, here and now.
With ev'ry storm, with ev'ry strife,
You guide us to eternal life.

Through lands of flame and seas of woe,
You hold us close, would not let go.
Your shining grace, a steadfast shield,
In ev'ry war, we did not yield.

You ready space within your gates.
You tend our fears 'til threats abate.
Our shields and swords are glass and foam,
We wander aimless, far from home.

Do not forsake us for our slights.
Our minds are vacant, dark as nights.
You are the way, you are the dawn.
With steadfast care, we carry on.

Lovely Maelstrom, our hearts true,
In faith, we march, we follow you.
With ev'ry breath, your name we cry,
Our goddess bright, who rules the sky.

–A Song of Praise by Grace Hallum

13

Returning to the Abbey of Mount Devour through the Glass of Infinite Realms, I can't gain my balance, and I totter down corridors, clinging to the slick walls. Beams of light shine down on me, filling these hallways and shifting darkness. I can't tell my foot from the shadow of my foot. Sometimes, I have to crouch and place my head between my knees. This shit's making me sick.

Pale-skinned Raqiel sentinels stand every ten paces and at every four-way corridor. These descendants of Mera and Onama say nothing as I stop, crouch, and lean, nor do their gray eyes shift in my direction. Do they ever leave these dungeons that thread through this abbey? Are they ever angry with their underground station in life? Do they ever wish they could see a sunlit sky and hear sounds that aren't merely echoes?

"And I used to travel through the Glass like that all the time?" I ask, my face hidden in the crook of my elbow.

Elyn, farther ahead, turns back to me. "You weren't Diminished then. Come on—we're losing time."

"Give me a moment." *Ugh*. My skin feels frustratingly clammy, even though I *just* took a bath. I peek out again from behind my elbow to stare at the wall across from me…a wall that soars overhead and ends somewhere in the sky. To make matters worse, the ground is too soft, and it feels like I'm walking on air.

My sense of space and my need for boundaries is…*gone*. I can't walk without nearly vomiting.

"Kai—"

"Yeah, yeah." I slide up the wall to stand, eyes closed. After pushing out a few breaths, I throw myself into the middle of the corridor and start on my wobbly way.

Elyn looks at me over her shoulder—the corner of her lip lifts just a bit. She wants to laugh. But she doesn't, and in silence, she leads me through one tall iron door after another. There are no longer torches or lanterns through these passageways. Her gold eyes and dove amulet are lighting the way.

No light glows from my own eyes or from my moth pendant, and so I must rely on her. What powers did my father manage to restore if I still lack the ability to find my own way? I guess I'm more broken than I thought.

"Did you get the answers you needed from Lord Megidrail?" the Adjudicator asks, reading my mind.

I give Elyn a one-shouldered shrug and scan the hallway for pots or vases just in case my stomach surrenders. "I didn't have a chance to ask him about our family or why he abandoned us. He didn't ask about my mother's end, either."

Elyn snorts. "Your mother's *end*? *You* caused your mother's end. *You* destroyed Ithlon. What questions did he need answered that weren't answered during the trial?"

My cheeks flush. "I didn't mean that. I don't know what I was thinking. Everything was happening so quickly." I pause, then add, "I did want to ask about the generals who lied to me about Mother being off-realm. Where are they now? You must know."

"Why must you know their locations?" Elyn asks. "Are you planning to kill them one day?"

I don't answer.

Elyn doesn't look back at me.

I tug my ear and clear my throat. "I don't know how many times I have to say this, but I didn't know that she was still on Ithlon when I launched its destruction. And I don't care if you believe me or not."

"If you'd known she was still in Gundabar Province, would you have called it off?" she asks. Even with her back to me, I know Elyn's scowling. Because to the Adjudicator, it doesn't matter that I'd been lied to. My destruction still hadn't been blessed by the Council of High Orders.

"Of course I would've," I snap. "Do you think I'm so maniacal that I'd kill my *mother*?"

Elyn doesn't respond to me but nods at the sentinels we pass.

"I'm trying to be better," I say, stumbling on a thicker patch of air.

She hears my scuffling boots and peeks back at me. "Are you gonna make it there?"

No.

"Of course." I flap my hand at her. "Keep going. We have only nine dawns."

"And you're gonna use six of them trying to walk down to the dungeons."

I chuckle. I have to stop and rest my hands on my knees again. "Do you know the significance of nine dawns and the nightstar's cycle?"

Elyn shakes her head—how does she do that without stumbling or clutching her stomach? "Something about the metals and gems and Selenova's mass and…" She takes a deep breath and pushes it out. "Doesn't matter. All I know is this: we don't have much time. For Agon to even agree to let us come down here and interrogate the Weapon tells me that this is serious. We can't stay long, understand?" She looks back at me again to confirm that I understood.

"No problem." I give her a wobbly thumbs-up from my place against another wall.

And really: this meeting shouldn't take long.

Waving my two middle fingers in the Weapon's face: that will take ten seconds.

Telling him to kiss my ass: five seconds.

Bathing in the toasty satisfaction of turning on my heel and abandoning him in this dungeon: timeless but only seven seconds.

"I know you're angry that he betrayed you," Elyn says, walking backward now, "but it's up to you to not let that betrayal ruin the rest of your life."

"Thanks, Mom." I throw myself to the middle of the corridor, overshooting and blundering into the wall across from me.

She's right, though. Holding on to that hurt means living like these dungeon-dwelling Raqiel, guarding my hurt feelings and never feeling the warmth of freedom kiss my face.

Elyn smiles as she watches me bumble from wall to wall.

I laugh. "Stop looking at me and showing off—I'm gonna throw up on your shoes."

If I vomit in her presence, I *know* she'll never let me forget that.

Elyn tries not to smile and jams her lips together. She turns away from me and marches on in silence.

But silence makes me have to think more as I navigate these janky-lit hallways.

"Why don't the sentinels down here cover their faces or wear red ribbons like the cardinal-bird ones that follow you around?" I ask.

Even as a free defender, I'd rarely interacted with the Raqiel. Living with the Fynals, though, I'd see the guard all the time. I had a crush on one—Eston, son of Athigor. He smiled at me once, and it had been the smallest, most inconsequential lift on the left side of his beautiful mouth. We held each other's gaze for the moment it takes one to blink…

"Just a different branch of Raqiel," Elyn says now. "They're all trained in warfare. The cardinals just have additional skills. They understand more languages. Can identify a mortal threat quicker than the Raqiel of the dungeons. The other 'red-bird' ones serve all the Adjudicators throughout the Aetherium—and have done so since the first conflict ages before even our own parents' births." She pauses, having provided a distraction from my sorry state. Then she asks, "Better?"

I say, "Yes," and I am better. I haven't lurched or weaved in twenty paces. Sure, I'm taking tiny half steps, but I *am* forging ahead.

We walk in silence on that hard-soft ground, through those tall corridors that have no ceilings, and into deeper shadows and shifting, glowing light. Elyn slows her pace—the darkness has grown even darker here, and her eyes can barely penetrate the gloom. The temperature in this passageway has also dropped. Frosty clouds puff like dust from our noses and mouths.

"Does keeping the prison this cold somehow stop him?" I ask.

"Yes, the cold weakens Miasma and whatever spells Danar Rrivae has endowed him with," Elyn whispers.

"The holding cells we passed didn't have prisoners," I say, just realizing. I look back over my shoulder but only see darkness. "I remember jailing several immortals who broke the laws of Vallendor. You tried those cases."

Tiny Aver, a Dindt, flayed the skin off a mortal woman who'd rejected him at a tavern.

Ryany Ashtod, another Dindt, killed a mortal family in the saffron fields of Peria.

Three Mera Diminished—Maxilla Sonuaria, Nicata Eulinari, and Lanicon Laniconia—burned down a village just because it was there. Six people died.

A pack of rowdy gods on holiday terrorized, tortured, and raped mortal women over the course of three dawns.

A few of these losers had even claimed *under oath* that they were doing my bidding.

But even on my worst days, I never tolerated rapists, and Elyn actually had to direct the Raqiel to keep me from beheading the leader of that assorted pack of evil.

"They have been moved to cells at the Abbey of Threka Realm," Elyn says. "We don't know enough about the Weapon to guarantee those prisoners' survival here. This may be a jail, but we aren't cruel."

"I'd be okay with leaving the rapists down here," I say.

Elyn turns to grin at me. "As the Adjudicator, maybe I'll take the Lady's recommendations once—*if*—she's reinstated and bring them back." I manage a small smile in return.

We stop at the end of the corridor and turn toward the only occupied cell in the dungeon.

"You have a visitor," Elyn announces to the darkness.

Nausea—the first sign of Miasma—coils in my belly once again, but this feels different than the motion sickness I'd finally recovered from. This nausea feels like tiny, shrimp-like creatures swirling around my guts and chomping away at me with razor-like teeth. Yes, this queasiness bites. As I tiptoe closer to the cell, my skin pebbles from the cold. In this darkest darkness, a weak glow thrums from my pendant.

"Kai? I feel you here." Jadon's voice sounds scratchy, rusty, as though the cold has leeched every drop of oil from his body. His gaze is filled with light as weak as he is, an indicator of his state. He sits on the edge of a narrow bed. Piles of quilts and books are stacked across the stone floor. He wears a simple tunic and breeches, not the outfit of a prince or demigod. His greasy dark hair has grown and flops in his face even after he sweeps it away with his left hand. His marked right hand glows, a reminder of his lethal heritage. Even if this is a jail, it's the jail in the abbey of the gods, and he doesn't belong in this immortal space. He doesn't belong to me, either. He is otherworldly.

Yet I dreamed about him nights ago. We'd lain together in that bower, holding each other right before the world around us exploded. He'd told me, "Time is life," and "For love, for change, for all that yet breathes," and then he caught fire and his last kiss had filled me with flames, and…

And now, seeing him again…

My blood boils, and then it ices. My heart booms, and then my heart goes still. Jadon Rrivae Wake spins me round.

"You look strong, Kai," he says, standing up and moving toward the bars. "And you're still beautiful. I don't wanna look away."

"Cheers to me, then," I say, poking my tongue into my cheek. "Obviously, you can't see the new cuts and bruises on my face from my fight with the Sea of Devour's most aggressive residents."

"I can see them," he says, "and I said what I said."

"You've either made yourself so sick that you've tricked yourself or you're lying to me again. Or both. I'm thinking both. A self-deceived liar."

Elyn snickers and drifts back into the shadows, remaining close enough, though, to provide light for me to see this beautiful liar.

Jadon smiles. "I'm hoping that you've come down here to free me, and to tell me that—"

"I'm not here to tell you one damned thing," I blurt. "I don't know you, sir, nor do I trust you. I'm not even sure why I came other than to laugh in your face about your offer to *let me* stand beside you as you ruled *my* realm. I believe your precise words were...

"'I won't destroy the world with him, Kai. Nor will I rule this realm with Gileon. I want to share Vallendor with you. I want to rule this realm with you by my side and make Vallendor what it *should* be.'"

Those words are seared into my memory forever.

"Kai," Jadon says, fidgeting with the collar of his tunic, "about that—"

"You said all those pretty words while forgetting the most important fact." I cock my head and sneer at him. "*I* am Vallendor's Grand Defender. *I* am the Lady of the Verdant Realm. *I* do not *share* the administration of this world with anyone, especially with a man who doesn't even know who—*or what*—he is, especially with a man whose entire existence depends on the extermination of mine."

"I made a mistake," Jadon says, his face twisted and sweaty. "I'm sorry, okay? Since being in this stupid jail, I've had plenty of time to think about how foolish I was to even suggest that I become emperor. If it matters any, I'm—" He grimaces and stumbles backward, grasping his right arm.

"You're in pain," I say, staring at his right arm, which now sparks with amber light. I want to lift my hand to heal him, but I fight that natural inclination and keep my hands to myself.

"Every two days, I pray for death," Jadon says with a chuckle. "But that, I guess, isn't Supreme's will. So I'm now asking you for the opposite. I ask for my life. Save me, Lady. *Kai*. I don't want to live as Miasma or as my father's tool."

I blink at him. "Now which father are we talking about? The awful one or the immortally awful one?"

Jadon drops his gaze and cradles that offending right hand now that festers with inked elements. "Do you really think I had a lot of choice? You know that I tried to escape my path, my destiny. That Maford was supposed to give me a future, but then you showed up and..."

Kinda destroyed Maford? And what I didn't burn down, Elyn demolished.

"You're right," I admit. "We ruined your hiding place. And I'm sorry about that. But if Olivia hadn't stolen from me, I would've never chased her into that stupid, raggedy town, and you and I would've never...*met*."

My throat tightens, and I look away from him to collect my thoughts. Imagining a life without Jadon... I was fine before him. I'll be fine after him. Yes, I'll be fine...

"Kai?" Elyn says, spurring me. "Time."

"We're not here to lament the past or to wish upon stars," I say now. "Your father continues to breed new otherworldly. Resurrectors. Why? And how do we stop them?"

Jadon blinks at me, and hope drains from his face. "You stop them by killing them."

"No shit," Elyn mutters, stepping out from the shadows. "How do we *kill* them?"

He doesn't answer her.

"How do we kill them?" I repeat.

"Blades and spells," he says, tapping his foot to a song that only he can hear. "More spells than blades. Don't know. They aren't invincible."

"And what are the spells?" I ask, taking another step forward. My stomach drops, and spit floods my mouth.

"Kai," Elyn says, "no closer."

Jadon sits back on the bed with a smile playing at the corners of his mouth.

What's that smile about? Is his advice a trap? What else does he know that he's not sharing?

"Wake's army," I say, swallowing the pool of spit that had gathered beneath my tongue. "Where are they headed next?"

"I'm in *jail*," he snaps. "How would I know?" He pauses, then asks, "Do you ever think about me? Do you ever think about the good things we did together? Our entire life together wasn't a *complete* lie. You couldn't have forgotten, not after all we've been through."

"Are you kidding me right now?" I ask, gaping at him. "Do you think that I, *the* Kaivara Megidrail, Grand Defender, Blood of All, go through my days anchored to memories of you? Do you think that my day begins and ends with—?"

"Okay, okay," he says, his eyes squeezed closed, his hand held up. "You've made your point. *Fuck.*"

"Mind your words," Elyn growls.

"If you want me to slowly waste away down here, fine," Jadon says. "I understand. I'm a danger to the realm. But if you're a truly compassionate god, if you still care for me just a little, please do one thing for me: save Olivia. Maybe Gileon will let her go if she returns the book that she stole from Castle Wake."

He pushes up his sleeves—the veins along his forearms are now twitching. "There's something in that book that Gileon needs. That's why he searched all of Vallendor for us. It wasn't because he loved Olivia, I know that for sure."

"And where *is* your brother?" Elyn asks.

Jadon runs his fingers along his twitching veins, still snubbing her.

"You ignoring the Adjudicator won't help your cause," I say, "and doesn't put you in the best light. Recognize her authority right now or spend the rest of your miserable life in this dark, dank cell…or worse. Test me. *Please.*"

The light in Jadon's eyes flares at me before they land on Elyn.

"Why does Gileon need the book?" the Adjudicator asks again.

Jadon flexes the fingers on his right hand. "Pride? Anger? I don't know what drives him, especially now. All I know is that he wants it back."

The artifact, WISDOM, is fastened to that book's cover—*that's* what Gileon wants.

Elyn and I turn away from Jadon. I beckon the Adjudicator to follow me back into the corridor. "Does Jadon know the truth about the *Librum Esoterica*?" I whisper. "That it's not 'just a book'?"

She stares at me. "Don't know."

"If he did, would he tell us?"

"Don't know. Does he know that Philia Wysor still has it?"

My turn to say, "Don't know. But I'm more concerned that Philia's now staying with Separi Eleweg in Caburh."

The Broken Hammer Inn had been a needed waystation for us after Veril's death. There, Jadon and I had the chance to express our feelings for each other.

Yeah, I loved kissing Jadon. I loved sucking his lower lip and twisting my tongue around his and darting it back if he tried to catch it with his own tongue. And now, standing in this fucking hole in the mountain, I try not to smile as I think about our kissing game at the Broken Hammer. I try not to smile as I remember how his hands had roamed across my hips and how the game changed when his fingers found my favorite spot and...

Damn it, Jadon.

Though his words were lies, his kisses were not. Our explosions that night and everything we said to each other...all truth. I would've named a realm after this man. *Three* realms.

No, I don't wish death upon this man. At the same time, he doesn't deserve the entirety of my mercy, either.

I want to rule this realm... Yeah, he said that. *I choose you.* He said that, too. And now, his right hand burns with the immense power he inherited from the traitor, his father.

I push those thoughts away and whisper to Elyn: "If Gileon discovers that Philia still has the *Librum Esoterica*—"

"He'll return to Caburh," Elyn says, "and destroy the rest of the town—"

"—and slaughter the survivors, including Separi and her kin."

And then he'll claim the *Librum Esoterica and* WISDOM.

We need WISDOM to destroy the traitor.

"Are you done with me now?" Jadon shouts from his cell.

Elyn and I ignore him as we continue to strategize.

"You're here to show mercy, Kai," Jadon shouts again. "To teach and protect and love. I just… I need you to love me like you love all those who rely on your protection and tenderness."

Honey. That's Jadon's approach right now.

Because honey works when a hammer can't.

14

Even though Zephar frowns at me, I keep glaring at the ceiling of our tent. My chin quivers, a sign that I'm moments from breaking. That would be the worst thing that could happen in a Sanctum of Mera warriors, Diminished or not.

I take a deep breath and hold the air in my chest. *Don't cry. Don't whine. Don't beg.* I take in another deep breath and notice just how fragrant the air is here. Sweet figs and roasted dates. A fire crackles in the pavilion's hearth as someone sings about their mighty blade. All of this sits just a stone's throw away from me, and right now, I feel as far away from my life here as I did standing at that pond beside my father in Linione.

My return from the abbey had been so lovely, too. A new sarong made of soft pink silk had been draped across our bed—a gift from Zephar. The old tub had been replaced by a bigger tub made for two. Another gift from Zephar.

Now, though…

Shari sits at the tent's entrance, her tail twitching, her eyes glinting. She pants, then holds her breath, pants, holds her breath. Anxious, which makes me anxious, too.

I glare at Zephar and ask, "What's the point of going to Eaponys or anywhere else if the ultimate evil is roaming the realm? The *real* traitor, not the one you think is standing in front of you—"

"I didn't call you a traitor," he spits. "I'd never call you—"

"The *real* traitor," I continue, "is now creating stronger otherworldly that can't be killed. Again, I saw that creature at the sea reanimate right in front of me, Zee." I run my hands through my hair, then ask, "Do you think I was happy to hear that Vallendor will no longer exist if I don't kill Danar Rrivae by the nightstar's full ascent?"

Zephar sets his hands on his hips and turns away from me. "So what am I supposed to do while you're out saving the realm? Since your father refuses to grant *me* Spryte? Since I'm no longer allowed to go beyond Doom Desert province?"

"Please continue to prepare for war," I say. "Fortifying not only Gasho and the small settlements around the desert, but also the Sanctum. This fight will have no boundaries."

"And Eaponys?" he asks. "Will you grant me some freedom—?"

"Father didn't give me the power to lessen anyone's sentence."

That may or may not be true, but I don't want Zephar and the Diminished wandering the realm beyond Doom Desert.

"I'll be back to help with Eaponys," I say, touching his back again but feeling nothing—no desire, no angst. "We may need to pass through it to reach Danar Rrivae's hiding place."

Shari paces from the entrance and over to me, back to the entrance and back to me. Her fur spikes as she tucks her tail between her hind legs.

I squint at her. "She's upset."

Zephar looks over at his wolf. "Because you're leaving again. She hates it when you go."

I stare into the wolf's golden eyes. "I'm sorry, Shari-My-Love."

"No."

I startle. Did she say "no" or did I…? My amulet vibrates against my skin, and now, it shines with a barely there glow. I look back at Zephar. "There will be plenty of fighting and destroying in the coming days. I promise you that."

He rolls his eyes and folds his arms.

"Do you think this has been easy for me?" I shout, throwing my hands up.

He says nothing.

"I asked you a question," I ask, louder.

"Are you asking as my commander or as my love?" he asks, coolly, eyebrow high.

"Don't be like this, Zephar. Okay? Trust me, yeah?" When he doesn't speak, I gape at him and shake my head. "I'm doing what's being asked of me, what's required to save all of us."

My heart belongs to Zephar—but he doesn't want it anymore. I can tell.

I stomp out of the tent and head to the gravel path that leads to the narrow canyon separating the immortal and mortal planes.

So many people are waiting for me to act, to save them all.

Elyn remains at the abbey and awaits for me to return with the *Librum Esoterica* and its powerful gem, WISDOM.

Jadon waits for me to free and forgive him for his betrayals—against me and against Vallendor Realm.

Prince Idus, pacing alongside the special celebration ritual bed within the Temple of Celestial, waits for me to make him king.

Zephar waits to resume our life together, liberating one town after the next as we slowly make our way to destroy Danar Rrivae.

And the Gashoans wait for me to bless them with another baby and another cow.

Yet I stand here, as stuck as I was the last time, but now, I have the power to act.

Because someone else is waiting.

Me.

To return to Caburh and take the book from Philia. To corner the traitor and take his amulet and kill him. If I don't, Eaponys and god jails and celebration ritual beds and cows will cease to exist. No one else can do this work except for Elyn and me. So what am I waiting for?

The nausea that comes from using Spryte and from standing so close to Miasma flutters through me again. I grab hold of my knees and wait for the sensation to pass. My breathing tightens, and the urge to weep overwhelms me. *Don't do it, don't cry*. But I give in and watch as heavy teardrops thump onto the toes of my boots. Crying doesn't lessen the heaviness; it only grows heavier, and what I'm feeling is suddenly no longer queasiness or sadness, but worse:

Fear.

Fear of living an incomplete being.

Fear of failing and not being a perfect god.

Fear of death—not just my death, but the deaths of my father, Jadon, Ancress Tisen, the children of Gasho, Prince Idus…

Shari whines and barks, pulling me out of my head. *"Please."*

I frown. "Is that…? Is that *you*? Are you…*speaking* to me, Shari?"

She pants some more, then cocks her head. *"You must…"*

I kneel before the wolf, my amulet trembling against my chest. "Am I hearing your voice right now?" This voice in my head is as soft as smoke.

Her eyes shimmer as she holds my gaze. *"Yes."*

"Lady!" A woman's voice, not Shari's.

The wolf's ears twitch.

"Please come!" Yes, this call for help sounds like it's coming from a mortal woman, but she isn't from Gasho—still, she sounds familiar.

"Lady!" a man cries out. "Forgive my unbelief. Come now. Please hurry, I pray to thee, Lady of the Verdant Realm!"

I spin around, trying to determine where those prayers are coming from.

The woman screams.

Lively! The candlemaker's daughter from Maford.

With just a thought, I Spryte to the barren and brown fields behind Farmer Gery's barn in Maford. The land here has been crisped by the now-setting daystar.

In the beginning, Supreme had created this field, and every field across Vallendor, filled with thick-bladed grasses, plants, and flowers that ranged in shade from the whitest whites to the deepest blues. Back then, fruits, flowers, and trees held so much sweet sap that beehives were soon weighed down with honey. "Verdant realm" was more than just my title.

And now, this field—and almost every field across Vallendor—grows with rot and disease, and death and decay. Neither mortals nor animals can hide or slip through unnoticed in these grasses because every step snaps branches and blades. Every step makes leaves crackle and the hard dirt puff and wheeze underfoot.

Twenty paces away, I spot them: Jamart, the candlemaker, the one who'd been the kindest to me but had stopped believing in me after Maford burned to the ground, and Lively, who'd been jailed because of her belief in the Lady of the Verdant Realm instead of Emperor Wake as Supreme Manifest. I'd freed her from Maford's slimy jail.

Now, bloody and bruised, Jamart and Lively hover in the air, their toes not even touching the ground, their hands tied in front of them. Jamart's lantern jaw looks like it's been dislocated, hit so many times that the bones in his face have shifted. His daughter's eyes…bloody sockets where those eyes used to be.

Shit!

I run toward them. And I run…and run…but I can't catch up.

Something—or someone—keeps pulling them back and away from me.

There!

One thought and I've Spryted, and now I'm standing in front of them.

"I can't see you, Lady," Lively says, "but I feel your presence. You heard our prayers, Lady." She grins, delirious with relief.

Jamart dips his head and murmurs through his twisted mouth, "Please forgive me, Lady."

"Yes, of course." I reach for the knot around the candlemaker's wrists. No matter how quickly and forcefully I pull at it, though, the bond won't loosen. "Who tied you up like this?"

Both shake their heads and shrug their shoulders. But then Jamart's eyes widen.

I look back over my shoulder.

Creatures with the legs and trunks of hares and the heads, eyes, and wings of owls hop around a nearby log.

I whisper, "What the…?"

More of these creatures soar and circle the treetops and land on the highest branches. They stare at me with large, owl-like eyes, and they cock their heads just like I'm doing.

Some weird shit.

I turn back to work on the knot—

But Jamart and Lively have moved away from me again.

I run toward them and…run and run…and I'm forced to slow down until I'm not even walking.

A gray cloud forms in front of me. It's too high to wrap my arms around but low enough for me to lift my hand and scrape my fingers along its bottom. *Cold.* The cloud grows taller and wider, until it hides the dark sky.

"You're answering prayers again?" the cloud asks.

I pull the dagger from my ankle sheath as that gray cloud surrounds me. I can barely see the blade in my clammy hand through the mist.

The cloud thins some, and a man towers behind the candlemaker and his daughter. He, too, must hover—his feet aren't allowed to touch Vallendor's soil as long as I'm alive. He places one hand on Jamart's head and his other hand on Lively's.

I squint at him—but it's not his remark that confuses me. "I'm dreaming," I say aloud. "This…this isn't real."

"Oh, but this is *very* real, Lady," Danar Rrivae says. He wears his long gray hair tied in a crimson ribbon and a sleeveless black tunic that hides the countless spheres and vines that symbolize the realms he's infected—or successfully stolen. His bare skin is a mix of pale white and sickly violet. His green eyes are as soft as the fog swallowing us.

I glare at those markings swirling beneath his tunic and across his arms. Danar Rrivae is Dindt—an explorer and seeker. He isn't Mera. He also wears the crimson ribbons of Raqiel guards, who are descended from the Onama and Mera—again, Danar Rrivae is neither. Not only has he stolen realms, but he's also stolen traditions, stolen valor.

"Let them go," I demand, knowing that he won't, not until he gets what he came here for.

"You have something that belongs to me," he says, fire and ice blending in his voice.

I shake my head. "There's nothing on Vallendor that you can rightfully claim."

"The *Librum Esoterica* longs to be at home. Give it back to me."

"I gave that book to Syrus Wake," I say. "It belongs to *him* now."

• • •

On that day, we stood in the heart of Brithellum, in an open arena with high archways framing the sky. The *Librum Esoterica* rested on a pedestal of polished obsidian, casting its light across Syrus Wake's face.

Priests and Renrian scholars, including Veril, Separi, and Adjudicator Saerahil Fynal, had assembled to witness Syrus Wake, twenty summers old, kneel before me.

The *Librum Esoterica* had levitated between my hands as I said, "Syrus Wake, you stand at the threshold of greatness. This book is the key to the wisdom of the ages but also carries the burden of truth. You, young king, are entrusted to guard it, to seek its counsel, and to wield it not for power, but for balance and understanding, for the protection of your people."

As soon as Wake's fingers closed around the book, the gem WISDOM flared with brilliant light. A matching silver band with an indention that matched WISDOM'S size formed around the new king's left ring finger.

"It will not open for ambition nor will it open for pride," I'd warned him. "It will yield only to those who seek knowledge for the sake of the realm, and even then, only in times of great need. Remember this, my chosen king."

But that was then, and this...*this is fucked up.*

"Syrus Wake belongs to *me*," Danar Rrivae now says. "But rest easy, Kaivara. I came to bargain with you, not to fight."

Those owl-hare creatures hop away from their log and over to Danar Rrivae, Jamart, and Lively.

"These creatures shouldn't be here," I whisper, gripping my dagger tighter. "Not in this field of lesser creatures. Not on Vallendor." I pause, then ask, "What are they?"

"Minulles," the traitor says. He clucks his tongue.

The creatures look at him and call back—and that call sounds like its name. Men-*yool.* Other owl-hares hop out of their underground dens and purr to each other. Men-*yool.* Men-*yool.* Then they corner a field mouse and eat her.

"See?" Danar Rrivae says. "Good riddance. No one likes mice."

"That field mouse dug burrows that kept the soil loose. She spreads seeds and scavenges and—" I glare at the traitor. "This is what you do: destroy order."

"Funny coming from you, of *all* gods." His hand leaves Jamart's head and slips down to the man's neck.

"I saw your new creatures lurking around the Sea of Devour," I say, my pulse racing, eyes on the traitor's hand. "They flew with leather wings. Brought beasts that I'd slain back to life. How did they do that?"

Danar Rrivae chuckles but doesn't answer my question. His amulet, a twisting red-tipped vine of moving metal, glows against his black tunic.

"You destroy order," I say, "but you keep chaos flourishing."

"Who are you to accuse me of destruction and chaos, *Destroyer*?" He laughs and adds, "They call you 'Maelstrom' in Caburh. Did you know that?" His other hand now disappears into Lively's tangled blond hair.

"That's just one of the many names I'm called. And what do those in Caburh call *you*?"

His face turns hard as stone.

"They call you nothing, since they credit me for all of your…" I wave my hand at the minulles. "How awful for you, to do all this work for a Diminished Mera to get the glory."

The traitor's rage makes more mist that crawls over my skin like oil.

"Let the candlemaker and his daughter go," I say, "and I will personally write a song just for you. I'll make children learn the words, and they'll sing it at festivals and…"

Jamart's crooked mouth opens wide, and his eyes burn with pain, so much pain that he can't even cry out.

So I cry out for him. "Stop! What do you want?"

"We can heal this realm," Danar says.

I squint at him. *"We?"*

"Yes. *We* can heal Vallendor and save ourselves."

My eyes dart to Jamart—his face has relaxed some. Danar's grip on him has eased.

"Ambitious realms need ambitious minds," Danar continues. "Verdant realms need verdant minds. I won't surrender in my quest for Vallendor. You refuse to give her up as well. But what if…? What if, *together*, we force the Eserime to heal this place? We make them bring back clean, sweet waters and banks of crystal-white sand. What if we made them give us a sky as blue as the restored sea and rich soil that nurtures those blue flowers you love but can no longer grow here? You want all of this, Blood of All. So do I." The picture he paints is tempting, beautiful, but the prisoners in Danar's hold tell a different story.

Lively clasps her clenched hands at her lips. "I turn to only you, Lady, because you love me most of all." *Praying*.

"Imagine the orders working together," Danar Rrivae says. "Those loyal to you, those loyal to me. Imagine, just for a moment. Close your eyes and picture…"

I close my eyes against my will, and I see myself standing on the banks of a river with soft sand— *No.* I force my eyes open again.

The land must be made anew. Forcing Eserime to use their gifts won't be enough. Only Mera can bring enough fire and winds to cleanse a realm. Only after that can the Eserime heal the soil, singing over the smallest dewdrops to coax life to return. Those dewdrops grow to become lakes and oceans that nourish plants that then nourish animals of the land and sea, and then mortals… That's the order of things.

But Vallendor isn't so far gone that it needs cleansing fire. In this, Danar Rrivae sounds like Zephar. And yes, there was a time I, too, thought about burning Vallendor down to its roots and starting again, but I have learned from that mistake. Good still exists here. Beauty still thrives here.

"That's what I want, Kaivara," Danar Rrivae says. "That's why I'm here. To complete all that you'd aimed to do for this realm. They didn't want you to succeed. You were too young to be allowed that much success and control. Others aimed to outshine you, and they needed to stop you, the genius Mera-Eserime girl who could command and swing a blade better than any pure Mera.

"You know...I wasn't the first to be labeled as a 'usurper.' There were others who fought and died—and failed—to set realms on the right path. You and I, though... Our causes were different. We didn't want to destroy realms for the sake of destruction. We loved the beings of those worlds, and we wanted better—"

"What do you want?" I ask, sounding like Uncle Agon. "Right now. At this moment."

He doesn't speak.

Lively's lips move, but she makes no sound as she prays.

"What were their names?" I ask, more softly.

Danar Rrivae raises his eyebrows as more mist rolls off of him. Behind me, shadows move and glowing coral light starts to pulse faintly in the fog.

"Indis, my beloved," Danar Rrivae whispers at last. "My sons, Uriel, Kaleb, Golewn, and Aniya, my daughter. They were unjustly taken from me when you destroyed Birius."

"Jamart and Lively," I say, "they don't have anything to do with—"

"They have *everything* to do with you and me, and our struggle."

My hand squeezes the dagger I still hold, and my throat closes around the lump forming in my neck.

Danar Rrivae, Jamart, and his daughter drift closer to me, and their approach makes the hair on my neck stand.

"You were abandoned by your father," the traitor says, "because you were unlovable, because you were unteachable and prone to violence. He left you with Lyra and the Eserime in hopes that they could salvage something good from you. But then..." His lip curls viciously even as his eyes soften. "There's nothing worse than killing your own mother. The sad thing is everyone knew you would, but no one could stop you."

I shake my head. "That isn't true—"

"But then what were you supposed to do?" he asks, with innocent eyes. "It was in your nature to kill. Your parents had created a being who shouldn't have been, and the Aetherium was worse off for it. And the Council was so shocked that you destroyed realms without approval, that you thought that you were Supreme—"

"I've never claimed to be Supreme—"

"How it must eat you up inside to be called 'Diminished,'" he continues. "And then to see, firsthand, the death and the killing, the sickness of the land and sea, the animals and mortals...all of life here suffering. But to do something about it, you had to first fill out forms so some bureaucrat who hasn't been a Grand Defender in ages upon ages can tell you that Yorra or Ithlon or Melki weren't that bad?"

He squints at me. "When was the last time your father held a dying child in his arms? When was the last time Izariel witnessed the last of a beautiful species perish? Does he even know what a 'daxinea' is and what will be lost to Vallendor once she finally succumbs to the filthy air she breathes each day? Yet he calls *you* 'Diminished'?"

Lively's amber glow brightens, and she pants, unable to breathe.

"Why would Supreme allow this realm to suffer?" Danar Rrivae asks. "Where's the mercy in such torture?"

I close my eyes and grip the dagger's handle with both hands. *Lively is right there*, I remind myself, even as Danar speaks to my pain.

"You hesitate to do what you know is *right*," he says in that voice of heated ice. "Why?"

"You don't understand," I whisper.

"*I* don't understand?" he shouts, and now his eyes turn blood red. "You think I want to roam from realm to realm searching for my family? They're out there, crying for me. I can't—*I won't*—stop, and if, in my search, I can free others while taking what has been taken from me, why shouldn't I do that? There are beings who need help, who want better. Am I so wrong to restore hope and make them whole?"

Jamart's face twists, and his amber glow... He's dying, oh *fuck*, he's dying.

"Stop, please," I say, reaching my hands out to them, my heart in my throat.

"Do you want to save them?" Danar asks, icy.

"More than anything," I cry out, tears in my eyes.

"How far will you go to save them?"

I start running to Jamart and Lively, but they roll away from me. I don't stop running, though, even as my muscles cramp beneath my armor.

"What will you give to save them?" the traitor asks.

Beads of sweat roll down my face and sting my eyes and the cuts on my chin.

"What will you give up, Kaivara?" he asks again.

I keep running, reaching out but never catching up.

"I will let these two live," he says, "and three others of your choosing if you surrender Vallendor. Five lives saved for the five lives your father took from me—"

I turn, veering away from Jamart and Lively with a shout, and take a giant leap toward the traitor, my dagger ready.

Tempest sinks into a space that should be Danar Rrivae's ribcage. Yet nothing is solid there—no bones, no muscle, just a sucking, icy void.

I wince at the cold, but I lunge again, aiming this time at his neck.

No skin. Just space.

His eyes burn with that haunting scarlet heat, and he hurls fire at me from his hands.

I swat each ball away with gusts of wind.

He grabs my hand that holds the dagger and squeezes it.

I scream—his touch feels like fire and ice, burning and freezing. Light that isn't mine glows from the inside of my arm. I smell heat that isn't fire—no, this smells of earth and sky, and it rushes up my arm to my shoulder.

Danar Rrivae grips Jamart's neck until the man's head separates from his body. Then he lights Lively on fire.

I scream, "No!" over and over again, and I lob my own fireballs at him, one after the other. But in my anger, in my pain, every one misses that fucker, who now rolls away from me on that cloud, farther and farther away.

He doesn't even leave Jamart and Lively behind for me to bury.

Alone—even the minulles have abandoned me—I sink to the

ground in tears, and—

Pop!

I'm no longer on my knees in Maford behind Farmer Gery's barn. No—I'm now kneeling beside the stream in the Misty Garden, that liminal space between the Temple of Celestial and the Sanctum.

Did Spryte take my frantic desire to return to this garden, a place of peace and beauty, and instantly transport me there? If so, I need to work on controlling my— *Ouch!*

The arm that Danar Rrivae grabbed is now throbbing. All of me hurts. I bend to scoop water from that crystal stream and—

Shit.

My reflection…

My arm…

Crackles of lightning zigzag beneath my skin…

Maelstrom.

15

They're gone.

Those are the only words that my mind can form.

They're gone.

He killed them, right in front of me. He killed them, and didn't care who he'd be taking from their families, from this town, from this realm… Me. And even though I am immortal, even though I will never know what a human feels as she dies, these deaths feel like…parts of my lungs have been tied off. Like…my vision has dimmed—not by a lot, but enough that I notice. Like…I've left blood trailing behind me once again, but this time, I'm incapable of cleaning up the mess and must now accept the ugly.

My face stings as though Danar Rrivae had slapped me dozens of times and bit my cheeks afterward. I'm too stunned to even cry, and I stand there, in that field, shaking… Vibrating. My eyes cloud with tears. The air around me rolls with steam. My hands ball into fists but unclench because I don't have anyone left to fight.

What has Danar Rrivae gone to do? Find some other mortals to terrorize? Is this his plan? Target someone who I care about just a tiny bit more than the rest? Will Danar Rrivae use anyone vulnerable as leverage to get what he wants from me?

I let my head droop, sorrow washing over me like an icy river. I cry into my shoulder—poor Jamart, poor Lively—until I'm lightheaded. My tears fill the sky above me with thunderheads, damp and dangerous.

I stay still and try to take deep breaths—but not moving hasn't saved those I love. Moving and doing hasn't helped, either.

Shit.

I dry my face with my cloak and push out a long, hard breath.

I know what I must do. I've known all along, but he leaves me no choice. I must kill Danar Rrivae.

The moths that Spryte with me stay a little longer—they must sense my sadness and know that I've been suffering from vertigo as well as the ongoing effects of Miasma. Twenty paces away from the raggedy gates of Caburh, I wave my hand and thank them for their care. Looking at Caburh makes me forget my nausea. This place… it's not Gasho with its mud-brick homes and alabaster-smooth walls, palm dates and fancy baths with domed ceilings. No, Caburh, located southwest of Gasho, remains a riverside industrial trading hub founded by the Renrians ages ago.

The nightstar shines down on a town that stinks of smoke and funk from the tannery and forge. The stench of death has also seeped deep into the soil, into the banks of the Duskmoor River that winds through the town.

Even late at night, this hub of mercantilism, language and culture, travel and recreation buzzes with the languages of a dozen different provinces.

My boots clack against stones worn smooth by others who have walked this town. Back in the day, you could buy spells from women wearing green cloaks, sacred relics bartered alongside spices, onions, and salted fish.

I wrap my cloak tighter around my shoulders to try and blend in—and blending in *is* possible here. The streets teem with people from faraway lands, their skin tones representing every realm across Vallendor. They wear vibrant-hued clothes, and the languages flowing around me are a blend of words, grunts, and clicks. But they have one thing in common: everyone glows a deep shade of amber. Some will drop dead from Miasma before I leave this place.

So much has changed since I last walked through this town.

Fire was consuming the tailor's shop over there. A man's severed head had bobbed in the fountain across the street. The massive battawhale, Tazara, king of the night-dwelling creatures, had hovered over the town square while smaller battabies had fought fire-spitting cursuflies.

But for once, I'm not here to fight or to purchase leather or to exact revenge on anyone. I've come for a fancy storybook-encyclopedia—that's it.

As I head to the Broken Hammer Inn, I sense countless pairs of eyes following me. There's curiosity, yes, but also recognition—and fear. The watchers know who I am. Some even know that I'm not one to fuck with because they remember what I did during my last visit here. They remember that I fought both Gileon Wake's army and the attacking cursuflies. They remember that I sped away on horseback alongside Jadon Wake, following his brother Gileon and Olivia, who still possessed my stolen amulet. Those who remember stop their hammering and hawking to scowl at me.

"The abomination is back."

"How dare she?"

"What's left for her to destroy?"

"Take her head."

"No. Take her hands—her hands are the biggest threats."

I say nothing, shivering, though, as I listen to their most dangerous thoughts. They look up to me, not because of who I am or what I can do to them but literally because I'm tall and my hair is as big as the wool-haired, bargain-basement effigy someone made that they're now burning on an installment plan—straw Kai has only been torched to her shins. Some follow me through these streets not because of their love or admiration but only because they've forgotten my strength and power.

Follow a strange dog at your peril, Caburh. Right now, I'm an unpredictable bitch.

Enough townsmen surround me to slow my march to the Broken Hammer Inn. One man with a crooked nose and white, dandelion-seed hair steps in front of me.

My hands go clammy. *Come on, guy, I don't wanna fight you.*

He curls his lip and snarls, "You're dying today, Perversion."

"I haven't come to start trouble, sir," I say. "Yes, my last visit here led to unfortunate losses, and I'm sorry about that, but I didn't start it. The army of Syrus Wake came for someone else, and I simply defended myself—"

"A hundred souls died that night," a broken man with a broken voice shouts from behind me.

"Yes, I know," I say. "And I mourn them each day. My deepest sympathies to you all for those who were taken during the fight."

The man with the crooked nose and white hair squints at me. His fists clench and unclench as though he's already squeezing my heart or my throat, and he's ready for justice—or vengeance. "It's easy for you, isn't it?" Dandelion-Seed Hair spits. "To walk into this town with your fancy clothes and fancy swords while our homes still bear the scars of your 'defending yourself.'"

"What do you want, sir? All of you: What would bring you peace? What would restore the dead?" I ask, scanning those gathering around me, chills dancing up and down my spine.

Soot-covered faces, hands hardened by labor, eyes glinting with grief and rage. Faces scarred and swollen, amber glowing as intense as daylight. They look as scraggly and forgotten as the scraps of fabric discarded in the mud. They look as broken as the shards of furniture tangled up in hedges and ivy that continue to grow around them. Shoes, hats, and belts are found everywhere except on the feet, heads, and around the waists of the townspeople of Caburh. And their numbers are growing as they gather around to watch, swelling like a bruise spreading across skin. Their anger pulses and could explode with one careless word.

I need to move on, but I can't—their hearts are filled with agony even though their hands are heavy with metal. The townspeople need a goddess, and I cannot oblige. "The deaths of your loved ones were not my intention," I say with sincerity.

They scoff.

"She is the reason!"

"Cleanse us of her wickedness!"

"Destroy this abomination!"

Cleanse? Abomination? Those two words are never good together.

The angry townsfolk grip their weapons tight. They pull their lips tighter across their teeth, holding their hatred of me like they'd hold a baby rescued from a rushing river. They're ready to fight and kill me.

Don't they know? Mortals should never tempt the gods. Doing so surely brings disaster.

Fear fills me, not because of what they want to do to me, but because of what I can do to *them* without pulling the blade from my scabbard or the dagger from my boot.

They press in closer to me.

"Stop right now." I lift my left hand as a warning. Flames leap across my fingertips.

Some in the mob gasp. Those holding weapons lift their eyebrows in surprise, but their thirst for revenge compels them to take cautious steps toward me.

"I'm asking you one last time," I say and lift my right hand. I spot a broken cart and prepare to hurl fire at it as a warning shot.

"No!" a woman yells. "Don't!"

Separi Eleweg the Advertant, proprietor of the Broken Hammer Inn, stands at the edge of the mob. She's the one who just told me not to throw fire. Her thick braids quiver with anger, and the gold charms clamped on those locks tinkle with rage. Her eyes are flat and black, but her words are sharp and filled with horror. She doesn't wear her silk waistcoat or velvet breeches as she's done in the past. Like the other townsfolk, she's dressed in a simple tan tunic and frayed burlap trousers.

Just then, the broken cart creaks, and a little Renrian girl with white hair crawls out into the open with a kitten clutched to her chest.

I gasp and shiver. If I'd hurled that fireball, I would've… Exhaustion buzzes through me, another death averted by my tenuous self-control. *Too much. This is becoming too much.*

"She will kill each of you with her fire and wind," Separi shouts to the crowd. "Don't you remember? Don't you understand? She is no ordinary townswoman or traveler. Have you forgotten the terrible power that the Lady of the Verdant Realm possesses? Do you want her to burn down the rest of Caburh?"

Some townsfolk come to their senses and stow their weapons.

"Forgive us, Lady."

"What has happened to us?"

Others shout, "Fuck her!"

"False god!"

"Abomination!"

They grip their weapons tighter, ready to kill the stray dog, no longer caring that their lives may be consumed by flames if they take one more step...

"Lady," Separi shouts, "please show mercy. They—"

Don't know what they're doing?

Bullshit. They know how swords work.

They're angry and terrified?

Who isn't?

They're dumb shits who need to take it out on somebody, but since the real culprit who looks like them isn't here, they'll instead kill you, the tall, big-haired stranger?

Yeah. Sounds about right.

"Trouble has found you before, Caburh," I say. "But I don't want—"

A breeze whips past my face.

Something thuds to my left.

A man utters, "Oof," and falls back into the gasping crowd. His left hand clutches an arrow now lodged in his chest.

"Who shot that?" I shout, spinning around to find the assassin.

The crowd goes silent as the man with the arrow in his chest glows amber, and then...he glows nothing at all.

The hair on my neck bristles, and my mouth goes dry. My hands burn hot with the same fire that continues to burn down Caerno Woods. My gaze skips from dirty face to dirty face, and I listen to the thoughts of those now surrounding me.

"Supreme help us."

"She'll kill us all."

"Why is this happening?"

"Move away from her immediately," Separi shouts.

The crowd steps back.

"More! Give the Lady space!"

The crowd takes another step back.

Head bowed, Separi approaches me. "I apologize, Lady." The platinum fox amulet—a gift from me that had been worn by Veril—now dangles from her neck.

In my rage, my eyes skip from face to face, from thought to thought. My gaze soon slows and lingers on the non-tattered, too-new crimson banners hanging from rusted lampposts and splintered shop doors. In the middle of the banner is an embroidered golden tree that reaches up to coins and runes of wheat, hearts and sheep.

This is not the paddled colure of Syrus Wake found dangling around the necks and signposts of Maford, nor is this the moth displayed in my honor all throughout Gasho.

"Your visit is not entirely a surprise," Separi says, guiding me from the crowd. "I'm happy to see that you've survived your journey back." She pauses, then adds, "And I'm relieved that you've also survived Caburh so far."

We hug, briefly. "I survived my last visit and this one just now because of you."

Separi peers at me with strange black eyes. "You look different, Lady. You look…*more*."

I squint back at her. "And you look…*less*. Your eyes. Your fingers. You've changed."

"I'll explain once we're alone," she says. "You've been attacked recently. Which otherworldly?"

I chuckle. "How can you tell that otherworldly did this?"

"You always pause too long when you're attacked by the natural world—and they use that reluctance to do…" She nods at the scratches across my cheeks and chin. "To the inn?"

I scan the town, which used to be great, and remark, "It's bleak here." A bitter taste fills my mouth as I inhale the polluted air.

"A great depression has settled across Caburh," Separi says, her voice tight, her eyes easing from the swords and scowls of the citizens. "This isn't the same place my forebears established. The old gods—Emperor Wake, *you*—have fallen out of favor because..." She waves at the town's disrepair.

I point to the sigil that bears the mysterious golden tree. "Who does that celebrate?"

Separi squints at the banner. "A new god, I'm told."

"And this new god's name?"

Separi shrugs. "I started seeing that tree weeks ago as new crates of supplies arrived at the gates. The tarps that covered the wood, steel, and foodstuffs were embroidered with it. The grateful and starving cut up those tarps and made these banners, and now they're sewing that golden tree into dresses and tunics and forging pendants of golden trees. I'm sure some mediocre bard is composing a song about bushels of wheat growing like his lady's hair. And some holy man is crafting a prayer and rituals that include burning something or tying someone up to that tree."

"Next time. The arrow will land next time."

Who just thought that?

I spin around and look up, at the window of a brightly lit house.

A young boy—maybe thirteen—stands tall and defiant. His blue eyes burn with hatred, loathing in his heart. He stands there, rigid, sneering. He doesn't hold the bow, but I know he did.

And I want to shoot a line of fire at him right now instead of waiting for the fire I will throw at him ten seasons from now—that is, if Vallendor survives. His heart has already been poisoned with hatred.

"He's a child," Separi whispers. "His name is Dalbald."

"Dalbald will keep doing evil things," I say, eyeing him. "He's not scared of anyone or anything."

"But he's only a boy."

I meet Separi's eyes. "And Dalbald will be a stronger evil by the time it's right for me to kill him. I predict that, by that time, though, he will have murdered and raped in those towns outside of Caburh and across the realm, and then people—including you—will call upon me for help, but only after he's—"

"He's only a boy," Separi repeats. "And you may be wrong, Lady. Have mercy. Leave him be." She gazes at Dalbald and at the boy's mother now standing behind him with that same evil in her eyes.

The boy will kill her first.

16

Separi sends me a sidelong glance as we head south on the gunky cobblestoned road. "Tonight, Dalbald is a lucky boy."

The old Kai would've burned him to a fritter. That's what she *doesn't* say.

I cock an eyebrow. "My, my, my, what flat black eyes you have."

She nods to a Renrian who also has flat black eyes and fingers barely long enough to hold the handle of the bucket she's carrying. "Better to fit in than stand out nowadays," she says.

We pass a group of humans, their own dark eyes narrowed and filled with suspicion.

Separi quickens her pace. "They're wary," she murmurs without looking back.

"Of us?" I ask.

"Of everything." She rounds the corner and leads us down a narrow alley.

Before my arrival and destructive departure, the Broken Hammer Inn had boasted a white-and-gray quartz roof atop its three stories. Fat pillars of smoke had puffed out of its seven chimneys. Slick red double doors welcomed every visitor who wanted to relax in the jasmine- and toast-scented sitting room with its generous hearth.

The Broken Hammer Inn is still three stories tall, but four of the seven chimneys have crumbled, and the remaining chimneys are cracked and no longer smoke. Now, those same red doors have splintered and hang on rusted hinges. The acrid tang of burned wood has replaced the scent of jasmine. Ravens nest in the holes of that quartz roof.

"Once upon a time," Separi mutters, "guests could sleep peacefully here and enjoy a great meal."

"We'll make it right again," I say, more to myself than to Separi.

She laughs without humor. "Easy to say, Lady, but harder to do." Her gaze flicks to my face, searching. "Unless you're planning on staying long enough to help with that?"

I wince. "About that… 'Long enough' is such an intriguing concept."

The ravens caw and hop along the ledge as I near the inn.

"There is no death here, Lady."

"Not to worry, Lady."

"The Renrians are safe here for now, Lady."

I nod even though I know what those birds symbolize and what I smell… All can't be well here. I *see* that all is not well here. I don't need any more evidence than the few corpses I step over. I peer at the ravens who are still bowing and cawing and assuring me but…

That smell.

These bodies.

"You look troubled," Separi says.

"I'm being told one thing," I say, "but I'm seeing something different."

Separi unlocks the splintery red doors and opens them wide enough for the both of us to slip through. She immediately closes the doors behind us. "I can't let anyone in to see…"

I gasp.

The fireplace blazes, and the air, once again, smells of jasmine and toast. The walls gleam, and the carpets shine. Tables are neatly arranged, each with flickering candles that cast warm light, their flames dancing in the draft. Patrons scattered around the room, all with shiny lavender eyes, nurse mugs of tea, and eat toasted buttery bread. All stand as I pass and whisper, "Lady."

I've stepped into another world. "What happened here?"

Separi sees my astonishment and says, wryly, "Surprise."

We move deeper into the inn. Her boots shuffle softly across the polished wooden floor as she leads me to a secluded alcove by the roaring hearth. "This town has changed, but the Renrians have not. We enchant now more than ever. But visits here now require...*discretion*."

The Broken Hammer Inn has been enchanted, and the ravens were right. There is no death here, but there are Renrians laughing and playing flutes.

Separi's eyes have returned to their true lavender. "Right now, we're 'closed for repairs.' While the Broken Hammer was never a palace, it certainly wasn't run-down like this. The ravens are blessing us with their presence to keep people away. We've done the rest with our gifts."

We pass the center table. On my last early morning here, Gileon Wake sat at this table with Jadon across from him. That's when I discovered Jadon's identity: a prince, not a blacksmith by the surname "Ealdrehrt." Olivia Ealdrehrt was not Jadon's sister but rather Olivia Corby, a rich girl who didn't want to marry a prince she didn't love. It feels a lifetime ago.

At the bar, Separi pours me a glass of rum. "It wouldn't be safe for us to show our true selves. The humans of Caburh—and even a few Renrian sympathizers—blame us for this depression. They claim it's happened because of our so-called treachery. They believe that we conspired with you to keep them down, that we believe ourselves to be better than they are."

"Oh, but you *are* better than them," I say, chuckling. "You've given so much to Vallendor and the realms. Your influence moves beyond this space. What have humans done beyond killing each other, overpopulating the realm, destroying the forests and seas, and stinking up the place?"

Separi's lips quirk into a smile, though her eyes remain somber. "It's kind of you to say that, but the truth is more complex. Our work is often invisible to those who benefit from it and misunderstood by those who fear it."

I lean forward, resting my elbows on the shiny bar top. "Invisible or not, it's undeniable. You've preserved the Aetherium's stories—the rise and fall of its ancient cities, the wisdom of its sages. Without the Renrian archives, humans wouldn't even know how the nightstar affects the tides or the seasons."

The songs of Vallendor were nearly lost during the War of Flames. Renrians recovered them one fragment at a time, recording them in bound texts and teaching them among traveling bards, so that they could live again in the hearts of the people. During the Plague of Silver Ash, Renrian alchemists found the cure. While humans burned villages to purge the sick, the folk with the lavender eyes saved thousands of lives. Renrians recorded how to build aqueducts that provided clean water, and they placed ward-stones around the forest borders to keep the otherworldly from devouring travelers.

Separi lets her head fall with the weight of her responsibility. "I feel guilty for the subterfuge."

I lift my glass of rum. "I feel awful for what you have to do for your people's safety. And *I* apologize for bringing more attention to you and your home."

Separi smiles at me, but her eyes gleam with tears.

"What's wrong?" I ask, sipping rum.

"I not only fear for us," she admits, "but I also fear for Philia. They remember that she arrived here as a member of your party. That she, too, killed a few of Wake's men."

The rum burns my belly and rides up my throat. "Oh," I murmur, remembering.

Philia had held her own with a bow and arrow, killing at least six of Wake's soldiers before being injured in the fight. She stayed here with Separi and her wife, Ridget, as Jadon and I chased after Gileon.

"Is she doing okay?" I ask.

Separi beckons me to follow her behind the bar and down a flight of dimly lit stairs.

The young redheaded woman stands at the bottom of the landing. "Kai!" Philia whispers, her voice laced with relief.

Thinner now, Philia glows a brassy amber and wears the dulled sage-green dress that she'd worn on the day we first met in Maford. Olivia had sewn this outfit, and it now hangs on Philia's frame like a mother's frock on her toddler daughter.

"Phily!" I hop down the rest of the stairs and pull her into a hug. My spirit lifts—I didn't know I'd be this excited to see her again.

Separi stays up at the bar.

"Did Separi tell you that they're watching everything we do?" Philia asks.

"Yeah." I hug her again, and just like that, her glow transforms into a healthy blue.

Philia's secret bedroom is cramped, with only enough space for a bed and a small table that holds a few books and trinkets. The walls are bare, and the only source of light comes from a small window high up near the ceiling. The air smells musty, as if that window has never been opened.

Philia manages a quick smile, and a spark ignites in her eyes despite the fatigue that clings to her. "So..." Philia searches the empty space behind me. "Where are they?"

"Where are...*who*?"

"Jadon and Olivia?" Her eyes bug, and her face crumples. "Are they *dead*? They didn't survive the journey here?" Tears explode in those green eyes and tumble down her patchy-pink cheeks. "What happened, Kai?"

"I don't know where Olivia is, exactly," I say, "and Jadon's in jail. It's complicated."

"What's complicated about helping your friends?" she snaps.

"*Friends*?" I retort bitterly. "Two people who lied to me the entire time we spent together? A thief who stole the clothes *off my back* and the amulet from around my neck? A man who hid his identity from me even to the very end, shit you don't even know about because you weren't there at the Sea of Devour? *Friends*?"

"Since you haven't been helping them," Philia spits, "what have you been doing?"

Helping people make babies. Providing protection from travelers. Big Realm Shit.

"Helping the great city of Gasho in their recovery," I say instead.

"Ah," Philia says, lips curling. "I know about Gasho. You're content to just laze about where they worship you like you're some god—"

"I *am* some god," I snap.

A crack of thunder booms outside, rumbling against the walls of the inn and down into this room. Upstairs, the Renrians gasp and the startled ravens caw. Somewhere, metal pails clatter to the ground and glass breaks.

"Everything okay down there?" Separi calls out.

To Separi, I say, "No." To Philia, I say, "Are we really about to go down this road right now? Shall I take back the healing hug I just gave you? Those rheumy lungs and sore belly and failing heart—you want all of that back? I can do that. Or do you want me to do something more extraordinary than that?

"I could burn down this town, and then travel to the next town and burn that down, too. Shall I write a primer to remind you who you're talking so *flippantly* to?"

I smile without humor, and my nostrils flare as my hair scrapes the ceiling of this room. "'Laze about'? Beloved, you don't want me to 'laze about.' I haven't set out to willfully destroy shit in a very long time. That would be my version of 'lazing about.' Not giving a fuck and just...setting everything on fire without a care for who's in that house or in that inn and then turning over in bed and falling asleep in the arms of a big, sexy god who builds me tubs and writes me songs. That's my 'laze about.' Do you want me to show you a *working* god? An ambitious, overachieving, transcendent, and finicky Lady of the Verdant Realm?"

I've watched friends die. I've seen whole towns destroyed. I don't need this shit from her. Not today, not now.

In fiery, stony silence, I flop down gracelessly in the only chair in this small room and cover my face with my hands. I'm so tired. I take a deep breath, roll my head from one side to the other. The tightness in my chest and the headache that has spread to my entire body only grows worse.

"I thought you *at least* cared more about Jadon," Philia says, quieter now. "The way you both looked at each other..."

"Just stop, Philia," I say, blood draining from my face. "I don't have and you won't get the answers you want. The big storybook that Olivia stole. You have it. I need it. *Now. Please.*"

"You broke your promise," Philia says.

I cock my head. "What promise?"

"To rescue Olivia," she claims.

I scan my memory. *I'll wring that bitch's neck. I'll crush all ten of her sticky fingers.* I remember saying those things. I *don't* remember ever saying, "I'll rescue Olivia," not once.

Philia's eyes fill with defiance, and her face hardens with resolve. "Then I won't give you the book," she says, chin lifted. "It's taken you forever to come back to Caburh for me. And then, when you *do* show up, you don't even have Olivia with you. And now you expect me to give you something that belongs to her—?"

"That book *does not* belong to her," I say, my patience growing as thin as the walls of this room. I scan the area, and the air glitters around a chest hidden behind a screen. There's an enchantment in that space, and it isn't coming from the Renrians or from me.

Philia's gaze follows mine, and her skin flushes. She nods, acknowledging the tension now filling this cramped room. "I'm guarding it," she says, her voice low and steady.

"From what and for whom?" My gaze darts from the shimmering patch of air to Philia's face. "You plan to give the book back to Olivia?"

Philia's lips press into a thin line. "Umhmm."

I pause, the weight of what I must do pressing against my chest. "You have no idea what's at stake right now," I say. "If you did, you would give me the book."

She thinks about that and scrambles to the screen, opens the chest, and grabs the book. She clutches it to her chest like those out in the town square had clutched their swords.

I stay seated and prop my chin up on my fist. "You know...I can take that book from you right now without any effort."

Her mouth pops into an *O*, but anger turns her eyes into jade shards. "Do it, then. Kill me and be the one everyone says you are."

My ears hiss with her words. "And who am I?"

She swallows her words but still thinks them.

Evil. Devil. Maelstrom.

"*Maelstrom?*" I whisper.

That's what Danar Rrivae said.

I close my eyes against my internal flood of fire, and I wait…and I wait…and I wait until I no longer hear my bones crackling with flames. Then I take the deepest breath I've taken since waking up in the Rim of the Shadows high above Gasho.

"Please, Philia," I say, leaning forward. "I need that book. You told me once, in that meadow near Duskmoor River, that your mother had always prayed to me, that I'd kept her family fed and healthy. Do as I ask, for her." I hold out my hands. "You're in danger. Maford, Olivia, the *realm*, is in danger—and this time, it's not from me."

Philia considers my threat, clenches her jaw, and shakes her head again.

I leap up from my seat, take two steps across the room, and yank the book from her arms.

She yelps and clutches her elbows.

The book is heavy and solid, a symbol of its knowledge and power. The book's leather cover is adorned with dark blue, rich purple, and shimmering silver jewels. A dazzling gem embedded in the middle of the cover catches the light, its color shifting between blues, purples, and silvers. WISDOM.

I run my fingers over that center jewel and the rough, textured leather. My head pounds as I kneel before Philia and say, "I'm sorry." When she doesn't respond, I kiss her forehead, stroke her damp hair, and lift her chin. "This is serious, and I don't expect you to understand that."

Her face quivers, and a teardrop plops onto the back of my hand. Her shoulders shudder as a sob escapes from her chest.

"I promise to rescue Olivia," I say with great intent.

The young woman looks up to me, her eyes shiny with hope. "You said the word. You said 'promise.'"

"Yeah. I did." I sit back on my haunches. "And once I rescue her, I'll break her hands and wring her neck." I wink at the redhead, then turn my attention to the book. The jewels around its edges glow, but the mysterious gem in its center shines brightest. Why does Gileon need this book? He and his brother have already tried to usurp their father's rule. Could this gem help him succeed a second attempt? I pluck Tempest from my ankle sheath. *Maelstrom. Tempest. Coincidence?* and try to pry the silvery-blue gem from its setting.

No give.

"It's locked in," Separi says, now standing in the doorway. "It won't reveal the truth behind the fairy tales."

I shake my head. "I know, but I was hoping…" I drum my fingers against the book. "So if the truth remains locked… We need to take the ring from Syrus Wake, then?"

"No," Separi says. "We must take the ring from Gileon Wake." She lifts her right hand and waggles her ring finger. "He was wearing it on his last visit to the inn."

Shit.

Guess I'm going to Brithellum after all.

17

I slip upstairs with the *Librum Esoterica* now weighing down the satchel gifted to me by Separi—I can't leave it unattended. I pass through the busy sitting room to reach the bustling kitchen. There, Ridget and her family shell peas and peel potatoes. Their thick black, brown, and red braids glint with glass beads and rose-gold luclite thread, the strongest metal made by mortals. Each woman bows her head to acknowledge me, but they don't stop their work.

"I was hoping you'd come say 'hello.'" Ridget's voice crackles like a fireplace, sharp and smoky. She wears a saffron-yellow dress that complements her dark skin. On the day she married Separi, Ridget wore a similar dress with a corset of luclite and silk. Separi wore pale-green velvet breeches and a loose, blue-green tunic. In a clearing surrounded by towering trees, in light broken by leaves, I'd blessed their union and promised to watch over them.

Many seasons have passed since then, and I've broken my promise. I've broken many such promises to many humans who looked to me for protection. This realm they've helped to enrich is falling apart—and now there are people outside their home eager to slit their necks.

"I want to apologize," I say to Ridget, my stomach twisting from guilt as much as the food's aroma. "I'm so sorry that I've made you a target—"

"No," Ridget snaps. "They're simply using you as an excuse to perpetrate hate. Their rage has been building for a long time now, and it finally exploded the moment that first crate of wheat from the new god rolled up on the riverbank."

I grimace. "Still: just so that you know. I didn't come to Caburh for vengeance or to bring more chaos into this town."

Ridget taps the young woman working beside her, then points at a slab of bacon on the other counter. "A few glasses broke moments ago. And then this happened"—she points to the ceiling and to a thick crack zigzagging from one wall to the next—"while you were talking downstairs with Philia."

"I got a little angry," I admit. "Won't happen again."

"Emotion is bad now?"

I shrug. "I should show better control. I'm supposed to be an example, right?"

Ridget says, "Hmm," and stirs the shallots in the pan with a wooden spoon. "And who said gods were supposed to be perfect and free of emotion?"

My skin flushes as I remember what I did to those soldiers back in Caerno Woods after Veril's death. How I'd hurled countless fireballs at them even after it was obvious those soldiers were dead. That fire still burns.

The room shudders—like a bull has just rammed into the side of the inn.

The women in the kitchen gasp. They pause their work to gape at each other, looking worried.

"What was that?" I ask, creeping over to peek out the window.

And then, a steady knocking…

In the shadows, people are standing side by side at the walls of the Broken Hammer. They're all knocking on the inn at the same time. And they look…*different.* They glow but not with the amber glow of dying mortals. And "glow" isn't the most precise word, either. No, these people knocking on the inn's walls are filled with…*an absence of light*, but it isn't darkness.

Void.

And now, each of the Voidful knock on the walls of the Broken Hammer.

Ridget comes to stand beside me. "What are they doing?"

I squint at them, at their shredded hands, at their hollow eyes, how they place their ears against the brick walls trying to hear… "They're trying to get in." My heart flares, and I step away from the window.

"Get in?" Ridget laughs and returns to those shallots frying in the pan. "They'll fail."

These Voidful are looking for the door, looking for a weakness. Are they looking for me?

Ridget sucks her teeth. "Don't worry, Lady. They're just regular, hateful bastards wearing grimy tunics."

My mouth dries as I spin farther away from the window and shake my head. "Their light… It's different in these people."

Knock… Knock…

Ridget chuckles. "Ugly insides have a way of eating up anything beautiful. Think of them as apples. You know how the rot starts at the core? By the time the spoilage reaches the peel, you're thinking, *Oh, that's just a minor blemish.* But then you take a bite and…ugh."

Knock… Knock… Knock…

I look out the window again because maybe this is an illusion. Maybe my imagination has been affected by exhaustion and caused by my guilty feelings about…about…*everything*.

Outside the inn, the numbers of the Voidful have grown and—

I place my face against the window. Do I see who I think I…?

Fuck.

Jamart! The candlemaker's skin is covered with bruises. Dried blood crusts around his purple neck.

Lively stands beside him.

Both are knocking…knocking…

But they're dead…*right*? With my own eyes, I saw them meet their ends in that field behind Farmer Gery's barn in Maford. Danar Rrivae had squeezed Jamart's neck until…

I blink to clear my vision of what I saw, but as I open them, new tears blind me.

"Little do they know," Ridget is saying, "that if you were to show us your *true* power, this world would surely end." The Renrian narrows her eyes. "Don't know about you, but I'm not ready to go yet. So, if you don't mind..."

A lump forms in my throat at the plain and unassuming way Ridget speaks to me, and I reply, "Don't worry. I won't burn down the rest of Caburh because someone calls me 'Maelstrom.' I shouldn't destroy the forest because a single roach crosses my path."

She sucks her teeth again. "But where there's one roach in the forest, there are many." Ridget considers me with searching eyes. "Which means, then, that the forest must go. With fire comes life. Stronger life, tested life. Freedom."

Knock...knock...

I gaze at the beautiful, caramelized shallots in Ridget's pan. Then I gaze upon the kitchen's high ceiling speckled with grime, the once-sturdy walls now plagued with cracks. I shake my head in wonder. "How can you and Separi run such a lovely inn in this awful town? Why don't you leave?"

"Our ancestors founded this place," Ridget says. "Why should *we* abandon our home?"

"Because you and your family could be killed."

Knock...knock...

Eyebrows furrowed, Ridget exhales heavily and shakes her head. "We will continue to enchant just enough to make them see what their hearts cannot." She smiles at me. "Why don't you wash up for dinner? Your favorite room is ready for you."

I take one last peek out the window, wondering if this inn can truly withstand the Voidful.

The Voidful, including Jamart, Lively and...*Sinth, the Dashmala that I killed in Caerno Woods...* They all stand at the walls of the Broken Hammer, knocking and knocking.

...

Alone now in the room with the pearl-and-gold doorknob, I release a pent-up breath and regard the clean bedding, the wash area, and the cake of soap. Just an age ago, from this window, I'd had a view of tall, majestic firs and a river that ran swiftly with refreshing clean water. There had been wild turkeys in those woods on the other side of the Duskmoor. No longer. Sludge fills that river—nothing will ever live or survive in that water, not anymore. Those worrisome banners heralding the new god of the golden tree hang from every other post and doorframe. And the Voidful…

I don't see them anymore.

During my single night here with Jadon, we'd eaten a delicious dinner, and he'd blindfolded me and had laced honey across my tongue and he'd glowed with plum-colored light.

But then…

Shit happened.

I set the bag with the *Librum Esoterica* on the bed and cross over to the small washstand and mirror in the corner. My reflection shows a face worn thin with anguish and golden eyes dimmed by exhaustion. I dip my hands into the basin of cool water, and the chill shocks my skin awake. I splash my face, neck, and arms, and let my fingers massage my temples…

"What's that?" I lean closer to the mirror for a better view of the skin near my hairline.

Flaky.

I scratch at the spot, and the patch of flaky skin widens.

Shit—that stings.

I pinch at that small patch and peel— *Ouch!* Wincing, I peel that skin away to see a new layer of angrier-looking skin beneath. I spot another patch between my eyebrows, and I scratch at it…

Ouch. Fuck.

Okay, so I've been fighting and Spryting all around the realm, and I'm sure my body has tired from moving almost nonstop, but this… *decay* seems a little…*excessive*.

But I keep peeling and scratching until the wash basin is filled with dirty water, its surface flecked with pieces of me. And my face:

it's become a patchwork of old skin and new. What will I be left with once I'm done shedding?

I back away from the sink and sit on the bed. I push off my cloak, tight breastplate and tighter boots, and tunic and enjoy fresh air kissing my bare skin. My eyes weigh as much as a mountain, and I rub them to stay awake.

But all of me sags, and I whisper, "Fuck it," and lie across the bed. I stare up at the ceiling's wooden beams, and for a moment, I think about keeping watch, about the Voidful outside these walls, but my tired eyes shut, and my mind drifts…

Zephar and I ride horses and whoop with joy as we chase a behemoth worupine that shoots its poisonous quills at us from across the meadow. We pull the reins of our horses as the beast crests a hill.

"Let it go," Zephar says.

I cast an eye to the sky and to the gray clouds slowly smashing against each other.

"Are you hungry?" I ask, a twinkle in my eye.

"I'm starving," Zephar says, squinting at me.

Hunting makes us ravenous.

Hand in hand, we guide our horses through a valley nestled between a silver stream and ash trees. The air smells of wildflowers, but also of apples and lavender, even though neither grow here. As we round a bend, a man comes into view. He leads no horse and carries no sword. Tall and confident, he stands there, unwavering, his gaze fixed on us, his intent unknown.

Fearless, Zephar and I ride our horses over to the man. Once we're steps away from him, we dismount.

"What are you doing here?" I ask as Zephar takes my hand.

Jadon steps closer to us, his eyes on me.

"Make another move," Zephar growls at him, "and I'll break your fucking back."

Jadon, though, takes another step. He doesn't care about the man bigger than this realm.

My throat tightens, but not because I'm scared. No, I love Zephar's type of rowdiness, I love Jadon's clenching fists, and I can't stop smiling even though a fight is bubbling beneath this stormy sky.

Jadon finally shifts his gaze to the biggest threat before him. Remembering that he is, at least, a demigod, he presses back his shoulders and lifts his chin. The mark on his right hand glows like the daystar, and his jaw is harder than the earth beneath these lush grasslands.

Yeah, I remember Jadon's hand clenching on my ass, and I remember tasting me on his fingers and on his soft lips, and… "Can't we all just get along?" I ask now, my voice a whisper beneath my pounding heart.

"I will never 'get along' when it comes to you," Zephar whispers. His hand rests around my waist, and he bends to nuzzle my neck. His breath is hot on my ears and his cock hard on my back.

I tear my eyes from Jadon's and look up at my Mera warrior. "I don't ask for much," I say, searching Zephar's rum-colored eyes. I already feel drunk with power, with anticipation as my hands flutter like moths over his muscled chest, as my fingers drift from the destroyed realm of Melki over to the obliterated world of Yoffa and down to my favorite domain, the biggest realm of all…

Jadon and Zephar… I want to destroy them. I want to wear them both all over my skin.

"This monster betrayed you," Zephar says, his hand over my hand that now strokes and coaxes him.

Jadon doesn't speak—Zephar isn't wrong. So he stays quiet but lets his eyes dance over me.

Fuck, I love his eyes.

I step away from Zephar but keep one hand on his magnificent bulge while I peer at the silent prince of Brithellum. "Tell me, Prince Wake: what do you want?"

The sky presses down on us, and I look up again to those rain-heavy clouds.

"You," Jadon says. "I've only ever wanted you. In this realm, in realms beyond, there's only you."

I say, "Prove it."

I don't stop Jadon from kneeling before me. I don't stop Jadon as he kisses my belly and follows the inked vine curling higher…higher… until it becomes Mera letters that spell KAI MERA DESTROYER OF WORLDS. The prince of Brithellum pushes away my bandeau, and his tongue travels beneath my breast until his mouth covers my nipple. And then he bites.

I tense and moan.

Zephar's hand moves from my waist and pushes down my sarong. His fingers slide along my ass, dropping and then dipping into me from behind, and I gasp, and my eyes go wide, and I watch those storm clouds, and I'm amazed at how fat they are with rain, and I wonder who will explode first, those clouds or me, and I reach back and kiss Zephar, then turn to kiss Jadon and—

BAM!

A violent shudder shakes the meadow—

No. I'm not in a meadow. I'm in a room *at the Broken Hammer.*

I sit up in bed. "What—?"

BAM! BAM!

The windows rattle.

The banging is coming from the outside.

"Bring Maelstrom out here!" an angry man shouts.

"Kill the false god!" an angry woman shouts.

Outside in the hallway, footsteps bang up the stairs and down the corridor. The door to my room crashes open.

Philia, her face bright pink, her eyes bugged, stands in the doorway. "Kai, it's time to go."

18

I hop out of bed. "What's happening?"

How long have I been asleep? Waking up from my dream feels like bursting up from the depths of the coldest lake.

"You will not replace us!" a man shouts.

"Renrians eat babies!" a woman screams.

Neither asshole sounds like they're outside. They sound close. Very close.

Philia shouts, "They got in!" She sees my bed and its rumpled sheets before looking back at me and frowning. "Were you *sleeping*?"

My cheeks burn. I don't answer her question as I shove my feet back into my tight boots.

"That's how they broke in," Philia says. "Because you…you were asleep."

I mutter, "Yeah," and buckle my greaves around my calves. I throw a quick look at the young woman now judging me in the doorway.

She's dressed in black breeches, boots, and a long-sleeve tunic. Traveling clothes. She carries a backpack on her shoulder as well as a golden bow and a quiver of arrows, a gift from the Renrians.

"Philia," I say, "I don't think you should come—"

"Kill the redhead!" a man screams.

"She's unnatural," a woman shouts.

Never mind.

Philia takes a deep whiff of air. "Oh, no."

I sniff, too, and hurry over to look out the window. "What did these idiots set on fire?"

Down below, a mob wielding swords, pikes, and torches crowds the walkway in front of the Broken Hammer's porch. That effigy of me is now fully engulfed in flames. No more budget burning.

"You were sleeping?" Philia asks again, her face patchy-red, her eyes bright with tears.

I stop in my step and hold out my arms. "I'm sorry, okay? I fucked up, and I feel like shit." I sigh heavily, then rub my face, wincing at the sting of my peeling skin. I pull on my scabbard heavy with Justice and Fury and twirl Tempest around my fingers before slipping the dagger into my ankle sheath. My stomach growls as I check my armor once more—the dark gray is nearly invisible in this dim light. "Did I eat?" I ask Philia as I grab the pack holding the *Librum Esoterica* from the bed.

She pauses and thinks. Then: "No. Your plate is still on the table downstairs, untouched."

That's right. I came up to wash and—

"This is new." Philia taps the handle of Elyn's surrendered sword. *"Ouch."* She snatches back her now-red and smoking fingers.

"Never touch the weapon of an immortal." I wrap my hand around Philia's fingers. Her injury tugs against my skin like a fish caught on a line. Once I heal her, I release her hand and nod at the bow on her back. "You sure about this?"

She nods as she gapes at her healthy fingers.

"The Lady isn't real!" comes the shouting from outside.

"Maelstrom is hate!"

"Praise his holy name!"

Praise *whose* holy name?

Philia and I run down the hallway and down the stairs.

Separi, dressed in a full set of rose-gold luclite armor, stands at the inn's entryway. She holds out her hands and tries to appeal to the mob for peace.

Her brother, Vinasa, stands beside her. "Please," he says, the strain evident even in his calm, deep voice, "this is not the way." He's twisted his many braids into one thick ponytail; if he's the same stealthy fighter he was during the Great War, a stiletto hides in that braid, ready to slash.

Back in the sitting room, Ridget and the other Renrians adjust their white robes. Woven with luclite, these garments look like the rays of a daystar at dawn. The Renrians' staffs hum and crackle with violet energy.

I fell asleep. Tears sting my eyes at the thought of what they've faced without me.

Separi looks back over her shoulder. She sees me, and her face relaxes, relieved.

Ridget hurries over to me, her eyes narrowed.

"They knocked long enough to find a way," I say to her. "I should've stopped them instead of…" There are too many gruesome possibilities, so I merely say, "I'm sorry."

Ridget shakes her head. "You and I both know that Separi would've talked you out of fighting. I did, too, but not out of any mercy. I just didn't think these people were smart enough to find a way past our enchantments. Separi, though, relies on mercy like it's air.

"I want all of this hatred to stop, but I think they'll only stop once heads roll through the streets and their blood soaks the ground." She hands me a wrapped bundle of food. "For your trip. Remember to eat."

"Yes, ma'am." I turn to Philia and say, "If we are separated, meet me at that flat rock outside of town, where we saw that bloody spy."

Philia nods. "Yes, I remember it."

On our last trek to Caburh, a traveler had passed us wearing a helmet too small for his head and a leather tunic caked in dried blood. Later, we learned that he was one of Gileon Wake's spies.

I breathe a heavy sigh and march over to the doorway. The town stinks of fire, tar, and the musk of the frightened and the rage-filled.

I touch the small of Separi's back—*I'm here*—and nod to Vinasa. I stand between them as the crowd roars.

"False god!"

"Kill Maelstrom!"

"Rip her apart!"

"Hear me now!" I shout to the amber-glowing crowd, the strength of my voice cracking the cobblestone streets beneath our feet. This Kai-quake causes the commotion to dim. "I'm leaving now. Thank you for your...*enthusiastic farewells*." Then I step down off the porch, knowing that I'm exiting Caburh far from peacefully. I scan the crowds but don't see Jamart and Lively. I don't see the Dashmala, Sinth, either.

What I do see alarms me as much as the absence of those who have been killed.

Poisons cascade like waterfalls from the heads and hearts of the angry people calling for my death, and their diseased organs are moments from bursting. Their teeth cling to rotten gums like beads of water to a melting icicle. This is all Jadon's handiwork.

"You will die this morning," a man wearing a red wool cap shouts.

"You're a perversion, a disgrace!" A woman spits at my feet.

I crinkle my nose at the phlegm on the toe of my boot.

Philia shrieks, "Kai!"

I look up in time to see a man lunging at me with his ax held high.

Shit! I kick him in the chest. He stumbles back, resets, and rages forward again.

I kick him a second time, knocking him off-balance, before yanking his ax from his hand. I slap his face so hard that he hits the ground. One of his rotted teeth comes loose. I straddle him and raise my fist to punch—

"Defender!" Separi shouts.

I freeze right before my hand lands on the man's windpipe.

Another man leaps onto the porch with a howl, brandishing his broadsword.

Vinasa screams, clutching his belly and the sword now impaled there. Blood gurgles from his lips. Separi shouts, "Vin!" and rushes over to him.

Another man leaps at Separi, his spiked club ready to beat her down. I throw Ax-Man's hatchet at the club-wielder, and it slams into his forehead.

Separi reaches her brother in time to catch him before he hits the ground.

Someone else entangles the man who killed the Renrian in a web of lavender lightning.

I ram Tempest into the gut of a woman swinging a meat cleaver at me. Another woman tries it with a hoe, but that's *my* trick; her blood soon wets Tempest's blade.

The sea of angry city-folk swells and roars with wild energy, and the bloodthirsty tide rolls toward us.

Philia's first golden arrow sinks into the face of a man an arm's length away from me.

Separi hoists a woman from the ground and thrusts her skyward on the end of her staff. Another wreath of crackling lavender coils around a woman's throat, and her skin turns purple as she struggles to breathe.

I pull Justice from my back, ready to dispense it. These people aren't fighting me because I stole their houses or their goats. They aren't rebelling because I've forced them to bow and worship me. No, they're fueled by hatred and distrust and belief in a strange new god. They'll kill not only me, but Philia and the Renrians, too, if I let them.

Justice lands her first kill. But tides of hatred bear more angry townspeople toward us. They fight like we stole something of value from them, like their very lives depend on killing us.

I can't hear myself think over their cries and curses nor can I see clearly, not with all the sizzling lavender light glinting off metal, blood, and stone.

"You're dying, bitch!" A man wielding two curved swords rushes toward me.

I can barely see him through the curls melting into my face. I slide Justice into his gut and push my hair from my eyes. Then I shout, "Enough!"

The ground quakes again.

"Enough!"

Everyone, including the Renrians, freezes. Two men hold torches to the foundation of the inn, which starts to burn.

I thrust my hands at them, blowing out their torches with a gust of wind, and then I send the arsonists flying into the building next door with a violent blast. I throw a ball of fire at that storefront, followed by another fireball, and another and another…

"Lady," Separi shouts. The blood of her enemies and her brother streaks her breastplate. The sight stays my desire for destruction. I nod to Separi and turn to the mob.

"Hear me now! I don't know who or what you believe in now, but I don't need you to believe in me to save you or to destroy you. I *can* destroy you. Your homes, your shops, your lives—" I lift my right hand, and fire swirls from one finger to the next. "I can become the maelstrom you call me. Leave, now, and do not test me further."

A little girl with messy blue ponytails scampers from behind the crates closest to the fire. She hides behind the skirts of the woman holding a battle-ax, the same woman who'd shouted just moments ago, "Kill the dirty whore and rape her corpse." Standing with them is Dalbald, the boy with the bow, my would-be assassin. A sour-faced Renrian man holding a sword made of luclite stands behind this woman, the girl, and Dalbald.

Another young boy peers at me from beneath a cart, and other faces peek from windows that look down upon this square: young mothers nursing infants, Renrians holding frightened children. Elderly, stooped Renrians whom I've known since Vallendor's creation.

If I destroy Caburh—*burn this place down to new dirt*—I raze a town founded by the forebears of Veril Bairnell and Separi Eleweg. I would destroy a hub of industry and alchemy, of thought and education, a town polluted by outsiders who came and saw its greatness and claimed it for themselves.

I would destroy Nosirest, now named Caburh because of Leward Caburh's lies and violence.

I can't destroy this town, the home of those I love. Nor can I kill those who harbor hatred against those I love.

The angry townspeople closest to me retreat, their gazes still fixed on the burning men who attempted to destroy the Broken Hammer on my watch.

"Loyal Renrians of this city," I shout, "hear me now. In the name of the gods who watch from above, I shield you with eternal love, with my sword and my light. I cast my protection upon you so that nothing else will harm you in this town. You shall no longer fear any outsiders' blade."

A glimmering sheen of bloodred-and-gold light envelops each Renrian, who bow their heads in reverence. I'm relieved that it works, that my gift, this aura of protection, has been restored to me by my father.

I point at the remaining humans who still simmer with hate. "By seven dawns from now, you must leave this town. If you refuse, I'll return and remove you myself. Go forth and find your own space, your own path to prosperity that does not exploit the work of the Renrians."

"And where do we go?" a woman in the crowd shouts.

"I don't know or care," I say, "but you gotta leave."

The shouting resumes at my pronouncement, and a man dares to draw his sword.

With a burst of wind, I send him sprawling. Then I hurl a ball of lightning just inches away from his body. The ground cracks open, knocking everyone off their feet. My amulet glows so hot that everyone shields their eyes from its blinding light.

"Do you not hear me?" I ask. "I will kill *you*. This new god you worship doesn't care that you will die by my hand, that you are only spared today because I'm not the Maelstrom you fear."

I gaze at the sky, now orange and red in the early dawn. "You all have a choice to make: Do you choose to live? Or will you die for your unworthy god?"

19

I can't Spryte Separi and Philia to Castle Wake in Brithellum. If they're to come with me, we must travel that great distance the old-fashioned way: by horse.

Separi rides beside me, her face hard in thought. At 206 years old, she's older than Veril on his last day alive in Vallendor. Rather than smoking a pipe like he did, she chews licorice root to relax.

The *Librum Esoterica* glows from my pack like a beacon, revealing itself to those most interested in its power, including Danar Rrivae and Philia Wysor.

"Separi—" My chest tightens, and my hands tremble on the reins. "I'm so sorry about Vinasa. If there's anything I can do…" I know the words are meaningless, that I cannot replace him.

"He was my heart," she says, her gaze roaming the horizon.

"I should've been there—"

"You *were* there," she corrects.

I don't know what else to say, and Separi doesn't offer any suggestions.

Two Renrians she's loved have died for me, and we both know it. She doesn't ask the obvious question: *Who's next?*

I clear my throat. "I'll—"

"Bring him back?" she asks. "Change their hearts, make the mob throw flowers and honeycakes instead? What could you do, Lady, that would've changed the outcome?"

I don't have the answer. *Be better* is not enough.

No wolves or big cats snarl at us as we head east. No creatures with fangs and runny eyes or tri-colored feathers and scaly feet chase us into the desert. We find no animal shit drying on the path. No desperate bandits stumble from the brush to demand our coin or our bodies—but that doesn't mean that we aren't being followed. I feel another's presence—and a pair of eyes can be heavier than a pair of fists.

Dirt and blood cling to my peeling skin and crust the insides of my nostrils. I hate the tackiness of my fingers and the way my armor sticks to my skin.

Last time I traveled this trail, Jadon rode beside me and we weren't talking. I'd been furious with him after learning the truth of his biggest lies.

Now, though, I miss our conversations, our good-natured ribbing and flirting. I miss sharing meals with him, our long conversations as we lay beside each other, staring at the skies. I think about kissing him in the meadow before we'd been set upon by the gerammoc and aburan. And I think about our lovemaking at the inn. I remember his gifts of sweet treats, bouquets of wildflowers.

But through it all, he kept so much of himself hidden from me.

Beside me, Philia occasionally taps her bow, drawing power or comfort from it as she rides.

"Are you all right?" I ask.

She nods, silent and worried.

"You aren't alone," I say, though I'm no good at consolation. "You'll be fine. Think what you'll want to do once you and Olivia are home, wherever you decide home will be."

That makes her smile.

I asked neither of my companions to come with me, but Philia wanted to help save Olivia, and Separi wanted to help keep me alive. She knows that, despite my display of power, I'm not whole, that I could use her staff as well as her skills with plants and crafting—and she also knows that mine can be a lonely existence, and I appreciate her company.

Philia clears her throat and says, "Kai?"

I look over and see that clouds have formed in her eyes.

"I need to tell you something," she says. "Something about Veril and my family."

I wait a long time as she struggles with her words before prompting her to continue.

"Veril had a scar," she says.

"Yes, a small pearly one right here." I touch my cheek. "What about it?"

"Back when my father was mayor of Maford," she says, "he and his drunk friends broke into Veril's home one night. They demanded that he perform magic tricks, and sing and dance. Veril refused; he wasn't a minstrel or a fool, but my father and his friends didn't like that he told them no, and so... So they destroyed everything in his cottage.

"Pages of study? Gone. Powders to make new treatments and improve old ones? Gone. There was this one medicine he made for chest coughs? They destroyed that one, too.

"And then they pushed him over, and my dad..." Philia swallows and swipes at her tears. "My dad pulled out his dagger and—" She taps her cheek. "That's how Veril got his scar. Philip Wysor was an ugly man who made beautiful glass, and he got very sick and died the way he deserved: slowly and in great agony. The coughing powder he destroyed could've saved his despicable life."

Separi looks over to Philia, and then she glances at me. She touches Veril's fox pendant that hangs around her neck.

"I knew who my father was. I was scared of him, and I hated him." Philia dries her face with the backs of her hands. "But Veril...we didn't get along at first. I hated him because I was supposed to.

"But he made me want to be a better person, a better student. I'd go out to the woods to bring him herbs and plants. I'd watch him brew. He became like...like an uncle to me, one who knew so many things and appreciated that I was smart."

My stomach growls.

Philia hears my hunger and laughs. "My confession made you hungry?"

I laugh, too. "I think Veril knew how you felt about him. He would be proud to see you riding with me." Separi doesn't look at us, but she doesn't contradict me, either.

Philia nods, her expression lighter already.

We stop in a sheltered outcropping that overlooks the forest. There, we tie up the horses, and Separi prepares breakfast. We keep watch for any threats even as we eat.

I swallow the last bite of my sandwich and say, "So, Brithellum."

"Minimal casualties," Separi says.

On the dirt between us, the Renrian spreads out a map of Brithellum and weighs the corners with rocks.

"The walls are known to be impenetrable from the outside," Separi says. "Rocks fortified by ward-stones. The only way in is sneaking through."

"Here," I say, pointing to a tiny notch at the southern wall. "Gileon's suites."

Separi leans in, her eyes narrowed. "Yes, but it's risky. Too narrow for a quick escape."

"I'll have to take the risk. We need that ring."

"Minimal casualties," Separi repeats. "Wake is smart; he's integrated his soldiers throughout the city with families and innocents. Aphids among roses."

"Which means," I say, "that I must treat the entire infested garden."

"With fire, wind, and lightning?" Separi asks, eyes wide.

"Yes, unless they surrender Olivia or the ring first."

"I like Kai's plan," Philia blurts. "Fire, wind, and lightning if they resist."

"What about sparing innocents, Lady?" Separi asks.

"In this instance? Who is really innocent? Why should the wife of Wake's captain be spared just because she holds no weapon? Her husband *is* the weapon, and she holds *him* every night he returns to her with the blood of other innocents on his tunic. She feeds him. She loves him. She pays for her silk and wheat with the spoils of war. They hold hostages, like Olivia. Wake's army continues to destroy this realm as though it's theirs to destroy."

I touch my amulet to settle my suddenly queasy stomach. "I will give them a choice," I say. "They can give me Olivia out of fear, or they can do so out of love. If they choose neither, they will die. There is no compromise, not anymore."

Separi frowns but dips her head. "Yes, Lady."

Though I'd argued with Zephar about sparing innocents, here I am, days later, as merciless as he was. I clear my throat and add, "Minimal casualties."

"You can make a better threat," Philia says. "Demand that they release Olivia, or you'll destroy their precious, stupid little storybook, jewels and all."

"It's not a stupid little—" Separi starts to say.

"That's an approach," I say, speaking over the Renrian. "If I must, I will use the book as leverage."

Never in a million ages would I destroy the *Librum Esoterica*—but Philia doesn't need to know that.

The air feels heavy. We're still being watched—though I can't say by whom or what.

As we ride, the plains grow drier and grittier. The fine crystals in the dust glimmer in the daystar's light, blinding us. The trail curves to the west, then veers north again, ascending over foothills, and then sends us back down steep paths that bring some relief from the heat. We ride alongside rust-colored gorges that fall off sharply, down where the sharp rocks explode from the earth. I don't dare peek over these cliffs—gouges from the fingernails of desperate travelers mark the edge of the bluff.

I see no ravens. That's good.

I try not to think about Danar Rrivae, Jamart, Lively, Sinth, and the other Voidful whose bodies surround the Broken Hammer.

A ring of far-off blue mountains spreads seemingly forever, until it reaches that tallest peak lost in the clouds: Mount Devour. The Abbey of Broken Worlds sits at the peak, hidden in the clouds, unchanged.

Vallendor Realm already looks defeated. Everything around me is dying. Nothing lives here, no chirping birds or blossoming tree branches, no squirrels or crickets. The only sound is our horses' hooves on the winding path.

• • •

As the nightstar climbs high in the sky, we reach a town that has been smashed and burned, as though a fiery giant has stomped through it. The land sounds marshy—squelching like boots pulling out of mud—but there is no water here. The air remains dry, and the sky looks as fractured as a broken mirror. An arch of scorched white marble looms before us, with thick weeds threading through its many cracks.

But then I *look*.

Carts, horses, and people have all been consumed by flames, and their blackened remains now tumble across a charred meadow. Scattered across the landscape are wine barrels and tarnished mugs, chests burned down to their steel clasps, pots and kettles, knives and giant spoons, and swords that had clearly been useless in the town's defense—useless against…*me*?

Did I do this?

"No," Separi says.

I startle. "Did I ask that aloud?"

Separi squints at me. "Yes."

Philia giggles. "You're losing it, Kai."

"This is the town known as Fihel, Lady," Separi says. "Destroyed by mortals not long ago."

"Look." Philia points to a single banner hanging from the marble arch: the golden tree beneath a shower of coins and runes.

My teeth ache, dull and heavy in my head. If Fihel was destroyed by human hand, that hand was guided by this new god.

Who destroyed Fihel?

Who *is* this god?

I slide out of my saddle. The horses look skittish, uneasy at the stench of burning in the air. They're as ready to leave as my companions are.

"I hear you." I pet each horse's head and slip an extra sheen of protection over them. "But something's here that I need to see. We won't stay long."

Zephar had come with me because I wanted to establish another town like Gasho, with its aqueducts and centers of learning, and its reverence of…me. "I've been here before," I say. I may not have destroyed this place but… The last time I walked these soft dirt paths, there'd been cooing doves and other creatures filling the air with lively noise.

Something growls in the clearing ahead.

"Burnu," Separi whispers.

"Not again," says Philia.

Jadon and I had fought burnu—creatures that resemble both wolf and man—and we'd killed two of the four who had attacked us. Veril used his staff, Warruin, to kill the third. The one who'd escaped had a blue zigzag scar on his forehead.

The survivor, Zigzag, now prowls the clearing across from us. His white coat gleams as bright as his razor-sharp teeth. Clouds of icy air escape from his mouth.

"I want to try," Philia insists, reaching for her bow.

"Maybe not this beast," Separi says.

"Get ready, then," I say to the redhead, choosing this time to draw Fury.

The burnu bares his claws.

Separi pulls her staff from the horse's pack. Ascendance, forged of twisted gray metal and topped with a burst of light, already glows violet.

Philia nocks an arrow.

"Ready?" I ask her.

"Do I have a choice?" she quips.

"You always have a choice in what you do with your body," I say.

Philia purses her lips and nods. "I choose to fight."

We step into the clearing. I creep toward Zigzag and stop several paces away from him. "I remember you."

Zigzag growls at me and howls at the sky.

"Stand at my side," I whisper to Philia. "Let him come to you."

The burnu paces, wary of what I might do with a proper weapon this time. He remembers that, last time, a Renrian exploded one of his friends with a staff like Separi's.

My amulet glows and weighs heavily around my neck.

Zigzag draws closer, racing at us, bounding across the glen.

Separi's staff crackles as the creature's stench closes in on us.

"Now," I tell Philia.

She lets loose, and the air whistles, and the arrow bounces off the burnu's thigh like a thorn against a boulder.

The creature swipes his paw at her.

Philia jumps back, crying out in pain as his smallest claw slides across her leg, tearing through her breeches and the skin underneath. She clutches at her thigh with one hand, barely hanging on to the bow with the other.

Separi pushes the burnu back with her staff, pressing her advantage, Ascendence at the ready.

"Let Philia shoot!" I shout to the Renrian.

Separi stands down.

Zigzag pounces at Philia again.

The young woman rolls, scrambles back to her feet, but stumbles on her wounded leg.

"The joints between his legs and torso are the soft spots," I say. Right now, they glow a bright amber. "You can do it."

Zigzag launches himself at Philia again.

This time, she focuses on his left leg joint, an impossibly small target. She releases the arrow…which drives into the burnu's soft joint.

The burnu cries out in pain, black-green blood dripping down his thigh.

"One more time," I whisper. "The other leg."

The burnu roars again.

Philia shoots. The arrow lands.

Zigzag crashes to the ground, his teeth gnashing and his eyes bright with hate and fear.

We approach the burnu, now panting and snarling on his back. He's even more dangerous this close to death.

Philia pulls an arrow from her quiver to finish him off.

"Don't." I hold an arm out. "You can't kill him."

"Why not?" Philia asks, defiant, raising her bow.

"Because he's not yours to destroy," I say. My eyes scan the sky. *If a resurrector is nearby, he won't die for good anyway.* I don't spot a resurrector.

"How will I learn, then, if you won't let me experience everything?" She groans and grabs her hurt leg, forgetting her disappointment.

"If you want to experience *everything*," I say, watching her blue glow evaporate, "then you can experience dying from this wound."

Her twisted face pales.

"Or you can trust me," I say, "and live to fight and grow another day."

"Live," Philia squeaks.

I nod to Separi, who knows what Philia needs without my instructions. I hope she brought a lot of tonics.

I drive Fury through the burnu's heart, then turn back to the injured redhead. "Ease your mind. We won't let you die." *Please don't die.* I grip her bloody thigh with one shaky hand and accept a tonic from Separi with the other. "Drink," I tell Philia, my own strength depleting the longer I heal her with my touch. "Drink all of it. Immediately."

Philia obeys and lies back down.

Maybe I should've listened to Separi and kept the redhead somewhere safe until I'd killed the otherworldly.

Separi catches my eye, but I can't tell what she's thinking—about Philia's chances of survival or about me letting the young woman fight. Instead of speaking to me, she smiles down at the redhead and says, "I'll mend your breeches after I bandage your leg."

Philia nods, her mouth clamped tight, trying to be that brave shieldmaiden of Vinevridth.

I smile down at the young woman as Separi repairs both her torn skin and leather. "You name your bow yet?" *Please don't die.*

Philia shakes her head.

I gasp and say, "She deserves a name after all you've put her through."

A teardrop rolls back to the redhead's hairline. "Sub…Sub… Sublime."

I nod. "A lovely name." *Please don't…*

Her color shifts from the darkest amber to cornsilk.

I feel that tugging sensation again, like a fish on a line, but stronger and sharper this time. My heart beats sluggishly—healing Philia has taken something out of me that'll be slow to replenish.

I'll soon need all of me to fight Danar Rrivae. How will I make up this deficit?

20

The world turns dull and gray, and all light becomes pinpricks in the gloom. Shadows stretch longer and deeper, and the air grows musty and stale. Eerie, dense silence surrounds us, like we've been covered by a thick layer of dust.

The horses neigh and buck—but they don't leave us.

I jump to my feet, as if I haven't just drained myself healing Philia. "Now what?" My mouth tastes of corroding metal.

It sounds like the foundations of the realm are rearranging themselves beneath us, stone by stone.

Separi gasps. "This place isn't stable."

"Isn't it just...an earth-shake?" Philia asks, struggling to sit up.

"No," Separi whispers.

The ruins of Fihel ring with growling. Red lightning flashes through the sky and a man—no, a *being* as tall as the marble arch, with white hair as long as a river, stalks toward us. He wears a red loincloth, and smoke wafts from his nose. Blood drips from his lips, sprinkling the ground like scarlet rain. He wears black paint beneath his eyes. His long, pale arms end in blood-soaked hands.

"You aren't real," I say, my voice shaking. "I'm dreaming."

The giant's form shimmers like he's caught between the immortal and mortal planes. The edges of his form flicker, but each step he takes is sure and solid, leaving craters in the earth.

If I'm dreaming, why is the world splitting open under my feet, and beneath Separi and Philia, too?

The giant raises his massive blade and drives it into the earth. The shock wave sends me flying backward, and I land hard on my left arm. My breath is knocked from my lungs, and I taste blood on my lips.

Philia clutches at her leg, which looks inflamed and discolored. The burnu's disease is spreading through her veins like dirty water.

Shit. I wasn't done healing her.

"This is not your place," the pale giant says, his voice as full as woodsmoke and as heavy as the world.

Pressure builds inside my head, and I close my eyes before they explode.

"Look and see," the giant demands.

"Who *are* you?" I whisper, peeking at him. "Answer me."

"Look and *see*," he repeats.

I open my eyes and look up.

The *Librum Esoterica* is burning away my leather satchel. It shines on the bloody ground, but the book shrieks as if there's something terrible caught inside it, piercing as metal twisted until it screams.

The sound vibrates deep in my chest and scrapes at my ribs.

The ground beneath the book warps and trembles as if the dirt itself recoils from its presence. Violet fire licks at the ground in ragged arcs. Where the flames touch, the ground melts, not into magma, but into a pulsing black hole.

The scream from the book grows louder, seemingly echoing from all directions at once. I press my hands over my ears, but the sound echoes through my bones.

That black hole in the dirt widens until the ground crumbles away.

I'm pulled toward it, my breath catching as the air around me thins. "Stop," I whisper.

The shriek wavers for just a moment, but then it resumes, louder than before.

I squeeze my eyes shut. *This isn't real. Wake up, Kai. Wake the fuck up!*

Cold, white fingers pry my eyes apart.

I slap at the hand on my face and glare up at the giant.

He tilts his head back and roars. Behind him, a mass of equally pale-skinned giants swing their curved swords at Fihel's remaining houses and trees. All of it catches fire. The few humans who'd been hiding within those houses dash behind rocks and logs.

Are these giants the new gods of the golden tree?

Their chests are bare, their skin smooth and white as sandstone. Their feet look like marble, cracked and glowing faintly from within. With that unmarked skin, they aren't Mera Destroyers, despite the precision of crescent-shaped blades, each swing leaving faint trails of flame in the air. Their eyes are as black as that spreading hole. These giants move in unison, silent as shadows.

The air around me grows frigid; my breath puffs from my mouth in a white cloud. Frost forms on the tips of my fingers.

One of the giants tilts his head toward me, a predator's gaze locking onto prey. He bares his teeth at me, teeth flecked with armor, taffeta, splintered pine trees and giant cedars...

No, he isn't a Mera Destroyer; he is a *devourer*. This Devourer swings his blade at me.

I duck, but the pommel of his sword smashes into my back, knocking me off my feet. I scream as I slam sideways into the thick trunk of a tree. My back burns as I fall to the ground, numb, unable to move. I taste my own blood, and I want to vomit.

"Go to him and surrender," the Devourer demands.

I spit blood on the ground before him and growl, "I obey no one."

"Then you will die."

"I will *not*," I snap. "I've broken my chains."

I weakly thrust my hands in front of me—but no power bursts from my fingertips. No flame, no wind, no lightning. The world turns gray around me, my arms weighing as much as the realm. I drop my hand as the world spins...and spins...

I collapse, face-first, into the dirt.

"Kai!" A woman's voice.

I open my eyes to dirt and brightness...

A red cardinal flies so close to me that his wings brush my nose. I blink, shaking.

A hand appears. A gloved finger brushes my cheek.

Someone's shouting.

Gray suede boots.

The ground beneath me quakes. I look up and see those marble-skinned giants stalking toward the horizon. *Devouring.*

"Kai," the woman behind me shouts again. I lift my head, look back—

Elyn, in those gray suede boots, raises a sword of pure light. Her golden armor gleams against the darkened sky. Her eyes are as cold and sharp as her blade.

Jadon stands beside her, holding a giant broadsword—Chaos, with its silver blade and massive basket hilt. Beyond them, Elyn's guards strike down the Devourers with their pikes. But the slain giants rise again, their deafening cries echoing across the ruins of Fihel.

I cough and shake my head in a futile attempt to clear it. I swipe away the blood dripping into my eyes.

Am I still dreaming? How is Jadon here?

The giant closest to me roars, bearing down on Separi, who runs from the battle, dragging Philia in her arms, with my bag containing the *Librum Esoterica* on her back.

"No!" I gasp, staggering toward them, Fury clutched tightly in my hand.

Elyn and Jadon give chase. The realm slows all around us.

Elyn hurls a lightning bolt at the giant, which hits his back and explodes in a shower of sparks. The giant falters but changes course, swinging a massive fist at Elyn.

She ducks, moving like the wind.

Jadon ducks in between the giant's legs, slashing that enormous blade across tendons and bone in a spray of black-green blood. The Devourer howls in pain. He reaches for Jadon, but he is already gone, chasing the next giant.

This one Jadon left behind may be injured, but he isn't dead.

Lightning crackles through my veins. I swing Fury, and a beam of radiant light strikes the Devourer in the chest. He stumbles, and his skin hisses and festers where the lightning bolt struck him. His fiery eyes lock onto mine.

Why isn't he dying?

The giant raises his massive hand again, but before his blow lands, a flash of light shoots past me. Elyn descends from the sky on blue-and-gold wings, sword blazing as it sinks into the Devourer's neck. Flames consume him from the chest outward as she severs the giant's arm in one swing. He collapses to his knees, his cries of agony shaking the ground.

More giants pound toward us, and I spot the red-eyed creature soaring over the battlefield. As it bathes us all in golden light from its open mouth, giants that we killed rise to their knees, resurrected.

"We must destroy the resurrector," I shout to my comrades, pointing to the sky. "Destroy it and the rest will fall."

Elyn soars toward the leather-winged creature, her silhouette a blur against the sky. The resurrector flaps its colossal wings, its glowing red eyes trained on Elyn even as its light grows brighter, even as the dead giants stagger to their feet, their wounds knitting together in flashes of gold.

"Kai!" Jadon shouts.

Another Devourer lunges for me. I bury my sword in the giant's left leg.

Above us, the resurrector shrieks. Its massive head comes crashing down onto the bloody earth.

"Now!" Elyn shouts.

Jadon and I sprint toward the oncoming giant; I hurl a cyclone, and the giant topples. Jadon swings Chaos and cuts off the Devourer's head. We don't pause to celebrate. We keep fighting, and all around us, giants are slain.

One Devourer remains. He falls to his knees, his eyes flickering with hate.

Jadon, Elyn, and I stand before the giant. The Raqiel guards stand behind him. While Jadon's chest heaves with fatigue, Elyn stands tall and calm, her eyes and the dove hanging from her neck burning bright. I pause with my sword above the giant's head, Fury's black blade gleaming with blacker blood.

No. This execution requires Justice.

I pull that clean, silvery-blue sword from my scabbard. Elyn gasps at the sight of her old weapon.

"Who do you belong to?" I demand of the fallen giant.

The Devourer coughs, and his blood speckles my breastplate. "Bring him."

"Bring *who*?" Elyn says, the Devourer's face starting to burn and hiss in the light of her pendant.

The giant stares at Jadon. "Bring *him*."

"Who do you belong to?" I ask again, my heartbeat thudding in my ears.

"He will leave if you bring him," the Devourer says.

Both Elyn and I look over at Jadon, who says, "And if she refuses?"

The giant sneers. "Then he will snip your string, puppet. You will die, they all will die, and this wretched realm will come to its wretched end."

"And what if I bring him?" I ask.

Jadon and Elyn both exclaim in shock.

I quiet them with a hand as I hold the Devourer's gaze. "What if I bring him?"

"Then he will leave Vallendor to you," the giant says.

But if Danar Rrivae leaves Vallendor with his otherworldly as well as those flying creatures that resurrect… "Which realm will he terrorize next?" Elyn whispers, reading my mind, her eyes cutting to Jadon.

I swing my sword across the giant's neck.

My stomach twists on itself with hunger, but I don't want to eat. The smell of Ridget's pork chops makes me gag.

What's *wrong* with me?

I sit beside the fire and stare into the flames, while Philia, Jadon, and Separi eat, laugh, and recount their exploits to each other as if they're all the best of friends. Their joy feels distant, the weight of my thoughts impenetrable.

We'd left Fihel and found shelter in the forest again. Philia and Separi wove leaves and vines into canopies stretching between the trees.

Now, from a pit ringed by smooth stones, a fire casts long shadows across the ground. The trees look alive with glowing orbs hanging from their twisting branches—more of Separi's handiwork. Beyond the camp, the Raqiel guards keep danger at bay.

As I watch the others laugh, I can hardly breathe with nerves. The bag containing the *Librum Esoterica* sparkles between my feet. My concern isn't whatever awaits us in the wilderness. No, what I can't understand is why Jadon is here with us, rather than locked up in a cell deep in the abbey.

21

Elyn can't Spryte us all to Brithellum.

"I thought you were all-powerful," Jadon quips.

The Adjudicator cocks an eyebrow. "I am, but one in your party wouldn't survive being folded through time and space right now."

We all peer at Philia's injured leg, which remains the color of cornsilk.

"We need a moment anyway, to figure out…" I press my fingers against my temples. "To figure out *any semblance of a plan* and prepare for what comes next."

Elyn *can* return the horses to their stalls in Caburh. I offer them apples and my thanks for their swiftness and loyalty.

I beckon Elyn to walk with me. Once we're out of earshot of the others, I touch her elbow and whisper, "Thank you."

She cocks her head and regards me with those gold eyes. "For?"

"Healing me back in Fihel." I shake my head and stare out at the forest. "I've never…"

Tasted so much of my blood. Been in that much pain. Felt so weak during a fight.

I swallow. My mouth still tastes like old coins. "You helped me out, and I appreciate it."

She nods. "I'll be back." Before I can take another breath, Elyn has Spryted to Caburh with the horses and returned holding a knapsack.

"The family sends their love," Elyn tells Separi. "And they told me to let you know that Vinasa will receive proper rites. And Ridget also said that you must braid the Lady's hair in her stead. She said to use this—"

Elyn pulls out a skein of rose-gold luclite thread, a comb, and a tin of peppermint oil. "She says to take great care, as Kai is tender-headed." Elyn pauses. "You all do hair, too?"

Jadon huffs, his agitation palpable. "Can we get going—?"

Elyn holds up her hand. She stares at Separi and awaits an answer.

Separi takes the supplies. "Yes, we do hair. Would the Adjudicator like me to?" The Renrian eyes Elyn's frizzy white braid.

Elyn's eyes widen. "Could you? And do something new? I've had this braid a long time."

I laugh and weave my arm through Philia's. After the battle against the Devourers, we need the comfort, especially as the realm remains on the brink of destruction.

Little time passes, though, before our moods shift back to somber. Reality bites.

A jailer overseeing her prisoner, Elyn doesn't talk much as Jadon marches beside her.

The cool forest air flares with heat as Jadon follows several paces behind me.

Blue jays shriek, *"Lady!"* from their nests in threadbare trees. Orange-and-pink butterflies flit over sunflowers that lift their parched heads as I pass. The hard-packed earth turns soft under my boots.

But then the birdsong falls silent as the remaining leaves wither all at once on the trees, their branches turning brittle and snapping, sending those nests tumbling to the ground. The butterflies' wings stiffen into dull crystal, and they fall from the sky to their deaths, dashed against now-dead sunflowers. Burned seeds tumble onto the desiccated earth.

It's as though I was never here.

It's him. Jadon. *Miasma.*

What a cruel trick. My arrival brought the promise of life, only to be snuffed out by the weapon passing through twenty paces behind.

"Why don't we walk behind him?" Philia asks. "That way, you'd heal everything he's killing."

"We'd be in Miasma's wake," Separi says, shaking her head.

"You're still healing from the burnu attack," I say. "You'd be walking into certain death even if we waited for the wind to weaken his power. Even the wind dies when he meets it."

Philia's face crumples as she looks back at her old friend. "Poor thing."

Jadon, his eyes bright with regret, offers her a sad smile. He knows he's death. Beautiful death.

Soft rain soon falls through the pines and cedars. I breathe in the scent of wet, living wood.

Separi chews on licorice root as she tells tales of her days as a young and dashing Renrian. Once, she'd enchanted an abandoned chest of geld to resemble a pile of horse dung. "The bandits didn't know what to do," she says. "It looked like shit, but I'd forgotten to add flies, and there was no smell."

"So, did they believe you?" I ask, letting laughter bubble out of the tension of my throat.

"I convinced them that the horse that left this shit pile was on a special diet developed by the elves of Itheria." She blinks at me. "There *are* no elves of Itheria. There *is* no Itheria."

Once again, we make two camps, with Elyn and Jadon's camp downwind. The pine needles are cushion-soft under my tired feet. I sit between Separi's knees as she washes and oils my hair and then detangles my curls with the wide-toothed comb. Then she weaves those luclite threads into my braids. Under her ministrations, my neck feels strong, and my mind stops racing. I feel less prickly as I watch the fire glow orange against the dark sky.

"How can I feel...*comfort* right now?" I whisper to Separi. "Especially with Elyn and Jadon, who both betrayed me, just a stone's throw away?"

"Anyone can break your heart, Lady," says Separi. "Anyone can disappoint you. It's in your power, though, to figure out who you'll hurt for."

I silently accept a dinner plate of ham and potatoes with leeks and long beans from Philia. The ham tastes gamey, and the potatoes taste like dirt. I force myself to swallow the few bites, as I know I need the strength.

Separi's lavender eyes soften, and she chuckles softly. "You're not eating, Lady. Would you like Philia to prepare something else?" She tugs at the fox amulet hanging from her neck.

I take her hand. "It's not that I'm not hungry. It's just that..." I bite my lip. "I'm changing, Separi. I feel it. We need to get to Brithellum soon. And we will."

After dinner, I grab my satchel and wander away to survey Vallendor from a higher vantage point. I follow a drying brook upstream, where eventually it swells and brightens with silver fish darting through its waters. Bees hover over night-blooming jasmine and tuberoses. Though Jadon has walked behind me, destroying all that I'd revived, for *these* few moments, I witness what can be, what *will* be if I kill Danar Rrivae.

The traitor. But he hadn't been the only one to rebel.

We were all charged with watching over our mortals, and some grew bored with tending perfect worlds like this meadow and this brook. They enjoyed the destruction of a world too much or despised the realms they'd discovered. They started whispering into mortal ears, tempting them to fight, to steal, to make chaos in the quiet.

But who'd grow bored of meadows and brooks like these? Who could despise beauty, truth, good health, and riches beyond geld? Those who wanted disruption corrupted the realms with otherworldly, with sickness, with polluted waters and dying animals. They loathed Supreme, and they gained strength through their chaos and destruction.

They won't stop, not until every realm is destroyed—even if I succeed in killing Danar Rrivae.

I peel my armor off, and my stinging skin feels like it has also peeled away in strips. I step into the cold waters of the brook and sigh with relief as I apply soothing peppermint oil. Clean and scented,

I wash my clothes, then twist the towel that Separi brought with her around me.

The trill of a fife drifts from the camp below. *Veril!* My heart leaps, but then I remember: my counselor and friend has moved on.

"Hey." Jadon smiles at me from his spot near a small waterfall—the stream has slowed to a trickle even though it was flowing just moments before his arrival. But *he* looks lovely with his damp hair and clean-shaven face. "You're thinking too loud," he says.

I snort.

He walks toward me but stops a few paces away. "May I?"

Wary, I shrug and say, "Maybe." I sit up straight as though good posture will block Miasma.

Though I can feel the trouble he brings, I want to be near him again. He risked his life for us and fought beside me again, and the courage he showed melts most of my hatred.

"I won't stay long—I know what I am." He sits beside me. He takes my hand and brushes my knuckles over his cheeks. "Your skin…"

"I know." I blush, and the damaged parts of my face burn.

Jadon's gaze roams my neck. His eyes linger.

"There, too?" I ask, my fingers finding a patch along the curve of my neck.

He nods.

"Fuck," I say and tug at that unsightly flap in futility.

Jadon keeps staring at my neck.

I point to a far-off tree. "Hey! Look over there."

He laughs.

I don't. I fight off sudden tears.

"You smell good," he says.

It's up to me to figure out who I'll hurt for. But the ache along my thighs and hips isn't from pain.

I squeeze his hand.

We sit there, in the silence.

"I'm terrified, Kai," he whispers, at last. "I've never admitted my fear to anyone except you. At the end of all of this, where will you be? And what about me?"

I can't make promises. Even if I knew we would both survive, I don't know what comes next. "If we destroy TERROR and WISDOM," I say, "that will help us destroy him—"

"But destroying my father..."

Destroys Jadon.

We stare out at the valley, its carpet of green grass speckled with wildflowers.

He says, "Back when we fought those... What were they?"

"I call them Devourers," I say.

He nods. "Would you have turned me over to him?"

I don't look at him. "I have to save this realm at all costs." My words hang heavy between us, and I wonder if Jadon truly understands what they mean.

Jadon is not burdened with the job of saving anything. Even the grass beneath him dies, turning brittle and brown as if scorched by fire. Death spreads, clawing through the earth until it reaches me. A chill seeps into my skin, and the sickness stops with me. If I wasn't sitting here, Miasma would've continued to creep on...*devouring*.

"You see it, don't you?" Jadon raises his marked right hand, and then his left. "Everywhere I go, it follows. The land feels the death that I carry."

I nod.

"I'm glad that you're honest about that." He chuckles bitterly. "I've seen what I am. I feel this poison inside of me, and I fight it every day, but it's spreading because I'm alive. Soon, I'll destroy everything you're trying to save."

"We'll find a way to stop it," I say, "to stop him. You're not alone."

Jadon's eyes meet mine, and for a moment, I see the blacksmith I once knew, who'd fought beside me, who'd believed in something greater. But then his face darkens like storm clouds. "This sickness—it *is* me," he says. "You can't separate us. I'm the rot. I'm the ruin. The only way to save this realm is to destroy me."

He's right about that, too.

The sickness within him rises again, and the forest flickers around us—bright and green one moment, shadowed and dying the next.

I pull my hand away, and it's now speckled with small bruises. I lie back on the thick grass and stare at the pinpoints of light in the sky.

It's up to me to figure out who I'll hurt for.

I point to the brightest speck in the sky. "That's the realm of Lerango. It's not that different from Vallendor. Mountains, oceans, forests… The people hunt and craft, farm and sing. A cousin on my mother's side is Grand Steward there. Pretty easy job. And then…"

I slide my finger across the canvas of night, stopping at the bloom of light that sits on top of a pine tree. "And that's Sianiodin. I haven't visited yet—it's a real shithole. Swamps. Not just the landscape but the thinking, the *lack* of thinking, the corruption and depression. Once the daystar and nightstar decide to stop walking there, Elyn will go there to read the decree of destruction, and then the Mera will come and—"

I snap my fingers. "And that will be the end of Sianiodin. Maybe I'll get to visit before that happens and see it for myself."

Jadon's holding a wilted cluster of white tuberoses. He tosses them to me, and their deaths are quickly reversed as they land on my chest. He stares at me, full of thoughts that I don't try to untangle. I contend with my own knotted thinking. *I want this. I don't want this. Let go. Don't let go.* I brush the renewed bundle of blooms across my lips and hold Jadon's gaze.

His warm eyes focus on my neck again.

I drag the flowers down my chin, along the curve of my jaw and down to my throat. His eyes follow.

The towel I wear falls away. I skim the flowers along my breasts, down to my belly and between my hipbones.

"One of my favorite places," he whispers.

"I remember." I pause. Isn't he curious about where I've been, who I've seen? Who I've been with? I have to tell him. "I reunited with someone in Gasho from before."

Jadon doesn't speak for a long time. Then: "Him?"

"Yes. His name is Zephar and…" I swallow, but my mouth stays dry. "I was very happy to see him again. To see all of my warriors again."

"I'm sure they—*he*—missed you."

I search the skies for the words. There are no clues in Lerango and certainly not in Sianiodin. "Zephar and I reunited, but not in *all* ways… Not yet."

Jadon nods, staring intently at me, laid bare before him.

"Because I still think of you. I still think of us, and sometimes, I wish… I close my eyes and…"

He whispers, "Show me."

I imagine that my hand is Jadon's hand, that my fingers are his, and I imagine that he is caressing my skin, that these fingers are his, slipping inside of me and stroking me. My amulet burns so bright between my breasts that all of Vallendor can see its glow.

Jadon whispers my name, and I whisper his, and I can almost remember how he feels inside me. The earth rumbles beneath us, and I finally open my eyes and look at him. His eyes are bright, his gaze jumping between my hands and my eyes; I know that, like me, he wants his hand to be my hand. I'm a moment away from pulling him to me, into me, but that rumble inside of me becomes a crashing wave, and it slams over me, over and over again. He whispers, "Fuck," between breaths until he emits a staggered gasp. We lie there, both satisfied and unsatisfied, as the air chills our damp skin.

"Will I ever touch you again?" he whispers.

Who I'll hurt for…

"I don't know." I close my eyes, and a teardrop rolls back into my ear.

Even with my eyes closed, white light blinds me.

I sit up, my head swimming, fire igniting along my spine. With stiff fingers, I twist the towel around my chest, wincing as my joints protest.

Jadon sleeps, and the grass is brown and dead beneath him.

I stand, stifling a groan as my bones creak. I shield my eyes against that unrelenting white light with a sore hand.

The light glows brightest over at the bluff where red cardinals are fluttering, where Elyn stands at the cliff, her fists curled on her hips.

I totter over to her, pulse racing. "What's wrong?"

She looks me up and down, scowling. "You should see yourself right now."

Wait. Why am I now *looking up* at her? Where's the *Librum*—?

I bring my knees stiffly to my chest as my blood oozes through me like mud.

Elyn stands over me and shakes her head. "Was it worth it, Kai?"

My eyes fill with hot tears. "What's happening to me?" It hurts even to whisper.

"You're dying, idiot." Elyn stoops to press her hands on my stomach and the small of my back. "That luclite thread in your hair acted as armor and protected your head and neck. That probably saved your life."

A warm energy from Elyn's fingers travels up and down my spine, healing the broken parts of me. My mind clears, my throat loosens, and I can breathe again.

She helps me stand, and once I get my legs under me, she pushes me away. "You've risked all of our safety, you know that? I'm not here to be your nursemaid. I'm not Separi."

"I know." I stumble away from her like a new colt. "The *Librum*?"

She lifts my pack from the ground. "You mean the one in here? This same bag that I found sitting on the bluff, unattended?"

"Oh, no." I rub my aching temples with sore fingers.

"You *cannot* be this close to him, Kai," Elyn spits. "He draws strength from you like he pulled life from those sunflowers we passed. Those flowers died, remember? So did this grass, the birds, *everything*."

I sink to my knees. "I know—"

"No, you *don't* know," she says, the intricate braid Separi made loosening.

"You told me that we should be together—"

"I didn't mean go out and fuck Miasma." She throws up her hands, breathing hard.

"I'm sorry," I say.

"Shit, Kai." She clenches her fists. "Do you understand—"

"Yes," I whisper, my mind racing. "I love him."

"But—"

"He's the weapon, I know," I say, watching the grass turn green beneath my knees. "I'm sorry. I fucked up. But I've learned. I promise you that I have."

"Jadon's not just a weapon," Elyn says. "He is *the* weapon. He is certain death." Elyn kneels beside me. "The truth is cruel, Kai. I know how you feel about him, but Jadon Rrivae was not meant to live, nor to have a life with the Grand Defender and Lady of the Verdant Realm. What will happen if I'm not around to save you next time? You *will* perish, and Vallendor will perish with you." Her gold eyes soften, and she takes my bruised hand. "So don't do this again, Kai. *Please.* I truly am sorry about all of this."

And for the first time in a long time…I believe her.

22

"Beaminster never had a golden age," Jadon says as we approach a town just outside of the larger city of Brithellum. He still wears the borrowed armor of a man beneath his station—the prince remains a prisoner. "Not one person born in Beaminster changed the realm through music, art, or letters. Nothing was ever invented or discovered here." Instead of walking behind us, he and Elyn walk beside us, several paces apart.

Every tree and shrub in this province is a shade of red or brown, stooped, shaven, barren, prickly. Danar Rrivae's oven of malice has baked out all softness of life.

"But even in its best times," Jadon is saying, "Beaminster has always been an open-air jail." He explains that Beaminster was founded to house the worst of Brithellum, but they were all just mundane criminals without hope or aspiration. "The town suffers," he says, "because no one in Beaminster gives a single shit about making the best of what they have."

The gates around the city look like rotting teeth. Trash from years gone by—broken pots, splintered chairs, torn garments, dead rats—is piled high around those gates. There are no cottages with curtained windows, or churches or temples with gleaming walls. If there are honeycakes to be had, they would surely be filled with maggots.

Elyn's cardinals swoop around us, though the air here is also foul.

"Hostages are typically kept here," Jadon shares.

"And you know this because...?" Philia asks.

"Because *he* kept hostages here," Elyn says, eyebrow cocked.

"Well, I'm here to free Olivia," Philia says, chin high, "by any means necessary."

"Retrieving the ring is the most important task, Philia," Jadon says. "If we don't get that, no one will be free. We may have to search private homes to find her or Gileon or the ring. The town has a few hidden bunkers here, too. We'll likely have to fight. There's also sickness here. Not...*me*," he adds, when Elyn shoots him a look. "But some disease that congeals your spit, pits your skin, and fills your ears with tar. So don't get spat or sneezed on."

"Have fun," I say, smirking.

Philia's eyes widen. "Does that mean Olivia may have this mystery sickness? Could she die? Could she already be dead?"

No one speaks, because we have nothing reassuring to say.

Separi bows her head and touches my elbow. "Is there anything I can do for you besides aid in the coming fight, Lady?" She blushes and looks down at her shoes. "I know I've failed you—"

"Don't." I lift the Renrian's chin. "My mouth and body may have changed, but you provide me with more than food and company. You aren't failing me, Separi. Isn't it impossible for a Renrian to fail?"

She chuckles as she fixes my buckles and my hair. "No, we don't fail."

I grin and lower my voice. "The threads in my hair saved my life. I did something foolish last night, but your braid-work kept me more whole than I deserve to be."

"Last night?" Her eyebrows scrunch. "Did I sleep through a fight?"

I wink at her. "A personal battle." I slip off my pack heavy with the *Librum Esoterica*.

"I'll hold it," Philia says, stepping forward.

"No," both Elyn and I say. We are so close to Olivia now that Philia could flee with the book to make a deal with Gileon herself.

"Thanks for the offer," Elyn says, "but I'll hold the Lady's satchel."

I roll my eyes at Elyn and hand her the bag. "Everyone wait here," I say.

"Why?" Jadon asks, his shoulders stiffening.

"Danar Rrivae knows that I'm in Beaminster," I say, "because the book is in Beaminster and the ring that unlocks the artifact is in Beaminster. He'll try to keep us from that ring. How, this time, I'm not sure. By staying back, you'll see just how many people you'll need to kill."

"You sound confident," Elyn says, surveying her own handiwork.

Elyn had brought fruit and vegetable tarts from the abbey along with cheese and bread. And I ate it all, until I could no longer stand. Though she couldn't stop my skin from peeling, she eased the sting with aloe.

I walk toward the raggedy gates and its raggedy guards. I smile as I close the distance between us. I'm not happy to meet these strangers, but I'm ready to enjoy the fight.

The four men wear Syrus Wake's twin leopard sigils on their tunics, which look like cast-off potato sacks. Their swords are rusty, their blades chipped. Were they ever *real* soldiers? Have they no pride? Have they even *named* their weapons? They gape at me with marvel and confusion.

The dark amber glow of these men alarms me. It's a miracle they're even standing. As I approach them, I notice the cloud of unpleasant smells emanating from them. The sour and rotting sweet of decayed teeth. Sickness and flatulence and wet and solid waste, the smell of people and animals shitting in the street.

"Greetings and salutations," I say, stopping a few steps away from them. "I'm looking for Prince Gileon Wake. I'm told he lives here on occasion. Also, I'm looking for a woman who should be with him. Big blue eyes, quick hands? Have you seen her around?"

"You better move along, you fuzzy-headed queynte," the straw-haired guard wheezes.

"Oh dear." I raise my eyebrows in surprise and amusement. "We're starting off like this? Let's begin again, shall we?" I take a breath and say, "Greetings and salutations—"

Straw-Hair draws his rusty sword.

"I'm looking for Prince Gileon Wake," I repeat.

Straw-Hair comes closer. And then a guard stomps past him.

I shake my head. "You probably should stop right there. If you take one more step, I'm skewering your round ass."

Ground Round pauses—but not long enough. Though the man called me a "queynte," I'm not furious yet. No, I'm feelin'... *righteous*.

Straw-Hair and Ground Round rush me with their swords held high.

In one smooth motion, I pull Justice from her sheath.

Ground Round's eyes widen at my sword's beauty—she's the last beautiful thing he sees before she cuts off his head. A feast for the beasts, a gift from the Lady of the Verdant Realm. I can already hear the grunts and cries of the hungry animals hiding in the desiccated fields surrounding the city.

Straw-Hair skids to a stop.

Still smiling, I look over to him and the other two guards. "Do you understand the language I'm speaking? Maybe you speak Shokata? Du avui indastend na nuw? Or maybe you speak...*Paraq*? Da I'ay yumlika pi mav?"

All three lift their swords, but their numbers will not save them.

I cock my head. "Is it something I said?"

Straw-Hair rushes to slay me with a sword too dull to slice cheese.

I step back, letting him enjoy swinging his toy at me. Not even a good wind comes from the sweep of his blade.

"Queynte," he spits, lifting his butter knife to strike at me a second time.

"That word again?" I swing Justice twice: the first time to take his sword and the second time to remove his left arm at the elbow.

He bleeds out even before he hits the soil.

I cock an eyebrow at the next two, their shamefully dull blades still in their hands.

The one with wheezy lungs looks at the bodies around us and says, "Fuck it." He turns and runs from me, but I close the distance between us and strike him down before he can sound any alarm.

The last guard—whose pudgy baby face fills with terror and determination—hops over dead Wheezy to rush at me.

I step back.

He swings wide, slicing himself in the shin. I put him out of his misery.

I step over his body and through the gates that these four dead men guarded.

No mosaic tiles. No lanterns on posts. No stalls of fresh produce. But in Beaminster, there's plenty to drink—fumes of rum and ale waft off the drunken men who rush toward me.

I smirk at the men's tunics and Wake's leopard sigil. So much for peace, piety, and progress.

Several drunken soldiers—not one of them sober enough to fight—pull their swords and call me names: harridan, whore, every slur they can think of.

I spot a sword with an intricate iron handle and hilt—this blade looks well-cared for. Unfortunately, the man who stole this sword from its original owner stumbles and impales himself.

Two more guards race toward me with less impressive swords but more assured movements. They fight without commitment or expertise.

Then someone's blade nicks my left cheek. I scowl at them.

The woman has a helmet of thick black hair. She smiles, pleased to see a pebble of my blood on the tip of her bright silver blade.

"Good job," I say. Then I drive Justice through one cheek and out the other.

The men try their best; a few succeed in breaking their swords against my armor. The remaining soldiers stumble away from me, sober enough now to understand that though I bleed, I will not fail. I'm unlike any opponent they've ever—

Something heavy slams into my back, sending me sprawling face-first into the ground. All the air leaves my lungs, and my back feels like shattered glass. My ears ring, and I see two of everything, and then six, and then my vision blurs with tears. I hear cheering, but they sound worlds away.

Maybe I fucked up coming here alone.

I turn my head, coughing as I move. High atop a decrepit inn, I see two guards load a catapult. That's what struck me.

Now that I'm prone, the guards on the ground raise their swords again, intent on killing me.

Yeah, I definitely *fucked up.*

I glance at the catapult again and squeeze my eyes shut. *Get up, Kai! Get the fuck up!*

They have a catapult and a legion of guards, however poorly trained. I'm just one person on her belly, seeing stars and hearing the roar of blood in my—

One man kicks dirt in my face.

I thrust out my hand and scream because my arm feels hot and broken. I manage to throw him skyward in a burst of wind.

Two more men rush toward me. My power blasts them away, too.

Lightheaded, I cry out as I get to my knees, thrusting wind at clusters of belligerent men on either side of me. They're thrown against rotting wood carts and the crumbling walls of houses that should've come down seasons ago.

On the rooftop, the men load the catapult's basket with a boulder.

Anger roils through me like volcanic steam, and now I see clearly again. My body vibrates with pain and anger. I want to be up there on that rooftop—

Pop!

I find myself on the rooftop, looking out at the roof of the tavern and the crumbling houses around it. Moths flit around my aching ankles, leaving behind glittery dust to mark my sudden ascent.

Spryte, bitches.

The soldiers who'd been loading the catapult stumble backward, startled to see me standing beside them. The catapult can't help them now.

"No backup plan?" I ask.

I thrust my hands at these two men, sending gouts of flame at them and then at the fighters down below. I ignore the pain in my back and arms and fling balls of fire everywhere, until all is lost in smoke and silenced by the thunder of burning lumber.

No one moves because everyone is dead…*except for her*. Another woman wearing armor. On the ground, the lone survivor holds a bow, an arrow nocked and ready against her cheek.

I hop down from the inn, my back and hips screaming. I point to the only buildings that have escaped my flames.

"Prince Wake," I say to the woman. "Is he in one of these buildings?"

She doesn't speak. She doesn't release her arrow, either.

"Answer me," I shout.

I can sense her fear as she says, "No, he's on the perimeter. In the camp."

"Are you lying to me?" I ask. "If you are, I will kill you, and then I'll find your kin and kill them, too. I will burn your hometown to the ground. So I ask again: are you lying to me?"

"I'm telling the truth, Lady." She nods so hard and fast that I won't have to break her neck—she may do that herself.

I beckon her to me, and even that simple gesture is painful.

She obeys. She's about Philia's age, and the protection she wears is not made for a woman—the armor barely accommodates her breasts and digs into her hips. She glows a dark amber, and her thrumming heart inches closer to death.

"Your name is Grace Hallum, yes?" I ask, swiping at the blood trickling down my tender cheek.

"Yes, Lady," she says, her head dipping.

I scowl at my blood on my fingers, shimmering ruby red with life against the crusting brown blood of the mortals I've slain today. I hold out my stained hand. "Nice to meet you, Grace."

She kisses my hand. Immediately, her amber glow transforms into a vibrant blue. Her chestnut hair shines like the picture of health.

"You were about to make the worst decision of your life," I say. "It would've also been the *last* decision you would've ever made. But you learned, Grace Hallum, and you chose wisely. Remember, though: some gifts can be rescinded."

I squeeze her hand and release her. I nod toward the broken gates where hungry beasts have already begun scavenging the pile of corpses. "Tell my friends out there that they can come in now."

"Yes, Lady."

I limp toward that perimeter camp with my bruised back to her. Grace Hallum's feet pound the dirt as she runs toward freedom.

23

Elyn, Philia, Jadon, and Separi join me in the burning town.

"You just can't help yourself, can you?" Elyn hands me the bag holding the *Librum Esoterica*, then places her palms on both of my shoulders. She breathes deep, then moves her hands to my hips, and finally to my back. That sensation of crawling ants travels all around my body until there's no place left for them to go.

I take a deep breath and sling the bag over my left shoulder, which cries out in agony, as a flash of pain makes my legs quiver. I squint at Elyn and gasp, "You missed a spot."

"No, Kai. That entire arm…" She shakes her head and whispers, "You aren't well."

I try to smile, but she doesn't blink. "Do you understand what I'm saying?"

I swallow and blink away the tears welling in my eyes. "Yeah. I understand."

As Elyn brushes ash off my armor, I stare at the charred inn, the guardhouse, and those creaky houses that ought to be demolished. I'm hardly in better shape.

"We need to hurry," Elyn says. *Because I'm falling apart.*

I look over to Philia. "You should've stayed back at the—"

"No," the redhead says. "We're so close now. I'm not leaving without Livvy. She's here." I follow her eyes to my bag, where the *Librum Esoterica*, the key to Olivia's freedom, is stowed. Philia is at her most desperate, and I hope she chooses wisely.

I hope she proves me wrong.

There aren't many soldiers left in Gileon Wake's regiment. Four sit at the entrance to the barracks, and not one of them glows with life—not blue, not amber. Does Wake know that his men are dead—and considering the maggots in their eyes and mouths, that they have been dead for a while?

The camp smells of urine and smoke. The ground is thick mud, littered with scraps of armor, broken weapons, and rotting food. Flies swarm everywhere.

Some soldiers sleep in mold-covered tents that sag under the weight of damp rot. The tents themselves are mismatched, patched together. Other soldiers sleep out in the open, sprawled on tattered bedrolls or directly on the cold ground, barely hanging on to life.

Campfires burn at every thirteenth tent. Men huddle in silence around these fires, their faces gaunt and their eyes hollow. The amber glow that marks them flickers like dying candlelight. There's no camaraderie, no drunken songs or shared laughter, only coughing and curses.

One of three bloodhounds lifts her head as we pass.

Daisy! My old friend.

She sniffs the breeze. She stands, and her tail wags hard and fast at my familiar scent.

"Sweet girl," I say, "Daisy, my lovely one!" I wave my hand over the other hounds' noses, and they dip their big heads in recognition. I kiss Daisy's forehead and offer her and her brothers leftover pork cooked by Separi and boar jerky cured by Philia.

"Can your noses even work in these conditions?" I ask her.

"There's nothing alive to search for," she replies sadly.

"We'll be back," I assure her and the boys.

We move on, sneaking past the armaments, the mess tent, and a small tarp covering cords of firewood.

Command tents cluster near the center of the camp.

"Gileon will be in there." Jadon points to the fanciest of the tents, the one made of heavy, green wool. A banner hangs limply from a crooked pole, that twin leopard emblem faded and stained with mud. A gold-threaded colure has been embroidered into the tent flaps. A plume of smoke rises from a hole in the center of the tent. Two imposing knights guard the entrance.

Jadon eases out a breath. "Hope this goes without bloodshed. I hope he understands that neither of you cares if it *doesn't*."

Because we're leaving with that ring—his finger still in it or not.

My gaze stays on Gileon's tent. "It's made of wool."

"Yeah," Jadon says. "And?"

I shiver. "I'm allergic to wool."

Jadon laughs. "Kai, be serious."

I don't laugh. I don't even crack a smile. "You don't remember my rashes that day I sheared farmer Gery's sheep back in Maford? It was part of my punishment for causing a public disturbance." I shiver again, remembering the hives on my skin.

Jadon tries to swallow his embarrassment. Too late. "Just…don't touch it."

I roll my eyes. *That* would be a stupid legacy. *She could wield fire and wind in her hands. She could hear others' thoughts. Pity she met her death after an encounter with soggy wool.*

We walk toward the tent, hands ready on our swords.

Soldiers watch us approach, but none move to stand.

Philia whispers, "Why aren't they fighting us?"

"They're contending with a greater threat now," Elyn says.

Some soldiers' eyes widen once they see me. They whisper, "Lady," believers again now that death is in the air.

"If everyone dies, what will happen to…?" Philia looks back over her shoulder at Daisy and her brothers.

"Maybe," I say, "you and Olivia can be their mommas. Give them a good home."

Philia smiles at that, though her eyes wander toward my bag again, to the key to Olivia and their happily-ever-after. I clutch the strap a little tighter.

Some men groan; others emit rattling breaths that might well be their last.

"Step away if you're smart," I warn a half dozen more Dashmala soldiers who've hurried from their own grubby tents to guard Wake's fancier one. "If you choose to stay, you *will* die."

"She's the one who killed Sinth."

"Drove his own pike through his mouth, she did."

Like Sinth, these soldiers have yellow eyes, scars, and bony ridges growing along their jawlines. Their race is derived from my own, the Mera. They're fighters, with big weapons and bigger egos.

The two soldiers whose thoughts I overheard back away from me and run.

Four foolish Dashmala unsheathe their swords. One lifts his chin and says, "I'm not gonna let some mudscraping—"

I fling him into the sky. *He will never walk this land again*, I think viciously. I glance behind me, to make sure Philia is watching.

"Who's next?" I ask.

Another soldier looks at me, looks at the sky, and runs after the two men that fled. The remaining two lift their swords, ready to fight.

I flick my hand, and they are flung behind me. I'm sure they'll land *somewhere*.

We reach the two Dashmala guarding Gileon Wake's tent.

Neither knight is dying from the sickness hanging over this camp; the Dashmala are not as susceptible to most human diseases. But their swords are useless against the wind bursting from my hands. I slam one of them into the ground. The other Dashmala, also the size of a mountain, blocks me from entering Gileon Wake's tent. "You—"

I flick my hand.

He crashes into the ground behind an outlying tent, and the campground shakes.

Jadon holds open the flap to his brother's tent.

My stomach drops. I duck as I step inside, not only because of my height, but because I'm careful that no part of me, not even my hair, touches wool.

This tent is nicer and larger than most people's homes; even with Jadon and the others standing behind me, there's still space to move. There's a wash basin and a wine barrel. A small wooden chest and a sword-stand are on the opposite side. Spotted leopard pelts drape across a bed. The wool traps all the heat from the fire, as well as the heat of the volcanic rock the camp was built upon.

Gileon Wake brandishes that same broadsword he carried the last time we met, a sword that stands taller than him. "Don't come any closer," he shouts, his voice tight with fear. "Or I'll…" He gawks at Jadon. "Brother?"

The prince was already a small man before, but now he is a shadow. His armor hangs loose on his gaunt frame like an ill-fitting shell. The broadsword wavers in his hands, its weight clearly too much for him. His skin, once sun-kissed and healthy, now verges on sickly gray, with deep hollows beneath his cheekbones and dark shadows under his dull blue eyes. Even his stance is off-balance, his knees buckling slightly under the effort of standing. The man who once commanded legions now looks like he's fighting just to remain upright.

In two steps, I'm standing behind the emperor's youngest son. I yank the prince's sword from his hands and twist his right arm behind his back.

Gileon yelps, his pulse frantic beneath my fingers. Nonetheless, he tries for nonchalance. "Jadon, tell her to release me immediately. I can't talk if I'm being assaulted."

"You may not remember this," I say, "but you still owe me a couple of thousand bodies to make up for Veril Bairnell's death."

"Let me go," Gileon demands.

"You're the son of the emperor," I say, "and he's the circle in the middle of the colure. He's Supreme Manifest. Isn't that what you all have told the realm to believe? And if you're the son of Supreme, you should call upon your inherited godly powers and force me to release you. Go on. I'll wait, but I'm only gonna squeeze you harder."

"Kai," Jadon says, "we can't. He's…"

Family.

"Please?" Jadon adds.

"Now, *that's* a powerful word," I say, nodding but not relenting. "Before I let go…" I lean harder into Gileon and ask, "Where's Danar Rrivae?"

He growls, "I don't know—"

"I'm not fucking around." I tighten my grip on his arm, and Gileon yelps.

"He was at Castle Wake, but he's moved on," he gasps. "To where, I don't know."

I release the prince and peer down at him, slumped on the ground. "Do you wanna keep toying with me?"

"You don't know how to play our game, Ser Wake," Elyn adds, "and so you'll lose. Trust me when I say that cooperation works best in this instance."

"What is your father planning to do next?" I ask.

Gileon doesn't speak as he rubs his bony arm.

"Tell us," Elyn says, her voice hard.

Gileon snorts. "The nerve you have, demanding *anything* from me."

Elyn cocks her head. "Is that a 'no, I'm not telling you'?"

Even under duress, Gileon Wake still has the strong chin of a boastful man—and he's about to get it knocked off.

My stomach gurgles, and my mouth fills with spit. Philia's skin is taking on a green tinge. The effects of Jadon, of Miasma, in an enclosed space.

"I can't change what's happened, or this legacy of ours, but..." Jadon leans in closer to his brother. "Are you with us or against us?"

"Us?" Gileon points to Jadon and then at me. "You two are back together?" He grins. "Now how does *that* work?" He glances at Elyn. "Everyone who betrayed the Lady gets to fuck her over again?" He eyes Philia. "Oh, yeah. You betrayed her, too." To Separi. "I don't even know you, but I'm sure you haven't been as faithful as you should've been." His eyes settle on me again. "You *are* a merciful god."

Elyn's freckles darken. "Enough. Will you live or die today?"

Gileon's grin widens, but there is no humor there. "Unlike you, brother, I have no goddesses protecting me from Danar's threat. Even as you merely stand here in whatever protection they've placed upon you, I feel the threat of Miasma bleeding into my dying body." He adds, "Time is life, and I have no time left for anything but death."

Time is life. In my vision, Jadon had said those words, not Gileon.

"My slow death has been assured," Gileon continues. "A punishment from your true father for *my* betrayal. He is *not* merciful." He pulls down his collar to show us his neck. The skin there is a canvas of pink, purple, and black.

The smell of Wake's rotting flesh fills my nose and turns my stomach, adding to my nausea.

Jadon notices my smallest movement, and he scowls, stomping over to his brother.

Gileon doesn't cower away from the bigger man. "Do it," he whispers. "Feels like minnows are nibbling at me, killing me one tiny bite at a time. I open my eyes each morning with a delirious sadness that I've seen another dawn. I despair every night because I still live and will sleep again, but never the eternal sleep I desire.

"I've tried to end it with my own hand, but Danar Rrivae has kept me from that relief. No soldier will do as I command and run his blade across my neck. I've stood on a field with the most vicious otherworldly, beasts that wouldn't hesitate to rip a newborn from her mother's arms, and yet they walk past me as though I'm a rock or a tree, not even worthy of their notice."

"This..." Jadon turns to Elyn. "This sickness isn't me. This isn't Miasma."

"You're wrong, brother," Gileon says. "It's you. *All you.* You're changing." He gazes at me. "Lady, by the look of your skin...he's killing you, too."

"The signet ring," I demand, my throat tight.

"Gileon, where's Olivia?" Philia asks. "We have the book."

"Yes, I see it." He squints at my bag. "It shines."

I say nothing, but I burn with rage. At Philia. At Gileon. At myself.

"Why do you want it back?" Elyn asks. "I doubt you care that it belonged to your family."

Gileon shrugs. "It holds the answers to everything. There's unlimited power in those pages. Not that the *Librum* can save me, not anymore. I don't think anything—or anyone—can save me."

He smiles. "Is this merely another nightmare? Only one way to know." He lifts his softening hand—there, on his left finger, sits a silver band with a large blue jewel. He peers at Jadon. "Kill me and you will have the ring."

"Do it," Philia shouts at Jadon. "Or I will."

"You don't have to die today, brother," Jadon says, shaking his head. "We can fix it. Fix you. Be a family."

"It would be best for *you* to do it, as family," Gileon says to Jadon. He then frowns at Philia. "Miasma is supposed to end me, not some bitch with a borrowed bow."

He turns back to Jadon. "Here you stand, with the power to do one more thing for your little brother." He chuckles weakly. "Remember playing the hiding game with Mother? We didn't find her that last time..." His blue eyes, clouded in contemplation of certain death, now brighten with memories. "I miss her."

Jadon dips his head. "I miss her, too."

Beaminster is filled with broken people, including this man standing before me.

"Elyn..." I whisper.

"I know," she says, moving closer to me.

In two steps, Gileon slips behind Philia and holds a stiletto to her throat.

Philia is too startled to shriek, but her eyes bulge with fear as the tip of Gileon's sharp blade presses against her neck. Her mind twists and screams, *"Let me go! Olivia never loved you! I'd kill you if I could."*

"Where will I go after this, Adjudicator?" Gileon asks Elyn. "After I open my eyes, where will I be?"

"Gileon," Elyn says, "I'm not *your* judge. Your fate is not mine—"

"Tell me where I'm going!" Gileon shouts. "Or I will slit this bitch's throat. I have nothing to lose, and I can take this whore who stole my fiancée—"

Jadon thrusts his own dagger into Gileon's decaying neck.

Gileon's dead blood gurgles around Jadon's knife like sludge, rather than spurting like that of a vibrant man with a healthy heart. The prince's blue eyes brighten, grateful for his coming release. His mouth moves, but he can no longer speak.

Jadon catches his brother before he falls, kissing the dead man's cheek as he slowly lays Prince Gileon Wake onto the rug.

Philia lets out a sob and stumbles over to Separi.

"It's all right," the Renrian murmurs, holding the trembling young woman.

Elyn slips the ring off Gileon's finger. We all leave the tent, allowing Jadon his privacy as he mourns his brother alone.

Even this rotten air is healthier than the air in the tent. Elyn and Separi tend to Philia and me. Both of us are weak from our prolonged exposure to Jadon.

"We can't take that long again," Elyn whispers.

The signet ring will unlock WISDOM from the *Librum Esoterica*. *It holds the answers to everything.* Gileon Wake said that. Searching for those answers, though, will take me an age and—

"I'll read the *Librum* as quickly as I can," Elyn says, catching my thoughts.

Jadon, gray-faced, pushes aside the tent flaps and steps out into the light.

I want to hold his hands and bring them to my own heart, but he'd take my heart—and my life with it. He's taken so much already.

24

Separi's not fucking around.

"You could've endangered everyone in that tent," she shouts at Philia. "What if they didn't want him to know they had the *Librum*—?"

"But he already *knew*," Philia retorts. "You're being a—"

Separi's lavender eyes narrow. "Take care what you say next, young miss."

Elyn and I jam our lips together. We'll let Separi go off because she's right.

"I'm not some *young miss*," Philia murmurs.

"You're still talking?" Separi snaps back. "I may choose peace most of the time, but you continue and I'll…" Her lips twist, but no words escape them. Her anger renders her speechless.

"Philia," Jadon says, "know when to talk and know when to shut up. Now's the time to shut up. Gileon would've taken the *Librum* and done who knows what with it. Just like he held a blade to your throat and forced my hand."

"But no one knew that was going to happen," Philia protests.

"I knew," I say.

"Me, too," Elyn adds.

"We all knew, Philia," Jadon says, "and now Gileon is dead. Anyway…" He points to the dip in the land ahead. "Olivia's down there."

He leads us to an underground warren guarded by two dead soldiers. Elyn gently relocates the men with puffs of wind.

The entrance is a jagged wound in the earth, its edges lined with splintered wood and rusted metal spikes. The smell wafting from this opening is worse than the camp above—thick, cloying, and sickly sweet.

I glance back at the campground, at its decaying tents and shambling soldiers, and dread floods my heart. If this is what Wake's men endured beneath the daystar, what horrors must the prisoners face in the darkness below?

You're changing. That's what Gileon told Jadon. But how? Is the power he carries growing stronger? Does the wind carry it like pollen, allowing it to take root in a land far away? Or is Jadon diminishing like I am?

Elyn won't let anyone touch the heavy bar that keeps the doors to the prison closed. Since she's not of Vallendor, nothing, not even the death coating this place, affects her. But even she doesn't want to put her hands on that rail—something slick and oily has seeped into the wood. Instead, she uses wind to lift the bar, tossing it into the fire that continues to burn down Beaminster.

The doors swing open and…

"Sweet Supreme." Philia slams her hand over her nose.

The jail reeks of rat droppings, human waste and rotting flesh, rank water and vomit. All of it makes my eyes water. Skeletons and decaying bodies crowd every cell we pass. Unlike the jail at the abbey, torches and oil lamps burn bright.

As we descend the uneven stone steps, the air grows colder and heavier. The slick walls are streaked with dark stains.

"How can anyone survive down here?" Philia's voice quavers as she peers into the gloom.

No one answers her question. No one wants to open their mouth.

The tunnel widens as we reach the main chamber. Iron cages are stacked against the walls, many of them bent and broken, their bars crusted with rust and dried blood. The prisoners inside the cells are skeletal and covered with sores, their hollowed eyes barely blinking as we pass.

Who *are* these poor souls? What have they done to be locked up and forgotten down here? Jadon might think my questions are rhetorical, but no, I want to know. Did they murder entire families? Did they burn down holy places with worshippers still inside?

We continue to walk the long corridors in silence, passing a few open cell doors. Did some of the prisoners get to leave before the worst happened?

The few living prisoners look up as we pass them. One man, his face grimy, his eyes hidden behind scraggly hair, whispers, "Celestial, help me." His amber-shine could light a meadow on the darkest night.

I step into his cell and crouch before him. His name feathers into my mind.

"Divine," he murmurs. He tries to bow his head, but his pain is a constellation of yellow sparks. He bears the pain of seven men.

"Be at rest, Ebelar," I whisper.

He closes his eyes, and a breath slips from his parched lips.

Behind me, Philia whispers, "Is he dead?"

Separi shushes her.

This place is evil.

No one complains any time I stop at a cell. No one hurries me as I say the doomed one's name—Scorsca, Thilos, Nenji, Igal—and end their pain.

At one point, Elyn stands behind me and touches my shoulder. That healing sensation crawls from where Elyn touches me, across my shoulders, arms, and back. "You grow weaker each time you do this," she whispers. "Remember what's happening to you. My help is less effective each time…"

My eyes fill with tears, but not from the stench. "I know. And thank you."

She squeezes my shoulder one last time before she lets go.

We reach the last cell, and the iron door is still locked. It's occupied by a young woman with a gaunt, dirty face and big blue eyes. A once-beautiful dress, now tattered, clings to her thin, amber-glowing frame.

The fabric used to be a deep, shimmering sapphire, but none of that color remains, stained as it is with grime and streaks of dried blood. It hangs limply from her shoulders and hips. The skirt is shredded, the hem caked with mud.

I imagine that, once upon a time back in Maford, she'd danced around her sitting room, her voice proud and playful as she named this dress DECADENT or OCEANSIDE.

Now, this young woman gapes at me from the floor. Her expression slips from surprise and joy to fear as she remembers all that she did to me.

With only a thought, Elyn opens the door.

Jadon rushes past the Adjudicator and into the cell. "Livvy." He pulls his adopted sister into his arms.

Olivia's glow slips into a shade of brown.

"Jadon, no," Elyn says.

He releases her and scrambles to the other side of the cell. But knowing that he's Miasma, that he's just lessened the length of her days, does not temper Jadon's joy at finding Olivia.

Philia enters the cell, her eyes bright with tears. "Livvy?" She kneels in front of her beloved and touches her cheek. Bursts of purple light flash from both young women.

Olivia croaks, "Phily?"

Philia and Olivia crash into each other like the softest waves against a lakeshore.

Phily swipes tears from Olivia's grimy face. "I love you so much."

"I must look frightful," Olivia says.

Philia giggles. "You may not see them, but…" Her smile dims. "I have so many scars now. Big, ugly ones. I've been fighting to get to you, and… I fought a burnu!" She shakes her head, unable to speak, embarrassment now coloring her cheeks.

Olivia tries to smile but looks to Jadon. "What about Gileon?"

Jadon shakes his head and looks away.

"What have you decided?" Elyn whispers to me. "Mercy or…?"

I grind my teeth as my heart rises up against my anger. The Adjudicator waits in silence as I agonize over what to do about

Olivia Corby.

"Life," I whisper, finally.

Elyn nods and places her hand on the small of my back, since my decision means extending more of me for her to live. Then she says, "Olivia, we need to go."

Olivia shuffles over to me, her cheeks red, her head bowed. After I touch the top of her head, after her glow shifts from brown to blue, she whispers, "I'm so sorry, Kai. I never thought… I'd hoped…" She manages to look up at me and offers an earnest smile.

I don't return it. I want to break her neck, or at least her hand. Sure, I've healed her, but I can still take a little of that gift back. I'm still angry, and the ground rumbles beneath us. The bones of the dead rattle like pebbles in an empty cup.

"Lady," Separi whispers.

"Kai," Elyn warns.

But I'm not the first one to spit angry words.

"Do you know how much we all risked looking for you?" Jadon asks, his joy soured.

Olivia nods. "I *do* know, and I can never—"

"That's right," I interrupt. "You can never repay any of us. You can never make amends, nor repair what's been broken. And you did all of this because you're greedy. How much time did I waste chasing you across the realm? Veril died because of you."

I touch my fingers to my vibrating amulet. "You can't steal from others and think that your theft is harmless just because no one's bleeding. And you can't decide that because you've been hurt, you have the right to hurt someone else."

Olivia lowers her head.

"Look at me," I shout.

Somewhere, a wooden beam cracks and stones fall to the ground.

Olivia looks up at me.

"I only came here because *she*"—I point to Philia—"asked me to, because I promised *her* that I would. Your decisions have cost lives. I've granted you life so that you may learn and do better. However…" I bend down until Olivia and I are nose to nose. "Touch something of someone else's again and I'll see that you regret it. Now, *that* is a promise to you that I certainly won't forget. Do you understand me?"

Olivia whispers, "Yes."

We return to the surface, to smoke and thick ash that stings our eyes. Shadows dance across the charred landscape as fires burn everywhere. In the distance, we hear the howls of bloodhounds anxious about the encroaching flames—and that's where we head.

Daisy wags her tail to see us again, and so do her brothers.

"You came back for us!"

"It smells absolutely awful!"

"I told you that I'd be back," I say to the hounds.

They howl, sniff my legs, and lick my hands.

Now, Elyn has questions for Olivia. "Why did you take the book?"

Olivia shrugs. "Because it looked expensive. Like I could get a lot of geld for it."

"Did you ever hear Gileon or his father talk about the book?" she asks.

Olivia shakes her head. "Not once."

We all peer at Jadon.

He shakes his head, too. "It was always just a book."

Philia and Olivia decide to return to Caburh with Separi.

"We can do glasswork and tailoring there." Philia blushes and grins at the Renrian. "That is, if we're welcomed."

Separi squints at the couple. "Will you listen to counsel? Not insist on forcing your way and forcing Caburh to be what *you* want?"

The young women nod and say, "Yes, ma'am."

Philia clasps Olivia's hand. "We've learned a lot out here. I think… I think we're ready to do things differently this time."

Olivia kisses Philia's hand and says, "We'll earn all of your trust back, Kai, Separi. Promise."

Separi studies the two women for a long moment, her expression vague. Finally, she exhales and nods.

Philia releases Olivia's hand and comes over to hug me. "Promise me that you'll visit."

I roll my eyes, pretending to be annoyed, pretending that her hug doesn't hurt my skin. "Another promise, Philia?"

Her face shines with love and devotion. *"Promise."*

I smile. "Fine. I promise to visit."

Satisfied, she closes her eyes. She bows, then slips onto her knees and folds her hands at her lips. *"Oh, Guardian, gentle Lady of the Verdant Realm, hear the humble plea…"*

Watching this young woman grow is almost worth the journey. I touch the top of Philia's head as she prays, my heart full of her love and the love I now have for her. She's grown from a thief, conspirator, and petulant girl into a fierce, devout warrior. Once she's finished praying, I pronounce, "You will live a long life of joy, Philia Wysor." I shift my gaze to Olivia. "Do better and perhaps you will, too."

Separi takes my hands. "The threat in Caburh. Seven dawns are left."

I nod. "And I'll check in on the eighth." I turn to Elyn. "Are they strong enough to…?"

Worry flashes across Elyn's face.

I wince. "We don't have a lot of time," I say.

Elyn's expression doesn't change even though she acquiesces.

"Ridget and I and the others," Separi says, "we'll make sure they heal."

Before they leave, I let the bloodhounds slobber all over me again. I laugh and say, "I love you, too." Daisy and her brothers will live long lives until they're ready to cross over their own bridge.

"Before you go…" I place a hand on Separi's shoulder. "We *will* need you and your kin to fight with us."

The Renrian nods. "I'll go and prepare them for your call. All of the Vallendor Renrians will do as you ask, Lady. Here—" She takes a scrap of clean gauze from her bag, sprinkles droplets of a pink tonic onto the cotton, and presses it against my still-bleeding cheek.

"That woman-fighter back in town," I say, feeling the medicine's sting. "Can you believe she cut me?"

"How did you reward her success?" Separi asks.

"I told her 'good job,' then drove my blade through her face," I say.

Separi replaces her hand over the bandage with my own. "The cut should be better by dusk."

"You've been a great help to me these last days," I tell her.

She nods, but she doesn't smile. "Gileon Wake… That man sat in my inn and yet, moments ago, he didn't even remember my face."

Nothing I can say will take away the sting she feels—everyone wants to be remembered. Still, I say, "You and your kin are the stewards of Vallendor's story. Take up your pen and pay him back that way." I hug the Renrian and add, "I'll always remember you—hopefully, I will never have to wander the realm without my memories again."

Elyn calls my name.

Separi hands me the last vials of tonics that she'd prepared for this trip.

Elyn says, "It will be a treacherous battle, Separi."

The Renrian dips her head in acknowledgment. "But the traitor must be destroyed. If there's a war that requires sacrifice, it's this war. Our forebears, the Onama, didn't help evolve the realms only for Danar Rrivae to destroy them." She bows to Elyn one last time and says, "Just as we were there in the beginning, we'll be there to erase the threat at its end."

Philia, Olivia, Separi, and the bloodhounds gather around the Adjudicator. The cardinals flit around the group. In a blink, they are gone.

Jadon stands several paces away from me, his shoulders slumped. His loss is still fresh.

I say, "Hey."

He looks up with hope in his gaze.

Before I can say anything else, though, Elyn and her sentinels are back.

"That took forever," I say.

"I'm slowing down in my old age," Elyn says, pretending to wince as she rotates her shoulder. "Are we ready?" She looks over at Jadon.

"Back to the abbey?" he asks.

Elyn nods, but before we get underway, she turns back to me. "You told Olivia that your search for her distracted you. But dealing with her, wandering Vallendor, fighting, losing, and loving—all that has only galvanized your purpose. You're becoming the mountain this realm deserves."

25

Elyn dares to smile at me.

I dare to smile back.

In my heart, we dance down that long catherite corridor of the Abbey of Mount Devour. But we temper our joy right now because all my limbs ache, because Danar Rrivae knows that the *Librum Esoterica* is now at the abbey. We hold in our joy because Jadon just killed his brother—and because Jadon is death and can also die. *Snip your string, puppet.* That was the Devourer's threat.

At least, I'm not trailing blood like I did the last time I walked this corridor. Small mercies abound.

The silence in the aerie feels heavy and still. Agon the Kindness stands at the narrow window, his red robes spotless and bright. He isn't looking out upon the realm but rather reads a massive book.

"Look who's back," I shout.

Uncle Agon looks over his shoulder. His expression remains unreadable upon seeing Elyn and me—his only reaction is the tightening of his hands around the book.

"What's wrong?" Elyn places Wake's ring and the *Librum Esoterica* on a worktable.

"He thought we were gonna kill each other," I say, smirking at Agon. "Admit it, Uncle. You thought only one of us would make it back to this room, huh?" I chuckle and add, "Guess what, Uncle? I can now leap a tall building in a single bound."

Agon gives me a small shrug. "You used to be able to *fly*."

My head snaps back like he's punched me in the throat.

Why can't this man just be *nice* to me?

He closes the book he holds with a snap. "And the Weapon?"

"Should be here any moment," Elyn says, squeezing my elbow, encouraging me to keep calm and to mind my mouth. "He did as he promised. Thank you for placing your trust in me."

I focus on taking regular breaths. Really: why couldn't he just say, "That's great, Kai," or "I'm glad you're coming back into yourself, niece"?

The door opens, and five Raqiel sentinels the size of ancient oaks march into the room, their sharp-ended staves reflecting the light. Jadon is swaddled in a strifalite-threaded jacket that restricts his hands and cuffs that restrict his feet. He hobbles between two guards and looks at me with dulled eyes but manages a quick, hopeful grin.

This will work. He will be freed. I will have one more ally in this fight.

Agon shuffles over to a worktable and a metal instrument producing flame. He picks up the ring with a pair of pliers and holds it over the fire until the gem sags and melts like shiny blue ice. *Plop...plop...plop*. The melted gem turns the flame bluer and hotter.

I whisper to Elyn, "Is that supposed to happen?"

Agon keeps the ring over that flame until only the silver band remains. The inset that held the blue gem has uneven edges that resemble the teeth of a key. Agon peers at the leather and jeweled cover of the *Librum Esoterica*, squinting closely at the purple-blue-silver jewel in the middle of the book. He presses the ring's empty inset against the face of that center gem. Bright light erupts in between the stones and...with a *pop*, the purple-blue-silver jewel snaps out of the book's cover.

My eyes widen.

Jadon gasps.

Elyn whispers, "Wow."

Agon positions the gem in the worktable's clamps and tightens the screws.

The gem emits a high-pitched squeak—like a bolt or a wheel in need of grease. The sound pierces the room.

We all shudder.

The gem made that same sound in Fihel as lavender fire consumed it. Was it in pain? Angry? This can't be just a jewel.

"Celedan Docci awakens," Agon whispers, "and he knows that his end has come."

I lean closer for a better view. I glimpse a faint silhouette no bigger than a mosquito, lost in the vibrant color.

The tiny god—Keeper of Knowledge—pulses with light, and his delicate and translucent wings flutter in rapid bursts. The energy that emanates from him is strong and heavy. He twists, curling in the confines of his jeweled prison. His tiny face is a blur, and his voice a faint whisper in my ear. "I rhuirn lud fa hasa." *I should not be here.* "I rhuirn lud fa fuiln." *I should not be bound.*

I frown and reply, "I cac' arlnmassa iya'au homo." *I didn't imprison you here.* "You went willingly." Celedan Docci had been eager to provide wisdom and knowledge to Syrus Wake. For more than fifty seasons, Celedan shared with the young king all that should be known to mortals…but then, he began telling Wake more than he should've.

Like all men, Wake craved more: more power, more land, more knowledge.

With his own desire to remain revered, Celedan Docci taught Wake the prayer that hastened Danar Rrivae to Vallendor. Danar hadn't previously read any of the *Librum Esotericas* on *any* realm he'd stolen, but this time, he read Wake's. That's when he learned the secrets of breeding animals and—with the Keeper of Knowledge fueled by his own twisted ego—learned the secrets of mating with mortals to create…

I glance over at Jadon.

Syrus Wake then turned to Danar Rrivae for wisdom and power instead of Celedan Docci and the *Librum Esoterica*, and both god and book were tucked away in a dusty library down in Castle Wake.

The answers to the realm still exist in this ever-growing book. Elyn's Onama forebears ensured that Onama learnings were automatically added to pages of already-acquired knowledge within the *Librum Esotericas*. From how to properly summon a dragon on Realm Sadaadea and coralopes on the realm Exalter to how to restore worlds like Vallendor.

Now, Jadon shakes his head. "I've read this book all my life, and then I read it again after Olivia took it. I don't remember seeing formulas for otherworldly or lists of special words. I remember bedtime stories and fairy tales, including an awful one about this hairy giant who we all thought…"

Was Kai. Yeah. The tale of Inocri and the two asshole kids that harassed her and forced her into servitude if she wanted to live.

"That's what Celedan *wanted* you to read," Agon says. "Remember: he is a Keeper of Knowledge, after all."

"And now," Elyn says, "this keeper of knowledge must pay for his treason."

Celedan Docci still struggles within the clamped stone, and the heat of his hate still rolls over me. "Yui heya fadseirran na, Lenirr." *You have betrayed me, Lady.*

I take a step back and say, "No—*you* betrayed *me*, Keeper."

Agon tightens the clamps again, then says, "Adjudicator?"

Standing beside Agon, Elyn glares down at the tiny god and lifts her chin. "I am Elyn Fynal. As Grand Adjudicator of Vallendor and the Nine Realms, Sentinel and Divine Mediator, with the approval of the Council of High Orders and the blessing of Agon Laserie the Kindness and Grand Wisdom of Vallendor, I sentence you, Celedan Docci, Keeper of Knowledge, to death."

Celedan Docci shrieks. "Yuis rewr esa naelai lrrarr. Yui err wairr naia." *Your laws are meaningless. You all will die.*

Agon grabs a mallet with a head made of linionium. Without

ceremony, he brings the mallet down upon the jeweled home of Celedan Docci.

A fracture corkscrews across the gem's body.

Agon brings the mallet down.

Celedan Docci cries out again as the jewel cracks into jagged halves.

Agon strikes a third time.

The gem—and the Keeper of Knowledge within it—shatter into powder.

We hold our breaths, our eyes locked on the glittering surface of the worktable, waiting for something—*anything*—to happen. The silence stretches on…

But nothing happens on that worktable surface.

Finally, Agon whispers, "Iasca'o." *It is done.*

Behind us, Jadon makes a gagging sound and collapses between the guards.

Elyn whispers, "Shit," and retreats to tend to her prisoner.

Agon and I remain standing at the table, watching the powder that was once Celedan Docci dissolve… We wait there until there's nothing left. Only then do we both release our breaths and sag against the worktable. Exhausted, Agon smiles and nods at me. "Well done." He glances down at Jadon, but I can't look away from my uncle yet. His smile and his approval make my eyes cloud with tears. *Well done.*

Jadon, the Weapon, still sits on the floor. His skin, now flushed from his ears to his neck, turns from pale gray to healthy bronze. He lifts his head, his eyes swirling with color and slowly settling to become lavender. He peers down at his right hand, and the marking there—the elements, each in their own circle—fades. He dares to smile as his connection to his traitor-father becomes a mere memory.

With the guards' help, Jadon rises to his feet like a man coming out of a drunken stupor.

I walk over to him and stand closer than I have since our night together at the Broken Hammer. I experience no rolling nausea, no buckling knees, not even a headache.

"Do I make you sick?" he asks, his voice hoarse.

"Because you're annoying or because you're the son of the traitor?" I ask.

"Both."

I laugh. "It's almost the end of the world, but I feel fine."

We've overcome so many obstacles. Stepped over so many bodies. Said goodbye to too many friends. But now…

I'm glad that Supreme didn't just end me with one grand punishment.

Jadon is mine, this time for good.

Elyn and I retreat into our separate bedrooms.

I shudder as I strip out of my pewter armor, trying to avoid my reflection in the mirror. Even with just a quick glimpse, I see that my body is a quilt of different skin tones and textures. If I dared to look any longer, I'd never leave this chamber again. But I have work to do—work that doesn't require smooth, even-toned skin.

Fuck that—I miss my smooth, even-toned skin.

The warm bathwater melts my tension and aches, and soon, I can't tell dirty water from flakes of my skin. After gently toweling off and applying that aloe-vera-like gel and kastat rose–scented oil to stave off further deterioration, I pull on a simple black tunic and black suede breeches. The soft fabrics soothe my skin…and my ego.

Elyn meets me in the corridor, flawless and graceful as ever in her dove-gray tunic and breeches. "How are you feeling?" she asks.

"I'm not hurting as much as before but…" I motion to my face and hold out my peeling hands. "The diminishing continues." I let out a shaky breath and add, "I have something for you." I grab my scabbard from the trunk and pull Justice from her place beside Fury. "You've earned her back."

Elyn gapes at me, then at the perfect silver sword. Her eyes fill with tears that match the glistening of that silvery-blue blade. "But you won her from me."

"I did win her," I say. "Did I say that I'd never remind you that I won her?" I pause, then add, "I *will* remind you. So take it. Please."

She swallows, her chin trembling as she takes Justice from my hands. She whispers, "Thank you," and studies the engravings on the blade. *Arbiter. Judge. Truth. Mediator. Justice. Life. Death.*

Elyn and I take our time walking back to the aerie, relishing the comfort and calm we haven't experienced together over the last several seasons. Laughter—about nothing at all—bubbles up between us, and we're again moments away from linking arms.

The Raqiel guards had taken Jadon to bathe, and he now stands in the aerie, clean and unsure of his station here. His long, disheveled hair has been cut and combed, and his face is grime- and whisker-free. He wears a simple blue tunic, breeches, and boots. Despite the unremarkable clothing, his stance has also softened. His eyes are hooded, and he shoves his hands into his pockets. He looks...*relaxed* now, like he rules the realm but doesn't allow it to consume him.

Agon tells us that he'll search the *Librum Esoterica*, now stationed upon a wooden block in the Abbey, for the words that will kill those resurrectors.

"I was planning to read it myself," Elyn says, starting to flip through those thick pages.

"You have greater tasks to complete," Agon says. "Time hasn't stopped for us."

Though he stands in this aerie, relaxed and open, Jadon Wake Rrivae is still the enemy, the Weapon, the son who'd worked—*forced or not*—beside his father, the traitor, to destroy Vallendor—and to kill me.

"He must remain imprisoned," Agon declares, dousing our early celebration with this sobering truth.

As the tattoo on Jadon's hand continues to fade, there's nothing we can do about the blood that still flows through him as Danar Rrivae's son.

Are his other tattoos also fading? I'd kissed the irregular rectangle on the left side of his chest, and I'd licked the script that runs along his ribcage. *With death comes life*. Will he be free of them, too?

I ponder this as Jadon and I follow Elyn and the Raqiel down the stairs and back to the Abbey's dungeons.

"I've wanted to ask you," Jadon says now. "Back at Beaminster, down in those jail cells. How did you know all the names of the prisoners?"

I shrug. "It's my job."

When I don't say more, he offers a thoughtful, "Hmm."

I want to ask him about Beaminster's jail, too.

What role did he play in building it? What role did he play in keeping it open? Did he ever imprison someone in that dank, awful place? If so, how could he be that cruel?

Those questions sit on my tongue, ready to emerge. I clamp my lips together, though; I'm not ready to hear his answers. Not right now. Instead, I ask, "Do you feel any different?"

Jadon squints at me. "That will be up to you. You make me feel all kinds of ways, Kai."

"I'm not at my...*most delectable* right now," I say, remembering my patchwork reflection in the mirror.

"If you say so," he says, smirking.

The dungeon's darkness slows our walk until Elyn and the guards become the light that guides our steps. At least it doesn't stink in this jail. At least there aren't rotting bodies or suffering prisoners here. Compared to the jail in Beaminster, this prison in the depths of Mount Devour might as well be a fancy inn.

Finally, we come to the end of the corridor, and the Raqiel opens the cell door. Jadon's stacks of books and quilts have remained in their place.

"Sorry about this," Elyn says as Jadon enters his cell.

"I understand," Jadon says. "This is a sacred space of order and power, and you can't have a diseased weapon running amok among the better gods."

Elyn says, "Yeah. Something like that."

I whisper to her, "Can you give us a moment?"

"A *moment*? You fought giants and soldiers, wolves and bear-men, and you're asking for only *a moment*? Is that how you reward your success?"

"Okay," I say. "Several moments."

"But you can't stay down here," she says, wagging her finger at me. "So don't even ask."

I smirk and spread my arms. "Does this look like a place I'd beg to stay?"

Elyn rolls her eyes.

I cock an eyebrow. "Don't you have a god you want to see before Selenova rises full and we all die trying to save Vallendor?"

Elyn's freckles swirl across her flushed face. "Not really."

"I saw What's His Face from Astes up in the sitting room," I say.

She wrinkles her nose. "He smells like Separi's chewed licorice root."

I wrinkle my nose in sympathy. "What about Calyx? He looks good. Well-rested..."

She tilts her head. "This *could* be the end of Vallendor, huh?"

"In the most awful way," I say, stepping into Jadon's cell. "Consider it while you can."

Elyn closes the door. "I'll leave some of the lights on." She grins, waves a hand, and three bulbs of flame materialize in the air.

"Actually..." I grimace and shake my head.

She sighs and dims two of the lights.

My moth amulet rebukes my desire to hide in the dark and conjures its own golden glow.

Jadon and I stand there, listening to the footfalls of the Adjudicator and her guards... Once I can only hear our own breathing, I say, "Hey."

He leans against the wall and crosses his arms, his eyes glinting. "Hey."

I step over to him.

His arms snake around my waist. "You're beautiful to me, okay? In every way."

I press against him and smile as he hardens beneath me.

"You don't believe me?" he asks.

"I don't want to think about that right now."

"Several moments" isn't a lot of time, especially with all that I want us to do to each other. So we need to take the quickest routes to those destinations.

Both tattoos are right where I left them, and I lick each. "I'm *back.*" I look up to Jadon and purr, "When we make it through this, I'm gonna bring *you* to your knees."

"That a promise?" he asks.

"A promise and your dream come true," I say. "Because, as you can see, I'm a merciful god."

He stares at my lips before bending to kiss me. "Make my sword stronger than ever," he whispers, "and let me fight beside you for all time. Gift me with unmatched strength, and I'll write songs about you."

"Is that your prayer?" I ask, nibbling his lips.

"Mmhmm."

"Done."

He plants kisses along my shoulder blade.

I lose my right hand in his hair as my left hand pushes down his breeches. His breath, hot and urgent, warms my skin as his nose nudges beneath my tunic. Our lazy urgency makes me breathless, and I close my eyes as I guide his hand to that place on me where it needs to be.

He lifts me up, and now I'm against the wall, and he's strong enough to hold me, and I'm free enough to push down my own pants, and we're agile enough to bend and twist until he's inside of me. And after a moment, I don't even mind that my back scrapes the wall—the rhythm of our fucking adds to my pain, and I whisper words into his ear that make him move faster, faster…

He fills me with breathtaking colors, and gasps fall from my lips in between my moans and encouragement.

Yes, he pulls my hair.

I bite his lower lip because he likes it, and yeah, I like that, too.

We sink to the bed because this wall has become the size of a moth's wings as we love each other down. And I keep my eyes open as he brushes a teardrop rolling down my cheek, and I lock my arms tight around his neck because I never want to forget the way I feel right now beneath all this hurt, beneath all my decay.

And I ride and he pulls and we bite and our breathing quickens, he whispers, "Fuck," and I whisper, "Ost." I move quicker, spurred by his mortal curse and my Mera one, and I'm trembling and ready as he presses deeper and…

The world turns bright, and I cry out and lose my breath, and he groans and shivers and we clench each other, so neither falls onto this hard, cold ground. We rub our noses together, and I keep my eyes open to study his face.

We hear the guards' steps and kiss each other good night. This may well be the last time.

It's like we've discovered a new realm. Maybe after we save Vallendor, we'll settle that new realm, Jadon and me. Yes, if I become whole again, if his own change finally comes, that's what we'll do.

We have seven dawns left.

26

Uncle Agon stands at the aerie's lone window flanked by two Raqiel sentinels, all watching as I tumble down, falling through clouds, breaking through the gauzy film that separates the Abbey of Mount Devour from Vallendor…

I close my eyes and pull myself into a tight ball. But my eyelids don't block the thrumming glare of the daystar.

My visits to the abbey and to the realm Linione weren't supposed to be this way. I was supposed to be bathed, fed, outfitted with new gear. My father was supposed to hold out his arms, and I was supposed to run to him, and we were supposed to cry—from the anguish of my situation, from the joy of our reunion.

He was supposed to help me beat the One. He was supposed to love me.

Someone, finally, was supposed to love me.

But Father betrayed me, just like everyone else betrayed me.

The Council of High Orders.

My uncle.

Elyn.

Vallendor.

Supreme.

I'm alone. Again.

I'm falling, and I don't know how to stop. Somewhere down there is the bottom, fast approaching. Fear pumps through me like water. I'm speeding up, my descent uncontrollable. There's no one to stop me, no one to help me. I'm alone.

They told me that I was too quick to act, too quick to judge, too impatient to make the best decisions, that I needed to consider the consequences more carefully…

But Vallendor still exists.

I am *not* the One.

Their anger at what I've decided, in what I've accomplished, of who I am, is a weight on my chest in this freefall, pressing down on me so that my undoing comes faster.

I was told I was strong, smart, and powerful, but I've been condemned for being strong, smart, and powerful, and that's why I'm falling now. Ultimately, on *my* end, no one, not Agon, not my father, not Supreme, truly wanted me to succeed.

I was meant to fail. It was my destiny to fail. They knew I would fail. I was lured here to complete my failure.

Is this really happening?

No one slows my descent.

No one will catch me.

I'm not meant to survive.

A whirlwind of my own spite and my own hatred consumes me, and I can barely breathe. I see nothing now but shades of red and black. The vision of my body smeared across Vallendor burns in my vision, and I shout, *"No!"* I twist upright, my feet and legs ready for this collision. I will not die. I will not break like a brittle plate or crumble like stale bread against the realm's pantry floor.

I no longer fear hitting the bottom. No, I *welcome* the impact. I *dare* this earth to claim me. The rocks and trees of Vallendor should fear their *own* doom if they fail to protect me.

A smile crackles across my face as I squint at the ground racing up to meet me and—

BOOM!

The world explodes around me. Boulders break apart, and solid ground is hollowed in one big crater. Full-grown trees come crashing down, no longer high and mighty. New rocks and logs, dirt and splinters rain down from the sky, but none of it vexes me, not one piece of gravel, not one clump of turf, not one mote of dust.

Nature knows I am the Lady of the Verdant Realm.

Welcome to my world—

I'm pulled from sleep, from that dream of…

There's no turning back.

What's that?

A dull roar vibrates through my bedroom. I sit up in bed and look to the narrow window bright with moonlight, to the chaise lounge lined with crimson-and-gold pillows, to my clothes and armor folded atop the chest at the foot of the bed. My back still aches.

Someone pounds on my bedroom door, which bursts open.

Elyn, in her tunic and breeches, stands there with mussed hair, backlit by torchlight. "Are you okay?" she asks.

Behind her, Raqiel guards shuffle along the corridor.

"Yeah," I say, throwing off the quilt. "Did something happen with you and Calyx?"

"Huh?" She frowns, caught off-guard by my question. "It's not that."

The worry on her face makes me hop out of bed.

"People are falling ill," she says, grabbing a breastplate from her guard's hands and buckling it on. "Something's invaded the abbey. Hurry up and get dressed."

Invaded the abbey?

That's impossible.

I pull on my clothes and turn so that Elyn can buckle my pewter breastplate. A small piece of the plate around my waist cracks and crumbles between her fingers.

I gape at the fracture and the disintegrating metal. "Why is my armor…?"

She dusts off her hands and says, "No time, Kai! We need to go."

I hear fear—in her voice, in the footsteps of those running down the hallway. And I hear something new: moaning and crying. I grab my scabbard, and the leather holder feels loose.

Elyn and I make our way through the abbey's hallways. Columns of Raqiel guards hurry in every direction. Senators still wearing their nightclothes poke their heads from their own chambers or collapse in the doorway, their eyes gunky or filled with blood.

"Who's invading?" I ask. "Who are we fighting?"

"This invader wields no blade," Elyn says.

I can't believe her, with the shrieks in the air… Only otherworldly can bring about this sort of terror. I still draw my sword, convinced that a ram-headed sunabi or a bear-man aburan might roam the halls of the abbey, striking down the gods of the Aetherium.

But there is no blood on the guards' spears and swords. Nor are there gory remains left by a gerammoc or a burnu.

There's blood, though, shining bright on the tile floors, and it's the super-red-blue blood of the gods.

We pass a man slumped against a door, his back arched in a final, agonizing spasm. We pass another woman twisted on the floor, her tongue clenched tightly between her teeth, her bulging eyes wide open.

The Abbey is becoming a tomb.

"What's happening?" I ask Elyn.

Before she can respond, a woman staggers from door to door, coughing and gurgling. She wears a mauve gown that gathers and separates like trousers. She coughs once more before collapsing at my feet. Her copper skin looks pale, her face tight like she's struggling to breathe. It's Nimith, the steward who led me to the aerie just days ago. She gapes at Elyn and me, her eyes filled with fear.

I reach for her.

Elyn shouts, *"Don't!"*

Nimith closes her eyes and becomes one more body we step over.

We reach the holding cells down in the bowels of the abbey.

"I've protected myself but…" Elyn grabs me right before we approach the first jail cell. She whispers, "In my name, be shielded now.

No plague or poison shall claim you." She touches my cheek.

A sheet of ice prickles across my face, down my neck, and spreads across my chest, arms, and legs. My moth's thorax glows and pulses like the light from Elyn's dove.

"We don't know," she says, her eyes bright with tears.

Fear.

My breath catches, and I whisper, "Thank you."

We creep past the jail cells, the light cast by the stewards like Nimith dancing across the cold, jagged walls. That glow twists and then disappears and is replaced by sickly blue light that doesn't come from Elyn.

I exhale—no cold clouds gather around my face. No, there's something else in the air, and even with Elyn's protective ward, it pushes at me like insistent smoke.

She and I exchange worried looks before she shouts, "Jadon Wake Rrivae."

Silence and then… "Yes?"

We exhale with relief—but it's short-lived.

He sounds…*bigger*, thicker, muddier.

Elyn and I forge ahead, stepping cautiously, hearts in our throats, as we near that strange watery light like a pond reflecting shadows in a cave.

Jadon sits behind locked bars, resting on the edge of his bed. He's the center of that underwater light, and his tunic and breeches look tight against his frame.

Is he *growing*?

"How do you feel?" I ask him.

He looks at us with dull eyes and lifts his right hand.

The tattoo there—those circles and the elements within them—has returned. Worse, that tattoo has spread to his wrist. That watery glow… it comes from his inked right hand.

Elyn steps back. "Oh, no."

My throat closes. "It didn't work."

Jadon shakes his head, and his dulled eyes glow brighter.

"We should return to Agon," she says.

"Don't leave," I tell Jadon. "We'll be back. I promise."

Elyn and I race past the dead and dying: Vepaz Sirhhen, senator from realm Oron, Sielel Bezal, senator from realm Reilaph. Idwant from...

The door to the aerie is open, and younger monks congregate around Agon. Barefoot, they wear simple green robes and cropped hair. They speak in hushed tones as their eyes dart between Agon and each other.

My uncle spots Elyn and me, and he shakes his head. "Even in death, Celedan Docci is more powerful than we imagined." The remains of the Keeper of Knowledge—silver dust again even though his body had completely dissolved—glow on the worktable, now surrounded by ten Raqiel guards.

"How is that possible?" Elyn asks. "We destroyed him."

Agon shakes his head.

"Jadon's marking," I say, lifting my hand. "Not only has it returned, it's spreading. And there are dead everywhere and..."

Agon's gray eyes brighten. His owl amulet pulses in time with my moth and Elyn's dove. Soon, a shimmer wraps around him and everyone in this aerie.

Fear.

"Until we understand what's happening here," my uncle says, "the Weapon needs to leave the abbey immediately. We have only six dawns left, and Danar's amulet must still be destroyed."

"Where are we supposed to take him?" Elyn asks.

"We'll figure that out," I say, already retreating out of the aerie.

"But the *Librum* may know," Elyn protests.

"There's no time left for study," I shout.

I still don't know how to kill the resurrectors. I still don't know how Danar Rrivae is creating these otherworldly, old and new. I don't know if destroying the traitor's amulet will have any effect or if any of us are meant to survive this.

"Go!" Agon shouts. "The Weapon must leave the abbey before everybody's killed. And if you *don't* remove him, we'll have to evacuate this realm. You understand what that means."

Losing protection from the orders means we lose this war. Losing this war means Danar Rrivae wins. Danar Rrivae winning means Vallendor as we know it is no more.

Back down in the dungeon, Elyn casts a ward around Jadon to contain the danger he presents. As we speed through the corridors, those closest to us fall to their knees, many taking their final breaths. We break into a run to escape this sacred space. We climb the seemingly interminable stairs and hurry across the sitting rooms now teeming with bodies in various states of living and dead. We rush through the chapels and anterooms and finally down that long hallway with the catherite floors. We burst out into the open air, and soon, Jadon, Elyn, and I find ourselves standing in that dell of blue flowers. No red cardinals join us—the Raqiel must stay and protect the Abbey.

Jadon sinks to his knees, the marking well past the bones of his wrist now. The blue flowers beneath him tremble before they wilt, and their vibrant color instantly drains to gray. The grass also recoils, browning and withering despite the shimmering protective shield encircling him.

I watch helplessly, knowing this is terribly wrong, scared that I can't stop the inevitable—but that I must.

Breathless, Elyn rests with her hands against her thighs. Her hair sticks to her sweaty neck and face.

The color of Jadon's eyes wavers from blue to lavender to translucent to blue to lavender to no color at all. "What do we do now?" he asks.

The slow roll of Miasma pushes past the shields Elyn and Agon set, making me woozy. To wait for the spell to pass, I rest my hands—

Shit.

Bruises shaped like dead flower petals speckle my hands. My knees ache and creak as I rest upon them.

I force myself to look away from my hands—right now, I'm more worried about vomiting than about those spreading bruises. But then I stare at the dell's dead blue flowers…

Vallendor is dying right beneath my feet.

Jadon says, "What do we—?"

"I don't know," Elyn shouts, her mouth twisted. "What do *you* think we should do? Or are you content with just sitting there, letting shit happen, waiting for Kai and me to do all the work? You get to go around destroying the realm while we come behind you, cleaning it up only for you to do it again."

"You think this is easy for me?" he shouts back. "Do you think I chose this path—?"

"Poor you," Elyn spits. "Will someone please think of poor Jadon Wake—"

I squeeze shut my eyes as the two bicker about what was supposed to work, why it didn't work, why this isn't his fault, why this *is* his fault. "Quiet," I finally shout. "Listen to me."

Both shut their mouths as the ground keeps trembling and those blue flowers keep springing to life only to die again.

My dream...

I'd been falling, headed toward my death until I righted myself.

"I don't have an answer but..." I place my bruised hands on my hips and limp over to the bluffs that overlook the valley and the Sea of Devour. "But I know someone who may."

PART III

LOST IN PARADISE

Celestial, your power bright,
You are the star in darkest night.
With gratitude, our voices raise
In song and praise, we sing your ways.

From ancient roots to futures blessed,
In your embrace, we find our rest.
To you, we offer all our days,
Our endless love, our timeless praise.

Celestial, your power bright,
You guide our ways, your eyes our sight.
Our songs of praise are only weeds
That pale compared to your great deeds.

We thank you for the pledge of life.
We praise you for your guard 'gainst strife.
We dance with joy for your great gift.
You bless us by your grace so swift.

Your voice commands the storms to still.
The mountains bend to your fierce will.
In every heart, your light remains
Through fire, floods, through endless rains.

–A Song of Praise written by Grace Hallum

27

This landscape looks utterly unfamiliar to me.

I don't recognize these dead blue firs scratching up from the parched earth to the early morning sky, nor the clumps of chaparral and sage clustered in this clearing. The sandy trail I walked last time to Malik Sindire's settlement? The dirt wasn't this orange. Even the path itself feels more brittle and crooked than it did days ago. The air is thick with dust, and something smells like it's burning. And even the horizon feels different. The hills look like they've shifted away from us, leaving gaps in their place.

None of this looks familiar, and not only due to the holes in my memory. No, Vallendor is falling apart every time I blink.

My chest feels tighter with every breath; time is twisting my insides as it's twisting the realm. Everything that I thought I knew about this province, and even about my own body, has changed since three dawns ago.

It is also possible that I'm just losing my mind.

With my hands on my hips, I try to orient myself, using the Temple of Celestial as a starting point. But I'm still lost.

"Why is it so *hot*?" Elyn asks, sagging onto a boulder. "It's still the early morning."

"Feels like we're sitting on the top of the daystar." Crouched, Jadon lowers his head, his sweaty hair now a limp curtain. "Feels like all the heat decided to come and live here."

"And you *like* this weather?" Elyn asks. She fidgets with the buckles on her breastplate, tempted to shuck her armor altogether.

I glare at them both. "Stop whining—it's a dry heat. It's usually not this arid or hot, but the world is dying, remember? So move the fuck on." Yes, the weather is weird, and my already-sensitive skin is broiling. By the end of the day, I'll look like a roasted pig.

"You sure this Malik's house is up here?" Jadon asks, sitting down against a boulder.

"No, I'm not sure," I admit. "This time, we came by Spryte instead of walking the trails, but that shouldn't matter." I turn again to the Temple of Celestial, but nothing rings true here.

"Maybe we should start where you walked from the last time," Jadon suggests.

"The Sanctum of the Dusky Hills." I bite my bottom lip, reluctant to start over on that path when we are already racing against time. Instead, I wander toward the cliff and peer out at the valley.

There's the bridge to enter the city. There's the canal that circles Gasho. There's the Howling Wolf Inn with the floor of crushed date pits. There's the grove of date palms.

Elyn comes to stand beside me and whispers, "There's something you're not telling us."

"Two problems. First: the Sanctum is the dwelling place of the gods," I whisper back. "No mortals may enter there—and if they try, they die."

Elyn glances back at Jadon. "He isn't completely immortal. Shit. Is that also true of the Yeaden's dwelling?"

"No idea, but at least I won't have to worry about the second problem."

"What's the second problem?"

"Zephar."

Elyn gasps as she realizes the danger of my old lover meeting my new lover, who is the son of two traitors, a deadly disease, the scion of a corrupt emperor, and a demigod whose very existence threatens the realm, which, by default, threatens me.

"Zephar may just kill Jadon on sight," Elyn says now.

"And while the thrill of two men fighting over me is kinda sexy," I say, "we can't allow Jadon to be harmed, at least not until..."

"We have Danar Rrivae's amulet." Elyn nods. "So you thought we could just pop up the mountain and find this Dindt's settlement without—"

"Having to risk our necks? Yes. Because he *is* of the Dindt order, which means he's explored other realms and he's observed life and will know more than what we know now."

"Can we at least find some shade?" Jadon complains from behind us.

Elyn studies my face. "Your skin... You need to..."

I sigh. "Yeah, I'm cooking."

Behind us, Jadon lifts his tunic to wipe his sweaty face. "How do people live in this oven? There's nothing here except sand and—"

"Nothing here?" I snap, marching over to him. "Before your fathers fucked everything up, *everything* was here."

"Kai," Elyn starts.

"Sweet-water rivers that made fertile land," I say, standing over him, "which meant abundant food, which meant abundant trade. Trade brought people and people brought new ideas. Writing and craftsmanship gave them poetry and mapmaking.

"And these people knew how to worship a god. They built that fabulous temple and those breathtaking gardens, and the daystar kissed their skin with love and colored them until their bodies said, 'Enough.'" I bend down until Jadon and I are eye to eye. "So...*nothing here*? These people, this land, is *everything*. *Everything* is here."

Jadon holds up his hands. "Sorry. Relax."

My skin fucking hurts, and I'm fucking lost. I won't be relaxing for a long time.

Elyn points out across the valley. "Look."

I follow the line of her finger.

A sandstorm. It looks like a living thing in the desert, dark and swirling, a chaotic mass of dust and grit blurring the horizon. It *is* a living thing.

Zephar and the Diminished are fighting otherworldly now.

I smile the tiniest smile. "Perfect." The nightstar hides behind a thick veil of swirling sand. I heave a sigh of relief. "Let's head to the

Sanctum. I'll be able to find Malik Sindire's dwelling from there."

Elyn smooths her unraveling braid. "So that solves one of our problems. What about...?" She looks back at Jadon.

Still overheated and miserable, he's now tucked his head between his knees. If Elyn and I leave him here alone, the heat and otherworldly will take him. If we bring him with us, the Sanctum itself may crush him.

I think for a moment, then say, "I know a place."

The smallest chamber in the Temple of Celestial is tucked away, not frequented by the priests or the Sisters of the Dusky Hills. Its narrow entrance is hidden behind a cluster of stone columns weathered by the passage of time and by sandstorms like the one now raging across the valley. The room smells of frankincense, and the only light comes from a single, flickering oil lamp. A dense film of dust covers the cool stone floor and the intricate carvings on the walls.

The space feels claustrophobic. A person is not meant to live here for long. Without windows, there is no sound from the outside world, just the steady drip of water from a hidden bath. In one corner sits a low stone platform draped with a thin, faded cloth. This ledge served an unknown purpose once upon a time. This chamber meets our current need: keeping Jadon safe from being killed by otherworldly or by Zephar.

Ancress Tisen and the Sisters of the Dusky Hills quickly tidy up the space, leaving behind gifts for Jadon once they finish: clean tunics and loose pants, wine, soft towels and scented soaps and oils for a dip in that hidden bath. Once a prince, always a prince.

Elyn wanders around the chamber, worry in her eyes. "Last time we left him in the abbey's dungeons," she says, "gods perished, and he's changed even since then."

The markings on Jadon's hand have spread, and his eyes have turned an eerie violet, and even his voice makes me shiver—and not in a good way.

"There's nowhere else, Elyn. This has to work."

She says nothing.

Jadon settles on the pillows and sighs. After telling Jadon not to go anywhere or touch anything, I close the door.

"Don't worry," he says from the other side. "The air hurts out there. And there's food, water, and wine in here."

"No one crosses into this chamber," I instruct Ancress Tisen. "If they do, they will die. Understand?"

Ancress Tisen nods, then turns to bow before Elyn. "Lady of Law and Light! It's an honor to be in your presence."

The rising god Lumis has started his ascent above Doom Desert's slot canyons, and his golden light slices through the dust. The rock face resembles the gods who have visited this place: a crag resembles the nose of the Lady of Storms on the realm Camua; a wide, uninterrupted span of rock resembles the forehead of the Lord of Dreams and Despair on Realm Sthury.

The sandstorm roars in the distance, which means that Zephar continues to do battle down in the valley.

Elyn follows me up the trail that ends at the pavilion.

As we near the Sanctum, the blended aromas of roasting meat, caramelized sugar, and strong drink grow stronger. They awaken my senses, and the hunger gnawing in my stomach sharpens. My belly rumbles. Have I eaten today?

The distant hum of voices and clinking cups grows louder, far more pleasant than the screech of Zephar's sandstorm.

"Stop right there." The Diminished archer Carana stands at the entrance of the pavilion, bare-chested, and lifts his bow, a tall weapon made of blackened fierer wood. A twisted-metal arrow is nocked, ready for a trespasser.

I look behind me: is a trespasser following Elyn and me? No one else is on this road.

So who is he addressing? The Adjudicator?

"She's with me," I say to Carana. I slow down but don't wait for his approval.

"Stop right now," Carana repeats, his golden eyes cold. "Take another step and I'll shoot."

"Are you talking to me?"

"Do you know this man?" Elyn whispers.

"Yeah," I say, "and I don't understand why he thinks he can prevent *me* from entering my own dwelling."

Carana pulls back the bowstring—it's so tight that I can hear it hum.

I cock my head. "Have you lost your mind, Carana? You dare to draw your—"

His arrow whizzes in the air, that twisted tip aimed at my neck.

I swipe my hand, batting the arrow away with a breath of wind. The bolt drives into an oak tree, and the trunk cracks like a peal of thunder from the impact.

Elyn shouts, "What the *fuck*?"

Blood roars in my ears as I stomp toward that asshole.

Carana pulls another twisted-metal arrow from his quiver.

In three steps, I'm standing in front of him. With one hand, I grab him by the back of his head and with the other hand yank him closer by his thick neck.

Yes, he is Mera by birth. Golden eyes. Muscular build. A single orb on his shoulder—the realm of Gathela, the only realm he's destroyed, known for its beautiful grassy steppes…and its gleeful murder and torture of children, the elderly, animals, Eserime, trees… An awful place that I didn't have the honor of destroying myself.

This man just tried to kill me *and* Elyn Fynal, the Grand Adjudicator and Lady of Law and Light, the worst person to threaten. My hands cup both of his ears, and I drag this warrior closer to me. "Welcome to your last day alive. Hope you had fun."

He sneers at me and spits, "You're not strong enough to—"

I growl and twist his neck.

He crumples to the ground.

"You've been here three minutes," Zephar shouts from behind me, "and you've managed to kill one of my warriors?"

He, Shari, and a small contingent of Diminished walk up the path, their hair, dark and wild, shining with the sands of Doom Desert. They move with the practiced grace of warriors—every step deliberate, every motion purposeful. Their hands rest on their weapons, ready for the next fight...*and it better not be with me.*

Zephar's lips curl into a thin smile as he eyes Carana's lifeless body at my feet. A flicker of respect hides beneath his scowl—a recognition of my strength. The others stop a few paces behind him and await his next move. Their loyalty is obvious by the way they tightly form at his back.

"Did you see him shoot at us?" I ask, restraining myself from kicking the dead warrior's corpse.

Zephar raises his eyebrows. "What can I say? He was young and dumb." He spreads his muscular arms and adds, "And what can *I* say? I'm old and dumb."

I step over the dead archer to reach Zephar. He smells like dust and oranges.

Two warriors move Carana's body out of the way. They'll dress him and burn him—but I won't perform death rites, not for a treasonous Mera. Elyn could sentence him posthumously, but we don't have the time.

"Windwolves and hydrasalts attacked another caravan," Zephar says. "We hadn't placed wards on the road they traveled, but I don't think it matters now. The otherworldly are growing bolder. Seems like they don't care whether they live or die."

"Neither did your archer," Elyn says, nodding to bloody sand left by Carana.

"I would apologize about killing him," I say, "but I won't because I warned him and he tried me anyway."

Zephar shrugs and kisses the top of my head. "Nothing to apologize for. I'll come up with something to tell his kin."

"How about the truth?" Elyn says, eyebrow high. "He tried to kill us."

Shari bounds over to me, and I stoop to nuzzle her face. "I told you that I wouldn't be gone long," I say to the wolf.

She licks my cheek, and her coarse tongue sloughs off the first layer of grime from an already-long day—but that lick also sloughs off some of my peeling skin.

I want to cry out from the pain, but I need her affection too much. I dry my tears on her coat and take a few deep breaths.

"Elyn," I say, scratching behind the wolf's ear, "remember Shari?"

I need to distract and delay her. She's thinking about Jadon and Zephar. Will she comment on my entanglement in front of Zephar? Or will our old friendship keep her mouth shut? She's kept my secrets in the past, and I've kept hers.

Look at the wolf, Elyn, and shut up.

The Adjudicator takes a step back from the wolf. "Shari, daughter of Riya. Warden of the Unseen Step. You've…grown."

"So, Elyn," Zephar says, "do I have you to thank for whisking my love away from Gasho again? There's always a threat with you."

"Where corrupted men breathe," she says, "there will forever be a threat about."

I take Zephar's hand. "I've been to the Abbey of Mount Devour."

"What?" He peers at me and whispers, "What happened to you?" He starts to reach for whatever he sees on my forehead but changes his mind, his hand falling to his side.

"The threat against Vallendor is real," I say. "I also traveled to Linione to see my father."

Zephar takes a few steps, his eyebrows furrowed. "Why?" He stares at the warriors awaiting his command behind him. "Why are you here with Elyn?"

"We're all in this fight together," Elyn says. "We must put aside our differences to save this realm."

"Is that why you've stowed trash in my temple?" he asks.

"Trash?" Elyn looks at him, her head cocked. "Where, exactly, is *your* temple?"

"The asshole eating our food," Zephar says. "You didn't think I'd notice a stranger within our gates?"

"That 'trash' is the traitor's son," I say. "He's the Weapon—"

Zephar's eyes widen. "You've put fucking *Miasma* in the temple—?"

I hold up a hand. "There's reason." I tell him about Celedan Docci, the hand tattoo and Jadon's strings being cut, and the threat that abounds if he's harmed. "I gave clear instructions to the Sisters," I continue. "No one will approach him—they'll die if they do."

"Understood." Zephar runs a shaky hand through his hair. His anxiety is a rare thing.

"Thank you for your understanding, Zephar," Elyn says. "I'll be sure to let the Council know of your kindness and hospitality."

Zephar considers her and decides instead to swallow the retort on his tongue. "I'm honored that the Adjudicator is visiting the Sanctum. I'm sure you'll find it to be the nicest prison in all the realms."

"There are sixty-seven thousand realms," Elyn says. "I'll get back to you on that."

"Can we not?" I ask, forcing a smile. "We have work—"

"You're a guest here, Adjudicator," Zephar says to her. "If you have a better Sanctum to insult, maybe you should go find it."

Elyn turns to squint at me. "Your taste is so...*specific*."

Zephar places his hands on my shoulders. "What's that supposed to mean?"

Elyn holds my gaze. "One day, the Lady of the Verdant Realm will get her shit together and find someone worthy of her station."

Zephar snorts. "And what does Vallendor's Grand Librarian know about love? And taste? And life?"

"I know she's worthy of an equal," Elyn lobs back.

Zephar squeezes my shoulders. "She's a prisoner here just as I am."

Elyn's smirk blossoms into a smile. "*Kai* led the rebellion. You simply...*carried her purse*."

Zephar releases me and steps back. Heated waves of anger roll off of him.

I close my eyes and hold up my hands. "Listen—"

"Kai? A word, please?" Hands clasped behind her back, Elyn marches to the overlook. "Grand Librarian?" she snaps. "I've studied under the most esteemed Adjudicators in the Aetherium. I've written the laws of more places than those lands where he's broken laws. I've saved the lives of the worthy and decreed the deaths of those who've caused harm. *Grand Librarian?*"

Sweat prickles my underarms, and I feel my heart shrinking in my chest. "Grand Librarian—that's better than 'fucking tablet-carrying guttorply.'"

Elyn snorts. "Jail has improved his character, but he remains an ignorant, arrogant *guttorply*. I know more about this realm and his own order than he ever will."

I peer at her with my arms folded. "And yet you don't know *shit* about how to kill the resurrectors, the Devourers, or Danar Rrivae."

"Shall I leave you to it, then?" she asks, with ice in her voice.

I groan and squeeze the bridge of my nose. "I don't miss your bickering with Zee. And you've been on a tear. That outburst at Jadon up in the glen?"

"Was I wrong?" she asks.

"Not at all," I say, "but you could at least be—"

"Nicer? More patient?" Her eyes roll wildly, irritation in every loose tendril of her silver hair. "You're gonna keep losing, Kai, because if he's beautiful, you won't be able to tell that he's your enemy. He wasn't good enough for you then, and he sure as fuck isn't good enough for you now."

I cross my arms and lower my head. "Which one are we talking about?"

Elyn whispers, "Both of them! Jadon *and* Zephar. Is it possible for you to fall for someone *not* set against Supreme? Someone I don't have to put in jail?"

I chew the inside of my cheek, then look out to the city below.

The temple bell chimes, a call to the faithful that echoes across the rooftops and fades into the dusky hills. The walkways fill with those faithful now gathering for morning prayers, and the sweet scents of thyme and lavender waft from the temple. Gashoans move toward the courtyard, their heads bowed, their hands raised in quiet devotion, their voices blending in a soft hum of prayer that rises in the stillness of the morning. The rhythm of their chanting almost makes me forget that Miasma is tucked in one of the temple's chambers.

Elyn sighs and says, "Jadon was born to be bad, but Zephar's *spoiled.* His daddy is an asshole, and his momma is an enabler and a climber who only wants to be the mother-in-law of High Lord Megidrail's only child." She shakes her head and sneers. "*His* temple? I thought the temple was named after *you*, to worship *you*, *Celestial.*"

I stare at the scented smoke billowing from the city below. "That wasn't lost on me."

"And who was the fucker shooting at us?" Elyn hisses.

My head falls back, and I watch the stars fading from the lightening sky. "Yet another question." I pause, then add, "I told Jadon about Zephar."

"Are you gonna tell Zephar about Jadon?"

I sneak a sidelong peek at Elyn. "Both are breathing right now, and neither is bleeding to his death. So I'd say no."

"Are you gonna tell Zephar that you also destroyed Beaminster with another man—Jadon—or should I?"

I turn to her. "Don't you *dare.* And *technically*, I destroyed Beaminster alone."

Zephar leads his warriors and Shari up to the pavilion.

Elyn and I stand in silence and watch the priests shuffle into the courtyard with their heads bowed. The Sisters of the Dusky Hills dance in formation across the courtyard's mosaic tiles, their movements fluid and graceful, their faces serene, their arms lifted toward the sky. They twirl in time with the rhythm of guitars and hand drums, their robes flowing out around them.

"In all seriousness..." I squeeze Elyn's hand. "Thank you for your concern. Feels like old times again."

Elyn's lip curls. "Do better, Kai. Stop fucking with the beautiful, toxic assholes." She pauses, then tugs a lock of my hair. "*Now* it feels like old times."

28

We don't have much time.

"I know," Elyn says, "but you need to eat. Remember: you're weakening and can no longer eat mortal food." And so we stay at the Sanctum for breakfast.

The rich aroma of tender lamb mingles with the scent of crisp, golden chicken. Sweet honey and nectar adorn cakes and dough balls piled high on the platters set around the pavilion. The Sanctum looks golden in this light.

The music playing was composed by my great-uncle, Sacha Laserie, as he watched over his shepherds throughout Ithlon. The melody is light and infectious, bouncing around the pavilion like a child's ball. The soft plucking of strings, the gentle thrum of drums, and the lilting notes of a flute blend in perfect harmony.

And we rush now
With blue light of darkness
To save one milky-drop of life.
We clutch this realm with hendassa strong as fierer!

My mother taught me these lyrics, and now I'm blessed to recall her sweet voice as she sang. The faces of Mera warriors and Eserime healers shine with laughter.

It's as if all is well here. Great music. Delicious food. Yet something is out of tune.

"Are you certain that I'm welcome here?" Elyn asks.

"While there aren't any Onama around, there *are* other Eserime," I say, nodding at the pods of healers enjoying the festivities. "So at least *some* of you is welcomed."

We laugh.

"And this is *my* Sanctum," I say, serious again. "I can invite whoever I want."

But no Eserime have come over to speak to the Adjudicator. She is the enemy even though she didn't sentence them to be here—they came to Vallendor voluntarily.

I, too, feel like the enemy even though this is my Sanctum, my realm.

Shari is brave enough to join us, and she places her head in my lap. That low, anxious whine rumbles through her again.

Elyn scratches the wolf's snout as she sends her eyes back around the pavilion to linger on the Diminished. "Sometimes, I forget that you all are so…*big*," she says. "Sometimes, I forget that this isn't even your true size."

I sip from my cup and say, "When it's time to destroy, you'd never see our faces from the ground. I'm a little smaller than some because my mother is Eserime. Those two"—I point to two bronze-skinned women warriors—"Imlodel and Dayjah are big, but they both have Yeaden grandfathers. In their true form, they're as tall as redwoods, and even they are short compared to Zephar and the other full-blooded Mera. The Eserime are puppies compared to even the smallest Mera." I pause, then add, "But Mera—even Diminished—can be whatever size is needed."

"I'm shocked seeing my order here," she says, chewing on her lower lip.

"I believe in accepting the help of allies."

A man laughs heartily from a firepit closest to the tents. His laughter sounds *misplaced.*

I look over in that direction, but I can only see the side of Zephar's face and the back of a stranger's head.

Elyn follows my gaze. "Who *is* that?"

I shrug. "Let's go see."

Tail down, Shari trots with us, her body pressed against my leg, that low growl vibrating against my calf.

A sour taste clings to my tongue, and my skin prickles as we near the chairs and hearth.

The stranger seated at the smaller fire is Mera, fair-skinned with blond hair. Since he wears a long-sleeve brown tunic, I can't see how many realms he's destroyed. The stranger stops talking the moment he sees Elyn, Shari, and me approach.

Zephar smiles, his expression strained, and stands up. "Everything okay?" He glowers at Elyn and taps his thigh for Shari to stand beside him.

The wolf hesitates before she slinks over to him.

"That depends on your definition of 'okay.'" I nod at the stranger.

The stranger acknowledges me and eyes Elyn. "An Adjudicator wandering the prison. How bold of you."

"A Mera visiting my realm without paying his respects first to me," I say, voice tight. "How bold of you, and stupid, to sit in my settlement as though you belong and deserve to be here." My fingertips burn hotter the more I consider this man's blatant disrespect.

Zephar lowers his head. "Kai, that's my fault—"

"Who are you?" I ask, staring hard at this man who *still* has not shown me any deference.

Standing this close, I glimpse more of his skin—but I can't see a vine, a star, or a title. He's not a young man, nor is he old. What has he been doing all these ages? His sword leans against his chair and was crafted by the great Yeaden who forge all Mera blades—it gleams cold, sharp, and unforgiving. But the hilt looks untouched, pristine, the leather pale and smooth, not darkened from use, never raised in anger or duty. The stranger's breastplate sits beside his sword, and it looks just as sterile as the blade. There, in the breastplate's center, is an "X" made of fiery crossed blades.

I don't know this symbol.

"He's just an old friend," Zephar says now. "We haven't seen each other in seasons."

"How lovely," I say. "Shall I reach out to this old friend's mother and share that her son remained seated in my presence?"

Yes, something is out of tune. Shari growls, a confirmation.

There's an unfriendly glint in the stranger's gold eyes. He stands with great reluctance, as if paying his respects is an inconvenience. "I'm Orewid Rolse, Lady."

"Orewid Rolse." I shake my head. "Doesn't sound familiar. You must be in the *administrative* offices on Mera." My eyes flick to his smooth hands and leather boots that have never stood in pools of blood nor in the cleansing fires of Mera devastation.

Shari barks at Orewid Rolse.

Zephar frowns down at her. "What's your problem today?"

I consider the stranger some more. This time, Shari growls.

Zephar tosses his "old friend" an apology, then takes Shari's collar. "I'll put her up—"

"The Adjudicator and I will be leaving soon," I say. "Goodbye." The words are sharp and final, a dismissal. I turn and follow Zephar with Shari trotting silently at his side.

Elyn lingers behind for a moment, her steps hesitant. She senses something.

The wolf and Elyn remain outside the tent as I slip inside with Zephar. The flaps close behind me, and the atmosphere inside turns heavy, stifling warm and thick with the scents of leather and sweat.

Even my home feels strange.

Zephar stands by the bed, his face cast in shadow, his gold eyes gleaming.

"Who the fuck is Orewid Rolse?" I ask.

Zephar doesn't flinch, unsurprised. He just stares at me, his expression unreadable.

I can feel that pull of a truth hanging just out of reach. Something isn't right.

Zephar tries to chuckle. "You ask that question like he's my lover."

"The way he sneers at me is totally disrespectful," I say. "Why is he here? We don't need his help."

"Will you calm down?" Zephar places his large hand on my shoulder. "He isn't here to help us. Like I said, he's an old friend that I grew up with back on Mera. You don't know him because he's... What did you say? In the *administrative* offices of our order?" Zephar cocks an eyebrow. "You never liked those types. Guess you still don't."

I snort and shake my head. "You're being a wiseass at the worst time."

"Will you trust me, please?" Zephar asks. "All is well, my love. Enjoy the quiet while you can."

"I'm not here to enjoy the quiet or to make new friends. We have shit to discuss, and your pride is standing between us."

Zephar crosses his arms and plants his feet apart. "What is it that you'd like to discuss, my love?"

"Don't."

He laughs, shrugs, and loosens his stance, placing his hands on his hips. "Better?"

My stomach becomes a tangled cord.

"Kai," he says, smiling. "What's on your mind? I wanna know what you're thinking before you race up the mountain to embark on whatever secret mission—"

"It isn't a secret mission," I shout. "The realm is ending—"

"Right. You said that." He points toward the hillside. "Where you're headed, they think that, too. And they run to the mountains to worship the charlatan wearing white as though the end won't find them there."

I squint at him. "That charlatan wearing white may know shit that may keep us all from dying, and yet here you are, laughing—"

"Sincerely, what could he know that we don't?" Zephar asks, arms out.

"How to kill those creatures that can resurrect the fallen, for one. What went wrong after Agon destroyed Celedan Docci at his bench? How did Danar Rrivae create those...*Devourers*? Zee, they're massive. They're nearly our true size. I would've been impressed if I wasn't fighting for my life." I pause, then narrow my eyes. "But I guess none of that really concerns you."

He shrugs. "I'm Mera, my love. Your second-in-command. I'm no ordinary Destroyer."

"True. But these are no ordinary otherworldly." I march over to my trunk and throw it open. My clothes, neatly folded and tucked away, still smell of lavender and tuberoses. Some of the fabrics have softened from wear, but they're all still rich in color. I push skirts and breeches and bandeaus aside.

"What are you looking for?" Zephar asks.

"Another pair of boots," I say. "These hurt. They're too small."

No boots. I close the trunk with a soft thud and walk over to another trunk closest to the tent's rear entrance. I catch a glimpse of the gardens beyond—and my breath catches when I see the tub that Zephar had built for me. The wood is splintered, and the once-perfect iron bands are now twisted and misshapen.

Shari nudges me.

"What happened to the tub?" I whisper to Zephar. "Who did this?"

His gaze follows mine to outside the tent. "I did that. I'm starting over."

"Really?"

He shrugs. "To make it bigger." He pauses. "Did I do something wrong again?"

I whisper, "I guess not."

Will a new tub or new boots matter six nights from now?

I take a deep breath. Standing again, I say, "I also need to say—"

"I apologize for saying 'my temple.'" He ruffles his hair. "You called it—I'm prideful, sometimes. When you're gone, I'm responsible for everything in the province, and so I tend to think 'my' and 'mine.' But you're here now, and even when you're not... The Gashoans built the temple to honor you, and I..." He smirks. "I only *carry your purse*."

I murmur, "I don't think that."

"She does."

"Since when do you care what Elyn thinks of you?"

"She was your best friend once upon a time."

"But that time has passed," I say. "Today, we are...reluctant partners."

Elyn and Zephar never got along. She resented that he thought of her as a "fucking librarian," and he resented her for thinking of him as a "strutting big dick who thinks with a fire-ravaged brain."

Now, Zephar pushes his hands through his hair and trudges over toward the tub. "Are you coming back?"

"Yes."

"When do we leave for the Sea? It will be a long walk, since we can't Spryte."

"I know. We'll leave tonight."

He nods. "I'll be ready for our departure, then." His hardness softens, and he scrutinizes my face again. "I'm worried about what's happening to you."

I offer him a sad smile. "I'm worried about what's happening to Vallendor."

He finally plucks the worrisome patch of skin from my forehead.

I whisper, "Ouch," and giggle.

He studies the fragment of skin, so tiny on his thick finger.

I leave him there, staring at that piece of me.

Shari follows Elyn and me past the pavilion, the eyes of many on our backs. She stops at the top of the path out of the Sanctum.

I kneel before the wolf and hold her face between my hands. "That fool up there upsets you."

She whines.

"Why?"

She pants and growls.

"Can she talk to you?" Elyn asks.

I shake my head. "No—she belongs to Zephar." I stroke her snout, wishing that she were mine. "I'll be careful," I tell her now. "I know there's something wrong here. I feel it, too."

Elyn and I trudge along the dusty path toward Malik Sindire's settlement. Selenova hangs low in the sky, and her white light casts long shadows across the hills. Tension crackles between me and the Adjudicator. Her first visit to the Sanctum didn't match the wondrous visit to the Misty Garden.

"We're almost there," I say now, alert as I scan the surrounding wilderness.

Elyn smiles tightly. "You sound like you're trying to convince yourself that you know where you're going."

Before I can respond, a figure steps onto the path before us. The Eserime healer who'd beckoned me on my arrival days ago wears a warrior's breastplate and an under-tunic embroidered with swirls of silver thread. She could be poor Nimith's sister with that copper skin and those gray eyes. She notices my hand reaching for Fury, and she holds out her own hands to save her life. "I haven't come to harm you."

She smiles at Elyn and bows deeply. "Lady Fynal, it's an honor."

Elyn stiffens. "And who are you?"

"Tatanye Lote." Her face looks calm, but there's a note of anxiety in her tone. "A healer now with Lord Itikin's—pardon me, *Lady Megidrail's*—battalion."

Elyn's brow furrows. "See, I don't understand this. The warrior who despises stewards—"

"Can we not?" I shake my head at Elyn. To Tatanye Lote, I say, "Were you trying to get my attention days ago?"

The woman nods. Her eyes flicker momentarily, and she swallows. "Strange, isn't it?"

I clench my jaw. "What's strange?"

Tatanye Lote whispers, "The Sanctum is…*shifting*. Something's happening here, something I can't explain. It seems as though I'm imagining it, that I'm the only one here that…that…"

I glance at Elyn—that unease I've felt has now been confirmed by this stranger. "What do you mean by *shifting*?" I ask.

The Eserime's lips twitch, and a faint frown tugs at the corner of her mouth. "There's something *wrong* with the power here. It's unstable. The threads that bind this place together are fraying." She looks directly at Elyn now, her gaze intense. "The other Eserime and I… We shouldn't be here."

"No, you shouldn't," says Elyn.

"Have you shared your concerns with Zephar?" I ask Tatanye Lote.

She slowly shakes her head. "The Eserime are here—or so we've been told—to heal the Gasho and other mortals that need our hands. But I believe we're here for more than that. That purpose hasn't been introduced to us yet, but my body can't rest with this mysterious threat on the horizon."

Tatanye Lote steps closer to us. "Remain watchful is all I ask."

Elyn studies the Eserime. "Why do you remain here if you sense this danger? And why did you come? I've not sentenced any Eserime to Gasho or Vallendor."

A faint smile dances across Tatanye Lote's lips, and her eyes glow with hope. "I'm honored to aid the Lady of the Verdant Realm in restoring Vallendor to its true purpose. That's why I came. That's why I've remained." She bows her head to me, but the excitement of her purpose dims and her bright gray eyes darken. "I must go before I'm missed."

We turn to watch the woman hurry back in the direction we came. Once Elyn and I are alone again, Elyn says, "I felt that strangeness, too."

"What did you notice?" I ask.

"The man you don't know," she says. "In addition to his ridiculous disrespect, I also noticed the symbol on his breastplate."

"The fiery 'X'," I say. "What is that?"

"There's not much literature yet, but that's the sign of the Crusaders."

"The faction within the Mera," I say, nodding. "But what are they 'crusading' against now?"

Elyn shrugs. "I have no idea, but are crusades ever good? Are crusades ever harmless?"

The Crusade of Broken Blades: to stop the expansion of Dindt explorers on the realm Taiko by the Dindt suborder of Honem. Twelve thousand killed.

The Crusade of Black Crowns: the Dashmala appealed to the Mera to come to Vallendor and kill the Gorga—which then brought the Yeaden to defend the Gorga. Six thousand killed.

The Crusades of Wrexen Cadine: Wrexen Cadine, an Adjudicator, led rogue Onama to capture the reliquaries on Linione. He failed. Seventy thousand were killed in that brutal massacre.

People always die on the other side of a crusade.

Yes, something is out of tune here.

29

Elyn and I finally reach the part of the mountain where Malik Sindire's glass- and white-stone-walled temple sits. The daystar is high in the sky, half-hidden behind clouds. He still casts hard light over the landscape—powerful even when he's concealed.

"*This* is a temple?" Elyn asks, shocked by the structure's simple lines, walnut doors, and the pools of still, clear water. "Looks more like the mountain retreat for Council meetings."

I take a deep breath; the air smells of pine and damp earth. "I noticed that it looks similar to the dwelling on Linione."

There's a restlessness in Malik Sindire's estate-temple today. As we approach, I hear the low hum of distant voices. I don't sense, though, the out-of-tune strangeness I felt at my own Sanctum down the mountain.

More people are milling around than during my first visit; some move between the shadows, a few sit beneath the trees. I don't recognize the people standing near the gates, lounging on the wide veranda, or draped lazily across the stone steps. They're all strangers, but they don't see Elyn or me as a threat.

When I catch their gazes, they simply nod and return to staring out at the trees or up to the cloudy sky. Blank-faced, they look lost in a trance, their thoughts floating beyond this realm. They all wear simple white robes adorned with symbols and tangled, shimmering patterns. They remind me of the gown that Nimith wore up at the abbey.

Elyn and I pass them without speaking. Malik Sindire waits for us on the veranda.

"Dyotila and Avish," I say. "Where are they today?"

"Gathering more berries, nuts, and fresh water for our guests." Malik Sindire's eyes linger on my forehead and the new patch of skin left bare after Zephar's plucked it. Tonight, the Dindt wears a gold robe with a rust-colored weave and matching slippers. He smells of sage and cinnamon, and his skin shines as though he's dipped himself into a vat of oil.

A smile sweeps across his face as he bows toward Elyn. "I've never hosted an Adjudicator, much less the *Grand* Adjudicator of the Nine Realms. Welcome to my home, Lady Fynal."

Elyn gazes around the temple grounds. "You have a full house."

"Demigods experiencing identity crises," Malik Sindire says, shrugging. His eyes continue wandering the new landscape of my face and neck.

"Kai told me that you visit Vallendor only twice an age," Elyn says. "That's not often."

Our host flicks his ring-heavy hand. "True, but I'm glad that my visit this time may benefit the Lady and her realm. My followers are also pleased that I've returned." He smiles as he regards his people. "Even during less dangerous times, they find my temple a refuge from the chaos in the hinterlands. And as you know, these are no longer peaceful times. The threat is real."

Elyn and I glance up at the daystar now moving toward the horizon. Soon, his partner will dominate the skies; she grows fuller each day.

"How dire has our situation become since we last spoke?" Malik Sindire asks me. When I don't immediately respond, he says, "Oh, dear," and he beckons Elyn and me to follow him. "Let's make our plans over a drink."

We pass more demigods sleeping on chaises and armchairs. If they were scared before, their faces no longer show it. They are soft and unlined, blessed and unbothered.

We settle on the glass-walled patio that shields the interior of the temple from the outside world.

"Zephar thinks your followers are a doomsday cult," I say.

Malik Sindire looks over to me. "Is doomsday not upon us?"

I open my mouth to respond but think better of it and seal my lips again.

"Lord Itikin is usually a clever strategist," Malik Sindire says, "but in recent times, he's grown willfully ignorant. A grasshopper who thinks he has all the time in the world."

I furrow my brows. "He hasn't been himself lately."

"Even some in his camp see that all is not well," Elyn says.

"Dyotila and Avish have also told me similar tales," Malik Sindire says, nodding.

"I'm referring to someone else," Elyn says, "the Eserime healer who met us on the road."

I give Elyn the slightest headshake, angered by her carelessness.

"Really?" Malik Sindire says.

Too late.

"She expressed her concern to us," Elyn says shakily as she realizes her mistake. "But then, as you said, who isn't concerned about *everything* nowadays?" She chuckles.

Malik Sindire says, "Hmm. Yes."

Elyn mouths an apology.

I nod, irritated. Malik Sindire and Zephar won't be bonding over mugs of mead anytime soon, but I don't want to endanger Tatanye Lote's life in any way.

"If it matters, Lady Megidrail," Malik Sindire says, "I'm pleased that you decided to follow your head and not your heart. Zephar Itikin is a most…*persuasive* god. You are a brave woman."

"You've heard our arguments, then," I say.

His eyes flit around the room, amused. "Such marvelous echo in this part of Doom Desert. Who needs fools or songs when we can all listen to the new chapter of 'Kai and Zephar'?"

I laugh heartily. Elyn rolls her eyes.

Malik Sindire chuckles. "Will she boot him from the Sanctum? Will he destroy the closest town? Will they grow into their true sizes and battle it out? Who knows?"

"I apologize for our highly entertaining disturbances."

"Don't ever give in to guilt or to someone else's plans," he says, now serious. "Though you owe Zephar Itikin nothing, Kai, you will give him life through your wisdom. He doesn't understand, but only because he doesn't *have* to understand. He doesn't *have* to make decisions like yours. That's not his legacy."

"But what if walking away was the wrong choice?" I ask.

Malik Sindire shakes his head. "If you continue to search for answers, people will ultimately forgive your honest choice. Isn't that right, Adjudicator?"

Elyn grunts. "Sure."

"You, Kaivara, are on the path that will change the course of this realm."

"According to man's prophecies," I say. "You've said that before."

Malik Sindire clutches his heart. "*Man's prophecies?* Didn't you just return from the Abbey of Mount Devour to learn more about how we'll all die if you don't stop the traitor? Did you forget that the Council will send the most powerful Mera to destroy Vallendor if you fail? That your father, too, will be annihilated—?"

I hold up my hand. "I'm changing the course of this realm. I understand."

"Yet all Zephar Itikin can think about is toppling some cottages and burning down some poor farmers' wheat fields." The Dindt rolls his eyes. "Such a tiny mind in that big body. The Lord of the Shielded Fount and Prince of Lissome Blades can be a…*hejelink.*"

"Asshole" in Yeaden.

That makes Elyn laugh. "Hejelink, indeed."

"Are there any additional updates," Malik Sindire asks, "besides the quiet buzzing of whispered concern?"

Over glasses of wine the color of late afternoon skies, I tell him about all that's happened since I left here with his gifted armor and a new dagger—from reuniting with Jadon Wake Rrivae at Mount Devour and claiming the signet ring from Gileon Wake to destroying Celedan Docci, to Miasma sweeping through the abbey.

"And where is Wake Rrivae now?" Malik Sindire asks, his

eyebrows knitted.

"In the safest place I could think of," I say. "Cloistered at one of the smaller sanctuaries down in my temple."

"Your temple?" He tugs at the collar of his robe. "But..."

"We know, ser," Elyn says, holding her glass idly between her fingers. "Our choices of location were few. He presents a great threat, and we wonder if, by destroying Celedan Docci, we've made the problem worse."

"We didn't have the chance to consult the *Librum Esoterica* before the wave of death swept over the abbey," I add, draining my glass. My face stings from the strong wine—a better sting, though, than the kind in my cramped toes. "I must admit that I regret giving the *Librum* to Syrus Wake back then."

Malik Sindire flaps his hand between us. "It's not your fault he abused the power of knowledge to gain terrible power and conspired with the traitor to gain even more."

"Maybe some things shouldn't be written down," I say, staring into my empty glass.

"First," Malik Sindire says, pouring more wine into my glass, "books, even the worst ones, are magical. If the mind can capture abstract concepts in a form others can grasp, we are better for it. And second, *you* didn't write the *Librum*. The Adjudicator's family, the House of Fynal did—and they will continue to be the stewards of that knowledge. While you are Blood of All, Beloved, you aren't a scholar. I don't intend to offend you, but this is not yours to grieve."

I snort. "Fikx vai."

He smiles and lifts a finger. "I didn't say that you weren't *smart*. You can curse in seven thousand languages. Are you content in books and papers, your fingers stained with ink?"

"No."

He chuckles. "Exactly. So, the Weapon: you said that the marking on his hand has spread. Can you describe it?"

"Do you have paper and ink?" Elyn asks. "I can draw it better than describing it."

Malik Sindire sets before Elyn sheets of thick white paper and different-colored inks.

By the time I've sipped half of my wine, Elyn has drawn a remarkable depiction of Jadon's right hand.

Green, red, black, yellow, and blue inks that comprise a hand with one fingertip a flame. Another fingertip as ice. Water. Earth. Darkness. A drop of water disturbs a pool that ripples out, out, out to create rings within rings.

How did she have time to study his tattoo so thoroughly?

"And his skin has turned the color of paste," Elyn shares, "and his eyes change from blue to lavender to no color at all."

"And there's this glow that emanates from him now," I add. "Like the light in an underwater cave. Watery and..."

Malik Sindire studies the drawing in worried silence.

Elyn finally takes a long swig from her glass. The old Elyn's dead and gone.

"And this marking faded," Malik Sindire says, "right after Celedan's destruction? And then it returned and spread?"

"It's now up to here." Elyn points to her wrist bone.

"And according to Agon the Kindness," Malik Sindire says, "Selenova at her fullest will galvanize the mark's full power?"

"Yes."

"Did he tell you why?"

We both shake our heads. "Do you know the reason?" Elyn asks.

Malik Sindire looks up at us, his face flushed. "Linionium," he declares. "It must be."

"The mallet that Agon used to destroy Celedan Docci was made of linionium," I say.

"Correct." Malik Sindire shakes his head. "The ink used in Jadon Rrivae's marking was infused with linionium, which derives from the very element Supreme used to create the first realm. That ink is indestructible."

"Even against our swords?" Elyn asks.

"Catherite," Malik Sindire says, "was the second element that created the first realm, and the metal used by the Yeaden to craft the weapons of the gods. Not linionium. And there's a reason: only linionium can destroy linionium."

"But what if we were to forge weapons from linionium to counteract the linionium in Danar Rrivae's amulet or in Jadon's marking?" Elyn asks.

I press my fingers against my forehead. "Forging one sword of linionium can take half an age," I say. "It's unforgiving. Willful. Only the hottest fire on Linione Realm can coax it to bend. There's no time to forge linionium blades."

Elyn crumples back into her chair. "So we're gonna die."

Malik Sindire gasps. "Giving up already, Lady Fynal? The greatest battles don't happen only on battlefields. I'm not concerned with facing the traitor with blades and spells. What's most worrisome is…" He picks up Elyn's drawing of Jadon's tattoo. "The linionium ink used to create this beautiful mark…makes him the most dangerous, most powerful weapon in the realm."

The old man peers at Elyn and then at me. "Destroying Celedan Docci simply transferred his linionium to the closest source of power."

"Are you saying that Celedan was made of linionium?" I ask, brows furrowed.

"Come with me." Malik Sindire leads Elyn and me to his office, a dim space with true walls of stone rather than glass. The only illumination here comes from a single candle on his desk and a few shafts of pale light from the narrow skylight.

We stand at his desk covered with scrolls and ink-stained quills. The air smells of aged paper and incense; the walls are lined with shelves filled with books, faintly pulsing crystals, small glass vials filled with mysterious liquids, and artifacts that gleam with a light all their own.

The Dindt opens a thick, brown, leather-bound book with a cover embossed in intricate symbols faded from constant touch. The paper within the tome is aged, thin, and fragile. The ink, though, has remained dark and sharp, and the text is written in fine, precise script. These words will survive even after the parchment disintegrates.

The pages are also filled with vibrant and detailed sketches of gods, spirits, and creatures from throughout the Aetherium. Some of the beings drawn here are graceful, their forms almost ethereal, while others are terrifying, with jagged, inhuman features and wings that span two pages. It's strange how the eyes of these drawings seem to watch us as we peer at them. These lines and arcs make the hairs on the back of my neck stand on end.

Malik Sindire continues to flip through the pages of this odd book. Each time he turns a page, I shiver. That naperone with its crocodile-like scales and lion-like head looks like it could step off of its page and into this room.

Uneasy, I comment, "Any minute now, I'd expect to see our faces in this book."

Elyn snorts.

"Oh, you're in here somewhere," Malik Sindire says absently.

"What?" Elyn says, eyes hot.

Malik Sindire doesn't stop to show us our entries. "Neither of you are ordinary gods from ordinary families. Why wouldn't you be recorded in a book like this?" He keeps turning pages. More gods and creatures, ethereal and graceful, delicate and light, monstrous, with eyes that stare right through me.

He's right: this is no ordinary book.

"Did you write or curate this compendium?" Elyn asks.

"Do the identities of the authors matter, Lady Fynal?"

Elyn frowns. "Yes. Not every god is a reliable narrator. Not every god is a scholar—"

"I don't mean to be rude," I say to Malik Sindire, "but we don't have time for a lesson right now on alchemy and literature—"

"Here we are." Malik Sindire stops at an inked depiction of a prune-faced man with translucent wings. He wears a simple loincloth, and his skin is entirely covered with letters and symbols of the Onama.

"Him," Elyn says.

"He's the reason we're in this mess," I say, my blood chilling.

"Do you want to know why that is," Malik Sindire asks, "or do you want to rush ahead and end the realm sooner rather than later?"

He pauses, then says, "Celedan Docci from the order Onama. You asked if he was made of linionium. *Not exactly*. Docci was filled with so much knowledge that his spine started to crack. The Council feared his loss, and the Onama healers arrived at a solution: fuse the Keeper with linionium. They also 'retired' him into the gem, WISDOM, which is why he volunteered to accompany Lady Megidrail's edition of the *Librum Esoterica* to Vallendor. He thought he'd live a long life with his new spine, on this new realm with the lovely Lady, sharing his knowledge with the dashing new king, Syrus Wake.

"But then he saw just how important his role was—Wake consulted him all the time but had grown disillusioned with knowledge that anyone could soon attain. So Celedan Docci called on Danar Rrivae. But that didn't keep Docci in the room. The young Corby woman stole the *Librum* from the library at Castle Wake.

"But then you found the book and Celedan Docci, and Agon destroyed WISDOM with him inside of it. Agon destroyed Docci's body, which was filled with linionium. Wake Rrivae was standing in the aerie, and Celedan Docci's spent power found more linionium in his hand to bind to."

"Had Jadon not been in the room..." Elyn says.

"The linionium powder would've simply diminished in time," Malik Sindire says.

And now, it's my turn to rub my face and say, "So we're gonna die."

"Kai, don't," Elyn says.

I throw up my hands. "Don't you get it? That..." I point at the drawing she made of Jadon's marking. "That ink will spread until Jadon's covered completely—he will be lost to us. If Jadon is killed, all that linionium will bind to the closest living source, which most likely will be..."

"Danar Rrivae," Malik Sindire says, "who wears TERROR, the gem of crystalized linionium. The marking on Jadon Wake Rrivae's hand—not Miasma—makes him the weapon."

"What are we about to face?" Elyn asks.

"Either Wake Rrivae saves himself by doing what his father wants," Malik Sindire says, "or he chooses the most difficult task: he kills the next source of power and the holder of the amulet—Danar Rrivae. But that practically guarantees Wake Rrivae's own death even though he'd save Vallendor. He's only a demigod. While Danar Rrivae could handle the total infusion of linionium, his son cannot. And since the light of Selenova at her fullest will only increase the power of linionium..."

"Jadon dies in every scenario," I whisper, my legs weak. *No.*

Malik Sindire wanders over to the window to gaze up at the darkening sky. "When given the choice by his father, Jadon Wake Rrivae will choose to save himself." He turns back to Elyn and me, his face inscrutable. "When faced with such decisions...all men choose themselves."

30

My father abandoned my mother and me on Ithlon Realm and chose to live his life on Mera without us.

Agon chose cloistering at the Abbey of Mount Devour instead of helping his sister to raise me.

Zephar's ego and impatience cause him to question my leadership and identity.

Even after I'd made him king, Syrus Wake chose Danar Rrivae as his god.

Danar Rrivae aims to kill me because he wants my realm…the perfect revenge against my father.

Jadon's choice will be to either obey Danar Rrivae and live, or disobey Danar Rrivae and die. If Jadon chooses to live, both of his fathers will use him to conquer Vallendor…and other realms known and to be discovered.

In each of these cases, the man chooses himself.

Walking this trail beside me, Elyn Fynal looks golden, strong, and worthy of an alabaster statue. The Adjudicator is not of Vallendor, not with those gold eyes and barely there wings only visible in this dying light—but she, too, has a stake in this fight. Her mother is Grand Steward of Vallendor. If we can't stop Danar Rrivae—and find Jadon—no one will ever be *of* Vallendor again, including Sybel Fynal.

"And I'm not letting that asshole destroy my mom," Elyn says, her enunciation slurred.

"You drank a little too much wine, huh?" I ask, also a little unsteady.

She snorts.

I squint at her. "You're talented, you know that? You draw like a real artist. You draw better than you fight."

She holds out her arms. "I fight pretty damned good for a judge."

"You know what would help *me* fight better?" I say. "Wings. And I've proven myself, haven't I by now? Don't I deserve to fly again?"

"Talk to the manager," she says, pointing to the sky. She narrows her eyes and looks back at the Temple of Malik Sindire.

"What's wrong now?" I ask.

"That guy back there. Who is he and why is my picture in his creepy book?"

"He's a visitor to Vallendor," I say. "A Dindt who travels—like Dindts do—and he collects shit from across the realms—like Yeadens do. Why does it matter?"

"How do we know that he's telling us the truth?" she asks. "About catherite and linionium, about Celedan Docci transferring his power? About the ink on Jadon's hand?"

"How do we know *anyone's* telling the truth about *any* of this?" I say. "We all know that catherite isn't as strong as fucking linionium. As for Docci?" I shrug. "We saw that *something* happened, which is why we're here and why dead gods now litter the abbey." I point to her. "You're starting to sound like me, questioning everything."

She widens her eyes. "No!" We both laugh.

Her smile fades, and now she looks small, too young for all this chaos, for certain death. It's her job to decide who lives and who dies across nine realms. But she also decides the fate of immortals on these nine realms who've made the wrong decisions. So much power too young.

Maybe I am, too.

"He worries me," Elyn says. "And I don't like my likeness everywhere."

I roll my eyes. "It's in a *book*. And if I had to count how many times my likeness—"

"Well, I'm not you," she says. "I'm nobody's lady or guiding light. *And!* I know of no arms-trading Dindt named Malik Sindire," Elyn says, her voice tight. "And he didn't wear any amulets worn by the Dindt."

Bees, spiders, beavers, hammer, angles…

"And you know every Dindt throughout the sixty-seven thousand realms?" I ask, eyebrow cocked.

"Yes," she says. "As a matter of fact, I do."

"You need to worry about one pendant," I say, "the one that we need to snatch off the traitor. Then we need to destroy him and then destroy Jadon before the freed linionium finds *him* and makes *him* unstoppable."

"One last thing," she says, holding up a finger. Her eyes are clear, sober now. "That name, Orewid Rolse. I'd heard it said before."

I nod, also suddenly sober. "And?"

Her face darkens. "He's dangerous, Kai. He hasn't swung a sword once to defend the Aetherium nor has he rebuilt any destroyed realms. Yet he goes around telling Mera that they are the master order, that Mera can't be proper warriors if they love outside their order, that the Mera bloodline must be protected at all costs.

"And he finds Mera men like Zephar, who are already experiencing some kind of…" She flicks her hand. "*…identity crisis* about who they are and who gets to lead and…Orewid Rolse riles them up so much that they'll kill whoever they think threatens them."

My heart jolts. "And what happened to those Mera who killed for his cause in other realms?"

"They were either destroyed or jailed in the abbeys on their realms." Elyn pauses, then adds, "There are some who argue that total destruction of these fanatics is for the best."

"Who is 'some'?"

"Your father. The Mera leadership. The majority of the Mera people."

"Why hasn't someone stopped Orewid Rolse?" I ask.

"Because he never swings the murdering blade himself. Because he can't make someone do something that's not already in their hearts or minds. Because he's never around long enough to be caught."

Elyn and I don't speak again as we rush toward the Misty Garden. Our breaths catch as we enter this beautiful yet mortal place. Mist curls around our ankles like hands pulling at us to slow down. I want nothing more than to give in and enjoy the quiet, the aroma of plums, the pristine waters, but we need to hurry. The Sea of Devour awaits.

We reach the temple, and our first task is retrieving Jadon.

A discarded ochre robe with embroidered sleeves lies rumpled at the temple's entryway.

I hold out my arm. "Don't move."

Elyn stops in her tracks. "Shit."

Wrapped in that robe is a body, lying motionless on the tile floor—one without an amber or blue glow. The only light on this body comes from a torch reflecting off the robe's thread.

"Oh, no." Elyn kneels beside the dead Sister.

I scan the empty chamber before us. Panic sets in as my eyes track slow-moving amber figures throughout the temple. They're sick, dying.

"This doesn't make sense," I whisper.

The Gashoans had been blessed again. They should be carrying offerings to the altars in the courtyard and up to the belltower. They should be preparing for nighttime prayers, lighting candles and replacing old fruit and flowers with fresh ones. These amber figures should be blue. These amber figures shouldn't be this still.

"What's happening, Kai?" Elyn whispers.

I shake my head and tiptoe ahead because we must retrieve Jadon. "I don't know."

Elyn and I come upon another crumpled Sister, pale-faced with blank eyes, slumped against a wall. She doesn't move; she doesn't glow.

My nerves flutter beneath my skin as we approach another body at the base of the alabaster columns. Another sister has collapsed at the entrance, and one more against the temple's golden-brown walls.

Elyn gasps as we discover more new dead.

I'm shaking and shaken by the time we reach Jadon's temporary quarters.

At the chamber's threshold, I cry out, "No!" and run to the open door of the small room.

Ancress Mily Tisen lies on her back with a bouquet of water lilies and orchids clutched to her chest. A teardrop still glistens on her cheek. She's now a hollow shape without the warmth of life, lightless.

I fall to my knees beside her and pull the young woman into my arms.

Elyn whispers, "Oh, no."

I free Mily Tisen's curly hair from her headscarf. Unlike those flowers in the meadows, my tears falling on her face don't bring her back to life.

"I'm so sorry," I whisper into her hair. No harm should've come to her or anyone in Gasho. This town, this temple, was supposed to be safe.

Elyn crouches beside me and touches the young woman's face. She whispers, "Thu lojh if shos rualum haus faukuk fir hur." *The light of this realm has faded for her.* Then she leaves me to mourn.

I shake my head, unsure of what to do with her. I can't just *leave* her here.

"But you must," Elyn says. "There's no time, Kai." She points to the chamber where we stowed Jadon. "You must see this."

I kiss Mily Tisen's forehead and gently lay her back on the stone floor. I leave those flowers in her hands.

Jadon isn't inside the small chamber, but there is a plate cluttered with olive pits, heels of bread, and a honey-dipper. An empty carafe of wine and a dirty cup sits on the ground. There, on the trunk: the folded clean clothes the Sisters left for Jadon to wear. On top of the clean clothes is the balled-up blue tunic and breeches that Jadon wore as he left the abbey. But there is no Jadon.

Shit.

A horn sounds, deep and commanding, cutting through the deathly silence. *Zephar's call!* Startled birds burst into flight against the nighttime sky, their bodies dark against the pale light of the nightstar.

"What's happening?" Elyn asks me.

"Trouble's found us," I say. "That's what's happening." I take a last look back at Ancress Tisen, and then I race out of the Temple of Celestial with Elyn beside me. She rushes back to the sanctuary. She shouts, "Kai—"

Soldiers wearing blue tunics and cloaks over copper armor pour into Gasho on what look like horses—but these animals have two spiral horns. *Howlthanes.* Horse-wolves bred for war. The uniforms of their riders may have been sewn for Wake's soldiers once upon a time, but the beings wearing them now have moldy skin in every tone and dull eyes that no longer flicker with life, even though these men *are* alive. They glow amber.

"These soldiers," I say, "aren't as big as the Devourers at Fihel."

Elyn's steps slow. "I don't have any Raqiel guards with me. I've been drinking."

I take her hand. "Don't worry—"

"I can't fight *that*—" She points to the soldiers. "I can't fight that and expect to—"

"I'll protect you," I shout, tugging at her shoulders. "Just stay close and be merciless, just like you did at Fihel. There are innocents here, so you can't throw wind and lightning indiscriminately. Just...do your best."

We can hear the cries of terrified Gashoans over the thundering of howlthane hooves pounding against the ground. Soon, these cries are swallowed by the noise of metal striking metal.

Pulling Justice from her scabbard, Elyn asks, "Aren't Zephar and your guards supposed to be—?" And just like that, Zephar and his—no, *my*—army of Diminished, black shapes against the pale light, drop from the heavens like a storm unleashed. The roar of their arrival splits the sky.

BOOM!

The earth shakes from the impact of their landing, erupting in clouds of dust and debris. The gods of destruction, each one a weapon in their own right, step from the rubble, their blades ready for destruction.

Gasho, once quiet and peaceful, has become a battlefield. Elyn and I race toward a town square now alive with shouting.

Thick smoke rises in dark tendrils, curling above the collapsing buildings. The stench of burning wood and flesh makes it hard to breathe as we push forward. The once-beautiful town square, with its fountains and market stalls, has been ruined again. The stone walls are cracked and stained, the fountains dry and still.

The alabaster-and-marble tub that Prince Idus had built for me shatters in the fight. The intricate carvings that adorned its sides—swirling patterns of moths and delicate flowers—lie shattered in pools of spilled water.

I won't let them take Gasho from me. My sword, Fury, sings as I grip her tight.

A soldier lunges at me. He smells like he'd been left half buried in the desert to die and was resurrected by expired tonics.

I swing, but Fury's blade bounces off his neck. I blink, surprised at my failure to cut him down.

The soldier smiles—the first sign of sentience—and lifts his sword.

I grab Tempest from my ankle sheath and slide the dagger into the living-dead's smile until he's truly dead.

Fury didn't even leave a scratch. *Why not?*

My hands shake as I grip my dagger. I jab and lunge, aiming for the necks, eyes, mouths, and every soft part of these living-dead. This is close work, and I wince every time blood or bile splashes across my hand. This blood stings, stinking like tar and vomit. I gag and try to clear my mind.

Elyn stays close by. Her swings grow tired, haphazard.

Fire and lightning would be too risky here. My Gashoans are already too close to the fighting—but they're being trampled and torn apart.

The Diminished fight with more zeal than I've ever seen in our seasons together. Five Mera warriors battle one living-dead who refuses to fall to blows that would've obliterated any other soldier.

"Off with their heads," Zephar shouts to the five.

He figured that out more quickly than Elyn, Jadon, and I did when we fought at Fihel.

Now, heads roll across the ground. It will never be clean, no matter how many rains sweep through the land.

Elyn reaches back for me, to make sure that I'm still fighting beside her.

I squeeze her hand. *I'm right here.* "Do you see Jadon?" I shout over the sounds of battle.

"Yes! Look!" She points south, to the perimeter of the city.

Jadon, wearing the sandy-brown leather armor of the Gasho, swings one of their curved blades. He moves slowly. He doesn't know how to wield this type of sword.

Elyn says, "We can't risk him—"

"Go!" I shout. "Get him out of here!"

Without another word, she launches herself into the sky, those faint wings catching the light.

My view of her is soon blocked by a living-dead warrior as tall as a date palm and as wide as a king's bed. I stagger backward.

He points at me. "You are to return the Weapon at once or—"

I plunge Tempest into the soft spot nearest to me: his groin. He shrieks and falls to his knees.

I step back.

Shari bounds from behind me, sinks her teeth into his sword hand, and forces him to drop his weapon.

Zephar's twin blades lop off the Devourer's head, and it rolls to a stop before me. Without a word to me, he plunges back into the fray with Shari at his side.

I scan Gasho. More lightless bodies: sisters, women, children, priests… My people. Tears spring to my eyes as the innocent fall all around me, by blade and by the horns of the howlthanes.

"Kai!" Elyn shouts.

I look back at her. "Where's Jadon? Go back and get him!" I say, dashing south before she can respond.

The thick smoke hides that this city is lost to chaos, but I don't stop fighting. I slide my dagger into the throats of three soldiers who block my path, and they fall without a sound. I keep moving toward the taverns, the palm grove, the aqueduct.

In the taverns, drunk men fight each other, while others rally against the soldiers. Other frightened Gashoans huddle in corners or hide beneath tables. There's no sign of Jadon.

I keep searching, forcing myself to push past the fear.

Jadon is still here. I feel him somewhere in this heavy storm.

Over in the palm grove, fronds rustle in the wind, but Jadon does not hide in their shadows. There are just more soldiers, more bodies, and the haunting sound of distant screams.

Down at the aqueduct, the sound of rushing water offers no comfort. Jadon is nowhere to be found.

I rush back into the city, stomach tight in frustration. As I near a coal bin behind a crumbling wall, a whimper catches my attention. I move quickly toward a clump of glowing amber forms.

A small group of women and children huddles together, their faces pale, their bodies trembling. In front of them, a soldier swings a flail; the chain whistles before the metal ball lands with a crack against the bin. The group screams.

I can't hear their prayers over the noise, but I know what they ask. I thrust my dagger into the soldier's cheek.

The Devourer clutches his face and staggers past a Mera warrior, who chops off his head.

Soon, the number of surviving Mera warriors and Eserime healers outnumbers the otherworldly. Soon, no otherworldly—including the howlthanes—have their heads.

Elyn returns to the town square, her golden armor now streaked with the black-green blood of these new Devourers. Jadon isn't beside her.

An Eserime healer's hesitation catches my attention. At first, I think I've imagined their continued sense of unease. As Elyn and I move through the square, though: the Eserime, normally efficient and unflinching in their work, now pause as they crouch over the wounded Gashoans. The healers' hands linger over the mortals' wounds, uncertain. Their once-constant murmured prayers and the soothing hum of healing spells have quieted to an uncomfortable silence.

One healer looks down at a Gasho soldier's torn leg, and her fingers tremble over the injury before she withdraws. She casts a glance toward the others, but none of them move to help the man.

"This isn't right," Elyn mutters, her gaze flicking between the healers.

"Why are they hesitating?" I ask, whispering.

We watch a healer pause before touching an injured soldier. She has yet to cast the soothing, restorative light that has always been the Eserime's gift and duty.

What is she waiting for?

"Something's stopping them," Elyn says.

The strange feeling settles deeper in my gut and twists. The world before me flashes, and I'm falling…the abbey so far away from me…

I crash into the earth, and I'm immediately surrounded by a herd of howlthanes. The creatures stab at me with their spiraled horns, but I roll this way and that way, avoiding their strikes. Their horns snag my armor as I tire.

BAM!

Horns yank my left greave off.

BAM!

Horns tear a vambrace from my wrist. More armor is dislodged from my body.

A large howlthane with horns thicker than a tree trunk stands over me. For a moment, the howlthane's eyes become Jadon's eyes, and the howlthane—Jadon—aims his spiraled horns right at my bare chest—

Shari licks my hand and brings me back to Gasho.

I'm having visions now even while I'm awake. If this vision is a true prophecy, then…

We won the battle.

We lost the war.

And I lost Vallendor.

Because when faced with such decisions, all men choose themselves.

31

Today, I lost Gasho.

"We still have time," Elyn assures me. "It's not over yet, Kai."

I pace and continue to scan the horizon for Jadon—but I only see ruined homes and shops, discarded swords and pikes, and bodies—too many bodies.

"How did he escape?" I rage.

Who gave him Gashoan armor? Who gave him that curved blade? Did *he* kill the Sisters of the Dusky Hills?

Why do I think he did something that horrible?

Because he is the son of two horrible men.

"He's grown bigger," Elyn says, using a discarded tunic to wipe off the blood drying on her golden armor. "I noticed that during the short time he stood beside me. He's taller, wider."

I lift my right hand. "And the mark?"

Elyn shrugs. "Couldn't see where the ink's stopped—but it's spread above the cuff of his tunic."

"Did you talk to the Eserime who weren't healing?"

"That was sadness," she says. "Shock and grief. They're overwhelmed and they don't want to disappoint you. They've come out of their trance, though."

"Without threats from you?" I ask, raising an eyebrow.

"Oh, I had to threaten," she says. "Gently, though."

Nothing fits together in this town, not anymore. Lone sandals sink into the mud, their owners unknown. Ears severed from heads are sprinkled like rose petals on slick cobblestones that have been gouged by blades and spiraled horns. The slain, already bloating from the heat, lie discarded beneath tables and beside altars.

What happened here? Will tomorrow be worse? Should we even try to right Gasho after the battle yet again, just five dawns away from this realm's possible end?

If Danar Rrivae doesn't take Vallendor from me, Jadon will—unless his strings are cut like the puppet he is. But Danar Rrivae will only cut those strings if he thinks I'm weak enough to defeat.

Am I?

Was Jadon captured by the Devourers to be returned to his father? Or did he leave Gasho on his own? And if he *did* leave Gasho on his own, what is he going to do? Where is he trying to go? Will he return to his mortal father, Syrus Wake?

And if he *wasn't* captured, if he willingly left, then he's betrayed me, again.

"We have five dawns left," I say.

"And we'll find Jadon," Elyn says. "We must. Meanwhile, you have to convince Zephar to join our cause. If he does, I will reduce his sentence and restore his rights to travel freely—here and throughout the Aetherium. I may even approach the Council of High Orders and suggest a promotion for him." Her words are measured, like all deals brokered during wartime.

But then I study the twisted wreckage of the town square, the broken bodies littered across the cobblestones. The flickering shadows of Mera and Eserime moving like smoke across this destroyed town. I'd pay almost any price to end this destruction.

Elyn and I try not to flinch, try to stand tall for the sake of the townspeople looking to us. But our eyes can't stop searching for something in this carnage that will restore order here and across my dying realm. The day is ending, and the daystar does not bring the light it once did. Instead, it casts a sickly glow over Gasho and the surrounding desert. Red light bleeds across the horizon and seeps into the cracks of the broken city. The buildings, once proud and grand, are now ragged silhouettes against the burning sky. Everything has been burned and torn apart.

Finally, the Adjudicator nods. "I'll bring as many Raqiel as your uncle will allow, because...this is the end. Meet me in Agon's aerie after you talk to Zephar."

She places her hand on my shoulder. "Thank you for protecting me. Maybe, after we've won this fight, we'll laugh together about me needing your help." She flicks her wings. "I'll look one last time for Jadon. He's here. He must be." She takes to the sky.

I watch her glide away until she's swallowed by smoke and light.

Once this war ends, I will write a strongly worded letter to the manager about how my experience here in this realm left me wanting, how by the end of every day, my armor was covered in blood. The food tastes rank now, and given what happened to this realm, I want my time and money back, or even a trip to one of the nicer realms. I'd also appreciate a new sword.

I stare at Fury's black blade. No nicks. I tap the edge, still sharp even though it bounces off these new otherworldly. Yet my dagger, Tempest, has had no difficulty tearing through muscle and bone.

Why?

A contingent of my Eserime healers—recently chastised by the Adjudicator—moves between the casualties. They place their hands over the hearts of the injured and offer prayers for the dead. I also touch hearts and heads as I make my way toward the Temple of Celestial, growing weaker with each one. Elyn isn't here to heal me, but I offer myself to my people—it's in my nature.

Zephar and the Diminished don't help restore Gasho like they did just days ago. They've already left for the Sanctum, leaving the Eserime to clean up the fallen town alone.

Why? Where is Prince Idus?

His body hangs from a date palm, still clutching his curved sword. The pool of blood beneath him looks darker than the others. He was the last in his bloodline and never became king, because I waited. These poor people relied on me for protection, and the enemy breached our defenses *again*.

Rage swells through me like an ocean on fire—rage at Danar Rrivae for destroying Gasho but also rage at Zephar, who prides himself on being a warrior with a big brain and bigger swords. How did he allow this massacre to happen? Where were the Mera guard who'd been charged with the protection of this sacred city?

I don't want to argue with him, but the longer I wait here, the angrier I become.

Because a cruel dawn draws closer to Vallendor.

The Sanctum no longer smells of sweet chamomile or soothing lavender but instead reeks of rot. The once-beautiful gardens have been trampled. The soil is tinged green and black with the fetid blood of dead Devourers.

Wait. I close my eyes to focus on a hum that shouldn't be possible.

Flies.

There shouldn't be flies in the Sanctum; corpses shouldn't exist in the dwelling place of gods.

There are now dead gods at the Abbey. Jadon. Oh, *shit.*

Up ahead, two Diminished guards stand at the pavilion's entrance. Even from the bottom of this pathway, they make me uncomfortable. Their flat eyes are more muddy than golden. My amulet thrums against my chest, warning me not to approach them.

I turn back. I hike over boulders and scale the cliffs to reach my tent. My muscles cry out and my left arm trembles. I'm weaker now from the fighting and healing down in Gasho. I can feel bruises spreading across my back with every move.

My amulet, though, keeps pulsing through it all, providing a necessary boost of power to compensate for my weakened muscles.

I sweat profusely beneath my unforgiving pewter armor. I will soon need new protection; the breastplate continues to erode, fractures grow on the greaves meant to protect my shins, the vambraces sag shapelessly around my forearms, and the scabbard holding Fury on my back feels soft enough to melt right off.

I keep climbing until I finally reach the bluffs behind my tent. Voices drift out from inside—Zephar's and…

"You told us that she'd be here." Orewid Rolse, the disrespectful oddity with the spotless armor and new boots.

"She's down in Gasho," Zephar says. "If you would've come when I told you to come—"

I peek through the tent's flap.

Orewid Rolse lounges on my—*my*!—chaise lounge. Four other Mera soldiers stand behind him, and they wear breastplates marked with those fiery crossed swords. Crusaders.

Zephar stands with Diminished from my own contingent. Imlodel, Dayjah, and Alan, but…

Something's out of tune.

Their skin bears crimson markings, but the color of their skin beneath the ink looks as degraded as the Devourers we just fought.

No, it's not possible. I sniff the air.

My tent stinks of dirt and medicines. *Like being left in the desert to die but…*

Oh, no. These Mera Diminished have been…

Resurrected.

How? I didn't see any leather-winged flying beasts soaring over the city.

Also inside the tent is Tatanye Lote, the Eserime healer who'd met Elyn and me on our trip to the Temple of Malik Sindire. She sits beside another healer, both women slumped over, their foreheads against their knees.

Oh, no. Are they using their order's powers to bring the fallen back to life? It's impossible, but I've seen many impossible occurrences recently.

"Will she return to you?" Orewid Rolse now asks Zephar.

Zephar smiles smugly. "Of course. Despite everything, she's still in love with me."

The men laugh and nod like they're comparing notes about conquests.

"Hard to believe," Orewid Rolse says. "One of the most powerful beings in the Aetherium moments away from losing it all for love."

Zephar snorts and folds his arms. "It's obvious you haven't been loved by me."

"She's lost her beauty. Her skin looks like an elder's quilt."

Zephar glares at him now. "Her beauty remains—that will never change."

Orewid Rolse takes a moment, then asks, "And what if she *doesn't* return? Or what if she slips by like she did before and kills more of your men?"

"Then you will go down to Gasho and stop her there."

Orewid Rolse glares at Zephar. "Since you didn't stop her before?"

"I was away," Zephar says. "He was one of my best archers— "

"And she *still* killed him. You had a chance to end her when she first landed outside of Gasho days ago, and you did nothing. Then, when the urts and cowslews invaded the city, your warriors had her surrounded and you did nothing. She keeps walking when she should be dead."

I gasp, recalling those footprints in the red dirt, the swords drawn on me as I was fighting those otherworldly on my first day in Gasho.

Fuck! I *knew* it.

Zephar tilts his head. "You don't trust me? She's nearby. You've seen how she looks at me. She'll do anything for me. Now, it's your turn to follow through."

When he doesn't speak, Zephar spreads his arms. "How many times must I say it? I believe in your mission. I believe we must remain pure and separate from the other orders to do our job—to wreak destruction as Supreme wants. I believe this with my whole heart."

Not only have the Crusaders invaded my Sanctum, they've also infected Zephar with their outrageous beliefs.

I didn't imagine that feeling of being an enemy in a place that's supposed to feel like home. The Mera who'd shot at me was supposed to kill me.

"Kaivara Megidrail is now the last one," Orewid Rolse says, "and she embodies everything that we stand against. She must die—and that seems to be underway already. She must die, and then she must live again for our cause."

Live again?

Zephar frowns. "I don't disagree. When she comes back to the Sanctum, then…" He waves his hand at the undead Mera standing behind him.

I creep alongside the tent until I gain a wider view.

The Diminished stand in two groups. Those standing with Shari had repaired Gasho the last time invaders came to the city. On that day, they'd cleared the aqueduct with good cheer. Just seven dawns ago, they'd burned the corpses of otherworldly and showed the Gasho children their swords and markings. Worry now shines bright in their eyes. Do they want this? Are they complicit in my murder—*and resurrection*?

Standing on the other side of the pavilion are warriors who'd been injured, who were once moments away from death. They wear their original Destroyer markings, but a new brand burns red hot in the middle of their bare chests.

Fiery crossed swords.

They stand there swaying, their eyes muddy, their unbranded skin mottled brown and green, like the scummy surface of a neglected pond.

My hands burn, and the urge to scream bubbles in my chest, like my heart might explode at any moment. I don't want to wait for help to arrive. I want to destroy them right now, Zephar included. But what would be the point?

I'm here on Vallendor for a purpose. The mountain can't sink into the swamp. If I fight alone, what would I gain?

The Crusaders are just one more problem on my growing list.

My relationship with Zephar is no longer an issue. We said goodbye a long time ago. I just didn't realize it.

"Tonight," Zephar declares, "I'll fuck her until all strength has left her legs. Then I'll take the amulet and the armor—I've already destroyed any protective clothing she's stored in these trunks—and she'll be as naked and powerless as the day Lyra Laserie gave birth to her filthy abomination."

Filthy abomination?

"You'll sleep with her even though she's betrayed you with the traitor's son?" Orewid Rolse says.

I reel in shock. Zephar knows about Jadon.

His face is still as stone. "She has no idea how close I've come."

Zephar lowers his head, his nostrils flared, his eyes shining with tears. "I'll do my part. I won't hesitate. Her infidelity just makes this easier for me. For all of us. My unhappiness isn't new, nor is it caused by the traitor's son—I'd taken a step away from Kai even before the Adjudicator deposited her in that forest outside of Maford."

I can't believe my ears. We were still together then. We were still in love. *Weren't we?*

This could all be a trick, I reason desperately. Zephar could be protecting me by trying to fool this Crusader into thinking he hates me.

But my heart and head agree for once: *Sweetheart, this isn't a ruse. Accept it for what it is. Betrayal.*

Is this what worried Shari? Has she been trying to tell me all this time? *You in danger, girl.*

Elyn and Sybel were right: Zephar isn't who I thought he was.

Neither is Jadon.

But now I know they are my enemies. And now, I will destroy them all—

Celestial!

A woman's voice cries out for me. She sounds like Ancress Tisen.

My pulse racing, I look over my shoulder at the desert outside Gasho.

Celestial! Please hurry!

Yes, that's Ancress Tisen calling me, praying.

But she's dead…

Right?

32

There's no one here.

Just me and a sea of sand.

Ancress Tisen is nowhere to be found, nor any other woman who could've sounded like her. Just rocks and dirt and wind.

I'm alone.

A sandstorm brews on the horizon, rushing closer to me…closer… I lift my chin, unafraid.

The sand melts, and Zephar Itikin strides toward me. His smile is too wide and doesn't quite reach his eyes. Dark, empty eyes without empathy, with no trace of the person they once belonged to. His eyes have seen too much, and he's felt too little. There is no warmth in them, no spark of recognition—only the cold, hollow gaze of a man transformed into something else, into *someone else*.

His leather tunic and breeches fit like a second skin. His twin blades—forged of catherite—rest across his back, their hilts gleaming faintly in the dying light. Zephar embodies control and discipline, but a dangerous emptiness clings to him now. He keeps smiling at me.

I wait to meet my newest ex-boyfriend.

"Don't we need to leave for the Sea of Devour?" he asks, grinning strangely.

"What are you doing here, Zephar?" I ask.

He cocks his head. "Looking for you, Beloved."

"You think I'm stupid, don't you?" I lift my hand to preempt his response. "Of *course* you think I'm stupid, and you always have. For so long, I *was* stupid. Not anymore. Today is a new day, a new dawn."

He shakes his head in confusion. "I don't know what you're—"

"How did you know that I was here?" I ask. "At this random point in the desert?"

"Does it matter? I'm here now." He sighs and rolls his eyes. "What are we bickering about this time?"

"Orewid Rolse is a Crusader," I say, "and you're conspiring with him to kill me, *Beloved*. *That's* what we're bickering about this time."

His expression remains neutral. "Then you know why I'm here."

"No," I say, "I've only heard rumors, but you have said nothing to me directly. I can't wait to learn why I must die—and why you must be the one to kill me."

Zephar's smirk fades.

"While I was away from you, I..." I swallow and continue. "I found companionship with someone else."

He doesn't react.

I want him to react, so I take a step toward him and say, cruelly, "I fucked Jadon Rrivae Wake. Last season and then two nights ago. I regret neither occasion."

His cheeks burn bright as he clenches his jaw.

I cock my head. "Now. Tell me all that you've wanted to say but have only whispered behind my back."

"For Vallendor Realm to reach its true potential," Zephar finally replies, his voice hard, "you must no longer be its Grand Defender."

"You question my leadership, then?"

"Your leadership is simply a symptom of the larger disease," he says. "Your father, Izariel—"

"You will respect your lord's name," I snap, my words hot enough to gather the storm clouds now forming above us.

Zephar's eyes flare, but he waits, inhaling and exhaling. He squares his shoulders, then says, "We no longer recognize his position in our order. *Izariel* broke his vow to his order when he sought companionship within another order, a weaker order, and compounded his offense by conceiving a daughter."

"Me," I say, bristling. "So?"

"Only Mera can be defenders and destroyers," he says.

"My mixed blood is no fault of my own—"

"I never claimed it was."

"And I've proven myself to be Mera—"

He snorts and rolls his eyes. "You're *here* because you were given Vallendor as Izariel's daughter."

"And you were my second because you're the son of Bezeph Itikin, my father's old friend, and because he and your mother wanted me to be your bride."

Bezeph, a former captain, had waged war beside my father since their first campaign. They'd been best friends until Bezeph's marriage to Mablinel, a Mera socialite whose family paid others to fulfill their required service. Once Father started to secretly see my mother, Mablinel conspired to expose their relationship. That is, until Father joined the Council of High Orders. *Then* she fostered the friendship and eventual courtship between Zephar and me and even allowed her daughter, Naelah, to fight alongside us. Naelah is no more, and Zephar remains a prisoner on the realm that he'd been assigned to protect with me.

"What did Orewid Rolse promise you and the other Diminished?" I ask.

Zephar doesn't answer.

"Will you fight with me against Danar Rrivae?"

He laughs but doesn't say "yes" or "no."

"Zephar," I say, "he is the common threat right now. Can't you put aside this stupid purification test in the face of the danger we're in?"

He folds his arms and lowers his chin to his chest.

"Orewid Rolse does this, Zee," I say. "He stirs up Mera like you who have otherwise been disciplined, and he appeals to your anger and desire to strike back. He blames those of us with the blood of other orders for your station in life, and you believe him. There are so many Mera in jail or wandering Anathema because of this man, someone who's never been jailed or punished in any way."

Still no response from my former lover.

"I've seen the living-dead Mera," I say. "Are you in favor of these abominations?"

"Mera warriors stronger than even you?" he asks. "Do you expect me to say no to that?"

"Are your *followers* interested in being living-dead?" I ask. "Do they get to choose?"

He squints at me.

"Orewid Rolse won't just stop at your fighters," I say. "Soon, it will be *your* turn to die and be returned to walk again. Is that what *you* want? You'd be the most powerful dead man on Vallendor. When I kill you, do you want me to bring you back, not as Zephar Itikin but as something you're not? Do you aspire to become a diminished Diminished?"

He snorts again and lets his gaze wander the red sands. "Anything else?"

"You continue this way," I say, "and you, too, will be punished. You will be destroyed. The Adjudicator will see to it—and so will the Council. So will my father. So will I."

He swallows, and his jaw tightens. Fear lights his eyes for a moment, but then he narrows his eyes and nods. Without a word, he turns back to the desert and strides into the storm of red sand.

My heart hurts.

I've lost him. His sword. His love.

My chest feels numb; all of me feels numb. Every time I take a breath, something inside of me rips and fills my eyes with water.

Moths flutter around me as I Spryte to the Abbey of Mount Devour. Though their numbers have dwindled, the moths that remain brush their wings across my cheeks before they depart. They are a soft and tender reminder that delicate things still exist here.

Elyn paces outside the Abbey of Mount Devour, her eyes scanning the horizon. Justice glints from the scabbard on her back. When she spots me, her manic eyes soften. "You're here." Her shoulders droop with relief.

But then she frowns as she takes in my crumbling breastplate. "I thought you were changing armor?"

I push my hand through my unraveling braid. "The plans have changed some."

The wind howls, and the long grass and bluebells surrounding the abbey tremble. Long ago, my mother told me that winds are the people's desperate prayers to the gods. Who do desperate gods pray to?

Two dawns have come and gone since I was last at the abbey. From the outside, this building rises like a spire from the crest of the mountain, a fortress overlooking a turbulent realm. But the abbey has become a mausoleum.

The sky above us churns with gold-and-algae-green light, swirling like oil on water, a sick sky.

"You find Jadon?" I ask Elyn.

She shakes her head. "You talk to Zephar?"

Hands clammy and lungs tight, I tell her about Zephar, the Crusaders, and the living-dead Mera. "The Eserime are being forced to become resurrectors," I say, shaking my head. "I saw them at the Sanctum: dead-eyed, mottle-skinned Diminished. Those fiery crossed swords have been branded onto their chests."

Imlodel and Dayjah both have Yeaden blood, and they'd stood in my tent...*dead.*

Elyn gasps. "How did they learn...? Are they working with Danar Rrivae?"

I shake my head. "I don't think so. But someone's read the *Librum Esoterica*—"

"Or they have some other book that we don't know about," she suggests.

"The Eserime working as resurrectors," I whisper.

"Who thought of that?" Elyn asks as we hurry down the long hallway.

"Did I unknowingly recruit them to my team?" I wonder. *I'll tear it down, rebuild it, and even bring your lost ones back to life, just believe in me.* "Did I do this, not realizing there could be disastrous consequences? Or did I recruit them, knowing full well the dangers but charging ahead anyway...?" Even as I walk, I squeeze the bridge of my nose, trying to remember...

"Kai," Elyn says, shaking her head, "I'm telling you: the Eserime coming here to work with Mera like this? It wasn't your idea."

"It must have been Zephar's idea, then." My heart hurts even more.

Zephar had already resented me: Orewid Rolse just gave him a direction, and the powerful imagery of fiery crossed swords to symbolize his hatred. Will he choose to hide his Mera markings, the ones he's so proud of, beneath those branded swords?

"Zephar also knew about Jadon and me," I say as we reach the now-abandoned great hall. "So I confessed to him. That's been fueling his animosity, too. To think that loving him was easy, once upon a time.

"Maybe I couldn't remember that I loved Zephar because deep in my heart, I knew that he didn't love me. I don't know what I could've done to prevent this. I should've paid more attention..."

"This isn't your fault, Kai," Elyn says. "Don't justify his hatred and violence because *he* can't get over you choosing someone else—"

"This is more than jealousy," I say, tears streaming down my cheeks.

"You're right," she says. "This is pure..."

"Hatred."

Elyn pales, but white flames flare in her eyes. "They truly believe that they rule the Aetherium. Fortunately, there are more of us than them."

I swipe at my wet face with my trembling hands. "I've totally fucked up Vallendor."

Sentinels still guard the Glass of Infinite Realms.

As Elyn and I made our way up to the aerie, we'd passed those other sentinels as well as the stewards and senators who'd survived Jadon's infection. They continue cleaning, disinfecting, and placing wards around the abbey's corridors and meeting spaces, its living quarters and jails. They are not surrendering. They are fighting to remain.

Vallendor hasn't been completely abandoned *yet.* I haven't been left here alone *yet.*

Agon the Kindness isn't working in the aerie, though. The space feels too still without his rustling robes and the sound of pages turning in those big books.

No powders and plants, books or bowls crowd the worktables. No forgotten sprigs or scraps of paper have been left on the floor. No lingering smells of crushed herbs; the fire that had consumed Celedan Docci no longer burns. The *Librum Esoterica* is gone: I see no sparkle of its presence. In fact, a third of the books that had been collected no longer sit on these shelves.

My heart kicks in my chest at the sight of this absence of study and craft.

The Abbey itself is being stripped away, book by book.

"I need a stronger sword," I say now, my eyes lingering on the empty bookshelves.

"I'll search for Agon," Elyn says, "and you go down to see Usese. He's still the abbey's blacksmith and armorer, and he'll do what he can to help us prepare. We'll meet back here."

I hear only one hammer striking an anvil when, in the past, I've heard thirty. The air in the forge is stagnant. No cloying, acrid smoke stings my eyes. The room feels too fresh to be a home of iron and steel. And though the furnace glows orange and blue, nothing is melting in those flames. This place is almost as still and cold as the aerie.

This silence is my doing, and the inactivity here will only spread.

Usese Ebrithin is the size of most Yeaden—muscled and wide, and tall but not as tall as the Mera. He's more of a bull than a horse. He keeps his black hair short so that it won't catch fire or get caught in his tools. His smock is as long as a dinner table; tailors must have used half a field of cotton to make his black tunic. When he sees me, the creases in the armorer's face deepen. His wide smile shows off teeth studded with jewels and metal.

"The Lady of the Verdant Realm!" Usese shouts. "The Grand Defender of Vallendor! It took your realm teetering on the brink of destruction for you to finally pay me a visit!"

I hug him; he's as solid as his anvil. "I'd wanted to come sooner but..."

"The living are toppling here like weak brick walls." He turns back to the single new war hammer taking shape on his anvil.

"I have a question for you," I say. "Do linionium-made weapons exist here on Vallendor?"

He snorts. "Certainly not. You think you got trouble now? Imagine what would happen if a linionium-made greatsword fell into the wrong hands." He glances at me. "Why do you ask, Lady?"

"I need a new blade." I pull Fury from my sagging scabbard and present it to him. "She's powerless against the new otherworldly that I'm now fighting."

Usese takes the sword, peers at the black blade etched with moths, and runs his finger along its edge. "Who forged this?"

I swallow, then say, "Jadon Rrivae Wake, and it was a gift. I accepted her, of course, unaware at the time that he was the son of both Syrus Wake and Danar Rrivae. Up until recently, Fury has proven to be a mighty blade. Now, though, she bounces off enemies that she used to slay without effort."

"That's because this sword was made by the usurper and traitor." Usese clicks his decorated teeth and shakes his massive head. "Agon shared that he's studying the *Librum*. Some of that knowledge has revealed that the traitor created new beasts that are invincible against mortal weapons. We're also just learning that blades like Fury can no longer harm a being that has been created by the one who created her, nor can she harm a member of the creator's family. Danar Rrivae has obviously imparted his son with knowledge gained from his travel across the Aetherium."

I shake my head. "But I've killed otherworldly before with her."

"Not this new generation of otherworldly," the Yeaden says, "which is why you're here now, asking about linionium-made blades. Have other blades cut down the enemy?"

Justice? Yes.

Zephar's dual blades? Yes.

The blades of other Mera warriors? Yes.

Even my dagger, Tempest, worked. Each of these blades had been made by immortal armorers throughout the Aetherium. Fury, the only sword that cuts as well as a butter knife, was made by a demigod and child of the traitor.

Shit.

"None were linionium," I point out.

"Catherite is still stronger than the steel used for…" He lifts Fury, then holds my gaze. "I'm sorry if this is unwelcome news, but she must be destroyed."

My nostrils flare and sweat pricks my underarms. "If you must." I close my eyes. I don't want to witness the end of this loyal blade.

"Lady Megidrail," Usese whispers.

I breathe through my clenched teeth before opening my eyes to look at him.

He holds a red cushion, and sitting upon it is a sword. "A gift from your father," the Yeaden says.

The hilt is wrapped in black leather. The cross-guard is embellished with a pair of small moths on each side, framing the blade. Another moth has been engraved on the dark metal cap of the pommel as though she's watching over the sword. And the blade…

"Linionium," Usese says.

The black blade tapers to a razor-sharp point. Ghostly moths spread along the length of the blade, shimmering in the forge's dim light, lifting her even though she is still.

So light. So beautiful. So *deadly.*

"It's as powerful as the Council will allow you to have." The Yeaden chuckles and adds, "Which means that it is *still* the most powerful blade throughout Vallendor. She is bound to you—and to you alone. Any person, mortal or immortal, who dares to touch her will die where they stand. Do you understand?"

My body shakes as I nod.

"And her name?" he asks.

I think about the power of this blade and the dread she'll inspire.

I think about the moths: transformation, death, rebirth, intuition.

I think about my place as Grand Defender and Lady of the Verdant Realm… Divine, Celestial, Maelstrom, Kielat, Aniel, Elenven, Lady of Courage, Goddess of Victory…

My mixed blood of warriors and healers, explorers and builders and scholars…the Blood of All.

All of it must end because one coming dawn brings more danger than all others.

"I'll name her…Cruel Dawn." I kiss the blade.

Usese bows his head. "And so she shall be known and recorded as Cruel Dawn."

And now I must return to work.

My first kill? Zephar.

And then Danar Rrivae.

And last, the man I love.

Jadon Rrivae Wake.

33

Elyn searches the aerie. She looks beneath worktables and scans the bookshelves, her face tight and her eyes narrowed. She mutters under her breath as she opens drawers and cabinets, as she paws through papers and maps.

I stand silently at the aerie's threshold and watch her.

She senses that she's being watched and spins around, wide-eyed. *Caught.*

"What are you looking for, Adjudicator?" I ask coolly.

She shakes her head. "Everything. Everyone."

I look around the bare room before gazing steadily at her. "No Agon?"

She exhales hard. "No, and the other wisdoms won't tell me if he's still here on Vallendor." She scans the aerie once more.

"And so you're looking for him in the drawers?" I step across the threshold with my hands clasped behind my back.

Elyn says, "Ha. I'm looking for any clues on his whereabouts, or about what we should do."

"Like the *Librum Esoterica*." I wander over to the aerie's sole window and gaze at the windswept bluebells below. "In your search, did you happen to find any other solutions?"

"We don't need the *Librum*," she says. She looks up and rushes over with a grin. "Usese gave you a new sword. Let's have a look."

I know she's changing the subject, but I slowly pull the blade from the sagging scabbard.

She gasps. "That is the most beautiful weapon I've ever seen, Kai."

"Anyone who dares to touch it—mortal or immortal—will die," I say, watching her. "It's the most powerful blade on Vallendor."

She snorts. "Unfortunately, it isn't the most powerful *weapon* on Vallendor. *Jadon* is still the most powerful weapon on Vallendor."

"And yet I'm still supposed to kill him...*somehow*."

She stares at me, tilting her head. "Yes, you're supposed to kill him. *We're* supposed to kill him. It was never supposed to be *easy*. What's wrong? Why are you acting like someone's plotting something behind your back again?"

I laugh without humor. "Because many people *have* been plotting behind my back. Because everyone I thought was a friend has now become my enemy!"

Outside the abbey, the sky continues to change, shifting from that sickly pink to a deeper indigo streaked with corpse gray. Impossibly, the Aetherium itself is rotting because of Vallendor's march toward ruin. The Aetherium is rotting because of me and my failures.

Bursts of lightning suddenly flash behind thick, swirling clouds. The wind picks up—these aren't frantic prayers of the realm-born calling on the gods for help. No, this wind slips through the cracks in the abbey's stone walls. This is Vallendor collapsing.

I hold my breath as I wait for the storm to break and unleash the violence building in the sky—and in my uncle's aerie.

Elyn says, "You can't be suspicious of me again. What are you thinking?"

"I'm thinking... She knows where to find Agon. She's looking for the *Librum Esoterica*. Killing Jadon can't be the only way to save Vallendor."

"What?" Elyn screeches.

"Zephar's betrayal changes everything."

"Kai—"

"I've accepted that I must kill Danar Rrivae," I say, holding up a finger. "He's told me that I must die for him claim Vallendor."

I hold up a second finger. "I've accepted that I must kill Zephar Itikin. He plans to strip me bare and murder me in my sleep."

I let my hand fall. "But Jadon has never expressed intent to kill me," I say. "*You've* said that Jadon wanted me dead." I stare at her and watch her begin to squirm. "My dear uncle has also said that Jadon means to kill me. You and Agon have plucked my wings and restricted my movements and lied to me about who I am, what I've done, and how my actions have threatened Vallendor and all the other realms."

Elyn and Agon control Vallendor because they control *me*. Anyone who possesses any more power than they do endangers the plans for this realm…a realm without me as Grand Defender.

I step closer to Elyn. She has to look up to meet my eyes.

We stare at each other for a moment before she relaxes, and a laugh bubbles up from her chest. "You're fucking with me, right?" she asks.

Before I can speak, a steward enters the room holding two bundles. Even with the chaos all over the abbey, he moves with an assured grace. His simple robes, a deep blue-gray fabric, blend into the shadows of the room. His pale freckled face is stern, and he bows low before placing the scented bundles on the worktable.

The parcels, wrapped in coarse linen and tied with thick twine, smell of fresh-baked bread, recently harvested herbs, and glazed sugar. Their intoxicating aromas fill the room, bringing warmth to this cold space.

Elyn quickly unties the twine and unwraps these gifts. Her eyes light up at the loaf of still-warm bread, its crust golden and perfect. "I asked for food and water for the both of us," she says, a little more relaxed in the presence of good food. She points to the second bundle. "That's yours."

I narrow my eyes at her again, still unsure. "They aren't the same?"

Elyn doesn't answer right away. "Yes and no. Yours is heavy on honeycakes while mine…" She smiles and pulls out a cookie with a thumbprint of purple jam. "Mine has these." She takes a bite and ties the bundle back up. "But I'll trade you some."

Cookies for honeycakes? No. Absolutely not.

This could still be a distraction. All of my friends are enemies now, so why not Elyn? Especially since we're no longer friends? What was she *really* looking for as I stood at the aerie's threshold?

I join her at the table and peer at my unopened parcel. "What if we don't kill Jadon—?" I hold up my hand before she can object. "What if I could control him instead? What if I could use Miasma against our enemies instead?"

She gapes at me. "You're…weakening, Kai. You aren't thinking straight."

"Bullshit," I say. "I don't know the cooks who prepared this pack. I don't know the ingredients in these honeycakes or the cleanliness of the water in this canteen. Who created these tonics? Who cut and prepared these bandages? Trusting anything and everyone is a thing of the past. That's not my mind *dying*. That's making *connections.*"

Elyn doesn't want me to control Vallendor again. That makes more sense to me than suddenly coming back into my life, acting like my best friend. She's still the same woman who said I'd never be the god that Vallendor needed and deserved. Does she think *she's* the god Vallendor needs and deserves? Is *she* tired of being a fucking librarian and a judge? Vallendor is already teetering on the brink of destruction, already mired in calamity, in need of a steady hand to guide her back on the right path. What I see as an end, she sees as the beginning.

Yes, Elyn sees an opportunity with Vallendor, which means she must kill Jadon—and me. Unless…she only wants *me* gone.

I remember how she looked at Jadon after that fight in Fihel, at the camp that night. I remember how gentle she was, touching him. She'd draped her hand on his cheeks and pursed her lips to blow the splinter from his eye, and there was joy, not duty, in her smile. She'd drawn that *intimate* sketch of his hand tattoo, in so much detail. She couldn't have drawn that without seeing it up close.

I don't want her wings. I want my own wings—my own power—back.

And I want the *Librum Esoterica*. To find the answers I seek, I'd study the book myself even though I'm no scholar.

"Where's Jadon?" I ask Elyn now. *"Where is he?"*

She grabs her parcel of food and frowns at me. "Something's bothering you, and I wish you'd just say—"

"Did you help him escape?" I ask, closing in on her again. "Did you promise him another gift, like last time?" At the Sea of Devour, I'd discovered she had promised Jadon that she'd remove his mark if he killed me. He failed, of course, and the mark remained.

"How was it that, back in Gasho, he was with you one moment," I ask, "and then, the next moment, he wasn't?" I wait for her to respond. When she doesn't, I add, "At the Sea of Devour that last time, you said that Jadon was the weapon who'd served both Danar's purpose and *your* purpose. What did you mean by that?"

Elyn flushes, realizing finally that something is off in this room, that something is seriously out of tune. The quiet hum of the abbey now feels suffocating. She glances at the door, then over to the window, as if she's trying to pin down what she hasn't been able to see until now.

"Is there someone in my life I can trust?" I whisper. I don't want to believe the answer—but reality sinks in with a cold, cruel certainty.

There's no one in my life I can trust.

POP! POP! POP!

The abbey shakes. It isn't supposed to.

Elyn and I exchange a brief glance. We rush over to the window again.

Stewards now take to the sky. One moment, they stand in the field of blue flowers; the next, they're gone in a burst of light. The whole abbey shimmies. It's obvious they're trying to get the fuck out of Vallendor *right now.*

A chill runs down my spine as I realize that this isn't a drill. This isn't a false alarm.

They're evacuating.

The corpse-gray sky darkens as the air grows heavier with evacuees. We've crossed the line of no return.

"We should go," Elyn says, eyes on the sky.

"Where are they going?" I ask, watching her and wondering what she knows that she isn't sharing. "If they're leaving Vallendor, why aren't they using—?" I point down to the Raqiel guards who remain standing at the Glass of Infinite Realms.

"Because they aren't going to another realm—"

I shake my head. "They can't just hide in the Between for too long. They wouldn't survive. They *must* be going to some other—"

"Kai, it doesn't matter right now—"

"It matters to *me*," I shout over her. "It doesn't matter to *you* because you haven't been sentenced to die here. You can leave Vallendor anytime you want."

She backs away from me. "I don't know what's come over you. Maybe you're just exhausted and hungry, but whatever it is, you need to snap out of it right now. There's too much at stake. I'm not your enemy, Kai."

"That's what they all say." I hurl my bundle of food out the window.

Elyn gapes at me. "Kai..."

"I've snapped out of it," I say, "and now I see that I'm alone here, that everyone I meet wants what I have, that they think they need it for their own survival. I'll have to save Vallendor on my own."

Only four moths flutter around me, and their delicate wings brush against my skin as though they're saying "goodbye." I land on the ground, on the highest bluffs at the Rim of the Shadows. I want to take off this armor—it's too hot, too heavy. I swallow, but my mouth is as dry as the desert. I blink, but no tears wet my eyes. Yet the world still blurs.

The thin air feels charged with an unnatural energy. The view below should be breathtaking, but the desert landscape sprawled out before me remains barren. The earth has withered, and the once-vibrant wild grasses crumble into dust with each gust of wind. The river that had briefly sprung to life is choked again with stagnant water.

The sky above me churns with dull golds and muted violets, a bruised sky to match the bruises that mottle my skin from my neck and back down to my smallest toe. Lumis, the daystar, the warmest of us all, casts a cold, distant light, and his rays are dim as an ember in a dying hearth. And as I sit here, on the brink of all things, the weight of Vallendor's death presses down on me.

The unnaturally cold winds carry the scent of death across the hills and mountains that tower over Gasho. The pine, walnut, and acacia trees have twisted into skeletons, their branches gnarled and barren.

I close my eyes, trying to wipe these images—evidence of a dying realm, an acute reminder of my failure—from my mind. I've lost this fight. What can I do other than sit here and wait for the end to come?

I needed an army to fight Danar Rrivae, and now I find myself alone in this battle.

The Renrians are required to fight for me—and Separi and her kin can't say no to the Lady of the Verdant Realm. But I won't ask.

Elyn will use the Raqiel against me just as she did in previous battles. She told me seasons ago that I'd never leave Vallendor if I failed to yield and obey her. I didn't believe her threat, and now I'm dying in this land of chaos. Who's the fool? Me, for not believing her.

And then there's Zephar…

I needed his blades and the Diminished—though in their new state, they are no longer mine.

Yes, I've lost this fight.

A growl sends me scrambling to my feet. I reach for my new blade.

A windwolf pounces on me from behind.

I roll away, but not fast enough. His paw snaps the pauldron off my left shoulder. The pewter armor, as cracked as it is, barely protects my skin and bone. Chunks of my breastplate, greaves, and vambraces fall into the dirt. I spot bleeding sores on my knees and the backs of my hands. I taste my own poisoned blood each time I swallow. Every time I blink, I see traces of someone I lost.

Jamart. Vinasa. Tisen…

My whole body hurts, screaming, "No more." I'm about to give my body what it wants.

The four otherworldly snarl at me, teeth wet and filthy with another creature's flesh.

I consider letting the windwolves take me, but my head shouts louder than my body, "Fuck dying by windwolf. If you're losing Vallendor, make your death an epic death."

Fine.

I hold up Cruel Dawn, even if it hurts both of my arms to do so. "Whose blood will stain this first?" I point Cruel Dawn at the wolf pacing in front of me. "Will it be yours?" Without looking, I gesture at the wolf lurking to my right. "Or will it be yours?"

"You may kill us," the pacing pack-leader says, *"but you will still fail."*

"Yeah," I say, "but you won't be here to say, 'Told you so.'"

The new blade swings easily through the air, slicing the head off a wolf who has no time to howl before he dies. Another windwolf leaps toward me, and I slide beneath him and cut him open along his belly. The steaming tangle of the wolf's guts splashes across the dirt before the rest of his body does.

The last two wolves pause as I stagger to my feet.

I blink and see Veril and Lively and Mother…

The greaves that had been protecting my shins lie on the ground, no longer adorning my calves.

"Care to join your pack?" I ask the surviving wolves.

"We will die anyway—today or two days from now." The windwolves howl again and charge at me.

"See you, then, in two days." Even as I slit one's neck and behead the other, I'm overwhelmed by sadness. Even the otherworldly have given up on the possibility that I'll save this realm.

Anger. Lowly windwolves no longer fear me, not even with my amulet or Cruel Dawn, the strongest blade in the realm.

Pain rips through me, sharp and insistent. My muscles throb, and the once-solid armor jostles against my body, now a heavy burden. Each blow jolts my ribs, my spine, and my arms.

Loneliness sticks to me more than any physical sensation.

I fall to my knees, a gasp of pain on my lips. My mouth tastes like burned butter and stagnant water, overripe berries and rancid meat. I taste anger, frustration, exhaustion… I taste good things polluted and turned sour.

Vallendor will never be the paradise it was intended to be because I was never the god it needed or deserved.

"So you're just gonna lie down and surrender?"

34

Jadon squints as though he can barely see me. His color-shifting eyes are now bloodshot slits. Other than the uncertainty in his gaze, he looks as though he already owns more than half of this damned realm. He's grown since I saw him last: he's as tall as the shortest Mera warrior now, and his cap-sleeved leather tunic and breeches are tighter on his muscular frame. His thick hair looks like he was carried here by the wind. The damning marking has spread past his forearm, now nearly at his shoulder, and it glows on this dawn like a newly created realm. His skin has deepened to the light tans of a peeling eucalyptus tree. He smells of smoke and sweat, and his voice crackles like flame in my direction. And then he smiles.

Trouble has found me.

My stomach twists, and saliva fills my mouth.

The protective shield that Elyn wrapped around me back on the night the abbey fell has dissolved. Now, the power that Jadon carries in his mere existence smothers me.

"I'm not sitting, I'm kneeling," I say, crawling away from the slain windwolves and staggering to my feet. "Do I look like the type to surrender?"

Jadon chuckles and nods toward the dead otherworldly. "You didn't look like you were having fun." He pauses, and his smile broadens. "Was it something they said? Or…" He cocks his head, and his gaze drops to my hand. "Is it because you're no longer wielding my gift?

Where's Fury, my love?"

My love?

I say nothing and take a step away from him. My thoughts grow foggy, and I can't tell if that is the effect of my own confusion or the insidious, creeping Miasma. The air around me feels heavy, pulsing against my chest and back like a living thing. My skin is damp and sweaty, my underarms sticky. The remaining pieces of armor that I still wear creak with every breath I take, those once-sturdy plates barely protecting me as they once did. A sudden, biting draft near my hipbone reveals a new breach that appeared when I killed the windwolves.

Just as I feared, bruises have spread across my side. The dull throb in my ribcage and the pain in my lower back are more than just external damage—death seizes me from my very core, just like the Voidful who'd surrounded the Broken Hammer. Apples rot first from the inside.

Jadon's blue and lavender eyes sparkle, and his smile becomes more of a sneer. "I didn't expect to find you here alone, Kai, not with only two dawns left." He takes a step toward me, closing the gap between us. "We need to talk." He points to my new sword. "As beautiful and as powerful as she looks, you might as well put her away. You can't kill me—"

"*Yet.*" I swallow the bile now burning up my throat. "And I'd rather not put her away. Thanks, though, for your suggestion."

This man standing before me, with those eyes and glowing skin… I don't know him. I wonder if I ever did. I'm trapped here with him, a beautiful disaster, without a solution, without an ally.

Not that any of my friends were allies.

Jadon exhales and squeezes the bridge of his nose. "It was never fair that you and I were pitted against each other. We've come so far." He shakes his head. "I've missed you so much, and it nearly broke me, willing you to come up here so that we could be together again. And now you're here, and now we're free to…to…"

He shakes his head again. "To love each other, especially since you and Zephar can never be. I may not be immortal, but I'll live a long life with you. I'll protect you—"

I hold up my bruised and now-swollen hand. "This isn't about your protection. Nothing is ever that simple. There's the realm and all the life that is mine to defend. That was my purpose, Jadon. *That* was my destiny, as futile as it might be. But my own fate? If Vallendor dies, I, too, will die. Living a long life with you has always been a dream. In the end, neither matters."

Jadon snorts. "How romantic."

And now it's my turn to stare at him. "My job never mattered to you?"

"*You* mattered to me," he says, his arms outstretched toward me. "You *still* matter to me."

"And Vallendor—?"

"Vallendor," he says, rolling his eyes.

"'Vallendor' means not only you," I say, "but also Philia and Jamart the candlemaker and Farmer Gery's dog Milo and Tazara the king of the night-dwelling creatures, and these canyons and that fucking tree down there… I loved and cared about it all, and even though we know this fight is over, part of me, the part that most wants to live, is still trying to figure out how I'll save this realm—even if I can't kill Danar Rrivae, who is bent on destruction just so he can challenge Supreme."

I step closer to Jadon even as nausea roils through me. "My love is bigger than yours. My commitment is *bigger*. My loss is *bigger*. This is just the truth. Do you understand? I want companionship. I desire friendship. I crave love. Once upon a time, for a blink of an eye, you gave me all of those things. But you lied to me, and you are still lying to me."

"What have I lied to you about now?" he asks, eyes wide.

I stare at him, at that tattoo of the elements slowly slinking up to his shoulder, eating away at his mortality. His markings boast of power while my bruises shuffle me toward death. This, too, goes against the natural order.

"Ask me anything right now," he says, "and I'll tell you the truth." He pauses, then adds, "If he lets me."

I squint at him. Him, *Jadon Rrivae.*

"Did you ever hold people hostage in that horrid Beaminster jail?" I ask.

He doesn't even blink. "Yes, and I regret it all," he says, as Jadon Wake.

"How did you escape my temple?"

He flushes, and this time, he blinks. "I struck up a conversation with Ancress Tisen from behind the closed door. I told her that she was beautiful even wearing that robe and stupid head covering. I asked her for more wine. She brought it over to me, and she and I stood there, hoping that something would happen between us. But then she realized that your warning about her dying if she came toward me was no rhetorical flourish."

He gives a one-shouldered shrug. "She died, and then I left." That is Jadon Rrivae's brutal truth.

"Who armed you?" I ask, lip curling.

"The Gashoan guard that I killed. And I took his armor, too. I've grown since then."

"Did you summon those Devourer soldiers?"

He laughs. "Fuck no."

"Who did? How did Syrus Wake know to send soldiers there?"

He shrugs. "Fuck if I know."

I pause, sensing dishonesty. "Have you seen your father Rrivae since you've left the temple?"

"No."

There's no hesitation, but something isn't quite right in that simple reply.

He sighs. "Are you done asking questions—?"

"Do you know that the traitor had other children?"

He opens his mouth, another flippant reply at the ready, but blinks at me then, lost for words.

"Three boys and a girl," I say. "A wife named Indis. They were killed when their failed realm, Birius, was destroyed. Danar Rrivae believes that they're still alive, somehow, somewhere. He truly thinks his family is being held hostage somewhere in the Aetherium, so he's destroying realms to force the Council of High Orders to return them to him."

Jadon Wake lowers his head.

And now he knows: to neither of his fathers will he ever be enough.

What does he think of that? I could read Jadon's thoughts once upon a time. I try to now, but all I can hear is bone grinding against bone, his clenching jaw and gritted teeth.

"He created me with my mother," he whispers, "to spite the Council of High Orders. Not because he desired Vallendor—or my mother—for their beauty."

I shake my head. "Danar Rrivae wants Vallendor for vengeance against my father, who approved the destruction of Birius. Every realm the traitor claims is important to members of the Council of High Orders. I'm High Lord Izariel Megidrail's daughter, and my father and yours hate each other most of all. You wouldn't even *be* here, in this predicament, if it wasn't for his spite, for his envy."

I pause, then add, "He never loved your mother, and he certainly doesn't love you."

Jadon smirks, but a scowl quickly replaces it. "Then I'll fight for *you*—I'll fight for the one who *does* love me. But then we must first build an army. I'll go to every kingdom not under my mortal father's rule and demand that they stand with us or die. There's King Exley of Kingdom Vinevridth in the south, and Queen Alinor of Kingdom Goldcrest in the east and..." Jadon's face hardens, and the cords flex in his neck. "I'll even enlist the last Gorgas and Jundum, Otaan and Dashmala throughout the provinces. If I must threaten them all with slow, agonizing deaths, then I will. It'll be their choice, their destiny. But, Kai, you need fighters, so their fates must be tied to yours."

I can't help but smile. "I do need fighters."

He'll do everything he just vowed because I can tell that Jadon Wake makes this promise.

Jadon gazes down at the canyons now carved by the harsh light of the new daystar. Those brutal rays cut through the dark sky and cast long, jagged shadows, twisting the landscape into something... *otherworldly*. The land below is a vast expanse of red and ochre, scarred by deep fissures and cracks—like the realm has begun to bleed under the intensity of the light. Dust swirls in thick, choking clouds. The canal is completely dry, the beds just lifeless grooves in the earth.

Jadon's gaze is fixed on the wasteland before him. His body tenses, his fists clenched at his sides as if he's willing the realm to change. "I won't let him take this place," he says, nodding, his voice thick with resolve. But the land around him echoes with doubt. "My fathers can only kick over a few chairs, but you, Kai, you own this house—and they'll both die knowing that." Then he takes my hand and kisses it.

I wince as the sting of his lips on my skin travels up to my wrist. Then he kisses the crook of my elbow, sores and all.

Lightning zigzags around my body and settles like a collar of heat around my neck.

His lips find mine, and I don't feel the blade against my neck until he pulls away from me. "Call off Elyn," he says, his grip tightening around the dagger's hilt. "You know she means to kill me, Kai, and she will. I don't want to die. You don't want me to die. You love me."

Tears fill my eyes, and my throat burns like it's filled with sand. "To love you and save Vallendor—I can't do both."

But then, I've lost Vallendor. So why not die loving him? Because I'm not ready to surrender, even though I've lost.

I've lost because I failed to recognize the enemy—and that included Jadon Rrivae Wake.

Now, he holds a dagger to my throat, and he won't need this blade to end my life. I feel my body chipping and tearing. I feel my muscles snapping. I feel my body screaming in protest as it dies, railing against the son of an emperor, the son of the traitor.

Jadon presses the blade harder against my neck. "Come with me, Kai. Let's live the life we've talked about. Traveling. Eating foods we've never tried. Visiting shitty realms before they're destroyed. We don't have to stay here. You have the power to take us to some other realm, don't you?"

"Yes." The Glass of Infinite Realms will take me anywhere I want to go. I blink, and a fat teardrop rolls down my cheek. "No." I'd never survive the journey with the traitor's son as my companion—he is Miasma and would kill me before we even reached another realm.

Jadon shakes his head. "You still don't understand how powerful I am now. I'm stronger than you. I'm *more* than you. What have *you* done to those who turn their backs on you? I could do the same, but I don't want you to choose death. I want you to join me."

In that dream, the one where Jadon and I lie together in the forest, I'd asked him to come with me, but he'd refused. And now, he wants me to join him as the realm burns all around us.

What if I said yes to him this time?

The realm would still burn all around us, but at least I wouldn't be alone…

But that's an illusion. I whisper, "I can't."

He backs away from me.

My neck stings from the blade and his poisoned lips, because of who he is. This new pain spreads across my chest and settles on top of the old hurts. The last plates of my pewter armor crumble into the sand; I'm back in just my bandeau and breeches as my knight continues to kill me softly. "You're wrong in this, Jadon," I say, sinking onto my side. "The love you demand from me isn't love. I'm not one of your hostages in that jail. But know this: I will hunt you down the ends of Vallendor, even in my march toward death, because I loved them."

Lively. Veril. Prince Idus. Even Gileon Wake.

I will wander Anathema in pursuit of those who did Vallendor wrong. Once I find them all and punish them for their sins, I will speak the word and pray that my dedication to Vallendor will be counted toward whatever reward or punishment awaits me beyond the gates of Anathema.

Jadon steps away from me but grips the dagger tighter. "I don't want to die. How is that wrong? I want to be with you. How is *that* wrong?"

"Neither desire is wrong," I say, whispering now as the world starts to gray. "But you can't always get what you want."

"I have no choice here," he growls. "Either I do as you say, or I do as my father says. Either path leads to my death. Is that my fate? It doesn't matter, because this time, I'm choosing me."

"You are your own savior now?" I ask, my eyes closing.

"Yes."

Now, I stare at the man who no longer resembles the blacksmith I loved or the prince who tended to me so gently in that cave. The warmth

I once found in his gaze has faded, replaced by a hollow, dangerous intensity that I no longer recognize. His anger and fear transform his smile into a sneer—sharp, cruel, and newly bitter. His brows furrow with frustration and pain. The muscles in his jaw tighten. He holds himself as a man straining between two realities, both destroying him from the inside out. Another rotting apple.

He stands rigid, a sour-smelling sickness rolling from him in waves. His vibrant eyes dim. The person I once knew is slipping away.

Where is the man who was my friend just a moment ago? The one who'd just promised to organize a motley army of Vallendor's mortals to fight for me? Where will *he* go in his death, beyond those gates?

"Is this goodbye, then?" Jadon asks, his face softer for just this moment.

I whisper, "This is goodbye."

"Then..." He scoops me into his arms, then presses his nose against mine. "*Hear the humble plea of Thy devoted servant seeking the grace of your Divine touch.* You are the realm to me, Kaivara Megidrail, gentle Lady of the Verdant Realm." And he kisses me.

I accept his prayer and his kiss, and he tastes of blackberries, rum, honey and...metal and blood and death.

He takes my breath away.

I push him away, and he lets me fall into the dust.

My throat grows tight. He stoops beside me. *"Look upon me with your Divine favor, quickening my sword and supplanting my weaknesses with your strength."* He's still praying even as he reaches for my amulet.

The amulet's thorax glows, and its light dances across his hard face.

I lift my hand to stop him. My skin is a dying mess of purples and yellows.

Jadon yanks the pendant, and the chain breaks around my neck.

Will he take my blade? Does he know he will die if he does, and the linionium in his markings will find their next source?

Is Danar Rrivae close by? Is he watching and waiting?

It doesn't matter anymore.

Ice crackles across my shoulders—my armor is gone.

I blink, and the world tilts until the sky is beneath me.

I blink and see Jadon's boots backing away from me.

I blink, the sky is gray.

I'm alone.

Linione.

No moths. Spryte depleted.

I blink, and a bank of fog surrounds me. Lights twinkle in this new gloom. The wind roars.

My heartbeat slows…

Those dead windwolves circle me. They laugh, and they howl.

You always fail.

35

I'm speeding through the Aetherium like a dying star, through the dust of realms that used to be and realms yet to come. Pain slices through my core and cuts into my heart, burning up my throat until it fills my body like broken glass.

I want to scream. I've never felt pain like this, and I never will again.

I want to close my eyes forever, but in Anathema, I will wander with them open.

I tried to do the best I could for the realm, for my people, but it was never enough, and now...I'm dead.

However...I glimpse a realm that I don't know. I want to turn my head away, but my neck won't move no matter how hard I try.

Ithlon Realm.

Heat surrounds me in this new land with its sea of crystal. As the flames around me die, I glimpse a colorful quilt on the seashore.

I see a tall woman bright with light, with glowing bronze skin, her wild curls the color of mulberries and cinnamon.

I see a man, his bare chest covered in the orbs and vines of destroyed realms, his eyes ever-changing pools of golden smoke. Sitting between them: a girl with still-soft knees and pudgy arms, her wild hair and his golden eyes. The girl piles wet sand to form a castle.

The world beyond this beach is a drab shoreline. There are no fish swimming in the sea, no birds flying across the sky, no slick-backed creatures slipping like arrows through water.

A basket filled with honeycakes, wine, and crabapples sits on that quilt. The knife by that spread isn't meant to slice food. It's a weapon of war.

Not far away, one raven perches on a boulder while another hops across a fallen, rotted tree. Their feathers are as glossy as the sea.

The man stands and scoops the tot from her piles of sand. He plants kisses on her ruddy cheeks and runs his fingers through her curly hair. He smiles, but there is regret in his eyes.

The woman stands, and the joy in her face melts into fear and worry.

His smile dies and his smoky eyes turn as flat and lifeless as the waters beyond this beach.

She presses her face against his large hand as she speaks.

What is she saying?

He kisses the top of the child's head. The girl pulls a lock of his thick hair. He presses his forehead to her tiny one.

A raven hops across that quilt and picks through the basket of sweets. The bird finds a small cake but then discovers the knife. It drops the cake, plucks the knife from the basket, and soars back into the dying forest.

For a moment, the woman watches the raven. Then she turns back.

Her loves have started walking along the shore without her, their heads pressed together like old friends.

The second raven swoops from the tree trunk and hops onto the quilt. A third raven joins it, the two birds cackling together like old women.

Why are you leaving her?

Why are they walking away from her?

Why is she running but not catching up to them?

A rock explodes in the sky, trailing a streak of fire. The meteor crashes onto the beach with an earth-shattering roar, and the land quakes beneath it. Sharp rocks scatter in all directions. The sky fills with swirling red clouds, obscuring the daystar. The sea of crystal waters turns murky, and the land of glass grows scorched and brittle from the heat pouring from the crater.

A misty breeze surrounds me. The violet light in the sky—*this can't be the same sky*—grows impossibly bright. I'm falling through space again, and in the distance, fast-approaching, I see my mother.

I see Veril.

I tried with my whole heart, wise one, and I failed.

And I sink through a bank of fog that breaks apart, and with a clap of thunder, the sky brightens to maroon and gold.

What a glorious light!

A woman shrieks somewhere beneath me. The stink of human waste and sickness fills my nostrils. And then I see blood splattering on the hard-packed earth. *Where am I?* A coop of chickens: dead birds and diseased eggs. The rooftops of houses have been ripped away, exposing the people to the heat and icy rains. The bodies of the livestock and their owners are covered with lice. Outside of town, corpses are piled like cords of wood, and animals nibble at the lifeless limbs of the dead.

The altars to the Lady of the Verdant Realm have been toppled and smashed. The paddled colures of Supreme—and Syrus Wake as Supreme Manifest—have been broken and stomped upon. These people no longer believe in anything.

There is too much despair. Too much disease and wickedness and…

Too much of *me.*

I stand in a realm of rain and sky painted in shades of gray. This is the realm of Melki, once a world of quiet strength. Its people had thrived under the rhythmic patter of the rain, finding comfort in the gloom, in the life-giving water. But beneath its surface, corruption had festered: they'd turned to sorcery, twisting the natural order to steal life from each other, in a quest for immortality. No one lived as they'd been born. No one's body worked as it should've: they'd become upright minulles and worupines, warped and unnatural.

I'd pleaded with the Council for permission to intervene. "Melki is unraveling," I'd argued. "The people can't see the cost of what they're doing." But the Council had refused me, so I defied them only so that I could protect the beings of nearby realms, beings who would be vulnerable to the sorcery unleashed on Melki. I couldn't wait for the

Council to see all that I saw. How many would die beyond this already-dying realm if I'd waited? When the priests of Melki unleashed their final ritual to grant themselves immortality by destroying the realm around them, threatening to siphon the lifeblood of children—who no longer resembled children—I had no choice but to act. My Mera army, Zephar included, called down a firestorm that consumed Melki until the realm was no more. It was too late to do anything else.

I blink, and I stand in a realm of mountains.

Yoffa had been a fortress of strength. Its peaks scraped the heavens and its mortals were hardy and durable. But their strength turned to hubris. The rulers all across Yoffa believed themselves untouchable and had carved deep into the mountains to mine forbidden minerals, to feed their deadly ambitions.

I'd watched in horror as the mountains cracked and groaned, as fiery rivers poured from the earth, consuming villages and forests alike. I'd begged Yoffa's leaders to stop, to turn away from their recklessness. They'd laughed, calling me a meddling goddess who didn't understand the value of their discovery. And so I shattered Yoffa's tallest peaks. The mountains bled fire one last time before falling silent forever.

I blink, and I'm returned to Ithlon, my home of endless green land and clear blue seas. The mortals there had lived in harmony with the land, tending to its verdant forests and sprawling meadows. But Ithlon's beauty had drawn envious eyes. Dindt raiders and Yeadens from other realms invaded regularly, tearing apart its harmony with war and conquest. Desperate to protect their home, Ithlonians had turned to an artifact discovered by the Dindt in a far-off realm—a Mera relic of destruction meant only for the gods' use.

I saw what was coming. The artifact's power would ripple outward, destroying not just Ithlon but every nearby realm. I pleaded with the senators of Ithlon to give up the relic, to trust me to find another way. But they were desperate, and their fear outweighed their faith. That artifact awakened, and its power spiraled out of control, out toward other realms…

I had no choice.

Diminished. Destroyer of Realms. Condemned for my actions. Stripped of my powers. Imprisoned on Vallendor. I was called impulsive, reckless, and deemed unworthy of the trust placed in me. And yet I knew I'd done what was necessary.

I explode past the fog and slam into something unyielding.

I'm no longer moving.

Rain pelts my face, and I wince as each drop rips at my skin. I stare at the sky, and the sky looks bruised. Yellows and purples and grays, and all of it glows bright… I want to close my eyes against the light.

A brightly colored bird hovers above me. She circles in that bruised sky with grace and drifts down to me until she's just out of reach.

Is it over? Is Vallendor gone?

Will this daxinea find her clan here in Anathema?

I'm still so tired, and I can't move or speak.

If I can't speak, how will I speak the word? If I can't move, how will I punish those who helped bring Vallendor to her end?

One of the daxinea's tail feathers could save me, but that would kill her. But if I'm now in Anathema, she, too, must be dead. The living do not abide with the dead.

Something heavy lies across my bare stomach. I glance down to see…Cruel Dawn. I didn't realize that she hadn't left me—with my body decaying, I just couldn't feel her presence. This sword…the only gift I have left of my father, proof that someone loved me. Even in Anathema, I must fight.

I need to move.

The daxinea flies closer, lifting her wings, shielding me from some of the rain that tears away my skin. The air warms because she's near. My bones and muscles no longer ache. I close my eyes, but that light still grows brighter and whiter… I still want to turn my head, but I can't because I'm dead.

It is my time.
Loosen me from the glades.
Let not the sting
And wonder of death's blades
Keep me realm-side…

At least I still have my memory of that prayer.

Do I need to use my time here to avenge Vallendor? Is that what's expected of me? Am I ready to see what's beyond this realm?

I close the eyes of my mind because I'm ready now. I'm ready with my whole heart.

Maybe my body will help grow a new realm, a place of life and love. Maybe Supreme will take all the best parts of me to seed this place, sprinkle my blood—the Blood of All—to spark new life.

But am I a good seed?

The daxinea pokes me with her crimson beak and bends to peer at me with bright golden eyes. *"Arise, Lady."*

But I can't rise.

The daxinea nudges me again. *"I will take you to the healing place."*

But I'm beyond healing now.

The Aetherium moves on, but where are the others?

"You are here for a purpose."

Tears stream from the corners of my eyes and slip into my ears.

"Come, Lady." The daxinea prods and pokes and forces me to sit up.

My armor's gone. Even my bandeau and leather breeches have disintegrated like strips of old skin. In Anathema, one is naked as a newborn again—

My head pounds, filled with tiny explosions.

"Come, Lady." The daxinea pries my arms apart and drapes one of my arms over her neck. *"Come."*

I shift onto my creaky knees as she lifts her wing to roll me onto her back.

With one hand, I clutch Cruel Dawn, and with the other, I hold on to her neck, nestling my face into her soft, shimmering blue-and-gold feathers.

"Where are we going, Lovely?" I whisper.

To see my mother?

To see Veril?

Sybel should be here.

Or have all three spoken the word, choosing to leave this place instead of waiting to reunite with me? Is Father here? If Vallendor is gone, he'll be here, too.

"Are we going to see my family?" I ask the daxinea.

She doesn't respond. She drifts up and out of the canyon, crooning a song as she soars.

Dawn only shines
When it shines through the haze.
You, Precious One,
Are the fury and blaze…

I know this song. I know this song because I wrote it just for her.

PART IV

METAMORPHOSES

Beloved of Aetherium, Vallendor,
Vallendor, twilight kissed.
Wolves stalk these shadows deep
And lambs stalk these shadows deep.
I blessed you with fire to light their way.
Arise from the ashes to light their way.
Arise from embers to light their way, that they may
dance through flames,
That they may pray, these flames are those that
curl and cleanse.

Beloved of Aetherium, Vallendor,
Vallendor, twilight kissed.
Cold nights spark your terror vast
And barren sands spark your terror vast.
I blessed you with stars to fill your bones.
Soar from the chasms to be restored.
Soar from the abyss to be restored, so that you may
Stay like the stone,
So that you may say, This void gives us a home to
Cultivate sands and souls.

Beloved of Aetherium, Vallendor,
Vallendor, twilight kissed.
Great waters flood your softer soils
And vines flood your softer soils.
I blessed you with steel to mute their strengths.
Direct your hand to find your way.
Direct your gaze to find your way, that you will
Blow like the wind.
That you may know, This bounty will meet our needs and
Sustain our lives here.

Cherished of Aetherium, my Vallendor,
My Vallendor, Verdant Realm.
Beauty thrives as you fall and scar.
I blessed you with dawn to bring you hope.

Find strength in darkness to keep your light.
Find strength in shadow to keep your light, that you may be
The path for others.
That you may say, Let us take flight to these
Endless skies.

–A Love Song from the Lady of the Verdant Realm to her Beloved Vallendor

36

My eyes creak open like a rusty iron door. The world is a blur, and shapes bleed one into another. As the haze begins to clear, tall beings made of light drift over me. Their hands dance over my body and their fingers trace invisible lines in the air. They never speak, but movements vibrate through this space to become low, constant hums.

I don't understand all that's happening to me. Who are they? Are they a threat?

Then I see Agon the Kindness pacing in front of a window, his hands clasped behind his back. His red robes rustle softly with each step.

And I see the Fynals, Elyn and Sybel, standing at the foot of my bed behind the healers. They both wear gray suede tunics and breeches, their hands clasped together tightly in one large fist. Elyn's brow furrows as her eyes dart between the healers and me. Sybel gazes steadily at me, but her lips are trembling.

Are we together in Execration? Are we in After-Anathema?

I blink and try to focus, to make sense of my surroundings, but pain and anxiety tighten like a vise around my body. This space is too small, too much. The chaise at my side is too close. The pillows beneath my head are too soft. Everything around me, too still. My thoughts, too fragile. This bedroom looks like my bedroom in the abbey, but is that how Execration looks for everyone?

Before I can understand where I am, the room blurs again, and I find myself caught between this world that I recognize and the certainty that this place can no longer exist. The realm known as Vallendor is no longer. Unless...

The Between?

I've been infected with Vallendor—its rot and decay have infiltrated my body, its death entwined with my life, and I can no longer dwell anywhere else—including Anathema. So I must've been shunted to this place instead.

I don't want to be here.

I turn my head, but fire spreads down my neck and floods my chest. I gasp but almost immediately am distracted from that acute pain because the man with golden smoky eyes has appeared at my bedside.

"You're here," Father whispers. "Rest."

"Here"? Where am I? I try to ask, but the pain returns, and I can't form the words.

I can't move toward my life or to my death. In the Between, I can't see a path to either, and I don't know where to climb.

I close my eyes and let the healers decide.

I rest in a field of bluebells that stretches on forever. The daystar casts warm golden light across an ocean of blue, and the petals glimmer like sapphire. The meadow smells sweet, and I take deep breaths, filling my lungs with crisp, clean air. I reach out to touch the flowers around me and am startled by my hands. They're too smooth, too soft, too small. A child's hand.

Elyn sits cross-legged beside me, grinning, her hair in two smoky white braids. She is also too soft, too small; she is also a child here. "You keep breathing all the air," she says, wriggling her nose.

I smile and lift my chin. "Nuh uh. You said that last time, so I asked Veril and he says we will never, ever run out of air. I can breathe as much of it as I want. So..." I close my eyes and take a dramatic whiff.

Elyn laughs, and together we lie back, our heads touching, on the soft grass in this field of bluebells. The daystar bathes us in warmth and security. Petals brush our skin like our mothers' kisses as puffy white clouds drift across the blue sky and morph into soft shapes—lions, boats, faces. Vallendor Realm will live forever as long as Lumis and Selenova make their treks, dawn to dusk, in the heavens.

I lift my hand to shield my eyes— *Oh!* My hand is bigger now.

"Do you see?" Elyn asks. "You're changing, Kai." Her voice is light, like a bird chirping at dawn.

"Yes, I see," I say. "But I don't understand *how or why* this is happening. Will you help me?" My voice is deeper than hers, like new smoke wafting from the earth.

"Will you help *me*?" Elyn says. "I asked you first."

"Yes, I'll help you, but— "

She pulls one of my many braids. "You got a big butt."

I snort. "Who came up with that stupid game?"

"Dunno. Stop saying 'but.'"

"I'm not strong enough yet," I say. "I'm not…all of me yet. What will happen to me, now that Vallendor is no more?"

Elyn and I roll onto our bellies to face each other. Now, she is a little leaner, her face narrower. She wears one braid instead of two. She peers at me with those gold eyes and says, "You *are* all of you. You just think some parts of you don't count." Her voice remains bird-like, but the bird has grown and lost the worm despite her early rising.

"You've proven yourself to High Lord Megidrail and to the Council of High Orders— "

I cock an eyebrow. "Do you have actual proof that the Council believes that— ?"

"Listen to me. You shouldn't regret what you've done to save Vallendor. Your efforts were sincere and accomplished with your whole heart."

She didn't answer my question.

"But Fihel," I say.

She pulls the end of one of my two braids. "Stop saying 'but.'"

I chuckle and slap at her hand.

"There's a reason that you keep thinking about Fihel," Elyn says, "and why you keep worrying about whether you destroyed that city. That's because every single hamlet, town, or province that you razed mattered to you. They were *all* Fihel."

I lower my head. "Which is why today—"

"Kai, they will not send you into this war ill-prepared. That is not in their interest, either."

"They will permit me to be all of me, then?" I ask. "Despite all my wrongdoings?"

"And what about all the *right* you've done? Does that not count?"

I consider all the bad things: I've destroyed provinces without permission from the Council of High Orders. I've allowed pride and impatience to lead me away from my true purpose. I've led others to ignore the Council's directives, which led to chaos and rebellion.

Then I tally the good things, ignoring Elyn's knowing gaze: I've been an exemplar of the power and grace of Supreme through my stewardship and protection of Vallendor. I've faced down tyrants who enslaved those they've conquered. I've blessed both believers and nonbelievers with coin, crops, and coupling. I've inspired arts, engineering, and cultivation among mortals, and I've celebrated and grieved with the mortals of this realm.

Is that not enough? Does the accounting not accrue in my favor?

I can't answer Elyn's question, and that failure brings tears to my eyes. I ask again, "Will I be all of me when this war begins?"

"Yes, but know that this fight won't end until you vanquish the traitor." Elyn sits up from the bluebells, a woman now, with strong hands and wisdom in her stern gaze.

"There are those on Vallendor and across the Aetherium, even, who don't want us here," she says. "They think we're disrupting the natural order, but if we're to survive, if we're to remain in our space, we must continue to fight. If we're to be good seeds in a land filled with brambles and thorns, we can't just surrender and slip away into the night." She touches my cheek and smiles. "Open your eyes, Kaivara. Welcome to your life."

• • •

My father stands on the bluff that overlooks the field of bluebells, a sharp silhouette against the sky. The wind tugs at his crimson leather shirt. The hide of his breeches has been softened by ages of wear. His boots are scuffed from countless journeys across rough terrain. He stands tall and unmoving, his gaze fixed on Vallendor, searching for something only he can see.

Like the inkings on his skin that represent the realms he's destroyed, Father's dark hair has meaning. His maze of twists and braids is meticulously woven, each braid telling its own story, marking battles fought. The plaits over his left ear: the map used to surround the instigators on the realm Graviel. The curved braids at his crown: the freedom road created for those who'd been enslaved on Realm Idwah.

Taught by the Renrians, some mortal tribes across Vallendor learned to mimic Father's braids of maps and memorials. Some have hidden rice, beans, and seeds within them, as a means of survival when they were torn away from their homelands.

I stand beside him in my bare feet, wearing a gown of light cotton. "Father?" My voice sounds strong but remains ragged around the edges. I'm not yet confident enough to look at my hands. Last time I did, they were swollen and bruised by Miasma. My face… I don't even want to think about how my face must look.

He smiles and looks over at me, then turns back to the field of flowers. "This place…"

"Welcome to Vallendor. Excuse the dust."

He takes a breath and touches his heart-spot before lifting my chin with his fingertips. "You look like your mother right now. That hair on your head… Do you still cry when someone else combs it?"

"Mmhmm." I bite my lower lip and push my fingers through my curls. Free of braids and threads of luclite, my hair blows in the breeze like the bluebells covering the field.

The Vallendor my father knew, once upon a time, no longer

exists. Beyond the still-pristine glen, sickly green clouds form above the Sea of Devour. Otherworldly—gerammocs, sunabi, aburan, and resurrectors—fight, die, and rise again all across the realm. Mortals—humans, Dashmala, Gorga, Jundum—die in their beds, set fire to the homes of their enemies, and raid towns, temples, and tracts of land not theirs. Children of every mortal race slash the throats of their playmates without mercy.

How are we still here?

Why hasn't the world ended?

"The last time I visited a realm other than Mera or Linione..." He stops speaking and remains silent for a long time. Finally, he adds, "That last day with you and Lyra, at the beach on Ithlon. She'd enchanted a perfect wedge of seaside for that day." He turns to me. "We were celebrating your third season."

As I lay dying on the Rim of the Shadows that overlook Doom Desert, I revisited that day spent on the shores of Ithlon Realm. Ravens had hopped from the trees onto our quilt—a warning of the age to come. Mother had stood alone on that beach as Father and I...

Now, his face falls and his eyebrows knit together. He knows what I've seen, and whispers, "I *did* love her."

"Then why did you abandon her?" I ask.

He shakes his head. "I'd already rejected one rule and married a non-Mera woman. I couldn't violate another without jeopardizing my role on the Council. Lyra couldn't reside on Mera, and my first duty was to the Council and to our order." He looks away from me. "You were the embodiment of my recklessness."

"Recklessness," I say, eyebrows raised.

"I knew what was expected of me, but I still did what I wanted without considering the consequences."

Recklessness. I suppose you could call it that.

"I regret that you became a target of zealots," he says. "Back then, the Crusaders were a small sect within the Mera, but they were still powerful. So powerful that Mera throughout the realms believed that the Crusaders would do as they threatened to do—travel the Aetherium and kill all those with mixed blood."

Father takes my hands. "That's why Sybel helped to raise you. We needed to keep you away from those fanatics. So we sent you back and forth between Ithlon and Vallendor and surrounded you with the Raqiel until you protested against that much protection."

"I remember." The tears come, and I can no longer see the clouds above or the fields before me. I close my eyes, and instead I see the woman with hair the color of mulberries and cinnamon, with eyes like ice and smoke.

"There are just two dawns left," Father says now, "and I came to bring you this." He presents me with a dagger. "She belonged to your mother."

In my dream of the Ithlon shore, this knife was stolen by a raven.

The dagger's slightly curved, polished steel blade is faintly blue-tinted, reflecting the sky. Etchings of flowers and vines embellish the blade, and the cross-guard spreads like wings. It's a perfect gift from a warrior to his healer love.

I shake my head. "I can't. I don't deserve it."

"She brought it with her that day to the beach," he says, examining the blade, "just in case the Crusaders found us and we needed to fight."

"But the Crusaders didn't end her life," I say. "*I* did, and I can never apologize enough for my arrogance, but I will again. I am so, so sorry, Father. Please forgive me."

"I forgave you long ago." He places his strong hand against my cheek. "I know you'd been encouraged by men who'd secretly become Crusaders."

My heart hammers in my chest. I'd been so gullible.

He shrugs, sighs, and finds a smile. "But that was then, and this is now." He holds out the dagger. "You have her hair—and now, take her blade, Kaivara."

With a shaky hand, I do as he asks. I turn it over. *Light.*

I don't deserve this gift.

I take a deep cleansing breath, then release it slowly. "Did Mother ever use this dagger?"

"To aid in her stewardship, she did." His smile broadens, and his gaze becomes distant. "I tried my best to teach Lyra how to use it to fight, but fighting wasn't in her nature, and she sent it back to me to hold on to for you."

My anger swells, pushing past the warmth of his nostalgia. "Was love not in *your* nature? Love for her or for me? There aren't enough Eserime in the sixty-seven thousand realms to heal—"

"Seventy thousand realms."

Wow. I'm determined not to let him get away with changing the subject. "There aren't enough Eserime in the *seventy thousand* realms to heal the rift between us, a rift that *you* caused by your choice."

"My first priority was to keep *you* safe," he whispers. "Your mother agreed with me, and she understood that meant we had to be apart."

"You both agreed, then, to surrender to fear," I say as a tear rolls down my cheek.

"If that's what love is, then…yes, we surrendered." He catches my teardrop with his knuckle. "This—" He motions to the bead of salted water he now holds. "This tenderness is all Lyra. She loved you, and I love you, and we protected you, and we gave you everything you would've enjoyed had you been allowed to be with me.

"And then, when it was time, I petitioned the Council of High Orders for you to claim your birthright. The Council had one stipulation: that you would train in the Mera way, in combat and destruction. But try as I did, and despite what the Mera wanted, you were still also Eserime and…" He sighs and rubs his temples. "It was just a matter of time before…"

"Before what?" I ask.

He stares out at the plains rather than looking at me. "Before your occasional failures. You felt too much at times and not enough at other times. Then and now, you're still gaining wisdom, developing your skill in combat, developing empathy… You're learning how to face your weaknesses and acknowledging the pain you cause."

"That's just showing fear, and it's why I keep failing."

"It's time you learned that what you must master is not fear," Father says, his eyes narrowed. "Everyone wants to rule the realm, but no one wants to first rule themselves. That fear you speak of—and your ability to accept it—is how you come closer to the state Supreme desires.

Being a good ruler, a *true* leader, requires listening to good counsel, and it requires that you care and love those who rely on you, whether they honor you or not. Sometimes, that feels like failure. *Feeling* means, though, that you still care."

I hold his wisdom in my heart. There, those words ache and sting, a bitter tonic that burns as I drink it. I suspect I had an inkling of this all along, but hearing his words forces me to see that it's his wisdom lodging in my mind and heart like a physical sensation. That burn fades, leaving behind a deep warmth—a peace mixed with sorrow.

I let my head fall, and a sob escapes from the deepest place in my gut.

Father embraces me, and his arms are solid and grounding, anchoring me in a way that I didn't know I needed.

"You did more than love the mortals of Vallendor at a distance," he says, his voice a balm against that sting and burn. "There were times you went too far in punishing them, and you've acknowledged your brutality, and you'll be tormented by your actions. Before that time in your life—and these last several days—you've brought these mortals into your life like a mother reaching back for her children. And because of that love, generosity, and commitment, I offer you one more gift."

I dry my face against my gown and try to steady myself by taking deep breaths. Once I feel as calm as I'm going to be, I nod.

"Some gifts can be taken back and never given again," Father says, "while other gifts can be taken but then returned, stronger than ever." He holds up my amulet—*no*, I realize, this isn't the amulet that Jadon stole from me. This pendant burns bright, and the rubies and onyx vibrate as though they are living gods. The jeweled moth looks as though she's slowly fluttering her wings, ready to break free from this smoky golden chain…

"Linionium," Father says.

I stare at him in disbelief.

"The entirety of your powers, Daughter, have been restored. Your sword and dagger have their whole power again. You are, once again, who you were always meant to be."

The amulet no longer dangles from his hand but now hangs around my neck.

Ice and flame crackle across my shoulder blades and down my chest to my arms, legs, and feet, and I take big gulps of all the air on Vallendor. My scalp flushes and spreads down to my forehead and across my cheeks. My body goes rigid as it fills with power and then in the next moment becomes smoke.

That's when—like a god—I see *everything.*

I peer past the veil to glimpse Jadon Wake Rrivae still growing in power even as he sleeps beneath the hedges at still-burning Beaminster.

I see Separi and Ridget and the Renrians in Caburh, fighting the stragglers pounding the red doors of the Broken Hammer.

I see the faint glimmer of armor worn by Devourers gathering in the canyons outside of Gasho.

"What will you name her?" My father taps the dagger in my hand.

I turn the blade this way and that, then say, "Victory." I pause before asking, "Are you certain that I will win?"

"I can't assure certainty." He holds my cheeks between his hands and peers deep into my eyes. "Your fate, Kai, is in your hands. It's up to you to prove once and for all, and to all the orders here and throughout the Aetherium, that you are mighty and wise enough to maintain the balance of this realm. That you can control and pacify all those factions that dissent—"

A horn blows.

I know that call.

Father points to the tablelands surrounding the Sea of Devour. "Starting with *him.*"

37

An army of living-dead Diminished marches ever closer to Mount Devour, a blight upon already-blighted land.

"I can't believe my eyes," Elyn says, shaking her head. "They forced the Eserime to do…this?"

I furrow my brows as I look out at the forty living-dead Diminished Mera making their way toward the base of the mountain. "How did they get here so quickly?"

"They must have had help from someone with enough power to Spryte many people at once." Elyn eyes the sky—it's darkened to match the sick-green tinge of the Sea of Devour. The land beneath her feet has been drained of life. "And—"

Her words catch in her throat. She swallows them, clenching her jaw. Silently, she marches beside me wearing new platinum armor and a blue cloak, her gaze locked on the path that leads to war.

Ten Raqiel sentinels dressed in red mail march behind us. No one speaks—the steady rhythm of boots against the earth and the distant rumble of thunder are the only sounds we hear.

The wind picks up, carrying with it the scent of mold and death.

The new armor I wear is the armor of my dreams: bloodred-and-gold catherite, with a breastplate adorned with vines and moths, and shoulder plates embossed with bursts of light. My crimson cloak has also been embroidered with protective runes: arrows and crossed spears, deer and dragonflies. And I own new boots that fit, too, conveying power and poise with every step.

My clean hair smells of lavender and peppermint, my braids threaded again with thin strands of luclite. A supple brown leather scabbard accommodates the weight of Cruel Dawn. An ankle scabbard worthy of Victory matches the larger sheath.

This new amulet thrums against my chest, the vibrant moth a protective shield against the sickness of my struggling realm—but not a shield against other gods. I can do more—no, *I can do it all*—but so can Danar Rrivae. So can Zephar Itikin—though as Diminished, he and his lissome blades have limits. I must press those blades to that limit, and then I must break them...and then I must break *him*.

Suddenly, an explosion louder than a thunderclap rolls across the firmament.

The clouds darken into banks of red-and-black mist.

We all shudder and gape at the violent sky.

"What's—?" Elyn's breath catches in her throat as another explosion rocks the land.

The first rocks that strike the ground are no bigger than fists and hit the ground like hail showers. The explosions grow louder as that mist rolls toward us.

The falling rocks are bigger now. The earth jolts with each strike, and fire flares every time a boulder slams into the ground.

I'm running out of time. Emerging from the smoke, the fiery meteors soon take shape, growing arms and legs...

BOOM!

These explosions are not meteors. They are Diminished, but they remain living Mera. Though they have been shrunken in size as punishment for their crimes against the Aetherium, they are still gods, still larger than any beings in this realm.

Yekaa...Yekaa...YEKAA!!

The destruction war cry of the Mera being shouted by a chorus of Diminished Mera.

"Kai!" Elyn screams.

A throwing knife flies to my right, headed low toward my calves.

I block that knife with my vambrace, and the blade cracks against that forearm armor. The impact sends a jolt up to my shoulder and neck.

That knife belongs to one of the warriors who'd joined me many seasons ago as I destroyed realms. Now, that warrior is a Crusader, wearing the brand of fiery crossed swords on their chest.

All the Diminished, living and dead, now shout, "Yekaa," and the earth buckles beneath our feet.

The Raqiel waste no time and surround Elyn and me.

Elyn grabs my elbow. "They're not here to help us, right?"

I shake my head, readying my blade. We're running out of time. Though the Diminished are here to kill me, time remains my greatest enemy.

The largest meteor strikes the ground.

My legs buckle again, and I push myself unsteadily to my feet.

Elyn stumbles back, but a Raqiel sentinel catches her.

The biggest Diminished of them all unfolds from that fiery ball. I recognize that hair, that body, those eyes.

"Zephar," Elyn and I say together. My lungs constrict in my chest, and my stomach rolls like waves across this sick sea.

Shari lands behind Zephar, her teeth bared, the largest wolf to ever stalk Vallendor.

"He's here to kill you," Elyn says.

"And I'm here to kill *him*." We are the worst exes ever.

"Kaivara Megidrail," Zephar calls out.

I take a deep breath, then stalk toward Zephar Itikin, Lord of the Shielded Fount and Prince of Lissom Blades. As I approach him, the trees around me shrink to shrubs, and the shrubs soon become patches of grass beneath my feet. In my god-size, I can see all of the provinces—from Weeton in the far east and Caburh in the south. The sky still roils with smoke, but I can see above the thickest layers. I swipe my hand across my body, scattering the smoke and making the trees and high grasses sway violently with wind.

Behind me, Elyn and the Raqiel have also assumed their true forms, ready to fight beside me to save Vallendor from both Zephar now and Danar Rrivae when we've defeated him.

"You need an entire suit of armor to fight me now?" Zephar cracks, unimpressed.

I peel off my vambraces and greaves and throw them to the ground.

"Kai," Elyn shouts behind me. "Don't take the bait!"

I unbuckle my breastplate.

"What are you doing?" Elyn shouts.

I pull off my tunic, and now I'm wearing only my bandeau. Arms extended, I turn before Zephar in a circle. "Tell me what you see," I shout, my words louder than any war chant.

Yoffa. Melki. Ithlon, all three realms destroyed without approval from the Council under my leadership. The leaves and vines that connect these to smaller orbs: Hastow, Pontin, Lemoor, Arton, and Fybury, realms that I destroyed under orders in my role as second-in-command to some of the men who would later lie to me about Ithlon and their loyalties to the Crusaders. The words DESTROYER OF WORLDS inked beneath my heart.

"I am Mera," I shout, glaring at Zephar and the Diminished who stand behind him. "From the moment I took my first breath until the moment I speak the word to Supreme. Each of you should be thankful that it's my mother's blood that keeps my hands to myself now, that the Eserime in me has kept me from burning each one of you for your betrayal."

"Put on your armor," Elyn hisses.

"I don't need any armor," I say, my teeth clenched, my hands burning as rage races like fire through my veins. I point to my opponents. "Your disloyalty will never be forgotten or forgiven. You will forever be Diminished."

And then, I unsheathe Cruel Dawn and hold her up before me.

Zephar's eyes widen as he regards the blade. "A sword of linionium," he gasps.

I cock an eyebrow. "Oh, this little thing? This is just a gift from my father. But this sword won't be the only way you'll leave this realm today."

Zephar snorts and says, "You're gonna be the one to die today, Abomination."

I roar, my voice a thunderclap. The ground trembles violently, and the earth buckles beneath our feet. Fault lines spread, swallowing trees and boulders. The land is seared with the heat of my anger.

Zephar roars back at me, his voice the crack of a whip vibrating through the ground. The earth shakes, harder this time, and tears open, into new caverns and canyons. Jagged rocks rise from the earth like sharp teeth.

Around us, the Crusaders scowl and sneer at me, and they raise their swords and spears and shields to the sky. Their voices rise in a collective, guttural, "Yekaa! Yekaa!" Louder and louder, and the air around them crackles, too, and the ground beneath them also trembles in response. Ready to fight. Ready to destroy.

New mountains thrust from the earth, their peaks splitting the heavens. The world is warping. We are reshaping the realm with our power.

In the distance, I hear the screams and pleas of mortals in Penem and Peria—two cities caught between gods waging war. Though their anguish echoes from a distance, their distress is real and cuts through the chaos. I feel their suffering, their helplessness. Their lives are unraveling as the land beneath them collapses.

This realm bleeds. I need to end this battle—for them.

Zephar has sixty Mera Crusaders and a wolf on his side.

I have ten sentinels and the Adjudicator of Vallendor. I am the only Mera warrior on my side, and I may just lose this fight.

But my blood is that of a Mera warrior who knows nothing of surrender.

And my blood is that of an Eserime steward who knows everything about healing.

Yeah, I'm fucked.

"You have me."

I know that smoky voice now in my ear. "Shari?" She is still standing beside Zephar.

"I was yours in the beginning," she says, *"in your true state. And I'm yours again, Mother. Some gifts can be taken back."*

A lump rises in my throat, but there's no time to think or respond.

Mortals scramble across the realm in search of safety, some running between the feet of Elyn and the sentinels like ants rushing from their overturned hills to find new dens before the floods arrive.

A screech fills the air and then louder and louder rumbling. An enormous ball of fire and black smoke careens from the east in a maze of red lightning. This ball is so bright in its blackness that the Crusaders turn their hateful gazes from me to watch its descent.

The earth shakes even before—

Zephar shouts, "Shields!"

The clank of catherite can barely be heard before—

This ball strikes the ground so hard that we all fall to our knees. Rocks and splintered trees rain down upon those shields.

This is no meteor. The man who emerges from the flames is taller than Zephar and all the Diminished, and not one patch of his skin is free of markings.

High Lord Izariel Megidrail wears crimson-and-orange robes, but beneath that fabric is the ink of a true warrior who can ascend no higher, whose smallest finger is covered with tales of the destruction he has wrought.

It seems that the world will never stop quaking as sixty—eighty—one hundred strong Mera land upon the flats of Devour. They wear bare chests or bandeaus, each bigger than Zephar and the Mera Crusaders who'd been punished and stripped of their stature.

My eyes cloud with grateful tears. Though I can barely see Zephar Itikin, I ask, "Did you have something you needed to say to *Izariel*?"

The Prince of Lissome Blades growls at me and glares at my father. "You dare—"

High Lord Megidrail slaps the air and strikes Zephar in the face with a burst of wind.

Zephar slams into the row of horrified Mera Crusaders behind him. The blow has ripped a gash across his cheek that spans from his temple to his top lip.

"That's for betraying my daughter," Father says, jabbing a finger at him.

He sends another blow at Zephar, who doubles over, clutching his stomach. "That's for disrespecting her rank." Father turns to Elyn. "Adjudicator!"

A cloak of fog billows outward, one that doesn't come from the sea or the daystar and is unlike anything seen in Vallendor. Elyn Fynal guides the fog as she commands the Raqiel guards to keep the Crusaders from leaving this arena. Then she lifts Justice, and immediately, two Raqiel guards take up positions behind her. "I am Elyn Fynal. As Grand Adjudicator of Vallendor and the Nine Realms, Sentinel and Divine Mediator, with approval of the Council of High Orders, including Lord Izariel Megidrail, I sentence you, Zephar Itikin, former Commander and Defender of Vallendor, Lord of the Shielded Fount and Prince of Lissome Blades"—she glances at the company that stands behind him—"and all of you…to death."

The Mera standing in formation behind me shout, "Yekaa!"

On the other side, the Crusaders reply, "Yekaa!" and race toward us.

The two sides meet as lightning flashes and whitecaps surge across the Sea of Devour.

I eye the setting daystar. Suddenly, with a loud clap, my shoulder is burning.

"Shit!" I shout, looking around for whoever threw this ball of flame at me.

Zephar!

I lob balls of fire back at him, each ball unerringly striking his chest. He falls back on his ass, his face twisted with shock.

All action around us stops as a ball of fire forms on Zephar's upturned palm. He's slowing the world to kill me, rather than using any extra time to reflect on what he's done and change his course before it's too late. No, he grins at that lovely, deadly fireball—

Shari lunges at him and bites that fiery hand.

Zephar shouts, "Ost!" and loses control of the realm's spinning. He gawks at Shari in shock.

A Crusader shouts, "Bitch!" and kicks Shari in the snout.

Both Zephar and I instinctively hurl fire at the Diminished who kicked our wolf. This is our last mutual act.

Shari hasn't forgotten her job, though, and she lunges again at

Zephar, biting down on his hand.

I narrow my eyes at Zephar as he struggles in Shari's ironclad hold. He pales from the pain of her teeth sinking deeper into his flesh.

"Release him, Shari," I say.

The wolf gives him one last shake before she loosens her jaw, dropping his bloodied hand. She sits on her haunches, her piercing gold eyes warily locked on Zephar.

The Prince of Lissome Blades grimaces, flicks his bloody hand, and climbs unsteadily to his feet.

But now, I am a titan, I am leviathan, larger than him, larger than he'd ever imagined I could be. Even now, I'm still growing taller—wider—*more.*

Like every battle, my shoulder aches from his fireball, my skin red and blistered, and all of my muscles throb. But my new amulet pulses against my chest, a steady, reassuring rhythm, humming with power. Its warmth spreads through me, and the pain of my injuries fades, replaced by a soothing sensation that wraps around me like a protective shield. A tugging sensation makes me look over my—

Wings unfurl from my shoulder blades. They are a breathtaking crimson, shimmering with golden luster. Energy hums through the space around me as moths the size of eagles emerge from the folds of my wings, their own soft wings dotted with glowing flecks. The glittering moths catch the air, and my feet leave the ground.

I rise. The noise and chaos of battle fade the higher I soar. The atmosphere around me is cool and crisp. The moths—loyal and powerful—spiral around me.

Zephar gasps as I fly above him. But then he swings his pair of swords. Heat shoots past me and into the sky, but then that energy falls back to earth and burns a hole in the ground the size of a castle.

I dodge that strike, and now I aim Cruel Dawn at him. The blade cuts off his right ear.

He screams and stumbles toward me, falling onto one knee a few paces away from me. I look down at him, recalling the other times I've seen him on his knees before me, wondering at how both of us have changed. He drops one of his blades and grabs my foot.

His touch burns like lava. I cry out in pain.

Lightning crackles across the sky.

I bring Cruel Dawn's pommel down on top of his head with an unmistakable *crack*. The impact against his skull reverberates up and down my arms.

Zephar releases me and rolls away, bleeding and racked with pain. He sends a wave of fire at me, wider than a river and twice as fast.

I dodge, but the flames are too powerful. They singe my head, and I smell burning hair. My amulet pulses again and heals the superficial burns on my face and scalp.

We're now fighting fire with fire.

Yekaa!

I light up the sky with more fireballs. Flames burst from my fingers like lava erupting from a volcano, and I drown Zephar in fire.

Every corner of the realm is subjected to his terrible cries. He falls backward as my fire consumes him. His hands, still clutching his pristine swords, turn to ash. His body becomes a thick vein of shining black ore that mortals of Vallendor could mine for ages.

Today, the realm loses its commander. And I lose someone else I loved.

Zephar Itikin, Beautiful Warrior, Breaker of Realms, Lord of the Shielded Fount, Prince of Lissome Blades, Warrior of the Righteous, Divine Xisi…and once upon a time, my Beloved Zee.

Farewell.

38

There is no time to mourn the loss of those who'd been born Mera true—the daystar will soon dip below the horizon.

We need the Renrians to add to our own numbers.

There are only five hundred Renrians across Vallendor Realm, most of whom live here in Caburh and deeper in the Kingdom of Brithellum—I haven't seen many of them in half an age.

The hacked-up door of the Broken Hammer creaks open, and Separi stands there. Her simple threadbare tunic has seen better days, but her smile makes her look almost whole. Ridget peeks out from behind her, slightly hunched. I remember the dress she wears. It was once vibrant green and has faded now into a dull, mossy shade. Her hair remains carefully braided, but her deep-set eyes reflect her exhaustion and fear.

Relief washes over both of their faces. Separi whispers, "You returned..."

Elyn and I push past the couple and into the inn, closing the door behind us before we continue the conversation.

Separi looks at me, then at Elyn, and then back at me. "Lady, you've..."

"You've grown," Ridget blurts. She sounds surprised, and her eyes widen as she takes in the changes—the way I've filled out, the height I've gained. She shakes her head, awestruck.

"We don't have a lot of time," I say.

I turn to my friends for a proper hug. I hold Separi and Ridget tight because they are dear to me—and because I'm about to ask them to make the ultimate sacrifice.

Ridget has a roast turning on a spit over the fire. A steaming pot of roasted garlic potatoes and carrots waits on the table. She pours us each a glass of rich red wine from a dusty bottle.

We all know now that neither Elyn nor I can eat their food. This dinner is an offering, like those made at the altars and sanctuaries throughout Gasho and around Vallendor.

After acknowledging their gifts, I take a deep breath and say, "Please, fight with me."

Both women say, "Of course, Lady," and bow their heads.

"The Renrians across Vallendor may be small in number," Separi says, "but we are mighty."

My eyes search the sitting room—there's no one eating, drinking, or playing music. It's entirely empty aside from us. "Where are Philia and Olivia?" I ask. "Down in the basement?"

"It was too dangerous for them to remain here," Separi says, peering at my sword with wonder. "My nephew escorted them to a hidden settlement north of town, just outside of Pethorp."

Separi takes a breath and clears her throat. She glances at Ridget, who says, "Tell her."

"Tell me *what*?" I say.

"I can't find Veril's fox amulet," Separi says, "and I've searched everywhere for it. The pendant was in my bag when we left Fihel, I'm certain of that. But when I returned from Beaminster, I searched and… I apologize for my carelessness." Separi's lavender eyes dim with embarrassment.

"You didn't lose it," Ridget says.

Elyn and I look at each other, and the Adjudicator says, "He stole it."

"Who?" Separi and Ridget ask.

"Jadon Rrivae," Elyn says.

"But was that the *real* Jadon doing something as shameful as stealing?" Separi asks. "His hand—"

"The unmarked and marked are *both* the real Jadon," I say. "You can't separate one from the other."

"That may not be accurate," Elyn says. "At least, not permanently."

We all pause to stare at her.

"Back in the aerie," Elyn says to me, "when you accused me of searching for the *Librum Esoterica*, I *was*, in fact, looking for it. Because as you know, there exist countless answers in those pages, which are constantly being appended. Agon had the book with him, and as you were healing at the abbey—"

"Healing?" Separi asks, eyes wide.

"Long story," I say.

"Agon and I both sped through the book," Elyn says, "and we found an entry on what to do about problematic demigods with troublesome markings."

I stare at her. "And?"

Elyn shrugs a shoulder. "Chop off the offending member."

I blink at her. "And?"

"That's it."

"So I still have to kill him," I say.

"You could chop it off and then try to save his life," she clarifies.

How the fuck do I do *that*?

High on the hillcrest that overlooks Doom Desert, Shari trots beside me as I ride Fraffin, the chestnut mare that I rode to Fihel. Behind me, all the horses' hooves clop against the earth as we rise above the province, drawing closer to the rolling expanse of this sea of sand. Below, the wind churns, dark and brooding, a deep reddish-green that shifts and pulses to its own rhythm. Sand dunes crash violently against the rocks, sending up dusty plumes that obscure the horizon. The edges of the world disappear into nothingness as the sand and sky become one.

Fifty Renrians ride in a loose formation, their figures silhouetted against the dimming sky. Their robes, intricately embroidered with luclite thread, catch the fading light of the daystar. Their drawn-up hoods protect their noses and eyes. The soft neighs of their horses blend with the roar of the sandstorm.

Separi rides behind me, her robes of rose-gold flow around her, and Ascendance, her twisted gray metal staff topped with a forged ball of light, glows faintly in the dying day.

Though the Renrians aren't a race known for brute force—they fill themselves with knowledge and wisdom—their staffs contain lavender current that can fry a mortal to their death.

Ridget, along with a smaller group of women and children, stayed behind in Caburh to continue tending to the work of a city at war—making tunics, crafting armor, and writing down the events of this day for all time. Their labor is as important as that of the warriors—their hands and words will shape the future in ways that steel can't.

The pain in my gut does not come from any sickness—no, this twisting comes from anxiety. Even though I'm at my strongest, I'm still worried, and I can't get the taste of worry-acid out of my mouth. I'm protected by the whole armor of my order and hold the mightiest sword in the realm and the dagger given to me in love. My amulet's power pulses through me, healing me from within, strengthening my bones, and still…

I have bubble-guts.

Shit…

And my mind won't let go of what just happened.

I killed Zephar.

I loved Zephar.

I killed Zee.

Our separation happened so fast—that's what I *want* to think. But the fracture between Zephar and me had always been there.

A difference of opinion.

That's how he is.

Our fights are legendary.

He makes me hot.

I was wrong.

Again.

The march down into the dusty bowl is a silent one. Elyn, beside me, rides Buttercup, the blond mare who'd also joined us in Fihel. Every horse in our service wears armor of luclite and has been shielded in a protective ward cast by the Adjudicator. The otherworldly creatures in this area—the smaller worupines, their quills bristling with strange poison, and the minulles, with their wide, glassy eyes, and their bodies a twist of owl and hare—scamper into their hedges, dens, and nests.

The long, sinuous bodies of snakes slide through the dead grasses and into dens. The few creatures of order—deer, rabbits, and ground squirrels—hide in their shelters of overgrown roots and hollowed-out logs. Their eyes are bright with fear, and they tremble as they wait for the storm to pass. And *that*! A scorpion the size of a crocodile rests in a bed of dying flowers. She doesn't move—she's too sick to move. Because she's the only one of her kind, she must receive additional protection.

I wave my hand as I pass all of these creatures. My fingers glide through the space, a summons to restore what's been broken and protect what has survived. The energy I use flows from my heart and spreads outward in waves as a soft, shimmering light that drapes across withered grasses.

The land slowly responds. The broken branches of trees straighten, and their leaves unfurl to reach for the gods of light once again. The flowers that have wilted begin to lift, their petals vibrant again.

The creatures around me stir, their trembling bodies slowly relaxing as the restoration spreads through them. Even the scorpion lifts her tail as blooms of pink, white, and orange untangle around her. The desert brightens, the sandstorm eases, the colors of the grasses deepen, and the air freshens now with the scent of renewal.

I feel the pulse of the land throughout my body. This fight is not just for those who walk upright but for all the beings that call Vallendor home. I must win this fight for them—if I don't, the most awful power will win, though his victory will be short-lived. Short-lived because the Mera *will* destroy him, but then they will destroy all within this realm—

from the High Lord of the Mera all the way down to the smallest worupine, minulle, and scorpion.

"Please tell me," I whisper to Elyn, "that you bedded Calyx before the abbey exploded with sickness and death."

She tosses me a tiny smile.

My eyes bug. "You *did*!"

"Ssh!"

"And?"

She puckers her lips. "I'll tell you the details later but… Obviously, it was good because he's got me out here fighting to save the realm."

I shriek and laugh. "Like that?"

"Kai…" Elyn pats her cheek. "He made me feel…*silver*."

My cheeks flush. "Wow."

"Yeah."

We reach the flats, and I lift my hand to halt our advance.

Up ahead, I spot a camp with banners fluttering in the wind. The dual leopards of Wake's regime have been embroidered on those flags, their sleek forms emblazoned in gold on deep red, their eyes fierce and unblinking.

A cry cuts through the silence.

Here we go.

Soldiers from our right and left charge toward us, their eyes burning with bloodlust. The camp quickly becomes a living, writhing thing. Soon, I hear nothing but the sounds of clashing steel, shouted commands, and the shrill cries of fighters and beasts.

The otherworldly of the desert—windwolves, hydrasalts, cowslews, and urts—rush from both sides toward Elyn, the Raqiel, and the Renrians, their glowing eyes cold and their bodies twisting with a power, their glows flickering from blue to amber as blades and staffs strike them down.

My sword strikes true, and the bodies of these soldiers, Wake's men, crumple from the force of my linionium blade and become heaps of black light. Feels like I'm pushing steel through fog. Yes, these fighters' bodies feel like they're made of foam and hope and not bone and muscle.

The otherworldly, though…

The ground shakes as massive worupines leave their dens, their bristling poisoned quills ready. They fire those deathly needles at Elyn and her guard.

Elyn summons the wind with a powerful sweep of her hands and sends the barrage scattering into the sky. Those deadly missiles slam into the necks and faces of Wake's army. Their bodies fall like chopped timber.

Shari romps and chomps, fearless.

The Renrians, their lavender eyes glowing bright, step forward with purpose. Half an age has passed since they fought in the Great War—but they move with the same fluid grace and power they once did. Their staffs, topped with carved animals—bears, eagles, the day- and nightstars—unleash storms of energy that cut through Wake's forces—soldiers and beasts—like sharp blades through brittle cloth.

The scent of battle hangs over us: acrid blood, spilled guts, all of it poisoning soil that already struggled between growth and restoration. No life will return here, not until the fires from the Mera roll across this land.

We all swing, slash, and summon. Wake's army has no chance here. They are worms trying to fight lions. One by one, stronger forces trample them until their blood soaks the earth. The otherworldly, for all their power, don't fare well, either. No resurrectors float over them to bring them back to life. Their bodies fall broken and scattered across the banks and flats of the Sea of Devour.

A soldier with a cruddy sword shouts, "For the emperor," and charges at me.

I flick my hand and send him flying into the slot canyons.

The daystar creeps toward the horizon.

We're losing time.

A herd of wolf-horse howlthanes races toward me, with its largest racing far ahead.

Where the fuck did they come from?

The howlthanes lift their heavy heads and bellow to the gritty sky.

"You must stop your incursion," I shout at them, my hand held out.

But the beasts keep charging, their hooves striking the muddy, bloody soil.

"Your creator sent you here to die," I shout to them, "but I'm offering you life. This realm does not belong to him. It belongs to me, the Lady of the Verdant Realm, and I'm promising you now—"

One howlthane me leaps at me, its mouth frothing with milky spit, its teeth sharp and filthy and fouled with meat and hair.

I rush forward on Fraffin and plunge my sword upward, right at the howlthane's heart.

The creature shrieks as its blood rains down on my hands and Fraffin's coat.

The howlthane is already dead before it slams into the ground.

The herd slows and skids to a stop, bellowing and waggling their heads. Their thoughts are as disordered as their bodies.

"I don't want to kill you," I whisper again.

But there are so many—and none are listening to me as they gnash their sharp teeth, as they call to the sky. *Creatorkillhelppleasepainnoplease.*

Danar Rrivae had no right to create these beasts.

Mercykillnopainenduslady.

I thrust my hands at them, and a massive ball of white-blue fire shoots from my fingertips and consumes the herd. The creatures catch fire, their cries immediately swallowed by my charged storm. I force myself to look—I don't want to, but I must witness their end.

And then I look around.

No soldier wearing Wake's tunics stands upright.

We've have cleared the field of fighters.

Panting, Elyn runs over to stand beside me.

"This was too easy," I say.

"Easy?" Elyn responds, still out of breath. "What—?"

"Those soldiers and otherworldly against our forces, they were already dead."

Elyn shakes her head, still not understanding.

I don't have time to make it clearer as I peer out across the land of the fallen.

Because now, here he comes.

Syrus Wake, Emperor and Lord of Vallendor and All Realms, the Manifestation of Supreme, the Divine and Most Holy, rides the most magnificent white stallion I've ever seen beneath the ass of a man. Wake's copper armor—no dents, no dullness—glints in the dying light, and his white cloak ripples like a glass sea. He glows a bright blue—and so do the soldiers behind him. He wears no helm to hide thick hair as white as a heron's feathers. His face bears no wrinkles or signs of age, skin too smooth to be believed.

The lie of Syrus Wake catches the light, and in those brief flashes, I see brown spots and crags, baldness and swollen veins. He was as young as me on the day I placed the crown on his head and presented him with his own *Librum Esoterica*. An age has nearly passed since then—he shouldn't be riding this horse. No, his ashes should be riding on wisps of memory and legend.

Time is not only my enemy—it's also his.

"Lady." The white stallion addresses me first.

"You're Vapor," I say. "I knew your grandfather, also called 'Vapor.'"

"The emperor calls me 'Snow.'"

"Lovely to see you, Vapor," I say, dipping my head.

The horse neighs and dips his head—he hasn't heard his name called in ages, and certainly not with the respect he deserves. Nature tells him now to kneel, but the jackass in the saddle kicks his haunches and presses him forward.

Vapor knows better.

But I know Syrus Wake, and this man won't stop hurting this horse until Vapor obeys.

I don't have time to play these power games. I hold up a hand and shout, "No need, Vapor." I hop off of Fraffin and tromp toward the emperor. "This won't take long."

Because there is no time.

Syrus Wake climbs off the horse and heads toward me. He chuckles even though his green eyes remain flat.

Yes, I remember this man who'd fought his way across Vallendor to take Beaminster, Tumunzah, Bolduf, and other lesser provinces. The scar across the bridge of his nose—that came from the battle at

Antleah. His missing left ring finger: from the fight at Aerie Fells. After being slit with a Dashmala dagger across his throat, the scar hidden now beneath his tunic, Wake stopped swinging a sword to conquer. And he lost that battle, and he lost Bacha as well as the southern regions of Vallendor, which went to the victor King Hamund Exley, ruler of Kingdom Vinevridth.

For a long time, Exley pushed back and won every attempt against Wake's army, retaining Maford, Pethorp, and all territory east of Caburh and south of Doom Desert.

But then Wake achieved knowledge by opening that book I'd given him on his coronation—and then, he'd wanted to learn more, and a certain Keeper of Knowledge said, "Hey, I know a guy..."

And now, Syrus Wake stands before me, so arrogant and certain of everything that even his cocky and disrespectful fingers don't tremble with fear. The mortal father of Jadon Wake doesn't resemble his son at all. Gileon and Jadon share their mother's lightning-blue eyes. Syrus Wake's eyes, though, remind me of murky water filled with dead things. Sea of Devour green. And now, those eyes stare at my amulet, which thrums and glows with absolute power.

"I'm here to proffer," Wake says, his voice sounding like clotted gravy.

I mock confusion, looking this way and that. "And who are you talking to? Surely you aren't addressing *me*."

The old man pauses, purses his lips, then dips his head. "Kaivara Megidrail, Grand Defender, Lady of the Verdant Realm, it's been a long time since my last audience with the most beautiful and most powerful being in the realm."

"Oh?" I say, wide-eyed. "*Now* I'm the most beautiful and the most powerful? The streets are saying that I'm not god enough for you. You listened, and look where it's gotten you: standing before me anyway with a prayer on your tongue."

"Not a prayer," he says, wagging his index finger at me, his voice dripping with condescension. "A *proffer*. That's when—"

"I know what a 'proffer' is," I say. "A proposal. A plan. A scheme. A fancier word, in my opinion, for 'prayer' because you, a mortal, can offer me nothing. You may have lived for a mighty long time, but to me, you're only dust."

The shadows on his face deepen. His jaw tightens, and the cords in his neck constrict—he's holding back an explosion.

Time… I'm running out of time.

Wake's top lip curls into a sneer that he tries to hide beneath a smile. "My…*prayer* is this: I will turn from Danar Rrivae and provide you my allegiance and belief. I will command my armies, including my very best captains and lieutenants"—his nostrils flare as he motions toward the men behind him—"to follow you. You, then, will rule beside me as empress—"

I laugh. "*What?* I will rule *beside* you?" I laugh and laugh and laugh some more.

Those shadows on his face now swirl like dark smoke. He's not a man who is laughed at.

"You see," I say, catching my breath, "I'm amused because your eldest son, Jadon? He made me that very same offer not too long ago. And your baby, Gileon? Had he lived long enough, he would've certainly asked for my hand and offered me a place beside him as well. The Wake men have one filthy habit in common: disrespect."

I shake my head and peer at those very best captains and lieutenants still straddled upon their horses. "The princes didn't get it. *None of you get it*," I say, glaring now at Syrus Wake. "I'm here because I'm the highest mountain this realm will *ever* see, and I've yet to stop growing. I rule *beside* no one."

Syrus Wake smiles at me, that condescension thick as slimy spit across my face. "You must not understand, Kaivara. I'm offering you—"

"*Kaivara?*" I take one step forward and swing Cruel Dawn, and she moves so fast, she catches fire as she cuts off the head of Syrus Wake.

Oh, the insufferable arrogance of men.

Syrus Wake's head lands at my feet, those dead, sea-green eyes still bright with surprise, that mouth still hiding its venomous sneer.

The gasps from those very best captains and lieutenants are as loud as the gasps from the soldiers standing in formation behind them.

"She killed him."

"He can't be dead."

"How do you kill Supreme?"

Their thoughts buzz in my ears as loud as the corpse flies now buzzing over the dead.

The horses, including Vapor, stomp their hooves, their eyes wild and nostrils wide.

"We're free!"

"He's dead."

"They too will die."

"Hold fast for now," I advise the horses. Then I snatch the head of Syrus Wake from the dirt and hold it up by that snow-white hair for his very best captains to see. "You have a choice on this day," I tell them. "Live and protect Vallendor from foes of this realm. Or…" I lift Wake's head higher. "You die alongside the charlatan, Wake."

Some soldiers bow their heads and immediately kneel before me. Others stick their blades between their ribs or slide their daggers across their necks. They prefer death to serving me. That's certainly a choice.

"For those joining me," I tell the survivors, "I will bind you to that promise. The moment your purpose turns from mine, you'll drop dead where you stand. An extreme punishment, yes. One relying on your fear of me, certainly, but you've already shown me your disloyalty. But this"—I hold Wake's head even higher—"is your prize if you show me your ass."

"Hey, Kai," Elyn says, coming to stand beside me. "We have a guest."

39

Jadon Rrivae Wake stands high above the desert, on the Rim of the Shadows. The ink that had started on his right hand now covers his torso and shoulder blades, but his left arm remains unmarked.

He wears my stolen pendant around his neck, and the moth now burns as bright as the daystar. He wears Veril's stolen fox amulet in a brace around his bare left arm, and the Wake family's signet ring that unlocked the *Librum Esoterica* squeezes his left ring finger. His eyes shine lavender, the second-most vivid light in Selenova's fullness.

Staring at him, Elyn says, "I thought your amulet was dead."

"I did, too." My gaze stays on the most powerful being conceived on Vallendor Realm.

"So what is feeding it?" she asks.

We both turn to my father, who has joined us for this last battle.

"Linionium," he says.

"From the signet ring?" I ask.

Father shakes his head. "Without Celedan Docci, the ring itself does not contain linionium."

"But if it's not in the ring," I ask, "where is the linionium?"

Father doesn't speak—is it because he doesn't know...*or because he does*?

"So what now?" Elyn asks.

I turn to her. "I talk to him."

"We can't use Jadon in the fight," she says, "not beyond using him as a threat against Danar."

I nod. "If he dies, we all die."

"We need Danar's amulet first," Elyn says. "Kill the traitor and then…"

"Kill Jadon before he can absorb Danar's power," I say.

She and my father peer at me with uncertainty. *Can you do this?*

My cheeks flush. "I will do what must be done to save this realm."

Elyn hangs back as I approach Jadon up on the bluff. She's a quiet anchor behind me. She gives us space, but she'll never be out of reach. "No stripping this time, please," she quips, a parting shot as I walk away from her.

I stop several paces away from Jadon, the distance between us too much and not enough. All that's happened between us lingers in this gap. I fear breathing the air around me. I'm not sure if he still has the power to weaken me. He's bigger than before, his frame wider, his muscles bulkier, but he retains that same elegance. He wears steel-gray mail tinted a subtle blue that shimmers like the ocean in a storm.

"I'm here to fight," Jadon says, his voice deeper, gruffer.

The greatsword he holds looks meaner than his old sword, Chaos—this new blade's teeth gleam with menace and hunger.

"You're here to fight," I say, "but for whom?"

Jadon gazes at me, his blue eye and lavender eye both flaring with pain. "I'm here to fight for *you*," he says. "To fight for *us*."

"I wish I could believe you," I say, "but you're wearing my amulet. You also held a knife to my throat as we stood on this very bluff. Yes, you're ready to love me, but you're also ready to kill me." I pause and then add, "All of Vallendor will soon witness your ultimate choice."

He remains cursed with Miasma—*no*, he *is* Miasma, he *is* the curse—and his power rolls toward me and pushes against my armor like the tide against the shore.

I take another step back. I'm no fool. Tides wear down mountains that stand in their way.

"I'll do anything for you," Jadon says.

"Now is the time to prove it," I say. "Everything's different. Times have changed because there *is* no time, not anymore."

"You killed the emperor," Jadon notes. "My father was a strong man."

"And your true father is stronger," I say. "And you're stronger than him."

Jadon holds out his arms. "You have nothing to fear—"

"You tried to kill me," I say, narrowing my eyes at him. "You took that from me." I gesture to the moth amulet hanging from his neck.

"Obviously, you didn't need it," he says, his blue eye glimmering. "Here you stand."

"It wasn't yours to take," I say, ice pooling in my heart. "And then to steal Veril's amulet from Separi? How much lower can you go?"

"As low as I need—and it's worked. Because here *I* stand."

"Unwilling—or unable—to help in this fight but hanging over us like a poisoned sword."

Jadon says nothing, but he doesn't look away—nor does he respond to my accusation.

I stare at the tattoo that continues to creep across his skin. Fire and water, earth and ice, circles and circles all slithering up his neck and down his left shoulder.

"You're willing to sacrifice yourself at the end of this?" I ask him.

"I'm willing to do what must be done." He presses his lips together and clenches his jaw. Both of his eyes brighten him. "And I will do it for love, for change, for all that yet breathes."

Caught off-guard, my breath catches in my chest as my eyes burn with sudden tears. He'd said that to me in my dream right before the world around us exploded. "We're done here," I say now, turning away from him.

"You may not believe this right now, but—" Jadon's nostrils flare, and that lavender eye flickers. "I do love you, Kai."

I look back at him over my shoulder. "I know."

• • •

Ithlon had been the last realm where I'd witnessed the awesome descent of my order in their god-sizes. That day had been an urgent cobalt blue and bright gold, swirling and luminous. That day smelled of copper and iron, of leather tanned over fire. The towns and cities and hamlets of Ithlon had shuddered beneath that falling sky.

I remember shrieking, wailing, burning. Collapsing.

Mera Destroyers, each of us as wide as six oxen and as tall as the oldest trees, stalked across the provinces, our giant red hands wielding two-pronged staffs tipped with fire. There were no shields. There was no obstacle great enough to stop this destruction. Flames wreathed our heads and around wings as crimson as blood. Our chests were adorned with countless swirling markings that glowed like flowing lava. With fire and molten rock falling from our mouths, we'd lifted whole houses as if they were loaves of bread.

The Eserime had stood in every city center across Ithlon, their faces twisted in horror as we marched over ridgelines and into their lives. They'd worn no armor, and their garments, light as air, could not protect them as they were launched into the sky. The air grew hotter as each steward flew higher, closer to Ithlon's daystar, Sandall. The god's glare was concentrated into a singular beam so bright that no being on the realm of Ithlon would ever see color again. No being on the realm of Ithlon would ever *be* again.

Dark clouds of deadly hot gases washed down every street, every river and mountain and across meadows and through canyons. There was no air to breathe.

This was death.

My mother, Lyra, had served as the Grand Steward and had settled in Gundabar, one of the biggest cities on Ithlon Realm. At that time, she'd been presiding over the start of fall harvests in this wealthy town covered in mosaics and statues. Most of the realm had been corrupted by greed, as some of its people gained immense wealth from trade and land. Even before the Mera came, festivals that were meant to celebrate community had become deadly traps of selfishness and vice. Slavery, rape, and murder spread like mold, consuming every home. Ithlon had failed and had fallen…but still not enough to be destroyed, according to the Council of High Orders.

But I grew convinced that the Council made the wrong decision—and other Mera Destroyers had agreed with me. So we destroyed Ithlon.

And then we were all punished, and I was alone.

Now, though, my father stands beside me as I fight for Vallendor's survival.

The nightstar begins her slow and deliberate rise, as if reluctant to begin her necessary journey. Full now, she glows with an eerie light, the orange of ripened pumpkins and the white of seashells bleached by salt and heat.

And beneath that dusky gleam are dead soldiers and Diminished scattered across rocks and new cliffs, impaled by spears, hacked apart by swords. In the city of Gasho: a dead prince. Dead priests, dead families, dead soldiers. No water. No food.

Amber light flickers from survivors of the last attack who had taken shelter in the Temple of Celestial. As Selenova rises above the horizon, windwolves and hydrasalts stalk them—another threat to this realm's existence.

The army of Devourers floods the land, stark-white giants with those blank red eyes, their pale skin stretched thin across their hulking forms. Their long arms hang lifelessly at their sides, their bloody-taloned fingers holding swords poised for battle. They wear chest panels made from the shells of the crocodile-like otherworldly, naperone, and loincloths stitched from the leather of every cow, lamb, goat, deer, and bison left on Vallendor.

The land is marred by their passage and the march of otherworldly everywhere, scarred and broken beneath their colossal weight, and once-fertile fields lie in ruin surrounded by splintered and twisted trees. The aqueduct has run dry again. The silence of this dead land is broken by the low, distant growls of Devourers standing in formation. *They* are the new river flowing across the desert floor and foothills.

"What has he done?" Father whispers, his gaze sweeping across row after row of countless living-dead warriors.

The leather-winged resurrectors circle above it all with their long snouts and sharp eyes, ready to give life to the fallen. Like the creatures at the Sea of Devour, the otherworldly here have swept through Gasho for supper, and they feast on the Gashoans who'd built me tubs and altars and praised my name.

I exhale long and loud, then look over to my father.

"You must finish the work," he says.

I cover my mouth with a shaky hand. I feel the weight of eyes on me: the eyes of soldiers who'd left Wake's army to join mine. I feel the eyes of Renrians who'd given everything to fight for Vallendor, for me. I feel the eyes of Raqiel sentinels, and Mera warriors, and Elyn Fynal.

I heave another sigh. "Let's finish the work."

Father lifts his sword, which burns with the fire of our order.

All the Mera cry out in unison, "Thak ak ail kuav!" *This is our day!* Their call echoes across Vallendor, stirring up red dust to swirl across the sky. But this realm answers with her own war cry—quaking beneath our feet, a demand that we win her at all costs.

The Raqiel guard hold the perimeter, and they focus on the soaring resurrectors above us.

Shari lopes over to greet me, and we nuzzle our noses. "I love you, too, Shari. Will you fight by my side again?"

She licks my cheek.

I wave my hand over her, forming a shield of protection.

Then Elyn waves her hand over the wolf—another shield.

Father pats the wolf's head. "Shari, I remember your mother, Riya. She was part of my litter on Mera." Then he offers the wolf a final protective shield.

"Kai," Elyn says, pointing to the north.

Danar Rrivae looms over Gasho. He wears a red-and-gray breastplate and his amulet of dark metal with crossed swords and compass points tipped with blood-like thorns. The pendant shines with the sickly red light of TERROR, the second gem we need. That jewel brightens as Selenova continues her ascent over Vallendor.

Although the traitor can't set a single toe upon this land, he is not untouchable.

Flanked by four Raqiel sentinels, Elyn marches to the front of our battle line. At her god-size, she is splendid and commanding in her platinum armor and blue cape. Justice crackles in her hand. "I am Elyn Fynal," she says, her voice hard as stone. "As Grand Adjudicator of Vallendor and the Nine Realms, Sentinel and Divine Mediator, with the approval of the Council of High Orders, I sentence you, Danar Rrivae, Seeker of All Truth, Veil Breaker and Destroyer of Realms, to death." She pauses, then adds, "Will you yield?"

Danar Rrivae stares at her, then smiles. His gaze moves past her. To this traitor, she doesn't exist.

I need no introduction. I march out to stand beside the Adjudicator. "Will you *yield*?" I shout.

Danar Rrivae glares at me, then flicks his eyes at my father. "No."

Well…

I lift my sword and shout, "Thak ak ail kuav! Dawn belongs to us."

There's no turning back now.

All around me, Mera warriors lift their swords and spears. We, too, are rows upon rows of fighters. We, too, are not of this world—yet we stand here to protect it. Fire and wind swirl around our weapons. One more cry—*"Yekaa!"*—and we charge straight into those undead giants, whose hollow eyes now burn with crimson light.

Danar Rrivae's eyes, once green, are now cold and gray. Two resurrector beasts with skeletal wings flank him while other creatures prowl low to the ground or soar overhead. All move with deadly purpose, their claws and fangs dripping with life-giving light.

Devourers meet Destroyers in a thunderous clash. Swords clang against swords, flames eat through bone, and the earth reverberates with the sound of heads of the fallen toppling to the ground. Devourers fall, but light soon swallows them, and then they rise again with mended flesh and mended bones.

Resurrectors at work.

Cruel Dawn and I make quick work of those Devourers lunging for me. We step and thrust, step and swing. *Yekaa!* I strike a leather-winged resurrector, knocking it to the ground without mercy. I then chop off its head.

Elyn and her guard fight as one, methodically cutting a path through the gerammocs and sunabi, the worupines and cursuflies, and advancing closer to our primary target, Danar Rrivae.

Shari fights beside me, clamping hands and legs in her jaws long enough for me to chop off their heads. She's a good girl, a deadly girl. Just like her momma, Rivya, and now me.

But the Devourers keep pouring forward. There are so many of them—rising, falling, and sometimes rising again.

The Mera, though, don't flag—this is what we do. We gain strength not from this realm, but from the power of the Aetherium.

Yekaa!

My father calls forth more wind and fire. Tempests and firestorms incinerate hordes of Devourers, reducing them to smoldering ash.

Elyn and the Raqiel guards close the distance to Danar Rrivae, who is enraptured with the destruction of my favorite place on Vallendor. There is so much quaking and shifting: new lakes where there were only oceans of sand. Another meadow, another valley, another new plateau.

The Mera sever heads and leave the fallen in mounds across the land.

Hope surges in my veins.

But Danar Rrivae remains, and he hovers above the ruins of his scattered and slain otherworldly. He lifts his hand, and shadows rise and twist around that hand, taking form as a massive, double-bladed scythe that pulses with a nauseating green-orange gleam.

With my eyes fixed on the traitor, I approach. Cruel Dawn blazes bright with lightning and eternal flame.

A far-off screech from the skies stops me in my step.

A meteor burning blue and lavender explodes from the clouds and crashes into the space between Elyn and me and Danar Rrivae.

Jadon!

He rises to his feet, demigod size now. He's not as big as Mera Destroyers, but he's big enough.

The nightstar shines now at her fullest. She would be glorious any other night. On this night, though, she's just one more beautiful villain.

We're out of time.

"Supreme has fooled you all," Danar Rrivae spits, his voice ringing across Doom Desert. "The false god has forsaken me and allowed my family to be captured without any explanation, without care or apology." He points to me, his lips twisted. "You're a fool for returning to the fold, to the liar, that so-called loving and merciful..."

He sneers. "Supreme allowed your beloved mother to die by your hand! Taken from you *by* you because of the lie told to you by your own soldiers and counselors, including the one you just slaughtered."

I stumble backward. "Zephar?" I gasp.

The traitor Danar grins. "You surely had to know that, Kaivara, or did you not want to believe your lover hated you from the very beginning? Everyone around you has lied to you. The Adjudicator, Miasma—they stand with you now, but they're both liars. Why is that? Do they think you're stupid? Or do they know you aren't valued? Do they know that you are the great experiment? Hmm? Maybe it's all those reasons, which makes you the most pitiful being in all the realms. I find it disgusting what they've done to you and what they're *still* doing to you."

"Kai," Elyn says, "don't listen to him. He's wrong about everything, including Zephar. He was never my choice for you, but he didn't know about your mother. He—"

"Is *this* what you want? Is this what you came for?" Danar snatches his amulet from his neck. "I don't need it." He throws it at me.

I duck, wincing, as TERROR flies over me, its heat singeing my skin.

The pendant instead smashes into the Destroyer standing behind me. Those compass points impale the warrior's neck, and he falls to the desert floor, dead.

"I will never bow down to Supreme," Danar Rrivae shouts, "nor will I ever heed the verdicts of the Council of High Orders. I will take this realm as my own just as they took my life from me. You may have slain my four children, but my strongest child remains." His eyes slide from Elyn to me and finally settle on Jadon. "I have one love left."

No unmarked patch remains on Jadon's chest, and his ink has now crept down to his left elbow. He turns to me, bloodied from battle, eyes glazed over from being consumed. "We were wrong," Jadon now says, his voice hoarse, his legs trembling. "That isn't TERROR in his pendant."

Elyn shouts, *"What?"*

"TERROR..." Jadon says. "TERROR lives deep within—" He lifts his tattooed right hand. In his left hand—still unmarked and guarded by Veril's fox amulet—he holds that toothed greatsword. He drops to his knees, thrusts out his right arm, lifts the sword...

"No!" Danar shouts.

Jadon's right hand falls to the dirt. His blood, red and black, splashes across the dirt as he falls to the bloody ground.

Danar Rrivae screams, "What did you do?"

With that bond between father and son severed, Elyn and I rush the traitor now gaping at his dying weapon, his dying son. I take to the sky and hurl handfuls of fire and wind at Danar Rrivae.

Elyn joins me, cardinals and moths lifting us both higher and higher. Together, we aim for the fallen god mourning the son he cannot approach. Elyn glides behind the traitor. She is the dagger to my broadsword.

I stand before Danar Rrivae, blocking his view of the child he created with the empress of Brithellum. "I'm here for a purpose," I announce. "The realm cries out for mercy, and I must offer relief. That means you die today."

Danar Rrivae's eyes widen as he realizes that no one has stopped for his grief.

"Tell me now," I demand. "Who runs this realm?"

He scowls and says, "I—"

"Wrong answer." I drive Cruel Dawn through his heart.

Elyn drives Justice between his shoulder blades.

I pull out Cruel Dawn from that dying heart, and I sever the traitor's head from his body.

Mera flames consume the rest of him, and the ashes of the traitor rain down upon Gasho.

I am Kaivara Megidrail, Grand Defender of Vallendor, and this realm and her people are safe once more.

40

The world is changed now. The daystar hasn't yet peeked over the horizon. The nightstar still lights the dark sky. No blue birds or nightingales sing, nor do children dance to our victory songs. There is no laughter, no mirth. This place still reeks of death. This land still languishes with disease. The waters remain poisoned, and the dead lie in mounds here in Gasho and all across Vallendor.

All because of our diseased hearts that desire power.

But Vallendor is ripe for change, eager for healing. The world is different now—and so am I.

But my army—from the mighty Mera to the fearless Renrians—smile because together, we overcame the brutality of Syrus Wake's reign as emperor and Supreme Manifest. We overcame Danar Rrivae's petty revenge as he sought vengeance against his perceived enemies and, ultimately, against Supreme. We conquered the worst barrier—my ego—to reach a place of hope. But there's so much work to do.

Again, the city gates of Gasho hang off their hinges like teeth hanging from diseased gums. Sybel Fynal, Grand Steward of Vallendor and the Lady of Dawn and Dusk, directs stewards from across the Aetherium to heal the mortal survivors of this gods' war. While the Eserime fill their gold pitchers with new water to replenish the soiled canal and wells, the Mera clear away the dead and burned, and cleanse Gasho with more purification fire so that all new growth blooms and thrives. The Dindt will soon arrive by the Glass of Infinite Realms to provide expertise to the survivors on rebuilding. They will also restore the exquisite bath that Prince Idus built for me.

I want Gasho to be rebuilt stronger than ever—and to aid in this, I will send select groups of mortals to the places where gods fell, to gather hardened blood that has transformed into new jewels. However, I will forbid them to dig farther than a day's work—any more would destroy the land and the creatures that live there.

I head over to Sybel, whose hands hover over the body of a living yet unconscious ancress of Gasho. "Will she survive?" I ask.

Sybel offers me an encouraging smile. "She and several others will pull through. This province is not entirely a graveyard."

I bow my head. "And am I closer to who I was meant to be?"

Sybel takes my hand in hers. "You are *more*. That's all we ever wanted." She squeezes my hand and adds, "Lyra would fall in love with you all over again."

My father talks with his generals, their voices low but firm, discussing the division of work that lies ahead. He's changed out of his dirty orange-and-red robes and now wears a sleek gown made of black fabric that drapes elegantly over his broad shoulders.

I approach the group, offering a quiet but heartfelt thanks for all they'd done for Vallendor and for me.

Father rests his hand lightly on my shoulder, a silent command to stay beside him until the other Mera leave us to carry out his orders. Once they leave us:

"How did it feel to fight again?" I ask him, smiling.

He chuckles. "My blood moved through my veins like lightning. But my heart aches... I don't miss this part." He gazes out at a realm that cries out for healing—the sick, the dead and dying, the choking smoke, the remnants of life crumpled and crumbling beneath the weight of destruction. Exhaustion lines his face. He sees that so much has been lost.

I see it, too. *But!* There's evidence of good things to come, a hopeful future after the chaos.

I point to the growing pool of water that would take humans half a day to reach. "That will soon be a new lake that will quench the thirst of those living here."

I point to the large gaps in the land to the west. "Those will be beautiful canyons. Though the dirt is now red with blood, it will one day become another place of new life and learning. A river will run through it all, and it will be one of the most beautiful places on Vallendor. And—"

I pause, allowing the weight of the possibilities to sink in. "Gasho will once again become a center for knowledge, for growth, for everything this land was before and shall be."

It will take time, but even the deepest scars will one day be flooded with new life.

And I'll see it through.

Still...my face falls as I consider another truth. "If I hadn't been defeated so many times—"

"Those defeats still moved you toward victory," Father says, lifting my chin. "And now, you stand here and Vallendorians will once again feel your love. They'll crave your touch, and that will lead them to each other."

I smile and say, "Yes."

"Lord Megidrail?" Another Mera general approaches with a large, heavy bag. She opens the pack and presents the contents to us: Danar Rrivae's scythe and amulet.

"Will you take all of it back to Linione?" I ask Father.

"Immediately." He nods back to his general and then turns to kiss my forehead. "Return to the abbey after you set everyone their tasks for the next age. Let's have dinner together before I return to Linione."

I nod, smile, and accept another kiss on the forehead. I say nothing as he steps back with a *pop!*

He's gone—only a lick of Spryte flame marks where he just stood.

Elyn stands at the entrance to the Temple of Celestial, her armor dull with dried blood, her hair stuck to her skull with the same gore, and her mouth set in a frown.

I groan. "Don't you bring me bad news now."

Her frown deepens.

My pulse flares in my chest. "*What?*"

. . .

"So where is he, then?" I ask, following Elyn back out to the blood-soaked desert, alarm hot in my throat.

"I don't know," Elyn admits as she leads me across this transformed landscape.

"Did they find Syrus Wake's head yet?"

Elyn says, "The otherworldly took it into the sea."

"Shit," I say. "What about Jadon's hand?"

Elyn sighs. "I don't know."

"His body?"

Elyn blinks at me and averts her gaze, staring intently at Shari trotting in front of us.

We stop where Jadon had collapsed after he cut off his hand. Then we follow a trail of vibrant red blood that leads to the canyons. We don't speak as we pass cratered ground, hydrasalts tails, date palm trunks, and broken blades. My mind spins. I thought Jadon was dead. That's why I'd delayed coming to claim his body but now...

The trail of blood ends right as the land rises to become canyon walls.

"Shari," I say, "find Jadon."

The wolf sniffs the air and bounds into the canyon.

Elyn and I run after the black wolf and into a sea of mist drifting through the passageways. My head hurts so much that my vision blurs. At any moment, my victory could slip into another defeat, because who will we find at the end of this path?

The buzzing of corpse flies grows louder than my pounding heart. Gore from the battles—soldiers, horses, otherworldly—is scattered throughout the landscape as far as my eyes can see, prizes hoarded by the windwolves and other scavengers of Doom Desert. There is no single trail of blood to guide us now, and every path has been spoiled with darkened and congealed blood. There are so many dead here, and Jadon could be in any of these piles.

A few soldiers who'd been taken for dead but lived now stagger through the canyons, hugging the walls for support. Not one of them wears a complete suit of armor. Not one of them moves faster than a tortoise.

I approach the most clear-eyed man, the one with the lightest amber glow, and grab his jerkin.

He wears Veril's fox amulet around his neck.

I snatch the pendant from him and shout, "Jadon Wake: have you seen him?"

"Lady!" His heart thuds once under my hand and then beats no more. His eyes glaze and his head lolls. He's dead.

"Shit, Kai," Elyn mutters.

I stow the fox pendant beneath my breastplate and then lay the now-dead man atop the closest pile of fallen soldiers.

If he had Veril's amulet, that soldier must've seen Jadon…

We move through the ravine, Shari in the lead, sniffing the air. She finds another survivor.

This soldier wears one of Wake's tunics and creeps along the wall as though lava has replaced sand.

This time, I keep my hands to myself and call out, "Hey…" *What's his name?* "Arnold!"

Arnold gapes at me and whispers, "Oh, Guardian, gentle Lady of the Verdant Realm, hear the humble plea…"

I don't want to interrupt his prayer, but windwolves lurk on the ledge above us, ready to eat the fallen.

This time, I gently tap the soldier's head, and his aura brightens to blue. "Have you seen Prince Wake?" I whisper.

Arnold, now bright-eyed and sweet-breathed, shakes his head. "No, Lady."

I tell him, "Go," and send a worried glance at the cliffs above us. "You will leave that man or else," I tell the wolves.

Shari sniffs the air, then releases a mournful howl that echoes through the chasm.

Elyn and I race behind Shari as she leads us through walls of broken rocks and broken soldiers. Bones lie scattered across the ground, crunching under our feet like dry twigs. Pieces of broken armor and torn clothes belonging to those who fought and died lie discarded and trampled in the sand. The smell of decay blends with the scents of earth.

We trek over the bones, though the sharp edges catch on our boots. We don't slow down even as the chasm grows tighter and the walls press in so close that sometimes we must move sideways. The world narrows. It's a blur of red walls.

Shari's low growls signal that we're getting closer. There is light ahead at the end of the canyon.

Moths the color of fire and forest flutter over a mountain of bloody rocks, severed hands, and bones from humans and beasts.

Elyn whispers, "Oh, no."

We burst into open air under an immense sky streaked now with finger-like clouds. We skid to a stop at the largest pile of scavenged bones I've ever seen.

I use the tip of Cruel Dawn to push through the heap of bones…

A blue-tinged mail breastplate. *Fuck.* Jadon was wearing this armor.

I continue my search and push aside…

A cap-sleeved leather tunic. "That's his, too," Elyn whispers.

I continue my search even though my shaky hand can barely hold on to my sword and…

No. A chain with the moth amulet.

I pull my old pendant from the mess. The black stone in the moth's thorax pulses with light. I stare at the amulet, unable to speak.

Elyn takes over the search, using Justice's blade to sift through the remains. I keep my eyes on the amulet until…

"He's not here, Kai," Elyn whispers.

Shari howls and pants.

Fifty paces away, a lounge of hydrasalts tears into some poor creature's leg. One of those three-headed lizards gnaws at a boot.

"That's Jadon's boot," Elyn says.

I watch the lizards eat until a curtain of tears obscures my vision. Those teardrops fall into the parched earth, and flower buds and blades of new grass sprout through the dirt. I cover my heart with a shaking hand.

I wish…that I could've made it right between Jadon and me.

I wish…that I could've healed him once and for all.

I don't regret doing all that I had to in order to save Vallendor. But he's gone, after making the ultimate sacrifice. *For you. For us.*

Danar had threatened to cut Jadon's strings at any time. Little did he know Jadon would cut his own.

Shari howls again, this time because she can feel the weight of my grief. She didn't know Jadon, but she knows my heart.

"We must leave this place," Elyn whispers. "We must go back and check on the living."

I nod and swipe my wet face against my shoulder.

The nightstar burns high above us in the western sky. Her silver light illuminates everything beautiful and horrible now twisted together in this realm. But past the stench of death, there's a new smell. Fresh honeysuckle and night-blooming jasmine now grow wildly around us—all here because of my fallen tears. Fireflies flicker and dance across this healing meadow, ready to illuminate the night and the path back to my people, back to my land.

"Look." Elyn points to the east, where Lumis will soon rise and bring with him a new dawn.

Out there, a figure sprawls across the red dirt. More hydrasalts circle this body, which now glows deepest amber, that shade right before life slips to death.

Who is that?

Elyn, Shari, and I run toward that body.

The lizards hiss and swipe at us. They know we're about to steal their dinner.

I shout, "Be still." Shari growls at them.

The hydrasalts hiss again, no longer so determined to keep their prize.

Because the body lying here…the man with that barely open lavender eye and matted chestnut hair is not theirs to keep.

This prize… This *man* belongs to me.

41

Before I can start the rebuilding of New Vallendor, I must take out Old Caburh's trash.

My arrival in what is now New Nosirest comes with a restored whirlpool of Spryte moths. Their wings flash brilliant reds and golds, and their glittering dust settles on my skin.

The town before me, though, remains a shadow of the shadow that it once was, its streets marked by violence and neglect. New Nosirest's buildings sag with age and decay. Their windows are shattered or boarded up, the walls cracked like rotting bones. This place stinks of smoke and sour sweat, stale alcohol, and the reek of blood that may never wash away.

Maybe the Mera should swing by and shoot some fire to cleanse Old Caburh's stench.

A few stragglers hiss at me, heckling and calling me names: Maelstrom, the bitch, the devil, the whore who dares to return but who won't fight fair, not with swords but fight with fists, fight like a *real* man.

I don't bother. Who puts on armor and weapons to take out the trash? Right now, I wear what every housewife in Vallendor wears to handle menial tasks: a housedress and a pair of sandals.

I hold my red-and-gold armor in my left hand, but in this moment, I choose to wield fire. The heat from my fingertips crackles, and with a flick of my wrist, flames leap from my palm, striking the barriers built around three taverns and a tannery. My fire burns several posters printed with "Kill This Evil" slogans and my likeness, tacked to standing posts. As the flames swirl around my fingers, I'm glad to know that this broken town will not suffer from people like this much longer. They'd made Old Caburh–New Nosirest such a miserable place.

The Broken Hammer Inn still stands, but its once-proud sign now hangs crooked, the wood weathered and decaying. Three angry men with axes—grizzled and wild-eyed, their clothes torn, their faces smeared with dirt and blood—hack at the battered red doors. Their frantic chopping is driven by anger and hate. They can't even focus long enough to hit the same place twice.

My sandals are silent on the cracked cobblestones as I approach the inn's porch. Unlike these three, I *can* focus, and my eyes seek out this trio as the fire inside of me builds with each step I take.

"I warned you, didn't I?" I say.

The men freeze, their axes in the air. They turn to face me, their shoulders hitched to their ears, their faces twisted in rage.

The gray-haired man levels his ax and spits, "Maelstrom, you bitch—"

I whisk him away with a sweep of my hand, sending him and his slurs to their deaths six hundred paces away.

The one with the permanent scowl shouts and rushes toward me with his ax raised.

With only a thought, I turn that ax on its wielder, and the blade lands right down the middle of the angry man's brow.

The third man drops his ax and runs away. He tries to make it home, but he shouldn't *have* a home here, not anymore. Did he not hear me the last time? I said what I said.

With a flick of my hand, I drag him along that broken cobblestone road and slam him into the side of a large wood crate.

And now that my housework is done, on to bigger things. Like making Vallendor the realm it deserves to be.

• • •

Twenty dawns have come and gone since I faced the traitor, Danar Rrivae. Now, on the twenty-first, Elyn and the Raqiel sentinels stand at the repaired gates of New Gasho. Her white pangolin-scaled armor reflects all the light of the realm and brightens the land with possibility and promise. The Gashoans, though accustomed to the presence of gods, have never seen such splendor as Elyn Fynal, Grand Adjudicator of Vallendor and the Nine Realms, Sentinel and Divine Mediator. They bow their heads in her presence—and then they gasp in awe as I come to stand beside her in my lemon- and orange-hued sarong.

Over in the courtyard, the city-folk of Gasho fete us with song and dance, hailing our renewal during this feast of thanksgiving. A quartet of girls wearing golden gowns, their hair combed into four puffy ponytails, stands before me and Elyn with their hands clasped before them, their cheeks ruddy. With encouragement from one of the girls' mothers and a wide smile from me, they clear their throats and sing.

All is right in Celestial's might.
All is right, all is right.
Where she is, there will be joy,
For every girl and every boy.
Find me safe in Celestial's arms.
Safe from harm, safe from harm...

I clap—*they are the cutest*—and my eyes fill with tears.

I accept the platter of stuffed figs offered to me by two girls with tufted ponytails that remind me of my own hair. They curtsy and giggle and call me, "Miss Celestial." Their smiles are brightened by their missing front teeth.

A short column of soldiers marches toward us, and even though not one man smiles, their eyes sparkle with pride in their service of this city again.

The city dwellers fall silent as Intendant Wosre, healed from his injuries, stands before us again and says, "With healing hands, she gently weaves our song of life. With cosmic sword, she fights the shadows that stain our night. She will return triumphant for battles seen and those not yet won."

Hopefully, Gasho—and Vallendor—won't see any battles in the coming age. That is my own prayer.

I scan the faces of the crowds and— *There!*

I spot Iretah, the woman I met on my first day back in Gasho. Nenefer is beside her, and she's holding her orphaned niece, Tymy, in her arms. I rush over to the small family. Iretah offers me Tymy. I hug the baby and take in her vanilla-and-soap scent.

"You kept your promise," the young mother whispers, her eyes bright with tears.

I kiss the top of her head and return Tymy to her arms. "Be well."

Elyn looks around one last time—to the gushing water fountains, the repaved mosaic tiles, the alabaster temple and belltower, and most importantly, the old and young faces of Gashoans, their bodies brimming with the blue of health…and hope.

Shari romps playfully with the Gashoan children in the long grass. Her energy in no way reflects the remaining work we must do in the seasons ahead. But these folks will do more than just survive in Vallendor—they will *thrive*, too. The youngsters laugh, their innocent faces bright as they reach out to the wolf. Shari nuzzles and yips and loves.

Around the city, the work already takes shape, like the spoiled dirt surrounding the town, now slowly being nurtured back to health, softening as tiny shoots of green push through the cracks. We've begun building dams and bulwarks to contain the growing lake—and the lake, once a trickle, now swells with life and spreads across the land, bringing with it the power to nourish the crops, sustain the people, and restore balance to the ravaged environment.

"We're not done," I tell Elyn with a small shrug.

"I'm not worried." Satisfied, Elyn turns on her heel. "Walk with me."

We head toward the grove of date palms, sweet-smelling from the plump fruit hanging now from their bunches.

"There's one last task I'm required to complete," she says, accepting a date from me.

I bite into my own fruit. Chewy, nutty, sweet. My eyes close with bliss.

"Kai," Elyn says.

I smile at her and then school my expression into something more solemn. "Sorry."

"Take a knee, please," she says, seriously.

Ah. My heart pounds as I kneel before her.

"You have reclaimed your position as Grand Defender of Vallendor Realm," she says, "the ten-thousandth of the seventy thousand realms. You are to heal this land and all that is in it. You are to observe the stewards here, guide them as they guide all mortal life. Share counsel with the Renrians in their wealth of knowledge and wisdom. You are to direct the Mera who have been charged as protectors of this realm, who are responsible for safeguarding this place from any threats, both mortal and immortal. You are to do all of this in accordance with our ways, as mandated by the Council of High Orders. Do you accept this charge?"

Tears of joy burn in my eyes. "I accept this charge."

"Then I bind you to this promise," she says.

Supreme placed gods in realms across the Aetherium to heal and protect the beings of our realms. To guide and teach—from treating each other with love and respect to protecting homelands from enemies. We are to bless the mortals with abundant harvests, offer warnings, and nurture visions. We provide protective barriers and intervene when needed—and deserved. If mortals didn't need us, then Supreme's decision to designate us as representatives would be pointless.

I take Elyn's offered hand, and she helps me to stand. We share a long, firm hug.

"Sister," Elyn whispers.

"Sister." I kiss her cheek.

We both exhale and take a deeper breath.

"So what did you want to show me?" she asks.

• • •

No white smoke billows from this cottage's chimney. The surrounding trees are now gnarled stumps and twist toward the ground. The front door lies flat and cracked across the threshold. I almost expect Veril to step out onto the porch to say, "What mortal nonsense *is* this, dearest?"

I close my eyes and think about the crowded hearth and comfortable chairs waiting inside. "He was a great man," I say, my throat tight. "An extraordinary teacher, and I still had so much to learn from him but…"

"Tomorrow, it will be better," Elyn says. "Where some see tragedy, Veril would see hope. And he'd be happy that you've returned here."

Shari barks, then lopes into the meadow behind the cottage.

"No killing," I shout after her.

I tap at a cocoon hanging from the splintered doorframe. The husk wriggles with new life. My eyes cloud with tears as I glimpse the forge in the dead garden. Jadon had gifted me Fury there. That large wooden tub—we'd kissed there as I bathed. Inside the cottage: the bedroom that had hosted me as I'd healed, and a hearth that had been tended by a generous old man who'd taught me languages, alchemy, and patience the moment I opened my eyes—at birth and near death.

I will make this place better, for Veril, for me. A nice place to stay as I rebuild Vallendor.

"Any news on Jadon?" I ask as Elyn and I lift the front door.

Elyn shakes her head. "I haven't seen him since Mother and the Eserime Spryted him to the abbey and Agon."

I say, "Ah," and swallow my tears.

He couldn't have any visitors—given how serious and dangerous his condition was. No one knew if he'd live—or be allowed to live, given his heritage, an irony I understood much too well—my own life had been threatened because of who my mother was.

Maybe I will hear something tomorrow. I've said this for twenty-one dawns now, with the hope that silence means I can continue to hope.

After making repairs, Elyn and I change into soft, suede breeches and airy tunics as the evening settles in. The cool breeze carries the scent of healing forest, and the twilight's softness flickers through the cracked windows. Before resting, we sweep away battaby skeletons scattered across the floor. The bones clatter, and I remember the horrors of their attack that day.

Soon, the warm kitchen smells of rosemary and peppercorns as Elyn prepares roasted vegetables and I tend to the hearth-fire.

"Hey," I say. "I'm sorry for my outburst back at the aerie. I shouldn't have treated you like the enemy. I shouldn't have mistrusted you, and I shouldn't have thrown those delicious pastries out the window."

Elyn says nothing for a moment. "They were the best pastries ever made, you fool."

I snicker. "I'm stupid sometimes."

Elyn shakes her head and looks back at me. "You had every reason to be suspicious, and…you weren't feeling well. I accept your apology, Kai." She places her hand atop mine.

I close my eyes and shake my head. "Zephar…I tried hard to get him to see…"

"To see *what*?"

"To see me? To see who Orewid Rolse truly is? To see through the big lie?" I shake my head. "The last thing I wanted was to kill my ex-boyfriend. Did I want to make him miserable? Yes, absolutely. But did I want to kill him?" I didn't, even though he thought nothing of killing me for being the product of my parents' love.

Zephar faked it. Not just his "love" for me but also his "respect." He pretended to see me as worthy of my order, but in truth, he held his breath, repulsed by my touch, repulsed by the curl of my hair, by my mother's nose in the middle of my face.

Any time we drank too much, Zephar and I would name our future children: Susan and Ronald, Lonnie and Mary, Joe and Joan, mortal names that made us laugh until we couldn't breathe. He'd play with my hair and he'd call me his love and he'd lie across my thighs and fall asleep. Now looking back, our coupling was not too different from the "celebrations" of Gasho. All politics and no love. Favor, yes, but no heart involved. The strongest wins.

He made a complete fool out of me as he and the other Diminished snickered behind my back, knowing that it was all a joke, a ploy to convince me we were in this together. He nurtured my natural tendencies to question and wonder, stoking them beyond my intentions, fostering rebellion in my heart, and I let him because he *got* me. I thought he understood me when few others did. He had my back, and I had his.

I try to smile at Elyn, but I can't hold back my tears. "You know…I was incredibly envious of you. Angry with you. Confused by you. You're so smart and so perfect—"

"I am," she says, winking. "Don't forget that I'm also breathtaking."

"I take a lot of breaths, dearest," I say with a smirk. "You're all those things, and yet I'd strayed so far from who I was—"

"No," she says. "Even though you became so dangerous that I'd sentenced you to death, you were becoming who you were meant to be. Questioning. Loyal. Compassionate. Frustrating. Driven. There are none like you, Kai, and in your own way, you came around to see all of who you are. The beings of this realm, in this complicated world under tremendous threat, they needed a champion like you to make it this far. The Grand Defenders of those destroyed realms are no longer here, but you are. And hope begins in the dark—didn't you say that? *You* are hope. *You* are the dark. *You* are the dawn. You are all those things."

We talk about her budding romance with Calyx; about the next realm she must visit; about those times as girls we'd run through the field of bluebells on Ithlon, the daystar Sandall high above us, the wind in our hair, and the freedom of the open fields stretched out before us.

The daystar soon drifts even lower into the western sky and paints the horizon in shades of burnt orange and deep purple.

Elyn stands with sadness in her eyes and takes my hands in hers. "Will you be all right here?" she asks again.

"Are you still worried about Orewid Rolse?" I ask. "All the Crusaders in Vallendor are dead."

"I know, but…" She bites her lower lip. "But I didn't see Rolse on the battlefield or among the dead."

I shrug. "Running away and dodging fights is what he does, right? Fucking coward."

"The Eserime are waiting for you at the Sanctum," she says. "With all this lovely quiet, remember that you have work to do."

I nod. "Don't worry—I'll join them soon."

We hug, and I tightly squeeze the woman I'd hated for too long.

"You'll visit?" I ask.

She walks down the pathway, and red cardinals immediately flutter around her. Two more sentinels wait at the foot of the walkway.

"Of course," she says, walking backward. "I helped save this place. I have to make sure you don't mess it up again."

"And we're visiting Sianiodin together, yes?"

She nods. "Right after Calyx and I…"

"Read every book in the abbey?" I ask, eyebrow cocked.

"Is that what it's called now?" Elyn says, smirking.

I wave and blow her a kiss.

She blows a kiss back.

Sister.

Friend.

Veril's amulet now hangs over the entryway to the sitting room. A new fire burns in the hearth, and the room smells of cinnamon and pine. The wooden floors sparkle, and outside the cottage's windows, the halved nightstar hangs against the violet sky.

Once word spread that I preferred living in these woods instead of the Sanctum above Gasho, the people of Vallendor started to make pilgrimages here. Now, Raqiel sentinels stand at the bottom of the crooked walkway that Veril had once hidden. I hide that walkway any time I tire of being Lady of the Verdant Realm. Tomorrow, I will join the Eserime, Mera, and Renrian council of Vallendor, and we'll discuss our plans for ongoing restoration. King Exley will request to lead this task, and Queen Alinor will request trade routes be rebuilt. Gasho and the new priests and ancresses have already asked that I attend their upcoming celebration.

Shari awakens from her nap in front of the fire. She stands and bounds over to the door.

Someone knocks.

I frown. It's too late in the day for visitors. I open the door.

He stands there with his right arm wrapped in pristine bandages. He pulses with a blue glow. His skin looks clear, the color of healthy eucalyptus bark. His eyes shine bright lavender, their color at his birth. He smiles and says, "Hey."

My heart stumbles in my chest and my knees buckle. I sink to the floor, whispering, "Jadon?" A sob bursts from my chest.

"Kai," he murmurs.

"Please say that you're really standing here," I say, "and that I'm not dreaming."

Shari's tail wags as Jadon pats her head.

Yes, he's standing right in front of me. There is a bag slung over his left shoulder. He wears suede breeches and a thick cream sweater to guard against the cold. The cable knit of his sweater tells the story of his journey across the realm—the son of a king, the town blacksmith, his life, his death, his life again. He winces as he helps me stand from the floor.

Plumes of amber flare around his injured arm and the space where his right hand used to be.

"I'm sorry." I pull away from him. Wide-eyed, I touch his arm, and it pulses blue again. "Are you okay?"

"I'm better now that I'm standing here with you." His voice remains deep and intoxicating, like a smoky rum.

I sweep that stubborn lock of chestnut hair from his forehead. "Can you—? Will you—?" I take a breath. "I don't even know what to say."

He touches my cheek. "I have something for you." He reaches into his satchel.

My mind races, my pulse hammers, all of me vibrates, and I can hardly think one thought at a time.

"I brought this for you." He holds out a large light-green flower with spiky stamens that resemble crowned cranes. The berries inside the flower are yellow and tinged pink. Nestled inside the bloom: a bee, her yellow-and-black fuzz flecked with pollen.

"She's a rare breed," he says, "and she makes honey on a tiny island south of Hamor. She and her hive feed on rose apple blooms that only grow on that island, but Agon told me that you can plant these flowers here and they won't disturb the blooms that naturally grow in these woods."

"Hello, there," I whisper to the bee. "Welcome to Verilwood. I will name you…Lyrabee." I smile at Jadon and say, "You remembered."

"That you wanted to keep your own hives for honey and use beeswax to make candles?" He nods. "And…" He reaches into the bag again, and this time, he pulls out a small canvas pouch. "Another gift."

I pull apart the drawstrings, confused by what could be in an empty bag. I shake that nothing into my hand and…

Seven brown seeds tumble onto my palm.

"Crabapples," Jadon says, his gaze sweeping across the garden. "Maybe…*there*?" He points to the spot where Veril's old crabapple tree once stood, heavy with fruit. During my recovery, Jadon and I had spent quiet afternoons beneath that tree.

"One more gift," Jadon says as he leads me past the garden.

I squeeze his hand. "I would like to say, 'You didn't have to,' but I've never been that type of god."

He laughs. "Nor will you ever be. Which is why…"

Out in the meadow, the soft green blades tremble in the breeze as a brown cow grazes on new clover. She looks back at me, her large eyes peaceful, unbothered.

Shari rushes out to greet her new sister.

I laugh and spin around to face Jadon. *"Really?"*

He grins and shrugs. "What do you give a lady who has everything, including her own realm?"

I finally—*finally!*—throw my arms around him. "You give her a cow and...you bring her yourself."

And tomorrow, I will wake up to a kiss instead of a kill.

Yes, Jadon will fit in nicely here at this cottage in Verilwood and in the new Vallendor. And so will Lyrabee and Clover, the Cow of Cottage Kai in Verilwood, now and forever more.

I kiss Jadon Wake Rrivae, and his lips are so soft, and sweeter than any rare honey in this realm and beyond.

His kiss makes me feel...*silver.*

CHARACTERS FOR *THE CRUEL DAWN*

HIGH ORDERS

Dindt

Explorers and seekers, this order travels through the Aetherium in search of new realms. Once they observe life in these new realms, they return to Linione, the first created realm, with knowledge. Green eyes.

Eserime

Stewards and healers charged with caring for the realms—from a single blade of grass to every mortal that breathes. Gray/silver eyes.

Mera

Warriors charged with destroying the realms for future restoration. Each wears markings that note those realms they've destroyed. Golden eyes.

Onama

The intellectuals of the original orders who impart wisdom and judgment across the Aetherium. They are the record-keepers and historians. Lavender eyes.

Yeaden

The gods of crafts charged with creating weapons and armor for the gods. They also build the abbeys located on each realm throughout the Aetherium. Black eyes.

MAJOR GODS AND DEMIGODS

Kaivara Megidrail

Grand Defender of Vallendor, Lady of the Verdant Realm, Destroyer of Worlds; Celestial, Our Lady of Might and Life; Lady Megidrail; Precious One; Divine, Warrior-Divine; Ancient One; sweet Lyra's baby girl; the One; Blood of All; Maelstrom; Abomination and Perversion. Daughter of High Lord Izariel Megidrail and Grand Steward Lyra Laserie.

Zephar Itikin

Beautiful Warrior; Xisi; Breaker of Realms; Lord of the Shielded Fount, Prince of Lissome Blades; Warrior of the Righteous; Divine Xisi. Kai's lover from the Before-Time.

Shari

Warden of the Unseen Step; Kai and Zephar's wolf; daughter of Rivya, the wolf of High Lord Izariel Megidrail.

Elyn Fynal

Grand Adjudicator of the Nine Realms; Grand Librarian; Lady of Law and Light. Daughter of Sybel Fynal.

Danar Rrivae

The traitor; the One. Seeker of All Truth, Veilbreaker and Destroyer of Realms. He is of the Dindt order but has appropriated the tattoos of the Mera and the crimson ribbon of the Raqiel guards. He brought to Vallendor animals from other realms and created animals to compete against Supreme. He conquered the realms Kestau, Kynne, and Fendusk. Can't set foot on a realm until he kills its Grand Defender.

Jadon Wake Rrivae

Son of Emperor Syrus Wake. Son of Danar Rrivae. Prince of Vallendor; Miasma; the Weapon. Former blacksmith of Maford.

Sybel Fynal

Grand Steward of Vallendor; Lady of Dawn and Dusk. Elyn's mother.

High Lord Izariel Megidrail

Representative of the Mera order on the Council of High Orders; Kai's father. Can trace his lineage to the first Mera of the original five races.

Malik Sindire

The God of Leisure; visits Vallendor every fifty years.

Orewid Rolse

Leader of the Crusaders, a sect of Mera who believe that only pure-blooded Mera should exist.

Agon Laserie the Kindness

Seer; Wisdom; the anchorite of the Abbey of Mount Devour. Lyra's brother and Kai's uncle.

Lyra Laserie

Grand Steward of Ithlon; Kai's mother, Izariel's wife, and Agon's sister; deceased.

High Lord Saerahil Fynal

Representative of the Onama order on the Council of High Orders; Elyn's father and Sybel's husband. Has spoken the word to Supreme; deceased.

Celedan Docci

The God and Keeper of Knowledge. Lives in the WISDOM gem attached to the *Librum Esoterica* of Vallendor.

Diminished

Mera Destroyers who have been punished and stripped of their full powers.

Devourers

Living-dead Mera warriors created by Danar Rrivae.

Raqiel

Guards of both the Adjudicators and the abbeys of the realms. They are descendants of the Mera and Onama.

Selenova

The nightstar (moon)

Lumis

The daystar (sun)

Council of High Orders

The most ascendant members of the original five orders sit on the Council. They dictate whose power remains and whose power is stripped.

RACES

Human

They've destroyed Vallendor with their greed, envy, and hate.

Renrian

Lavender eyes. They are derived from the Onama order. Archivers of the Aetherium's stories, the rise and fall of cities, and the wisdom of sages.

Gorga

Green-scaled race who roll painted rocks to decide their fates.

Dashmala

Derived from the Mera order. Large warriors with yellow eyes.

MORTALS

Veril Bairnell the Sapient

Renrian who'd served as Kai's teacher all of her life; worked as a healer around Vallendor Realm until his untimely murder in Caerno Woods.

Emperor Syrus Wake

Rules the empire of Brithellum. He was coronated as king by Kai when he was just twenty summers old. An ally of Danar Rrivae, mortal adopted father to Jadon, and biological father to Prince Gileon Wake.

Olivia Corby

Former fiancée of Prince Gileon Wake; pretended to be Jadon's sister; thief; girlfriend of Philia Wysor.

Philia Wysor

Also known as Phily; Olivia's girlfriend. A hunter and a tracker, she now possesses the *Librum Esoterica*.

Separi Eleweg the Advertant

Renrian and friend of Veril's. She is the co-proprietor of the Broken Hammer Inn in Caburh.

Ridget Eleweg

Renrian and wife of Separi. She is the co-proprietor of the Broken Hammer Inn in Caburh.

Prince Gileon Wake

Emperor Wake's second son, Jadon's brother, and ex-fiancé of Olivia. He chased Olivia from Brithellum to Maford because she stole the *Librum Esoterica* from his family's library.

Ancress Mily Tisen

A leader in the Sisters of the Dusky Hills; Kai's intermediary in Gasho.

Prince Rewyn Idus

Sixth of His Name, Starbound and Shadowforged, Chosen of Celestial; Gashoan prince.

Voidless

There is an absence of light in them, but it isn't darkness.

THE AETHERIUM

Comprised of at least 70,000 known realms.

REALMS

Vallendor

Nicknamed the "verdant realm" because it had green grasses, abundant trees and waters. It was the most beautiful. The 10,000th created realm.

Linione

The first realm created by Supreme. The Council of High Orders also holds court here.

Anathema

Also called "The Nowhere." Hell.

The Between

A place for gods who can't travel to other realms due to the harm they may cause any world.

Ithlon

Kai's birthplace. A destroyed realm signified by a seashell. Kai's mother, Lyra, was killed here once Kai led its destruction. Because it was so perfect, raiders came to plunder Ithlon for its riches.

Yoffa

A destroyed world signified by a mountain peak. Kai led in its destruction, with Zephar as her second-in-command. Yoffans had destroyed the mountains in search of forbidden minerals.

Melki

A destroyed world of rain. Kai led in its destruction, with Zephar as her second-in-command. Destroyed because Melkians had turned to sorcery to steal lifeforce from their neighboring realms.

Birius

Danar Rrivae's destroyed home realm. His family lived in this realm of savannahs and herbology. The people here stripped the land to create more poisons to kill rather than medicines to heal its people.

Fendusk, Kynne, and Kestau

Realms stolen by Danar Rrivae.

VALLENDOR

KINGDOMS

Brithellum

The kingdom and seat of power for Emperor Syrus Wake. Home to Castle Wake.

Vinevridth

Southern provinces ruled by King Hamund Exley.

Ohogar

Kingdom located in the Doom Desert province.

SPECIAL SITES

Doom Desert

Located in the northern part of Vallendor.

Gasho

Located in the middle of Doom Desert; the capital city of Kingdom Ohogar. In its prosperous times, Gasho was surrounded by marshland, with fresh water, game, and cool breezes. The people dug canals to irrigate the crops, but the otherworldly came and destroyed the city.

Rim of the Shadows

Located outside of Gasho, these nine-hundred-foot-high cliffs overlook the vast plain.

Temple of Celestial

Sits in the northern part of town. Massive dome covered in crimson, gold, and black tiles. A bell at the top. Each level features heavenly and realm-bound scenes depicting Kai's light piercing the dark sky and her might as she lifts her sword in battle. Two columns topped by Celestial holding the sword and Celestial holding the ball of light. Grand hall has high ceilings and is lined with stone columns. Murals depict legends—from the creation of Vallendor and battles to save it to paintings of Kai and Zephar in love.

Mount Devour

The gathering place of the gods visiting Vallendor.

Abbey of Mount Devour

The gathering place of the gods on Vallendor. Sits atop Mount Devour. One can see all of Vallendor from its windows.

Sea of Devour

The toxic sea at the foot of Mount Devour.

Misty Garden of Dusky Hills

Located in Gasho within the Temple of Celestial; reminds Kai of Ithlon.

Sanctum of Dusky Hills

Located in the forest above the Temple of Celestial. Past the entry, gods ascend a mist-covered trail lit by pearly light.

Temple of Malik Sindire

On the other side of the Dusky Hills; resembles a one-story mansion and was built by Malik Sindire's followers. Malik Sindire visits this temple every fifty years.

Caburh/New Nosirest

A riverside industrial town and center of trade founded by the Renrians ages ago. The Duskmoor River winds past it.

Fihel

A town northwest of Caburh and destroyed by humans.

Beaminster

A rotting little town east of Brithellum with decrepit gates, homes, and shabby soldiers. Everyone is sick and dying here.

Acknowledgments

Thank you, readers, for welcoming me into the world of romantasy. I've met so many of you, and your support, excitement, and open hearts have all meant so much to me.

Thank you, Jill Marsal, for still being my gladiator in this raucous world of words.

Red Tower, y'all are INCREDIBLE. Thank you, Liz—your brilliance is unworldly, and your heart is just as boundless. To the editorial, marketing, and P.R. teams, a big thanks for holding my hand, sending me out to the world prepared, for being friends and showing up. Special shout-outs to Mary, Sarah, Melanie, Hannah, Lindsey, Meredith, Heather, Curtis, Bree, and Britt!

To the ladies of BookSparks and Kaye Publicity: I'm so blessed to have you in my life. You send me all around this country, and sometimes, you show up in the audience as a bonus prize. Thank you, Crystal, Dana, Grace, Taylor, Ellie, Kaitlyn, Lauren, Erin, Amanda, and Lizzy!

I'm blessed to have great friends, and please know that I love you for showing up and putting books in strangers' hands. I owe y'all drinks.

To my family: I love you so much. Mom, Terry, Gretchen, and Jason, you've known me all of my life, and your support and love have never flagged. This year, with this new adventure, you being there for me, like… at so many events…made my Grinchy little heart grow six times bigger.

And Maya Grace and David, you both own that Grinchy little heart. You've gone above and beyond in your love and support and patience for all the new literary chaos I've brought into our lives. I can never thank you enough. I can never love you enough.

THE GODS LOVE TO PLAY WITH US MERE MORTALS. AND EVERY HUNDRED YEARS, WE LET THEM...

I have never been favored by the gods. Far from it, thanks to Zeus.

Living as a cursed office clerk for the Order of Thieves, I just keep my head down and hope the capricious beings who rule from Olympus won't notice me. Not an easy feat, given San Francisco is Zeus' patron city, but I make do. I survive. Until the night I tangle with a *different* god.

The *worst* god. Hades.

For the first time ever, the ruthless, mercurial King of the Underworld has entered the Crucible—the deadly contest the gods hold to determine a new ruler to sit on the throne of Olympus. But instead of fighting their own battles, the gods name *mortals* to compete in their stead.

So why in the Underworld did Hades choose me—a sarcastic nobody with a curse on her shoulders—as his champion? And why does my heart trip every time he says I'm *his*?

I don't know if I'm a pawn, bait, or something else entirely to this dangerously tempting god. How can I, when he has more secrets than stars in the sky?

Because Hades is playing by his own rules...and Death will win at any cost.

THE GAMES CONTINUE IN *THE THINGS GODS BREAK*, COMING SOON!

Doubling the Trees Behind Every Book You Buy.

Because books should leave the world better than they found it—not just in hearts and minds, but in forests and futures.

Through our Read More, Breathe Easier initiative, we're helping reforest the planet, restore ecosystems, and rethink what sustainable publishing can be.

Track the impact of your read at:

CONNECT WITH US ONLINE

@redtowerbooks

@RedTowerBooks

@redtowerbooks

Join the Entangled Insiders for early access to ARCs, exclusive content, and insider news! Scan the QR code to become part of the ultimate reader community.